Here's to the child and all he has to teach us.
Proverb

For my grandchildren who are my joy,
Daniel, Adam and Natalie.

CHAPTER ONE

The man was deep in thought, his dark head bent, his brow furrowed. He seemed to be studying his boots as they scuffed through the rich layer of leaves, russet and gold, orange and tawny pink which carpeted the woodland floor. Though he was not aware of it in his brown study, like the boy he used to be, he was kicking and shuffling his feet through the leaves, enjoying the rustling sound they made. It had been a particularly fine summer with less rain than was normal in this part of the country and the leaves were dry and crackling, satisfying, if subconsciously, that feeling he had known as a lad.

He was considering Miss Charlotte Gibson. He had been considering Miss Charlotte Gibson for the best part of the summer and the problem was that half of Fellthwaite, including the lady in question and her mama, were aware of it, though naturally they were too well bred to let it be seen they had noticed. That was the trouble with living in a small, close-knit community. You couldn't sneeze without it coming to someone's attention, who then told you, and everyone in Fellthwaite into the bargain, that you were in for an awful cold! Having paid Miss Gibson a certain amount of attention at several functions, and had her to dine a time or two, with her parents, naturally, at Howethwaite, his family home, he was well aware that speculation was rife in the district. She would make a splendid wife, it must be said, since she had been trained for it from the day she left the nursery. It was well known that she was already an

1

excellent hostess, brought up to it by her mama who was one herself. Mrs Gibson, who was the great-niece of a baronet, was well accustomed to entertaining men of high rank, not only from the gentry, but the aristocracy from which her own family came, and Miss Charlotte Gibson was sensible of her position and proud of her own worth in the marriage stakes. Her father, Mr Arthur Gibson, had vast wealth, come to him from many of the businesses which thrived in the district of Furness and Windermere. Copper mining, the manufacture of gunpowder, the mining of iron in High Furness, the quarrying of slate round and about Coniston, several farms which were rented to tenant farmers, not to mention coal from the coalfields in the west which stretched from Cockermouth to Whitehaven. He owned a bank in the centre of Ambleside and it was rumoured that the interest he earned from the loans he made kept his wife and daughter tricked out in the exclusive, and expensive, Paris fashions they were to be seen in about Fellthwaite, Ambleside and Grasmere. Ball gowns and afternoon dresses, at the right time, of course, walking outfits, outfits for their carriage exercise, dinner gowns, three-piece costumes, tea gowns and cartwheel hats trimmed with feathers, flowers, ribbons and vast amounts of lace and tulle. Charlotte was Arthur's only child and the gentleman who took her to wife, and there were many who were eager to do so, would have at his disposal, when Arthur had gone, an enormous fortune and the added bonus of the beautiful Charlotte Gibson herself.

James Buchanan sighed deeply and then shook his head, irritated with his own foolish indecision.

WHEN MORNING COMES

Lucy Dean is a young woman of eighteen years with no money, no job and four young brothers and sisters to support. James Buchanan is a young man of thirty-four years with a great fortune, who thinks that Lucy Dean is the most remarkable girl he has ever met. What could be more natural than their marriage? James—whom everyone had thought all but engaged to the wilful beauty Charlotte Gibson—proposes and a grateful Lucy accepts. But the surprising marriage that by turns charms and scan

WHEN MORNING COMES

Audrey Howard

CHIVERS PRESS
BATH

First published 1998
by
Hodder and Stoughton
This Large Print edition published by
Chivers Press
by arrangement with
Hodder and Stoughton
2000

ISBN 0 7540 2286 2

British Library Cataloguing in Publication Data available

Printed and bound in Great Britain by
REDWOOD BOOKS, Trowbridge, Wiltshire

Charlotte would make a splendid wife and partner. She was young, healthy and capable of bearing many fine children, sons among them, and really he didn't know why he was dithering about as he was. He needed a wife. He knew without being told that Mr and Mrs Gibson favoured his suit, for he was as wealthy and well bred as themselves, but they wouldn't wait for ever and if he didn't look lively they'd give her to some other, equally well-endowed gentleman.

He had driven from his home near Skelwith that afternoon, following the lane which led towards Ambleside and was on his way to see a client, the Reverend Edward Dean. It seemed the rector, whose church lay on the outskirts of Fellthwaite, had come to the conclusion that it was about time he made a will and James, who was a solicitor with a thriving practice in Ambleside, had been asked to call on him. The rector was a man in his fifties and though, as far as James knew, in the best of health, it seemed his own mortality had come into question, as it does when one is past one's middle years, and his thoughts had turned to putting in order his worldly affairs.

James couldn't have said why—perhaps because he was early for his appointment, or maybe the breathtaking beauty of the autumn day, or even the magnificence of the brilliantly hued woods through which the lane cut—but whatever it was it had made him brake sharply, bringing his motor car to a stop just off the lane and under the trees. He had his dogs with him, both trained to sit quietly on the back seat while he was driving; with a murmured word and a click of his fingers he ordered them out. They stood, trembling with anticipation, their

3

intelligent hazel eyes looking up at him, each with a paw raised waiting for permission to run free. They were big, handsome dogs, labradors with ebony coats which gleamed like wet coal. Their ears twitched and so did their noses, since there were dozens of scents to tantalise them and when he indicated with his hand and a soft murmur that they might go they bounded away like two children let out of the schoolroom.

He knew exactly how they felt. But then the life he led, the career he followed was his own choice and he could blame no one but himself if he was tied down for the best part of each weekday with legal matters, problems brought to him to solve by the less affluent of the district of Windermere. He had chosen to study law at the University of Edinburgh, though he was a man of considerable means and had no need to seek employment. The three sons of Alexander Buchanan, Johnny, Harry and Job, had inherited equal shares in Alex's business enterprises, which were many and lucrative, and when Johnny, James's father, had died his share had come to James. His cousins, Ben, Andrew and Alex Buchanan ran the Buchanan Copper Mining Co, the Emmerson Gunpowder Manufacturers near Elterwater and a bobbin manufacturing mill at Staveley, the latter two coming to the Buchanan family through marriage. His fourth cousin Paul was to be a doctor. With the income that came to him from the shares he had in these concerns, and others that he had set up himself, James Buchanan was that envied being, an independent man. He had no need to go each day to his office in Ambleside and if, sometimes, he longed to put on a pair of sturdy

4

boots, throw a haversack on his back and head for the long climb to Scafell Pike, to Helvellyn or the majestic peaks of Skiddaw, he had no one to blame but himself if he was unable to do so.

Lifting his head he breathed deeply, the air slipping like dry white wine down his throat and into his lungs. He could smell woodsmoke and the rich earthy aroma of the woodland where already the dying vegetation was beginning to rot down, ready to turn itself into the nourishment needed for next year's growth. Between the trees he caught a glimpse of the breeze-rippled waters of the lake, like moving silk, the flame of the autumn sun casting vivid colours of gold and rose and apricot across it and up on the fells at his back purple shadows were beginning to fall. It was not yet cold down here in the valley bottom but soon Coniston Old Man would wear its first fluted cap of snow, the whiteness creeping slowly down as winter approached.

The dogs had vanished into the rustling sea of bright copper bracken which carpeted the floor of the woodland on either side of the rough path. Leaves were falling as a small breeze tore them from their frail hold on the branches of the trees and when, smiling whimsically, he held out his hand, one spiralled down to land delicately on his outstretched palm.

There was a dog barking somewhere, not his, for this was the high, excited bark of a terrier, a small dog, and he hesitated since he did not wish to have company. He would turn back here, he decided, call his dogs to him and return to his motor car, for his appointment with the reverend gentleman was almost due. He abhorred unpunctuality since it seemed to him to smack of contempt for another's time and it would take him ten minutes to motor from here to the rectory.

Placing the tips of two fingers between his lips he gave a low but piercing whistle, one his dogs would hear but would be barely discernible to the human ear. He waited, his tall, lean frame lounging comfortably against the narrow trunk of a silver birch tree, both his hands pushed deep into his trouser pockets, one leg bent at the knee with his foot resting on the whitish bark.

He was not considered to be a handsome man, though there was certainly something about him that seemed to appeal to the ladies, other gentlemen had noticed. Of course, ladies were known to be romantic, intrigued by anything that did not fall into a category they could immediately recognise, though why they should consider it romantic to be sombre and grave, reserved and somewhat unapproachable the gentlemen could not fathom. His countenance was compelling, strong, unsmiling, but one that drew the eye to it, both male and female, though as yet none had caught his. To the female he promised something they could not understand but knew they liked, to the male a suggestion of mocking arrogance which told them he was not a man to be meddled with.

This was James Buchanan.

He had left his hat in the motor car and his dark, chocolate hair was revealed to be thick and curling, needing to be trimmed every week if it was to be kept in any sort of order. Even now it grew vibrantly, tumbling to his frowning eyebrows and catching in the collar of his coat. He was clean-shaven, his amber skin glowing with good health.

His eyes were quite beautiful, wasted on a lad, his old nurse used to tell him, the colour the softest grey, like the underside of a dove's wing, set in long black lashes. His jaw jutted implacably, his mouth was set firm, though a lift at each corner hinted at hidden humour. He was confident, vigorous, with a well-marked sense of his own infallibility, for James Buchanan had been looking after himself ever since his mother and father had drowned when the ice on Lake Windermere on which they were skating had given way. That was eighteen years ago. He had been sixteen years old at the time. His two uncles—brothers to his own father—and their wives, and his Aunt Amy, had done their best to keep a tight rein on him, even demanding that he take up residence with one of them, but he had refused to be tethered and, since he was a big lad with a mind of his own even then, self-willed as all the Buchanans were, they left him alone. They were all cut from the same cloth, job and Harry Buchanan, their sons and their nephew James, for in their veins ran the rich and tempestuous blood of Alex Buchanan and his wife Christy Emmerson, who were legends in the district of Furness and Windermere and beyond.

James was visibly annoyed when not two but three dogs scampered out of the undergrowth to his whistle. The third was no more than a puppy.

'What the devil have you got there, you idiots, and where in hell did you get him?' he exclaimed, pushing himself away from the tree.

The dogs, all three, wagged their tails energetically as they circled him, the puppy almost swinging himself off his feet in his ecstasy. He leaped up at James's knee, nearly doing somersaults in his efforts to reach his hand and James could not help but smile. The Border terrier, for that was what he was, was so small he could comfortably walk, or rather dart, beneath the bellies of his new-found friends. He had a short, rough, wheaten-coloured coat and eyes that were dark, with the keen expression of an animal that has been bred to drive the fox from its lair.

'Dammit, where in hell have you come from?' James muttered irritably, for he could hardly abandon such a young animal. The dog studied him, his tail slowing somewhat as though he were getting ready for a game, but already James could hear the sound of voices, children's voices and he heaved a sigh of relief mixed with exasperation.

'Dammit to hell . . .' He bent down and with a disgruntled gesture picked up the puppy which licked his face affectionately, and tucking it under his arm began to walk in the direction from which the voices came. His own dogs, subdued now that they had sensed his mood, padded silently at his heels.

'Thimble . . . Thimble . . .' the voices called, getting closer as he pushed his way through the crisping sea of bracken. He could hear the lilting sound of water tumbling across rocks coming from ahead, for you could not go far in this land of the lakes without stumbling across a ghyll, a beck, water erupting from the very ground under your feet. It gushed down runnels to join streams which foamed like spilled milk, making its way from hills and mountains to flow into lakes and tarns.

The puppy under his arm who went, apparently, by the absurd name of Thimble, lay there docilely, aware it was futile to struggle, knowing with the instinct animals and children have who means business and who does not. This man did!

They did not hear him as he stepped out on to the soft floor of the clearing, nor see him, for they were casting about on the far side of the rushing beck, calling the dog's name with increasing anxiety. There were six of them, four girls and two boys, all somewhat bedraggled, their feet bare, as though the loss of Thimble had interrupted some watery but exciting game.

'Thimble, you damn fool, where have you got to?' the smaller of the boys shrieked piercingly in the way of the young who cannot speak below a full-throated roar.

'Percy, you know Papa does not like you to swear, and need you scream so loudly? I'm sure you've damaged my eardrum, particularly as you were standing no more than six inches from it.'

'Sorry, Luce, but that's not swearing, really it isn't. If you wanted I could really swear. I heard Bibby say—'

'That's enough, Percy, and if Bibby knows what's best for him he'll watch his tongue.'

'Don't be daft, Luce, there isn't a cat in hell's chance you'd get someone to work like the old codger does and without wages too. When was the last time he was paid, tell me that? It's no wonder he swears so much and if he wasn't nearly a hundred he'd be off tomorrow.'

It was the second boy who spoke, a tall, dark, good-looking lad of about thirteen or fourteen, James thought, scrawny yet, but already showing signs of breadth to his shoulders. In fact they were all handsome children. They made a charming group, decently but shabbily dressed, the boys in

9

patched knee-length trousers in a particularly unsuitable shade of cream drill with open-neck, navy blue jerseys, long-sleeved and with a collar. The sleeves were pushed up to the elbow, the jersey hanging out of the trousers. The younger girls were in navy blue serge with sailor collars which had a row of white cotton braid round the hem and cuffs of the sleeves, again pushed up above their elbows. Their skirts were hitched up and tucked carelessly into the elastic of their sensible navy blue knickers.

'Now you're at it, Edward,' the older girl challenged. 'What you said was a swear word and is it any wonder if Percy thinks it's all right.'

'Hell's not swearing, Luce. Hell's a place and Papa mentions it every Sunday from the pulpit.'

'That's different and you know it.'

'Ooh, girls!' Edward shrugged his shoulders and sighed in deep exasperation.

The fourth girl was not at all like the others, either in colouring or in looks, and he noticed with half his mind that she had a limp, but the girl who had rebuked Percy and Edward was quite the loveliest thing James had ever seen. Dark, like the boys, like them all, but her hair, where the sun caught it, had the glossy sheen and colour of a horse chestnut, similar to the ones James had collected from these very woods and played with as a lad. It had evidently started out that morning brushed smoothly back from her forehead and plaited, a single plait which, where it still retained some order, was as thick as his wrist. Three-quarters of its lower length, which fell over one shoulder and across her breast to her waist as she bent down to peer for some curious reason into a

10

rabbit hole, presumably after Thimble, had come unravelled, curling vigorously at its end, and in the midst of this vibrant glory a scarlet ribbon dangled. Long wisps curled about her face and neck and there was a limp white flower of some sort pushed behind her ear. She wore a muslin blouse with a tucked front and a high neck, and a separate skirt with several deep flounces about the hem, both garments in white. Somehow James had the feeling that her outfit had not been made for her but had been skilfully altered to fit her. Like the other girls she had tucked the skirt up in some fashion and her legs, white and shapely, the ankle fine-boned, the foot slender, were revealed.

Hanging carelessly from the knotted branches of an ancient oak were six pairs of black stockings and in a jumble beneath it six pairs of black boots.

They had evidently been building a dam, for a neat line of rocks and stones had been laid from one side of the stream to the other. The water had already begun to rise at the back of it and there were small branches, twigs and leaves and a tangle of brush caught in it. A little brown grebe alighted for a moment, taking advantage of the children's momentary absence, then flew off with some wriggling insect in its mouth.

'I'll give that blasted dog the hiding of his life when I find him,' the older boy was heard to hiss as he poked about with a stick in the undergrowth.

'You'll do no such thing, Edward Dean. He's only a baby, and let me tell you he's more damned sense than you had at the same age.' The eldest girl's ban on swearing evidently did not apply to herself. She straightened up and threw back the burnished plait, and her young breasts, full and

11

rounded, strained against the muslin of her blouse. The peaks of her nipples were clearly visible and though James was certain she would be wearing some sort of undergarment beneath the blouse he could have sworn he could see the dark shadow of the areola about them. To his shame he felt his manhood stir and warmth spread up into his belly. She was tall, nearly as tall as he was, he would have said. He was quite mesmerised by the womanly magnificence of her, by her flushed and girlish face which was at such odds with her mature body.

His own dogs, one on either side of him, pressed against his legs waiting for his command and the one in his arms, a young dog who had exhausted his store of good behaviour, began to wriggle ecstatically, unable to contain his excitement at the sight of these people of his. It was as though he had been parted from them for a week as he struggled to get to them.

'Is this what you're looking for?' James asked, his voice brusque. 'Don't you think in future it might be advisable to keep such a young dog under closer surveillance?'

At once six astonished faces turned towards him and he had time to note that they each, except the girl with the limp, had brown eyes of different shades, though none was like the eldest girl's, which were the exact colour of old whisky. They were identical in shape and size, though, with thick brown lashes surrounding them, but it was to the eldest girl he spoke and it was at the eldest girl his whole male interest was focused. Her skin was a creamy white but flushed at the cheekbones with her exertions, without a flaw to mar its perfection. Not a freckle to blemish the satin-like finish, only,

12

as he watched, a small indentation at the left-hand corner of her mouth, the lips themselves giving the impression that they had been bruised to a rosy pink by a lover's kiss.

They looked at one another across the stream but though he appeared to have addressed his question to her it was not she who answered.

'Thimble,' the younger boy shrieked, the sound going through James like a grating saw, 'where in hell's name have you been?'

'Percy, what have I just told you?' his sister rebuked him, but her heart wasn't in it. It was an automatic response to the child's swearing. She was staring with great interest at the tall figure of the well-dressed gentleman in whose arms Thimble was struggling. She had thought them to be quite alone in this quiet part of the wooded inlet which led down to the lake and this man's appearance had rendered them all speechless with surprise, except for Percy, of course, who it was difficult, if not impossible, to shut up. She couldn't have said with any degree of rationality why they were struck dumb, for they were not a family who were shy or self-conscious, or even had any proper regard for the conventions of the day which said children should be seen and not heard. Papa, and Mama when she was alive, did not believe in the repression of a child's normal inclination to high spirits and she was well aware that some of Papa's parishioners considered his family to be out of hand and in need of proper parental control, which dear Papa seemed unable or unwilling to apply.

The dog in James's arms let out an agonised yelp, indicating that he wished to be reunited with his people on the other side of the stream. The

13

eldest girl laughed, a laugh at once high and joyous and Charlotte Gibson, who had a precarious hold on him at best, was sadly driven for ever from James Buchanan's mind.

'The little devil. I don't know what on earth we're going to do with him.'

'A bit of training wouldn't go amiss,' James remarked dourly.

'You're right, sir, but he is such a nomad it is hard to get a good grip on him. He has gypsy blood in him, I suspect, if a dog can have gypsy blood. We found him on Elsie's bed only this morning with a bone as big as himself which he'd stolen from Bibby's dog and how he'd got the thing up the stairs will for ever be a mystery. Where did you find him, Mr Buchanan? We were so busy with the dam, you see'—indicating with an airy wave the crumbling construction in the stream—'that we didn't notice he had gone. Of course he is only a puppy. Mr Henley gave him to us. He breeds them for showing, you know, and this one didn't come up to scratch, though only the good Lord knows why for he's a charming fellow, don't you think so?'

She gave him a smile of such brilliance and goodwill James had to work hard at forming an answer. Like some callow youth faced with his first encounter with the opposite sex he seemed to be lost for words.

'That is not the description I would have used,' he managed at last, his voice cold to cover his incredible loss of composure. 'You really must train him to remain at your side,' glancing down at his own obedient dogs who sat beside him without movement except for their eyes. 'He is likely to get into trouble if you don't.' He placed the struggling

14

puppy on the ground whereupon it leaped into the water and floundered to the far bank. It was seized upon by the younger boy who clutched its wet, wriggling body to his own already soaked chest, kissing it with a passion of childish love.

James did not notice. He was too busy watching the girl. 'You called me by name,' he said shortly. 'You know me? I'm sorry but you have the advantage of me.' His natural good manners were returning. 'Have we met?' Though it didn't show in his face the thought in his head was that he would surely have remembered if they had.

'Fellthwaite is a small town, Mr Buchanan, and your family, having been here so long, I suppose, is well known, whereas we are comparative newcomers. Yes, I'm afraid we're that dreadful species known as *offcomers*, and I do believe we shall all be in our dotage before we are considered to be residents of the town.' She beamed as though the thought worried her not a whit. 'Papa has been rector at St Silas's for the past six years. Only Percy here had the good fortune to be born here, the rest of us coming from a village near Buxton. A good friend of Mama's was related to the Forsythes— you know them?—of Dalebarrow Hall. Squire Forsythe had the living of St Silas's in his gift and offered it to Papa.'

She bent her head for a moment and her slipping hair hid her face but James saw her throat work, then she looked up at him, her eyes a pale gold dewed with tears.

'Our mama died when Percy was born, Mr Buchanan.'

The six of them moved closer to one another as though to give support in what was evidently a

15

great sorrow.

'I'm sorry,' he answered gruffly, not knowing what else she expected of him. Apparently it was enough.

'Thank you,' she said simply. 'Now I really must apologise for not making proper introductions. These are my brothers and sisters. This is Margaret who is twelve.' She smiled lovingly at the tall, awkward young girl who bobbed a polite curtsey. 'Margaret is my right-hand man, Mr Buchanan and I don't know what I should do without her since . . . since Mama went . . .'

'Oh, Lucy . . .' the girl said in smiling exasperation.

'No, Margaret, it's true.' She turned and took the hand of the third girl, a small but just as lovely version of herself who eyed him with a degree of shyness. 'And this is Emily who is eight and equally indispensable.'

The child bobbed her own curtsey, none of them seeming to wonder at the incongruity of their bare legs and feet which were turning to a mottled blue and pink with the icy coldness of the water they had just been splashing in.

'And this great lanky lad is Edward. Edward is nearly fourteen and if—well, we hope—that is, Papa hopes he will go to . . . to a decent school soon.' She stopped abruptly at a sharp look from her brother.

'Sir.' The boy bowed his head respectfully and James took his eyes from the girl for a moment to return the bow. Unconventional they might be, this flushed, dishevelled and decidedly damp family group, but at least they were mannered.

'This, of course, is Percy.' What more need she

16

say, her laughing expression asked him. 'He is five and a scamp,' but we love him dearly just the same, she had no need to add.

After a quick glance at Percy, which was all that was necessary in James's opinion, for he was not a lover of children, he returned his gaze to the oldest family member, unaware of the soft gleam in his velvet grey eyes which another woman, a more experienced woman, would have recognised.

'And this is my dear friend Buffy Tyson,' drawing forward the slight girl with the limp.

'Miss Tyson,' bowing slightly in Miss Tyson's direction. 'And you are . . . ?'

'Lucy Dean, sir.' She bobbed a quick curtsey as she had been taught as a child.

He did not know why but he did not like the 'sir', for it told him that Lucy Dean, probably no more than eighteen or nineteen, thought James Buchanan, who had just turned thirty-four, to be an old fuddy-duddy of the past generation, which he supposed he was.

He was not wrong. Lucy studied him in that unselfconscious way she had, which often disconcerted those on whom her intense gaze fell. He was an attractive man, she would not deny that, despite his age, but his unsmiling, sombre expression was, in her opinion, enough to quell the most light-hearted, giving them cause to cast back into their memories for some misdemeanour they might have committed. He was soberly dressed in a morning suit of dark, business-like grey, with a single-breasted waistcoat of the same colour, and a wing collar. Totally out of place for a stroll in the woods, she would have thought, though he did have his dogs with him. He wore no hat and a shaft of

17

afternoon sunlight burnished his dark hair to the rich gloss of mahogany.

'Miss Dean, a pleasure.' He bowed his head then straightened suddenly, since he had just become aware that these must be the children of the very gentleman he was to see that afternoon.

'Your father is Edward Dean, Miss Dean?'

'He is indeed, sir. Do you know him? Are you a member of our church? I don't believe I've seen you there,' twinkling as though the very idea of Mr Buchanan sitting through one of her father's sermons amused her enormously.

He did not return the smile, for James Buchanan worshipped no God and kept to no high-toned principles except those of honesty, decency and the belief that, as he interfered with no man, no man should interfere with him.

'No, Miss Dean, it's just that I'm to see your father this afternoon on a matter of business.'

'Business?' She was clearly surprised and if James had made the acquaintance of Edward Dean he would have understood why.

'Yes.' That was all he said, for it was not his custom to discuss his clients' affairs, even with that client's daughter.

'What on earth about?'

'Miss Dean, you must ask your father that.'

'I shall, Mr Buchanan, and at once. Come, children,' sweeping her brood up with the efficiency of a no-nonsense nanny. 'Dear God, I hope and pray he is not about to invest money; not that we have any, you understand . . .' Suddenly aware that she was perhaps revealing too much of her family's business to this perfect stranger, she picked up her skirts and leaped into the shallow

18

water, wading across with a great scatter of sun-filled diamond sparklets that flew about her in twin arcs.

'Come on, Edward, Margaret. Percy, don't drop Thimble, will you, darling. Perhaps Edward had better carry him until we get home. Why did we not bring his lead? Really we are the most disorganised people I know. Now, get your boots and stockings on. Yes, yes, I know your feet are wet, Emily, but just for once you may dry them on your skirt.'

All the while she was talking, with a total lack of selfconsciousness, she was pulling on her own stockings, hopping from foot to foot as she did so, then sat down on the exposed root of the oak tree and donned her ankle-length boots. Tying the laces about her slim ankles, unaware—as he was himself—of James's fascinated gaze, she stood up and stamped her feet then put her hands to the back of her head, the movement lifting her full, rounded breasts again, making James catch his breath and the blood to run warm in his veins. With a deft twist she re-plaited her heavy hair for an inch or two then, retrieving the scarlet ribbon, tied it in a bow. The plait fell to her buttocks. Instantly she was about her sisters, tweaking this and adjusting that, pushing a vagrant curl behind an ear and smoothing down the skirts of their mid-calf dresses.

'There,' she said, her expression declaring that the most critical onlooker would find nothing amiss with the Dean children. She had overlooked the drooping white flower which was still caught in her own hair.

'Allow me, Miss Dean.' To his own amazement he lifted his hand in what could only be described as a dream-like manner, and removed it, startling

19

her with his closeness so that her eyes darkened to a clear chestnut brown. The pupils widened dramatically and he noticed there was a fine black line round the iris. She smelled of something fresh and sweet, something he could not recognise but would never forget.

'Thank you, Mr Buchanan.' Her tone was polite, the tone used when one spoke to a gentleman, or lady, older than oneself. 'Now then, if you are bound for the rectory perhaps you would care to walk with us.' It was clear that the idea found little favour with her, since he was so serious, a condition the Dean family did not care for.

'Thank you, Miss Dean, but I have left my motor car on the edge of the wood so you see . . .'

He got no further. The effect his words had on the elder boy was electrifying. From polite boredom he exploded into life, cheeks blazing with colour, eyes blazing with the golden light of vivid excitement.

'You . . . you have a motor car, sir?' he breathed reverently.

'Yes.' Again his manner was brusque, for he guessed what was coming.

'What make?' the boy asked.

'A Rolls-Royce,' James answered reluctantly.

'Not . . . not a . . .a Silver Ghost?'

'Yes.'

'Gosh, did you hear that, Luce? Mr Buchanan has a Rolls-Royce Silver Ghost.'

'Really.' Lucy was evidently not as impressed as her brother.

'It can do seventy miles an hour, sir, did you know that?' Edward went on, clearly under the impression that Mr Buchanan could have no

20

conception of the jewel he had in his possession.

'I believe so, though I have not yet got up to that speed, not on these narrow lanes.'

Well, you wouldn't, Edward's pitying glance told him, not an old man like you, but all he said was, 'Oh, sir . . .'

He stood there, speechless with wonder and James sighed in defeat. He admitted to himself that it would be very pleasant to have the lovely Miss Dean sit beside him in the front seat of his elegant new motor car, but to take the lot of them, including the three dogs, was not something he relished, but how could he get out of it with the boy's beseeching eyes gazing into his.

It seemed he couldn't. Much against his will he said curtly, 'Perhaps I might offer you a—'

'Oh, sir, would you?' The boy was overcome with some deep emotion. 'I'd be eternally grateful. I've never been in a motor car, you see.'

'This is most kind of you, Mr Buchanan.'

During the short walk back to the vehicle Lucy Dean lagged behind with her sisters, her friend Buffy and younger brother, holding the hands of the two youngest, talking ten to the dozen, the four of them, laughing, pointing out to each other some wonder that they all seemed to find quite marvellous. A flock of butterflies dancing in a patch of sunlight, called, he heard her tell them, 'speckled woods'. A 'great spotted woodpecker drumming against the trunk of a hornbeam, and the antics of a daring dormouse playing acrobat in the branches of a tree. At his side Edward beseiged him with questions and bombarded him with information, for it seemed the young man was a passionate lover of the motor car, particularly the

21

Rolls-Royce, and meant to have one at the earliest possible moment. He knew every nut and bolt that held it together. When they reached it he circled it in wondering silence, touching with gentle hands the polished windshield, the black hood which was folded down, the lights, the distinctive radiator with its diminutive mascot, the 'Spirit of Ecstasy' perched upon it and even the spare wheel. James tried to curb his impatience but the boy's rapt admiration would not be hurried and he could do no more than stand and watch.

He did at least have her sit beside him on the short journey to the rectory, the wriggling and alarmed Thimble on her knee, while behind him his own dogs fought for space with Edward, who hung over his shoulder shouting instructions, with Percy who was as white as tallow with excitement and with the three girls who, now that they were actually aboard and going at the incredible speed of fifteen miles an hour, were not at all sure they liked it.

She did, though, Miss Lucy Dean. Her face was flushed to a rosy pink and her eyes shone like newly minted golden guineas. Her hair came loose again, whipping back from her face in a long shining banner of silken chestnut, her ribbon gone, and it was perhaps then, a mere half-hour after he had met her, that James admitted to himself that he must have her for his own.

CHAPTER TWO

'I think that's the best I can do, sir, bearing in mind that ... well ...there is very little in the way of assets. This house belongs to Squire Forsythe and it seems that from your stipend, with your family to support, there will be little hope of putting something aside for them ... when you are gone. Forgive me, I have no wish to be morbid but that is the purpose of this visit, is it not? To make a will. To ...to provide for your family in the future?'

'Yes, that is it exactly.' The benign and exceedingly courteous gentleman on the opposite side of the meagrely burning fire beamed triumphantly. 'You have it in a nutshell, Mr Buchanan.'

'But, sir ...' How did one address a parson, James wondered, placing his cup of tea on the low table beside him, a cup of tea which, had he not been told what it was, could have been washing-up water it was so weak. And how did one tell an obviously unworldly gentleman such as this one that the making of a will did not necessarily guarantee the beneficiaries of it security for the future. 'All my worldly possessions to go to my children, with my eldest daughter in charge of it, of course,' was all very well and good but if you had no worldly possessions, which seemed the case with the Reverend Dean, it was hardly worth the paper it was written on.

The rectory was a square Georgian box, very plain, very bare, the passage which led from the front to the back cool and dim, the long windows of the room he was shown to opening on to a surprisingly well-mown lawn. The work of the cursing Bibby, no doubt. In fact the grounds in which the house stood were quite magnificent, well kept and lovingly tended even if the gardener, or so it appeared from the conversation he had heard earlier, had not been paid his wages for weeks. He evidently took great pride in his work, for the flowerbeds, even this late in the season, were rampant with colour, mixed borders of antirrhinum of red and yellow and pink, long-legged chrysanthemum with cheerful daisy-like blooms, yellow-centred and white-petalled, petunias, showy with all the colours of the rainbow and, at the back of the borders, the great height of delphiniums in a rich, gentian blue. The borders led away like ribbons along the velvet lawn, turning the corner to the back of the house. Clinging in glorious profusion across the whole of the front of the house was a curtain of Virginia creeper already changing from the green of summer to shades varying from creamy yellow and pale orange to russet and gold and flaming scarlet.

The front door had stood wide open as James drove the Rolls-Royce along the neatly raked gravel drive and up to the wide, shallow steps. There was no one to greet them as the occupants leaped from the motor car and tumbled inside the house. At least the children, including Miss Lucy Dean, and the dogs leaped. James's well-bred, well-mannered animals, galvanised by the sense of whipped-up exultation with which the Dean family seemed to confront every happening, even the simple act of arriving home from an outing, cavorted about the gravel drive with the puppy as though they themselves were the same silly age. He could hear the children inside the house shouting someone's name, and one could have been forgiven for thinking that they had been away for a month instead of a few hours. Only Edward hung about the vehicle, still in a maze of rapturous delight, still proclaiming to James on the finer points of the engine, the speed available and the consumption of petrol as though James were the grateful passenger and he the owner. Did Mr Buchanan know, for instance, that only two years ago a Rolls-Royce had run from London to Edinburgh, covering just under twenty-five miles to the gallon, and not only that but had achieved seventy-nine miles an hour at Brooklands? It was a sorry day for the motoring world, he said sadly, when Mr Rolls was killed when his aeroplane crashed, and that was another thing. Did Mr Buchanan think that flying would become . . . ?

He might have stood on the steps for ever since there was no manservant or housemaid to show him the way. He was just about to ask the boy, who still stood in a preoccupied daze, where his father might be found when Lucy, filled with apologies, hurried back down the passage.

'Oh dear, Mr Buchanan, what must you think of me. I seem to have forgotten my manners . . .' as we forgot you, her youthful expression seemed to say. 'Please, do come in. Papa is waiting for you in his study. Will you bring your dogs in with you?' looking over his shoulder to where the labradors, the puppy swept up and carried away by Edward, sat side by side on the gravel waiting to be told what they were to do. 'Oh, look at them. Are they not splendid? Do you think we might eventually

25

train Thimble to be so obedient? No, I don't think so either, since we none of us has the patience.'

Pointedly he ignored her last remark with the contempt it deserved and said instead, 'No, they will stay outside, Miss Dean, providing they are in no one's way. If you are expecting carriage callers . . .'

She broke into helpless laughter, so rich and joyous he felt his own mouth tug at the corners, though he had no idea why she was so amused.

'Callers! Good gracious, no, Mr Buchanan. We are not a bit social here. Mama used to . . . to visit Papa's parishioners, those who were ill or in need and Margaret and I often go for a chat with old Mrs Jenkins or Mr Langley who worked in the garden before we came, but no one calls, not now. Not that we mind, you understand and of course Papa is too busy with his butterflies—he collects them, you know—to bother about it. No, we are . . . Oh, Lord, I'm babbling, aren't I. Buffy says I do that a lot, babble, I mean, but I seem to have so much to say and cannot get it all out fast enough. Do you find that, Mr Buchanan? You do! I don't believe it.' She smiled impishly. 'I'm sure you are just being polite. Well, if we don't get to Papa before he forgets you are here he is quite likely to wander off down the garden in search of a wall brown he spotted the other day. So, please come this way, Mr Buchanan and I'll send Elsie in with some tea.'

She led him along the passage towards the back of the house where sunlight streamed through the open garden door. He watched her as she walked ahead of him, outlined by the bright golden light, wondering if she was aware of the effect she had on

26

the male sex. Her back was straight, long and supple and she moved with the ease and elegance of a cat, her bedraggled skirt swaying with each movement of her hips. Jesus, she was a rare one, so innocent and yet with the sensuality one would only expect to see in a much older woman. So beautiful and yet so totally unaware of it.

The doors to the rooms on either side of the passage stood open and as he passed them, used as he was to the deep luxury of his own home, he was aware that each one was bare and spartan. It was all achingly clean, achingly barren, with no more than a strip of worn carpet along the passage and an ancient grandfather clock ticking sonorously against the wall.

Flinging open a door with the exuberance he had come to recognise as a feature of the Dean family, she stood back to allow him to enter.

'Mr Buchanan's here, Papa,' she called out from behind him, then, when James stopped abruptly, confused since the room was empty, she cannoned into his back. For a delightful moment he was concerned with the matter of turning to steady her, of telling her courteously that, no, it was not her fault, that really he should be more . . . careful. He was quite bemused by the nearness of her. Her perfume, whatever it was, was in his nostrils, her hair, still drifting in silken swathes about her face and shoulders was under his hand and it was all he could do, to his own consternation since he had never been an impetuous man, not to pull her into his arms and kiss her surprised, parted lips until she screamed, which he was certain she would not do. Not Miss Lucy Dean. Land him a backhander more like, if he was any judge of character. Afraid of very

27

little, he would have thought. The backbone and defender of her family, its support and mainstay since, it seemed to him, her absent father, after summoning James here and being told that he had arrived, had wandered off like a careless child. Not a man to be relied upon, James mused, and was it any wonder his family was as wild and unconventional as it was.

'Oh, for heaven's sake, where has he gone now?' Lucy asked no one in particular, certainly not him who, though he had kindly given them a lift home in his motor car, meant no more to her than any elderly gentleman who was owed respect. She darted across the room to the French window which led out on to a wide stretch of lawn backed by trees clothed in early autumn colours.

'Papa, Papa, where are you?' she yelled vigorously. 'Oh, there you are,' as a tall, spare gentleman in a clerical collar rose from a bench at the side of the lawn. 'Now, dearest, I told you Mr Buchanan was here and I've ordered tea.'

'Mr Buchanan?'

'Yes, Papa. Come to help you make your will, you have just told me, though why you should think such a thing necessary is beyond me at your age. You are years and years off needing it and we all agree that if we—'

Pulling herself up short, suddenly remembering James standing politely at her back, she continued breathlessly, 'Do come in, Papa, and let me introduce you to Mr Buchanan. We have already met, Mr Buchanan and I. In the woods, which I suppose is not a real introduction . . .' but what did that matter, her shrug said. I did tell you, dearest.'

She cast a somewhat despairing glance at James,

who stepped forward to clasp the reverend gentleman's hand. From somewhere in the house he could hear a female voice warbling a familiar tune slightly off key.

Early one morning,
Just as the sun was rising.

And another complained that if that 'dratted animal' didn't get out from under her feet she'd hand in her notice that very day. How was she expected to put dinner on the table by six when every minute she was terrified she might fall over it and Elsie was driving her mad with that song so would she kindly give over.

Lucy tutted. 'I'd best go and see what's troubling Mrs Hutton,' she said, but a timid knock at the door interrupted her. A little maid of about twelve, as fragile as a sparrow and as shy as a fawn, popped her head round it, a tray balanced precariously in her stick-like arms.

'Thank you, Elsie,' Lucy said to her, smiling warmly, 'that will be all,' as if the puny child had imagined she was to play hostess. 'I'll pour and then I must go and see what the children are up to.' Mrs. Hutton and her problems seemed to have been forgotten. 'I'm doing my best to teach Emily the fundamentals of fractions but as I'm not too sure of them myself it's an uphill task.' She did not explain what possible use Emily might have of fractions. 'We have no governess at the present moment, Mr Buchanan.' She said it airily as though one were expected any day now. 'So while Papa does his best with Edward and Percy I'm tackling the girls, but really, they are all quite ... well, I
29

wouldn't say wild, but they are not scholarly, are they, Papa?'

She smiled lovingly at her father and he smiled back in like fashion as though neither were unduly concerned with the children's lack of education since, this being their faith in life, something would be bound to turn up before too long. Besides, it was much more important to be well mannered, cheerful and willing, to keep a good spirit and be kind to those less fortunate than oneself than to know how to divide one number by another.

James held the door for her, bowing slightly as she left the room and for the next half-hour he and the reverend gentleman discussed the state of the Dean family's finances. At least James did, for Edward Dean seemed to imagine that, having told the solicitor how he wished to dispose of his worldly goods, whatever they might be, the matter was resolved.

James steered him back time after time from such subjects as butterfly-collecting which was the Reverend Dean's passion; a pair of bullfinches which had nested in his garden hedge last May, since it seemed bird-watching was another; the quaintness of the local dialect which he and his dear wife had found hard to understand when first they settled in Fellthwaite, and did not Mr Buchanan agree that October was the most beautiful month of the year in the district of the Lakes.

'Indeed ... er ... Mr Dean, but perhaps if we could return to the question of your will.'

'Of course, my dear fellow. My mind seems to wander these days, particularly when the subject is not one of a cheerful nature. Now, what else can I

30

tell you?'

'Have you, forgive me, perhaps shares in ... well, the railways, for instance?'

The reverend gentleman looked bewildered. 'The railways?'

'Yes, I have some myself and—'

'Have you indeed?' He smiled amiably, having not the faintest idea what they were to do with him.

'Yes, I just wondered whether you ..

'I'm afraid not, Mr Buchanan.' The rector was genuinely sorry he could not be of more help.

'Did ... was your ... perhaps your wife left something?'

'Left something?'

Surely no man could be so artlessly ignorant of the ways of the world as this one?

'Perhaps for the children?' James prompted.

'I don't think so, Mr Buchanan. I know she gave Lucy, my eldest daughter, if you recall ..

'Yes, sir.'

'...a very pretty pair of earrings but I'm sure they have no particular value, only in as much as they were her mother's.'

'Of course. How charming ... well ...' James looked round the bare room as though searching for inspiration. It was as well scoured and polished as the passage. It contained a large, square table with a Bible on it and at which, or so it appeared, the Reverend Dean wrote his sermons, a couple of glass-fronted bookcases crammed with crumbling books of great antiquity, a skeleton clock ticking on the mantelshelf and, on a small table beside the rector, a chessboard set out with ivory chessmen. A game was obviously in progress and James wondered who the players were. Two faded, red

31

brocade chairs in which they sat and from which the stuffing had almost gone stood on either side of the fireplace. There was a copper coal scuttle in the hearth with no more than half a dozen small pieces of coal in it, evidently to be eked out with care.

Set out on a table beneath the side window where they caught the northern light were a dozen glass cases containing hundreds of mounted butterflies.

James shuddered. He would have liked to discuss Miss Dean's earrings and indeed Miss Dean herself since there was so much he wanted to know. He had heard no talk in the district regarding her, nor any interest shown her by a young man but then, though she was quite, quite exquisite and evidently well bred, there was no money and young men, unless they themselves had considerable wealth, must marry an heiress.

The reverend gentleman, though the soul of courtesy, was beginning to fidget, presumably on pins to get back to his collection.

'So ... you will draw up the necessary documents, will you, Mr Buchanan? I presume I will have to sign something?' His smile reminded James of Lucy. 1f you like I could call in to your office when I am in Fellthwaite which would save you the inconvenience of coming to the rectory again.'

James's mind worked swiftly, formulating ideas on how he was to see Miss Lucy Dean again. He knew no one who was acquainted with her, otherwise he would have met her at some function or other. it seemed probable she did not mix in society, the gentle, backwater existence in which she and her family lived, and the signs of reduced circumstances he had seen in their home not lending themselves to the round of social gatherings the women of his family indulged in. There must be some way in which he could get to know her better and his shrewd brain would find it, but in the meanwhile he must keep alive the small beginning they had made today and the only way to do this was to meet her on her own ground, it seemed.

'Not at all, sir. It would cause me not the slightest inconvenience. In fact I am passing this way on Friday to another appointment so if I may I will call in then. The rough draft will be ready for your consideration. After lunch, perhaps? Say about two o'clock?'

Again the reverend gentleman looked somewhat confused as though he were not really sure of the legal implication of a rough draft and James was just beginning to think he might be either hard of hearing or slow-witted when the furious sound of dogs barking came in through the open window. It was some distance away but getting closer and mixed with it were the angry screeching and squawking of hens, raised excited voices, children's voices, and over it all the thunderous sound of a man provoked beyond endurance.

'Get them bloody dogs off my 'ens, yer young 'ooligans,' the voice roared and Mr Dean turned wondering eyes in the direction of the garden.

'Dear me, what . . .' he began, then stood up and moved hesitantly towards the open French window. James did the same, doing his best to show no more than polite interest though he was pretty positive that the barking, deep and throaty, came from his own dogs. There was accompanying them

33

the hysterical yipping of Thimble who sounded as though he were not at all sure he was having a good time but didn't know how to stop.

They all came hell for leather round the corner of the house with the speed and full-throated roar of the London to Glasgow express. The hens were first, beating their wings in frenzied madness, leaping in the air, feathers flying, then running when they hit the ground, jerking up again with their necks stretched out before them. They were a beautiful colour, a rich, glowing russet brown, their combs and wattles a clear scarlet. There were a dozen of them, Rhodes, James thought, though he knew little enough about the farmyard. They seemed not to have the sense to make for the safety of the trees but ran madly wherever they were driven. They were followed with ecstatic delight by his own two dogs who he had last seen sitting placidly by the front door. Their tails were lashing, their eyes were alight with joy, their mouths were grinning idiotically, for really this was the best game they had ever been allowed to play. At their heels, his own little legs pumping nineteen to the dozen, his wheaten coat a blur across the vivid green of the grass, was Thimble.

James groaned inwardly.

'Thimble . . . Thimble, you little devil, will you come here?' a female voice shrieked, high with laughter. 'Edward, what are those two belonging to Mr Buchanan called, d'you know?' the voice, which proved to be Margaret's, demanded. 'It's awfully difficult to get them to take any notice when you don't know their names.'

At Margaret's back were Edward, Percy and Emily and close behind lumbered a well-built, red-faced man in an overall and brandishing a garden hoe.

'I don't give a bugger what they're called, I'll throttle the lot o' them,' he was telling the world. 'They've dug up me cabbages an' trampled all over me sprouts an' if them 'ens ever lay again it'll be a bloody miracle.'

'Don't let Papa hear you swear like that, Mr Bibby,' Margaret told him reprovingly as she did her best to corner Thimble, who ran between her legs and nearly had her over.

'I'll 'ave that pup's 'ide, an' them an' all,' the incensed Mr Bibby shrieked, aiming his hoe at one of James's dogs. It caught him on the rump and he squealed and James felt the irritation in him turn to anger. It seemed to him that wherever they went and whatever they did the Dean family created havoc, which was all very well and nothing to do with him except when it affected something which belonged to him.

He could not abide cruelty to animals and what the gardener had done, no matter how he was provoked, had a nasty streak in it. His dogs had been trained to sit, to stay, to lie down, stand up, to walk to heel, and for the past six months, despite being less than a year old, had been exemplary in their behaviour. Now, what with free-roaming hens, an excitable and totally untrained puppy, four shrieking children, not to mention the maddened gardener, they had totally lost control and forgotten all they had been taught, and in a way it was his fault.

'Excuse me, sir,' he said politely to Mr Dean, no sign of the storm brewing inside him. Gently putting the reverend gentleman to one side and

35

stepping from the French window, the cold thunderclap of his voice brought them all, even, it seemed, the deranged hens, to a standstill.

'Holmes, Watson, come here to me,' he told the dogs in a tone of voice which brooked no argument, knowing, as his voice cracked across the lawn, there was really no need for such a show of force. He was allowing his own ill humour, and not just with this mêlée, he was honest enough to admit, to blur his usually clear mind. Miss Lucy Dean had, from the moment he had first clapped eyes on her, flushed, dishevelled, her hair rippling in a polished curtain about her, her great golden eyes catching the very sunshine in their depths, bemused him, bewitched him, cast a spell about him from which he could not shake himself free. It confused him, penetrating the reserve which was his nature, and it took the form of raging at his dogs on whom no blame could be laid.

They were all completely bewildered by it, children and animals alike, though Bibby seemed well suited, looking round and nodding as though to say at last here was someone who could put a halter on this lot.

'Here to me, now.' James's voice was harsh as he pointed at the ground in front of him and, both quivering and moving their tails placatingly, the suddenly silent black dogs padded obediently across the lawn and stood where he indicated.

'Sit!' They sat.

But Thimble was not so polite. Bouncing like a ball, his teeth flashing, his eyes glowing, his tail wagging, he raced across the grass and began to leap all over the unfortunate Holmes. Holmes, his anguished eyes on his master's face, though it took a great deal of self-control, ignored him.

Bending down, James swiftly picked up the wriggling, excited puppy, holding him round his plump body with hands of steel, his face glaring directly into that of the dog.

'Behave, I say.' His eyes were fierce and compelling. He gave the puppy a small shake and, surprised but not hurt, Thimble whimpered and became quiet. 'You are an ill-mannered cur and if you were mine I'd—'

'But he is not yours, Mr Buchanan,' a cool voice said, 'and I'd be obliged if you would hand him to Edward.'

'They was playin' 'avoc in my vegetable garden, Miss Lucy, an' all three need a good 'idin' in my opinion. If it 'adn't bin fer this gempmum 'ere'— Bibby nodded in an aggrieved fashion at James— 'Gawd knows what'd 've become of them there 'ens.'

'Thank you, Bibby, that will be all.'

Lucy Dean had appeared from some doorway further along the house, probably an outhouse, James thought, for she wore an overall and had a large wooden mixing spoon in her hand. What she had been doing with it was not immediately obvious, that is until the hens all surged in delighted anticipation towards her, cackling their goodwill, their fright forgotten. it seemed this was something they recognised and James guessed that Lucy had been cooking up the scraps on which they were to be fed. Her indignation at James's handling of her dog was plainly displayed in the stiff turn of her head on her neck, by the high colour at her cheekbones and the flash of temper in her golden eyes.

'Lucy, my dear . . .'

'No, Papa, Thimble is only a puppy and—'

'And will remain so until the end of his days, Miss Dean, unless some farmer shoots him when he finds him worrying his sheep.'

'You are being melodramatic, Mr Buchanan.' She raised her head higher and waved her spoon. 'He was harming no one.'

' 'E'd 'ave 'ad them bloody 'ens, beggin tha' pardon, Miss Lucy.'

'There is no need to use language like that in front of the children, Bibby. You know my father does not care for it.'

'Beggin'tha' pardon, Reverend, Miss Lucy, but them 'ens is—was—good layers as tha' well know an' Gawd only knows what they'll be like now. Useless, I reckon, after a fright like this 'un.'

'Thank you, Bibby, but as you can see they have come to no harm. Now, I'm sorry if Thimble and . . . and these two'—with a disparaging wave of her spoon at James's quivering dogs—'have damaged the vegetable garden. It was unfortunate that . . . that Mr Buchanan's dogs were left unattended and—'

James, to his horror and amazement, found himself to be quite incensed, interrupting her rudely.

'Miss Dean, my dogs, if not interfered with, will remain where they are put until I tell them to move. If yours is not stable enough to be let loose in the garden then he should be kept on a leash.'

What the bloody hell was he babbling on about, he wondered desperately and why did he feel the need to argue with this beautiful, spirited girl and all over a storm in a teacup? This was, of course, nothing to do with his dogs, the part of his mind that looked on coolly told him. So what was it about? his previously untouched heart asked him sardonically. You are making a fool of yourself, you who are normally so cool-headed. His dogs had, for a moment, lost control of their manners, and so, it appeared, had he. They were not used to hens, nor even children. His cousins, who all lived in and about Fellthwaite, Ambleside and Skelwith, had dozens of children between them, or so it seemed. He had lost count of the times he had been included, reluctantly on his part, in family christenings, in Christmas festivities where Ben or Alex's, Anne, Janet or Christine's offspring had squealed like hordes of piglets and raced about in what seemed to be senseless circles. His dogs had been left at home then, or, if the family event took place at Howethwaite, though he did his best to avoid it, were shut safely away from the excited hysteria that seemed to be the prerogative of the young. He always vowed at the end of such visits that when he had children they would be as well behaved as his dogs, or at least as well behaved as they had been up to today!

'Thank you for your advice, Mr Buchanan.' Her voice was icy. 'I shall bear it in mind. Now, if you will excuse me I was making the hens' feed and as you can see they are eager to be at it so I'll say good-day to you, sir.'

She was turning away, dismissing him, since he had proved such a tedious boor, her manner said, but he would not allow it. When he spoke again his voice was as icy as hers though he tried his best to keep it polite. He knew he was making a poor showing and he cursed his own nature which was to

39

be aloof, and his temper which could be quick. But somehow he must become better acquainted with Miss Lucy Dean and he knew he was not going the best way about it. Acquainted for what purpose was not really clear either at the moment, he only knew he must find some way to show himself in a better light than the pompous, self-opinionated fool she obviously thought him to be.

'I am just arranging with your father...' His voice was harsh, angry, truculent almost, and they all, including Bibby, turned to stare at him. The children, Edward with the squirming Thimble in his arms, Percy who was declaring loudly that he thought the whole thing had been great fun, didn't Emily agree, had been about to go back to whatever it was they were doing before Thimble had teased Holmes and Watson into lunacy. It really had been a good game and quite harmless since everyone knew what daft creatures hens were and the children couldn't understand what Mr Buchanan was making such a fuss about. Lucy was clearly displeased with him over something and now Mr Buchanan, as annoyed as she was, had something further to say, it seemed.

'Yes, Mr Buchanan?' Lucy's eyes narrowed suspiciously in that way they were all familiar with, a sort of warning that told them they were only a fraction away from going too far. 'You have not yet finished your business with Papa?'

'Indeed we have, Miss Dean, but—'

'Perhaps you have something further to say on the bad manners of our dog who you clearly believe led yours into mischief.'

James felt the irritation goad him. and he spoke through clenched teeth. 'No, Miss Dean, though I

40

must say if I had him for a few days he would—'

'No doubt be as submissive as yours?'

'Well behaved, I would call it.'

'Dear God, sir, you really will not give up, will you?'

'Nor you, Miss Dean.'

She lifted the spoon and the spellbound audience were amazed when, for some reason, Mr Buchanan began to laugh.

'Really, Miss Dean, I do wish you would stop brandishing that implement in my face. I meant neither you, your brothers and sisters, your courteous father, your gardener, your hens or your dog any harm but I have the distinct feeling that if I don't behave myself you might give me a good paddling, just like the one my nanny administered when I misbehaved.'

They watched, entranced, even Bibby, to see how Miss Lucy Dean, whose temper was quick but whose heart was warm, would respond. Would she unbend and begin to laugh, sharing the joke, or would she give Mr Buchanan a further demonstration of how haughty she could be? They were inclined to think the former, for the dimple at the corner of her mouth appeared for an instant and her lips moved in what might have been a smile.

'Lucy, my dear,' their papa suddenly interrupted, just as though the past five minutes had gone by him unnoticed, hens, dogs, children, all some sort of passing parade that had nothing to do with him. 'Mr Buchanan has been most kind and helpful. Though I know it upsets you to talk of wills, it really is necessary and now it is done and we can forget it. Put it behind us. Mr Buchanan has it in his capable hands and I have only to sign the papers when they are ready. You have no idea what a weight it has taken off my mind.' He turned to smile genially at James. 'I thank you, sir. Now I have matters to which I must attend,' making them sound as though the good of the entire country depended on his judgement, 'so I'll leave you in my daughter's capable hands.'

If James was astonished it did not show, for by now he was becoming used to the Reverend Dean's eccentricities. He held out his hand, saying as he did so, 'Then I shall look forward to seeing you on Friday, sir. The documents will be ready then. I trust you can find two witnesses?'

'Witnesses?'

'Yes, sir. Your signature needs to be witnessed by two people who do not benefit from your will.'

'Really, of course, how silly of me.' He looked vaguely about him as though two such persons might easily be found hiding behind a handy bush but his daughter came swiftly to his aid. She put a hand on his arm as though calming a troubled animal and he turned at once to smile with relief into her loving face.

'Mrs Hutton will do, Papa, and Mr Bibby.'

'Will they, my dear?'

'Mr Buchanan?' She turned her polite gaze on him for confirmation.

'Yes, of course.'

'There, then that's settled.' The Reverend Dean let out a great sigh of relief. 'Now then, Lucy, will you see Mr Buchanan out. I must get on.' Turning, he drifted back into his study, closing the French windows on a troublesome world.

Lucy handed the spoon to Margaret then turned

to James, indicating that he was to re-enter the house through the door which led to the narrow passage. Her manner was still curt. She did not speak and he had not the faintest notion of what was in her mind. The face, which had been so open, so sparkling with good humour and joy, had closed up, turned against him and he was at a loss to know why. Admittedly he had been his usual forthright self on the subject of her dog, but surely she had not taken offence at that, at least not enough to keep up this icy restraint she had pulled about herself.

The dogs leaped into the back seat of the motor car and lay down, still subdued and she watched, her face quite blank as he climbed into the front.

'Until Friday then, Miss Dean,' his face as expressionless as hers.

'Until Friday, Mr Buchanan,' she answered coolly and he wondered why he had the impression she believed he had tricked her into something, what he couldn't imagine, against her will.

CHAPTER THREE

James Buchanan sprang up from the armchair in which he had been sprawled and sauntered in what he imagined was a casual manner across Franny Buchanan's drawing-room carpet. He placed both hands palm down on the windowsill and peered through the open window to the long stretch of immaculate garden beyond it. The sky was the lovely, tender blue of autumn and the sun spread its serenity across it. The paths were carefully raked, leaves which were beginning to fall removed one by one by the Buchanan gardeners and the flowerbeds glowed with michaelmas daisies, dahlias and chrysanthemums. There were bees at work and a few painted lady butterflies drifted through the still air. James wondered idly if the Reverend Dean had any in his collection.

Frances Buchanan, who was the wife of Alex Buchanan, James's cousin, was not deceived by his air of carelessness, watching him with amused interest. He evidently had something of great importance, at least to himself, weighing him down and she waited patiently for him to divulge it. It was a Sunday, a day when James normally would be found climbing some mountain or other in that solitary way he had but today, for some reason best known to himself, he had turned up in her drawing-room with no explanation nor excuse. He had accepted tea and listened to her chatter but it was very evident that his mind was not on twelve-year-old Henry Buchanan's threat to run away from the well-known public school to which all the Buchanan boys had gone, nor Franny's plans for a dance she meant to give shortly. The possibility of rain did not concern him at all, the last thrown in to test whether he was really listening, which she knew he wasn't.

He sat down again and absent-mindedly accepted a third cup of tea, sipping it with so little enjoyment it might have been hemlock, then, putting his cup and saucer on the table beside him, he stood up and prowled about again. He studied some prints on the cream-painted wall, then fingered a small sculpted copy of Degas's ballet girl which stood among others on a low table by the

44

window. When he sat down on the stool in front of her piano, opened the lid and cast a haunted look at the keys, Franny stopped what she realised was just babbling and lay back among the cushions on her chair.

For several minutes there was silence but he did not appear to notice. He leaned his left forearm on the piano top and picked out a small tune with the index finger of his right hand, his brow deeply furrowed, his mouth clamped tight, his eyes a pale unfocused grey.

She could stand it no longer. 'James, if you continue like this I swear I'll scream out loud. For God's sake, leave that damned piano alone and come and and tell me what you are doing here and why you are in such a state. Oh, yes, you are. I've never seen you like this before and if I didn't know you better I'd think—'

'Do you know a family by the name of Dean?' He turned and interrupted her so brusquely she was startled. His voice was harsh as though he were angry about something, something he could do nothing about. it was not like him, for he had his life in a pattern of smooth routine which suited him to perfection, or so he would have everybody believe, but this, whatever it was, had him coiled like an overwound watch.

Franny was astonished. To give herself time to think she leaned over and took a cigarette from an engraved silver box on the table beside her, lit it and inhaled deeply.

'No, should I?'

'They're . . . he's a rector.'

'A rector! James, can you see me with—'

'There's a daughter.'

'A rector with a daughter! My God, James, am I to—'

'If you make one of your clever remarks, Franny, I swear I'll hit you.' His voice was savage with the bottled-up emotion he was doing his best to hide and which was warning her that he did not care to be trifled with. This was serious, important to him and he was in no mood for her usual facetiousness. His mouth was clamped tight and his thrusting jaw was clenched with a ferocious determination to be calm, and though she was besieged with the longing to question him, to know more about this rector's daughter, for the moment she had the good sense to keep her mouth shut. She raised one finely plucked eyebrow questioningly and waited.

'They're ... a decent family. A good family, if you get my meaning, but poor as church mice,' he said at last, shooting her a fierce, none-of-your-smart-remarks look from beneath his lowering brows. 'Reverend Dean has the living at St Silas's, given him by the Forsythes. Dalebarrow Hall, you know, so you see they have decent connections. I met them ... the father, on some business last week and it struck me that ... Goddammit it to hell, Franny. I'm not used to this.'

'Used to what, James?' she asked him innocently.

'Don't take that tone with me, woman,' he snarled. James Buchanan was an important, well-respected gentleman, not only in Fellthwaite but in the legal profession and had never in his life had the misfortune to be pinned down, squirming, and in a position where he had to play a part that he found downright uncomfortable. He did not beg favours, he gave them if he thought them worthy.

46

He asked no one for their help, and any problem he might have he solved himself. His dignity was suffering and he did not like it, neither did he like Franny Buchanan's sly smile. He was a proud man, proud of his family name, self-reliant and private and to be brought to begging from his cousin's wife to help him in the matter of ... of ... Jesus, what was it he wanted? He wasn't absolutely sure himself. He only knew that from the day he met her, Lucy Dean, in all her young, innocent, untouched loveliness, had come between him and everything that up to now had formed his pleasant, harmonious lifestyle. She was in his night dreams and his waking moments, thoughts of her interrupting the flow of his words during the day to the consternation of himself and the men with whom he did business. He could not get her out of his mind. He had not seen her when he visited her father with the documents concerning his will, and had been appalled by his own feeling of devastation at her absence.

'Is ... your daughter not at home, sir?' he heard himself asking the reverend, the yearning in his voice obvious at least to him, like some lovesick schoolboy hoping to catch a glimpse of the object of his devotion.

'No, I believe she and the children have gone to ...'

Edward Dean struck his forehead with the palm of his hand.

'Now where was it she said they were going? Dear me, my memory is appalling, Mr Buchanan. You must forgive me.'

'No matter, sir.' And indeed it did not matter, for if she was not here where he could see her it did not seem important where she was.

So, in his usual forthright manner, he must do something about it. Hell's teeth, he couldn't go about like this, could he? He must either put her completely out of his mind and resume his courtship of Charlotte Gibson, or take steps to get to know Lucy Dean; and since as a bachelor he could not ask a motherless young woman to his home, which was without a hostess, he must ask Franny for help. He could have confided in any one of his cousins, Anne or Christine or Janet, all married to well-set-up gentlemen, or to his male cousins' wives, Joan or Frances. The first four were conventional, straight-laced and concerned only with how things would look. So he had chosen Franny because he thought she would understand since she was the most—what would he call her?—sophisticated, worldly, uninhibited by the prejudices of their class with nothing to hold her back like the reputation of her children since she had none. He thought he could trust her to carry the thing off without revealing that it was at his behest that Miss Lucy Dean was being invited into their social circle, and besides, he could think of no other way to get what he wanted which was possession of the Reverend Edward Dean's beautiful daughter.

'I want you to take her up, Franny.' His voice was abrupt as he rose from the piano stool and returned to his chair. 'She comes from good stock and apart from a sad lack of cash is a most suitable young lady. She will not disgrace herself. She is a lady, clever and bright and you will find her . . . quite delightful.'

'As you evidently do and what I would like to know is what you have planned for this paragon?'

48

'That is my business.'

'No, it's not. Not if I'm going to get involved.'

James shook his head, giving a fair imitation of a beast tormented by flies. His face was dark and stormy and he turned away as though he didn't know how to deal with her obvious disquiet, a disquiet he shared, for he had no idea how this was to proceed. He only knew he had to see the girl again, talk to her, get some idea of . . . well, what? God, he wished he'd never clapped eyes on her, really he did, for he would have been so much more in charge of himself with Charlotte Gibson as his wife.

'And another thing to consider,' Franny went on, 'is will she be interested?'

'Christ, Franny, you're not to tell her it was me put you up to this.' He was aghast, leaning forward to glare into her face.

'I don't mean that, James. I mean won't she be surprised to find herself being called upon by a woman she doesn't know?'

'Of course she won't. Ladies call on one another all the time. They . . . well, they call to welcome newcomers and . . .'

'She's hardly a newcomer from what you tell me.'

'Oh, you can deal with that, Franny. You know how such things are done. She's only a girl and won't be able to resist.' His voice was full of confidence.

'A girl, you say? How old?'

'I suppose . . . nineteen.' He looked somewhat shamefaced, but then was it not the custom for a gentleman to wait until his thirties, or even his forties, and then to take a young bride with plenty

49

of childbearing years ahead of her?

'Young, James. You're thirty-four. I'm not implying that she's too young but may you not find her . . . well, her girlishness too immature for your sophisticated tastes?'

'Not this one, Franny.' His voice was quiet and very sure.

'Well, I suppose you know what you're doing. And as you say she won't be able to resist. After all, you are the county's most eligible bachelor.'

He frowned, his expression telling her he did not care for the implication that the lovely Miss Dean would take him only for that reason. 'You'll do it then?'

'It might be fun.' Franny lit another cigarette from the stub of the first and James watched her with faint distaste. He did hate to see a woman smoke and he was surprised at Alex for not stopping her. He certainly would not allow it in any woman of his.

'This is serious, Franny. I'm . . . well, it's serious and I hope you act in a proper manner. Miss Dean is a lady of some refinement and breeding and—'

'Oh, get off your high horse, James. You can be a real prig sometimes. I've said I'll do it and I will, and I shall be the soul of discretion, not to mention decorum.'

James Buchanan was not the only one to own a motor car in Fellthwaite. Just the same, when the dashing little Austin Ten two-seater drew up with a flourish and a spray of gravel at the front door of St Silas's rectory the day after James's talk with Franny Buchanan, those congregated there could not believe their eyes. To their knowledge the rectory drive had never before known the roar of

50

the combustion engine, the blare of a motor-car horn or the screech of brakes and now, within the space of two weeks two such machines had thundered up the drive.

Mr Buchanan's Rolls-Royce was a gleaming silver. This vehicle was bottle green, its panels decorated with fine bands of gold, its hood, which was down and tucked away in a sturdy cover, black, and at the rear was a railed space for luggage. There were polished brass lamps and hub caps, black leather seats but the most amazing thing, at least to young Edward Dean and old Bibby, neither of whom had a great opinion of the female sex, was that it was driven by a woman. They were all even more shocked by the way she was dressed.

They were riding their bicycles round and round in circles on the carriage turning space, shouting with laughter as was their habit, totally ignoring Bibby's roars to be careful with his bloody gravel which he had just raked, even Miss Lucy, who surely at her age should know better, as daft as the rest. They had assembled for a ride over to the Roman Station south of Ambleside which Lucy was interested in and a sorrier bunch of machines Bibby had never clapped eyes on, he had remarked gloomily when they were first dragged up the drive. If they got them hooligans to the gate he'd be surprised, he had told Mrs Hutton as he drank a cup of her almost black tea preparatory to making a start with the oiling can. Oiling can! They weren't fit for anything but the scrap heap which was where they had come from in the first place and had it not been for Master Edward's know-how and knack with a spanner, with bits of odds and ends of nuts and bolts, old spokes and lengths of wire, they

51

would never have been resurrected. Not one under twenty years old, falling to bits and held together by perseverance, cork and glue, as Bibby's old dad used to say when faced with some ancient farm machinery. Somehow the young rascal, with Bibby's help, of course, and a bicycle manual which he'd picked up in a bookshop in Ambleside, had made them comparatively roadworthy. Miss Lucy's was in the best condition, a Lady's Rover with a basket on the front, a spring saddle, a plunger brake and a dress cord to protect her skirts from the spokes. Miss Lucy, who needed her machine for shopping errands and such, since it was a long walk to the grocer and butcher—and they bought in small quantities for monetary reasons—used hers several times a week, but this morning, it being a fine golden day, they were off on some shenanigans Bibby wanted nothing to do with.

They all came to a screeching halt, mouths agape, eyes wide, machine crashing into machine, falling about like drunken sailors as they did their best to keep their balance, staring in wonder at the apparition which climbed from the motor car.

She wore knickerbockers! They were full, pleated round the waist and gathered into a band under the knee, below which were gaiters buttoned down the side. Her serviceable jacket of tweed was short and belted and she had on what looked like a gentleman's shirt with a tie. She wore no hat and her pale blonde hair, blown about by the speed of the machine she had driven, was carelessly tied back with a black velvet ribbon.

'Good morning. Am I speaking to Miss Dean?' she called out. 'Lovely day, isn't it? I see you are about to make the most of it so I won't keep you. I just felt it was about time I called on you. I know you have lived in the neighbourhood for a while but better late than never, I say. I was hoping to meet you and perhaps invite you to come to one of my afternoons. I'm sure you will like my friends. Mostly ladies of the district who would be delighted to make your acquaintance. My name is Frances Buchanan, by the way.' She grinned disarmingly. She was perfectly at ease, seeing nothing unusual in a woman dressed in trousers driving a motor car, nor in the fact that it had taken her six years to welcome newcomers to the area. As though to emphasise it she leaned her bottom on the bonnet of the Austin, drew out of her pocket a gold cigarette case and lit a cigarette with a lethal-looking lighter made of some base metal and dragged the smoke deep into her lungs. Folding her arms across her breast she narrowed her chocolate brown eyes against the sun's rays and studied them all one by one.

'Well, is no one going to speak?' she asked as the silence drew on, raising a fine blonde eyebrow and blowing out a perfect smoke ring at the same time. It was evident that Edward was vastly impressed.

Lucy was clearly amazed, but pulling her amazement about her she did her best to be polite as she had been taught. 'How kind of you to call, Mrs Buchanan,' she stammered, 'but I'm afraid you are wasting your time. I am far too busy looking after my family to go about in company.'

She knew she sounded rude, which was unforgivable, but she could think of no other way to discourage the astonishing Mrs Buchanan, who, it seemed, had taken it into her head to draw Lucy Dean into her well-bred circle of friends. Why, she didn't know and it certainly did not occur to her that James Buchanan might be at the back of it. Why should it? She had met him only once when he called on her father. A man almost as old as her father, at least it seemed so to her and his connection with this woman did not enter her mind. Now all she had to do was persuade Mrs Buchanan that Lucy Dean was perfectly happy with her own way of life, that she had no desire to receive or make calls as women like Mrs Buchanan did. Lucy was not a 'company' person. She had no company manners and Mrs Buchanan must be made to understand that, for she did not want her coming here again with her bright smile and outlandish clothes which she knew would shock Papa if he saw them. Lucy had no wish to mix with 'good' people though she knew she was one herself, for her mama had been a lady. No, Lucy loved long walks on the fells, cycling with the children, romping about the orchard and meadow at the back of the house. She was happy messing about with Bibby's hens, getting her hands dirty in the soil of the vegetable garden where she and Bibby were experimenting with the cultivation of globe artichokes, and to prove it she still had soil under her fingernails no matter how hard she scrubbed them. She had no style, as she believed it was called. Look at her today in her oatmeal flannel skirt and an old cream shirt of Papa's, her strong walking boots and thick, hand-knitted brown woollen stockings, her hair tied back into a twisted rope of tangled curls; but she was gloriously happy. There was a picnic in the basket at the front of her bicycle and the day stretched out before them, splendid with golden autumn sunshine, with the hyacinth blue of the sky.

But Mrs Buchanan was not put off by her rudeness, it seemed. 'Miss Dean, you disappoint me. I believe it is the custom to ask a caller to take tea.' She smiled composedly, telling Lucy that she was not to be turned away so easily.

Lucy was suddenly ashamed of her lack of manners. Her mama, who was surely watching from that gentle heaven where she now dwelled, would be appalled and she was just about to stammer an apology when her father's voice from the top of the steps interrupted her guilty thoughts. She turned to him in surprise, for it took more than a caller, when they had one, that is, to winkle him from his study. Standing beside him was Buffy and, bewildered, Lucy realised that she must have overheard the conversation at the front of the house and gone to fetch him.

He did his best to avert his eyes from Mrs Buchanan's knickerbockers.

'Mrs Buchanan, it is Mrs Buchanan, isn't it, or so Buffy told me.' His voice was gentle and courteous but there was a core of something in it Lucy had not heard before.

Mrs Buchanan turned and went up the steps. 'Reverend Dean. How do you do. A lovely day, is it not?' She held out a hand and shook his briskly.

'Indeed it is, but why are you standing here outside? Lucy, show Mrs Buchanan into the drawing-room and ... well, I'm sure Buffy could manage some tea ... or ... Do come in, Mrs Buchanan.'

Lucy's face was a picture and Franny Buchanan made a mental note to tell her that if she was to get on in society, as it seemed James intended her to do, she must make an effort not to let her every thought show so plainly. It appeared to have on it a mixture of consternation, irritation and plain indignation that her papa had so summarily spoiled her plans for the day, and she was right.

From where she stood Lucy could just make out a small corner of the lake, the deep blue sky mirrored in it and a small boat turning, its white sails like the wings of a gull. She could smell the sweetness of the bracken and fern and could picture the sheep trods up which, when they had finished with the Roman Station, their booted feet would climb. In her mind's eye was the tawny tapestry of autumn Lakeland spread out below right down into the vale where Grasmere lay. Fine waterfalls misted with silver spray, the strength and beauty of conifer and rowan. High fells where they would walk all day long without meeting a soul except for a taciturn shepherd and his dog and the scattered sheep they guarded.

Now, with a few polite and astounding words her papa had spoiled it all. It needed a whole day to enjoy the outing they had planned and by the time Mrs Buchanan had left the day would be half over.

The Reverend Edward Dean, his life sadly diminished by the loss of his beloved wife five years ago, had retreated from harsh reality and the responsibility of bringing up his children and, though he was was sorry about it, it was beyond his scope to change it. He could do nothing to ease his loss except become immersed in his obsession for catching and adding to his butterfly collection, and, in a lesser degree, bird-watching. He loved his children but without Evelyn had not the faintest notion what to do with them. So he did nothing,

56

leaving Lucy to muddle through as best she could. She did it very well. She had a practical streak in her come from her mother and though she regretted her brothers'and sisters' lack of a decent education, particularly the boys, what she could not mend she put to one side for later.

But deep in Edward's consciousness was the niggling suspicion that Evelyn would want to see, at the very least, her three daughters decently married and how were they to manage that if they did not go about, as was their right, in the society from which he and Evelyn had come. Lucy was eighteen and went nowhere without a line of her brothers and sisters straggling behind her like a mother duck with her ducklings. She was a beautiful and intelligent young woman and would make a fine wife, though how he would cope without her he didn't dare think. But that must not stand in the way of his doing his duty by her. He had no idea what Mrs Buchanan was up to but if it was to lead to the sort of social life Evelyn would have wanted for her daughter, direct her to people who would guide her in the right way of doing things, introduce her to young men of good family and thereby ensure that all three of his girls had a chance of making a decent marriage, then he must do all he could to bring it about. And if this strangely dressed woman who had so astonishingly and belatedly come to call could help him then so be it.

The boys, well, they must wait, though for what he didn't know.

They sat and drank tea and he let Frances Buchanan do most of the talking. His eyes were drawn again and again to her knickerbockers and gaiters, though he politely did his best not to stare. The cigarette she had been smoking when he first saw her beside her motor car had been stubbed out in the gravel before she entered the house and thankfully she had not lit another one. They discussed the weather, at least he and Mrs Buchanan did, since Lucy was tight-lipped at the waste of her day. They talked of Mrs Buchanan's love of motoring and motor cars, though he scarce understood her remarks about cylinders and chassis, about supension and mileage and of her intention to enter a race at a place called Brooklands if she could persuade her husband to buy her a twenty-five hp Talbot racer like the one that had taken the record in February of this year. One hundred and three miles in just sixty minutes, imagine that, if he could, until he began to wonder if he was perhaps being a little precipitate in entrusting his daughter to a woman such as this.

'Well now, Reverend Dean,' Mrs Buchanan said at last, placing her cup and saucer, the contents of which she had hardly touched, on the table beside her, 'shall we get back to the reason for my visit. I have been meaning to call for a long time. My mother-in-law was acquainted with your wife, did you know that? Oh, yes,' when the reverend gentleman looked astonished, 'and I thought it was about time I called on her daughter now that she is of an age to . . . enjoy society. I am holding a small dance at my home next Saturday. Nothing formal, I might add, and I'm sure she would enjoy it.' She ignored the look of frantic appeal on Lucy Dean's face, since she had promised James she would do this. Besides, she didn't care if the girl wanted to come or not, or if she enjoyed it or not. She was

58

keeping a promise, that was all, and it was up to James to do the rest.

'I have no children of my own,' she went on, 'and if I had they would be too young, but I do love to dance so I borrow my nieces and nephews. My sister-in-law, Janet, Janet Gunson, that is, has four handsome sons. Job is eighteen and the eldest. They have lots of friends, young friends, so I thought, well, other members of the family will be there and a few close friends, so do say you will join us, Miss Dean.'

Lucy turned to her father, her expression anguished. Surely he did not mean to force her to go to this dreadful affair of Mrs Buchanan's. Dancing which, she supposed, meant waltzes and . . . and the tango—was that what it was called?—and whatever else was fashionable at the moment, was something she knew nothing about. She could remember as a child—how long ago it seemed— she and Mama briskly circling the nursery, their arms about one another, laughing helplessly, which she recalled her mama did a lot of, and performing what she supposed must have been a polka, but she had forgotten the steps of even that.

No, she would hate it. The guests would all know one another, for they were a big family. Young men and women acting the giddy goat, which she and her brothers and sisters did all the time, she admitted it, but the idea of witnessing perfect strangers enjoying themselves in such a way, and worse still being asked to join in, was a horror to which she would not submit. Though she had not been among young ladies of her own class she was pretty sure they would not relish putting their white hands in the soil as she did, soil mixed with

59

manure, kneeling beside their gardener as she did, planting globe artichoke off-sets. Would they know what a dibber was and how far apart to plant? Could they discuss how to cook up hens' mash on the saddle-room boiler; how many greengages and damsons, cherries and pears they could expect on the trees in the orchard; the best way to milk a goat; how to keep a cow, which Lucy longed to do since the milk, and cheese and butter she would learn to make from it would be invaluable in stretching out her papa's pitifully small stipend. If Mrs Hutton would let her she would have tried her hand at bread-making, at preserving fruit, at making jam from the rich harvest of plums, which she thought would be immensely satisfying and yet here was Papa evidently prepared to plunge her into a round of social activities which she knew she would loathe. It seemed, from what he and Mrs Buchanan were discussing, she was to be fetched next Saturday at seven thirty sharp by Mrs Buchanan's chauffeur and be taken to Grange House on the other side of Ambleside where dancing and a buffet supper were to be held.

For a moment or two Mrs Buchanan was distracted by shouted laughter outside the drawing-room window which looked out on to the front drive. Holding up her hand in a peremptory fashion, well used to being obeyed, she strode to the window and her expression changed to one of deep annoyance.

'That boy is sitting in my motor car,' she exclaimed, menace in her voice. 'And why are those children making such a commotion?'

Lucy stood up and moved to stand beside her, and sure enough there was Edward in the driving seat of Mrs Buchanan's vehicle and, what seemed to make it worse, he had on her driving goggles. He was not touching anything, simply sitting there in a dream-like state, no doubt imagining that he was roaring round the track at that place Mrs Buchanan had mentioned.

And it seemed Thimble had escaped from the kitchen and made hotfoot for the front drive where he could hear his people's voices. His 'people' were doing their best to catch him, making it into a game, as they did everything, and threatening Mrs Buchanan's shining motor as they chased him round and round it.

Mrs Buchanan opened the window and her voice might have been heard in the centre of Ambleside, directing them to take that animal to the back of the house and if that boy would get out of that motor she would be much obliged. They obeyed without a murmur, proving that all they needed was a bit of discipline which they obviously weren't getting at the rectory.

She and Lucy resumed their seats and Lucy resumed her protest.

'I really don't think I can be spared, Papa,' she said desperately, though she could think of no good reason why not at such short notice. If she had known this was to happen she would have made damn sure she had a watertight excuse, but now all she could do was bluff and bluster, conscious that she was fighting a losing battle. Mrs Buchanan was very determined and Papa was putty in her hands. She was quite amazed that he was taking such an interest, was so agreeable to all Mrs Buchanan suggested and it was not until they were alone that he told her the reason.

'Have you ever considered what your life would have been like had your dear mama lived, Lucy? How different it would have been? From the age of thirteen you have looked after us all, managed the household and even, with very little help, brought up your brother who was a newborn infant. You have had no childhood to speak of, no young, carefree girlhood.'

'Oh, Papa, my life is as carefree as a bird's, or would be if you refuse to allow Mrs Buchanan to interfere in it.'

'Maybe it is, or you imagine it is, but you are a young woman of refinement, clever and bright and beautiful and . . . Lucy, my dear, I must say it, you are . . . ready for marriage.'

She shook her head vehemently. 'Oh, no, Papa, not yet. Not for years. The children need me, you need me and I cannot desert you. Besides, I'm sure all the young men I would be compelled to mix with next Saturday will be as brainless as . . . as . . .' She paused, running out of words.

'Yes, my dear? As what? Have you some member of the male sex with whom to compare them, these young men? You know only myself and Bibby, Edward and Percy, some of my parishioners and we can hardly be described as typical examples of—'

'I know what they will be like, Papa. All they will talk about are . . . are what I consider to be trivialities and I for one will be bored rigid by it. I won't fit in, dearest. Mrs Buchanan talks of having fun but I have no idea what she means by that. They will be strangers to me. I don't know how to do all these strange-sounding dances they do now and, Papa, you know I will hate it. Please, please, don't make me go. Please, I couldn't stand it.'

He had to smile. She was so passionate, this lovely daughter of his. About her family, her care of them and the servants, of him and indeed anyone who asked for her help. She would go to any lengths to give support and comfort to people less fortunate than herself and Mrs Hutton had been heard to declare the lot of them would starve the way Miss Lucy tried to feed every tramp and vagrant who knocked at the kitchen door. Give them the food out of her own mouth, she would, ready to do anyone a good turn and taking under her wing any lame duck that passed by.

Swiftly she knelt at her father's knee, her face flushed with entreaty, her hair tumbling about in a way that was familiar to Edward, for hadn't Evelyn's done the same? Her eyes were deep golden pools of entreaty and he could feel himself wavering. He didn't want her to become a part of the social scene, not because he was afraid it would spoil her but because he could not imagine his life without her in the house. He did not want her to meet eligible young men, to find one that suited her, to marry and leave them, for in a way it would be like losing Evelyn all over again. How would they manage, he and the children, without her warmth, her laughter, her blithe spirit which led them through so many tangles? Who would play mother to Percy or do their best to make sure Edward had a chance at a decent school? The girls needed her companionship, her guidance, her protective love, her leadership and yet she deserved her chance, must have her chance of a suitable marriage, for what else was there for her in this world of which she was a part? He could not hold her back and if she needed to be persuaded, even pushed, then he must do it for her own sake. The Buchanans were an old and wealthy family and to be befriended by one of them could do only good, not only for Lucy but for his other children.

'Papa, please,' she whispered directly into his face. 'Don't make me go. You know how I will despise such ... such affairs. I won't understand their ... their manners ...'

'You have lovely manners, child. Your mama saw to that.'

'I don't mean that, Papa. I mean the way they go about things. I shall do everything wrong.'

'No, you will not.'

'And I just don't know what to talk about if sensible conversation is forbidden. I've never met people like Mrs Buchanan before and ... well ... I just don't want to become involved.'

Her papa stroked her hair with one hand and with the other took hers in a warm clasp. His face was kind, calm, certain, and, though he could see she was very near to tears, his voice was firm with unusual resolve, he who had never been resolved about anything for a long time.

'I'm sorry, dearest, but I must insist. It is what your mama would have wanted for you,' and that was that as far as Edward Dean was concerned.

'This is all your fault, Buffy Tyson,' she ranted later, absolutely beside herself with rage. 'If you hadn't fetched Papa to the front door I could have refused her, politely, of course, and Papa would have been none the wiser.'

'Isn't that dishonest, Lucy Dean? I would say so, deceiving your papa who wants nothing but the best for you.'

64

'I wish you'd mind your own business. It's not you who has to play silly party games and prance about the floor in the arms of some callow youth who can't find his way round the room let alone up to the high fells.'

'There are more important things in life than tramping the fells, Lucy.'

'Is that so? Well, I can think of none.'

'You are being silly and you know it. Your papa knows best.'

'Does he?' Lucy's voice was savage. 'Well, I'll tell you this. I refuse absolutely even to try and enjoy it. I shall sit in a corner and speak to no one and never get asked again and that, Buffy Tyson, will be the end of my social career!'

CHAPTER FOUR

It was the next day and Lucy was still bemoaning her fate.

'I haven't the faintest idea what I'm supposed to wear, Buffy, and even if I knew I'm sure I wouldn't have it in my wardrobe. What do ladies put on for dances? Really, I can't imagine what prompted Mrs Buchanan to invite me, just out of the blue, so to speak, or even to call in the first place. She said her mother-in-law was acquainted with Mama but I can't remember Mama ever mentioning it, can you? It is very baffling. We're not her sort. We don't move in her circle. We don't move in any circle and I can't imagine why she should take it into her head to ask me to a dance in her home.'

'But why shouldn't she? Your mama and papa

are of the same class as she is and I'm sure you'll fit into any gathering of her friends. I'm only surprised you have not been invited out before this.'

'We don't know anybody, that's why. Only Papa's parishioners and there's not a party-goer among them. I just can't imagine what Mrs Buchanan is thinking of, asking me to Grange House.'

Lucy's voice was fretful and she twisted and turned in her chair as though she were doing her best to escape from a situation that was not at all to her liking.

'So you keep saying but this isn't solving the problem of what you are to wear on Saturday. Have . . .would you consider wearing something of your mama's? There is a trunkful of gowns in the attic and I'm sure between us we could contrive an outfit that would be suitable. What is the fashion nowadays?'

'Lord, Buffy, don't ask me. As long as I'm warm and clean in the winter and cool and clean in the summer that's all I ask. If you haven't the wherewithal to buy new dresses you don't take a great deal of interest.'

'I suppose not.'

The girl who spoke smiled a little. She was sewing a button on a shirt and she bent her bright head, using her strong white teeth to bite the thread, at the same time keeping her eyes on Lucy who had sprung up to stare moodily through the window.

The scene beyond it was enough to make the most cheerful feel moody. A mantle of fine rain drifted across the garden, blurring the trees that surrounded the house. It draped itself in moving folds about the heights of Loughrigg Fell and Ivy

Crag, the clouds from which it came dangling darkly beneath the lowering sky and rolling down from the tops in a grey swathe. The contrast to the vivid autumn sunshine of the previous day, when every peak from Loughrigg in the west, Rydal in the north and the Hundreds to the east had been sharp and clear against the endless, cloudless blue of the sky, was quite amazing. Then the fells had been ablaze with the colour of dying bracken, rich and russet, with red-berried rowans, with the whiteness of bent and grasses and the breathtaking purple carpet of the heather. Blackbirds had clattered in the hedgerows, the call of sheep could be clearly heard in the sharp air and the slender birches surrounding the silver blue lake had dipped their autumn leaves into its unruffled surface.

Now it had all vanished in the grey mists which drop so suddenly on the district of the Lakes, setting the Dean children to squabbling and sulks, since they did not care for the tasks their older sister had set them. They had no interest in doing the page of sums she had found and copied from an old arithmetic book belonging to her mother, who had also tried to instil some learning into her children, nor the composition, to be called 'A day on the fells', she had commanded them to write. They would rather be out, they had argued, even if it was raining and they couldn't understand why she was so concerned with this foolishness, since she was usually as keen to escape the house as they were.

They had not yet realised, and neither had she, how the invitation from Mrs Buchanan had confused and upset her. It had thrown a pebble into the smooth pond of her life which, though that life was threatened with anxiety at times, mainly over money, was always contented and peaceful, it had sent out ripples which widened and washed up against her normal blithe confidence. A part of her had no wish to go to Grange House, to become involved with the cream of Windermere society in which Mrs Buchanan moved, and at the same time, being young and spirited, another part was curious to see how that society spent its time. Those who attended her father's services were not young for the most part. Going to church on a Sunday was a habit they had formed when they were themselves children, taken there by their parents. It was a way of life going back to Queen Victoria's reign and before, one not easily changed by those who had grown up in it. But now, in these modern times of motor cars and flying machines, of telephones and electricity and all the other twentieth-century idiosyncrasies, it gave them a sense of security to keep to the old ways and going to listen to one of Reverend Dean's gentle sermons was one of them.

It was the only world Edward Dean's children knew, though it was becoming very evident that at least one of his brood was moving into the twentieth century and would not for long be content to remain in the smooth flow of the nineteenth which still claimed his father. Young Edward's fascination with the motor car and flying machine, and his oft-repeated declaration that he meant to devote his life to the design, creation and care of such things caused his father some heart-searching. A mechanic! That was the term used for the lads who spent their days with their heads under the bonnets of motor cars. A mechanic. His and his lovely Evelyn's son a man who did nothing but tinker with engines. It was unthinkable and so, in his usual fashion, he did not think about it. After all Edward was not yet fourteen and must first go to a decent school, a school where gentlemen went, though again how this was to be achieved had not yet been revealed.

Lucy turned and sat down on the broad window seat, her back to the window. Though her eyes wandered round the familiar bedroom where she had slept for the past six years she did not really see it. Like the long-skirted grey woollen dress she had on it was completely without adornment, and like the rest of the house, as though to make up for its deficiencies in comfort and embellishment, it had been subject to a great deal of scouring and dusting and polishing. There was a single, straight-backed chair on which her companion sat, a battered wardrobe, a washstand on which stood a plain white jug and basin, and a narrow bed. Everything was white from the counterpane to the curtains and walls except for the fireplace—in which no fire had ever burned—made of cast iron and ferociously blackleaded, The bare floorboards gleamed with polish. Beside the bed the room's only claim to comfort was a hookie mat made of hessian and scraps of material from the family's cast-off clothing.

The young woman sitting with Lucy went by the name of Elizabeth Tyson and she had been a part of the Dean family for the past ten years. She thought she was about the same age as Lucy but as the poorhouse where her mother had died, leaving Elizabeth at the age of seven or eight to fend for herself, had no records, it was hard to say. She and her mother had arrived in Buxton on a bitter day in

January, struggling through the snowdrifts which were a feature of the Peak District, her mother already racked with the dry, hacking cough which was to kill her. Who knows what might have become of her, she often mused, had Mrs Dean, wife of the rector of a small parish church a mile or so out of town, not herself been stranded by the snowstorm that day.

'That child cannot possibly be expected to lift that sack of potatoes, Matron,' for barely before her mother was cold they had set Elizabeth to work. 'Not with that leg. It is beyond her capabilities.'

Those were the first words Elizabeth heard Mrs Dean speak. Lovely, soft-voiced, sweet-faced Mrs Dean who had taken Elizabeth home to the rectory, fed her, bathed her, tucked her into a warm bed, kissed her goodnight as though she were one of her own children and didn't seem to care that one of Elizabeth's legs was shorter than the other. There was no name-calling in Mrs Dean's home. No 'gimpy' nor 'hoppy', only the endearing diminutive of 'Buffy', based on the infants Margaret and Edward's unsuccessful attempts to pronounce her true name of Elizabeth. She had been part of the household since. Everything Lucy was taught, which wasn't much in the way of academic subjects, so was Buffy. She could read and write and play the piano. She could sew and embroider beautifully, surpassing Lucy who got her silks in a tangle and her seams crooked. But for the first eight years of her life Buffy had lived among North Country men and women and no matter how hard Mrs Dean tried she could not erase their long-vowelled accent from Buffy's voice. She was and yet she was not a servant, helping in the kitchen, cleaning, even scrubbing when Mrs Hutton was run off her feet by the reverend's lively family, but at the same time she was a member of that family. Obsessively loyal to those who had taken her in, eternally grateful, devoted to their welfare, she would have died to save any one of them a moment's hurt. In fact when Mrs Dean was swept away on a tide of her own blood at Percy's birth she had howled her pain and anger at the injustice which had taken such a lovely, much-loved lady and left unworthy Buffy Tyson. It had broken her heart, but in the shared sorrow and support for one another, the comfort given to one another by the warm-hearted family, she had recovered, as they had, and her love from then on had been given to Lucy, who took her mother's place in the home and in Buffy's wounded heart.

Buffy was not pretty. For one thing she was painfully short-sighted and wore wire-rimmed spectacles which hid her one claim to beauty which was the size and shape and lovely colour of her long-lashed eyes. They were green, a deep sea green which in some lights turned to aquamarine. Her skin was as white as milk and scattered across her face, her chest and arms were hundreds of small golden freckles. Her hair could be described as no other colour but ginger and was tightly curled in corkscrews about her small head. Her mouth was the vivid red of strawberries, wide and serious, for Elizabeth Tyson had had little to smile about in the formative years of her childhood. The top of her head came just to the level of Lucy's shoulder. She wore a plain navy cotton dress with a white apron, its bib frilled across her small breasts, but no cap

71

since she was not thought of as a maidservant. There was no name to describe nor had she a given task in the household, so she provided service wherever it was needed. Companion and friend, playmate and nurse, comforter and adviser, scullery maid and cook at times, since Mrs Hutton was getting on and Elsie, though willing, was barely capable of deciding for herself which brush should be used to sweep the yard and which to clear the hearth.

'Come on, Lucy,' she said, her freckled face serious, 'don't just give up. You've been invited to this dinner and you've no choice but to go. If you don't enjoy yourself you don't have to go again, that's if they ask you.'

'You know I hate all that polite stuff, pretending to be interested in the silly things girls of my age talk about. I shall be bored to tears.'

'Oh, give over, do. You're just mad because for once you've got to do something you don't want to do. You have things far too much your own way, my girl.'

'That's not true, Buffy.' Lucy glared but her friend took no notice.

'Yes, it is. Now get your bottom off that window seat and let's scoot up to the attic and see what's in your mama's box.' Her brisk voice suddenly became soft. 'You don't mind ... I mean will it upset you to see your mama's dresses and things?'

Not one for sulking, Lucy took Buffy's hand affectionately as they moved towards the open door, accommodating her long stride to Buffy's lopsided limp. Her voice was low and sad as she squeezed Buffy's hand.

'No, I know Mama would want me to look my

best. I think, if she had lived, we would have been invited to many such occasions, for Papa would not be . . . as he is. So I must not let her down.'

*   *   *

She did look her best, they all agreed. They were all there to see her off, Bibby and Elsie and Mrs Hutton with Buffy beside her papa, watching with pride and a kind of fascinated awe as a uniformed chauffeur handed her into the back seat of Mrs Buchanan's rich blue Vauxhall which Edward said was called a Prince Henry and would Lucy look at the flutes along the bonnet. It was almost as splendid as Mr Buchanan's Silver Ghost!

' 'Ave a lovely time, Miss Lucy, dear,' Mrs Hutton called out, ready to sniffle, for it would have been grand if Mrs Dean could have lived to see the beauty her daughter had grown into.

'Bring us something nice to eat, Luce,' Percy begged her. He should have been in bed but with the usual disregard for rules the family applied, he was still hopping about in his nightshirt, Thimble clasped to his chest.

'Don't miss a thing, Lucy, promise. Emily and I want to hear about everything, positively everything that happens and what all the ladies are wearing. And the dances. Try and remember how to do them so that you can show us when you get back.'

'If you get a chance will you have a look at what make of motor car they're driving, Luce. Just a general idea, you know.' Edward prowled round the Vauxhall, his face cast in one of brooding concentration. He ran a finger along the shining surface of the bonnet and peered at its tyres as

73

though fully expecting a puncture. The chauffeur watched him anxiously. He did wish the little bugger would leave it alone, for if there was a scratch on it it would be his fault. He'd have liked to tell him to clear off but with his father watching he had to show restraint.

In her mother's trunk Lucy and Buffy had found, among other garments, a lovely dress of white mousseline with flecks of silver in it. Around the low-cut neckline was an edging of silvery lace and at the waist a broad sash to match. They did not know it but it had been made for Evelyn Dean at the turn of the century, a simple gown with a fluted skirt which had about the hem a broad band of silver ribbon. This Buffy had cut off and made up into a silver rose which, when Lucy's hair had been brushed up into a full, rather loose style framing her face, was placed in the coil at the back of her head. The dress fitted her as if it had been made for her, if perhaps a little short, but then dance frocks at that time had been worn just clear of the ground. Her mother's pearl drops swung in her ears.

To her own surprise she found herself admitting later to Buffy that she had enjoyed Mrs Buchanan's dance at Grange House. Not that she would like to make a habit of it, she stressed. They were all a bit ... brainless, the young people, Mrs Buchanan's nephews and nieces and their friends, but, again to her own surprise, she discovered that dancing was good fun and, what was even more astonishing, she had a talent for it, or so all her partners told her.

From the moment she was admitted by the poker-faced butler and greeted by Mr and Mrs Buchanan she sensed that this was not going to be

74

as dull as she had expected. For a start you could tell this was a party for young people. There were shouts of male laughter coming from a room off the wide hallway accompanied by girlish shrieks and giggles, the strains of lively music and what sounded like the stamp of feet on a bare wooden floor. It promised a definite air of youthful high spirits which drew her into the house more enthusiastically than Mrs Buchanan's smile of welcome.

'Come in, Miss Dean, come in and join the fun. We've just begun a two-step which is guaranteed to break the ice. It's called Alexander's Ragtime Band. Have you heard of it? No? Already the evening's developed into what my grandmother would have called a "reet merry-neet". "Lish as day-old lambs", they all are, as the saying goes. She was a Dales-woman born and bred, my grandmother. I remember her as a wrinkled face beneath her lace and ribbon cap. Stern, but with a twinkle in her eye which said, providing it was not offensive, she liked a joke as well as the next person. She was as outspoken as I am which is probably where I get it.'

Lucy realised Mrs Buchanan was talking to put her at ease, to get her over the doorstep and into the house without too much strain. Mr Buchanan, who reminded her of an amiable, shambling bear he was so big and dark, stepped forward and with old-world courtesy, though he was still only in his thirties, kissed her hand, smiling in a way that reminded Lucy of someone, though for the moment she couldn't think who it was.

'Miss Dean, I'm so glad you could come, and take no notice of my wife. She'll be telling you next we're to eat tatie-pot and clapbread at supper. She is very proud of her northern heritage and sometimes labours it to death.'

'There is nothing wrong with tatie-pot, darling. I've eaten it many times as a child before my grandparents Graham began to go up in the world. We were not always as you see us now, Miss Dean, or at least my family weren't. Now then . . .'

Slipping her arm through Lucy's, she drew her across the hall towards the doorway from where the sound of merriment came. A male voice begged someone to 'Watch where you're putting those enormous feet, lad,' and a female's, high with excited laughter, informed him that it was her feet which were being punished, not his. They did not stop dancing as Lucy was ushered into the room.

'It was a large room. Once it had been two but Franny Buchanan, on her marriage to Alex, with her love of parties, dances, balls, anything that smacked of fun, had persuaded him to demolish a wall and make it into a room big enough to hold such entertainments.

Grange House had been bought for them as a wedding present by Alex's father, Harry Buchanan, and was situated in its own five acres of gardens to the south of Ambleside. There were fields all about it, with a drive that led from Borrans Road up to the house. A big house suitable for a family with many children but in the eight years of Alex and Franny's marriage none had come along. Her mother-in-law said sourly at first that it was Franny's love of riding that prevented her from conceiving and later that it was the fault of that contraption she drove about in, referring to her smart little Austin Ten motor car. She had even proffered her own carriage and horses in the hope that a more gentle way of getting about might do the trick. It had not.

The carpet of what was usually the formal drawing-room had been removed, the chairs, sofas and low tables pushed back against the wall and, to the music of a lively record played on a gramophone housed in an exquisite wooden cabinet made in the style of Chippendale, a crowd of young people were energetically throwing themselves about the room, or so it seemed to Lucy. They were now dancing to the tune which came from the most successful show in London, 'Hello Ragtime', arms and legs flying, their faces flushed, their eyes bright with laughter. With the enthusiasm and vigour only the young possess it had become an overheated romp, to the alarm of several mamas who watched.

'As you can see, Miss Dean, there is little decorum at my parties and my sister-in-law is not happy about it,' nodding her head in the direction of Mrs Angus Gunson, once Janet Buchanan, who was watching disapprovingly as her son Job steered an over-excited Marion Mossop about the polished floor. She was the mother of four of the young men dancing. 'She is not at all pleased by the high spirits of her sons, nor their partners. Now then, let me introduce you to some of the young people not dancing.'

'Thank you, Mrs Buchanan,' Lucy managed to gasp, the first words she had spoken beyond the initial greeting at the front door. Her eyes were wide and startled, her mouth open in a small O of astonishment. She and her brothers and sisters made a great deal of noise in the old nursery at home. They laughed and became over-excited in some of the games they played, but the sheer volume of noise here, the shrill chatter of the ladies not dancing striving to be heard over the din, the bright lights which must be electric, she decided, the warmth, the colour of the dresses of the young ladies who were whirled about the floor, quite took her breath away. There were groups of young people lounging about the edge of the floor, the gentlemen in immaculately tailored evening suits, the ladies in the very latest fashions, for they were all from wealthy, or, if not as wealthy as the Buchanans, old families from the neighbourhood.

Colours were strong this year with no pastel tints, emerald, cerise, saxe blue, mauve and sulphur yellow being very popular. The gowns were generally of a one-piece design, straight and tubular with a tunic or overdress, scooped-out necklines and short sleeves. Waists were high with a look of the Empire line about them. Bead fringes were common, and gold and silver embroidery and sequins. The fabrics were lovely, soft and drifting, very flattering, chiffon and gauze, lace, net, silk and voile.

But the most enchanting, the most expensively dressed was Miss Charlotte Gibson, and James Buchanan, to whom she was chatting, wondered what demon of mischief had made his sister-in-law invite her here to the same party as Lucy Dean. He, naturally, had known Lucy was to be a guest, having engineered it, but Charlotte had been something of a shock and his face, though quite without expression, seemed set in intransigent lines which only Franny understood.

She smiled sweetly as she introduced Lucy to the

78

other guests.

'Mrs Mossop . . . Frederick, and that is Marion on the floor . . . Roderick . . .'

'Mrs Askew . . . Rosalyn, Louise, Roger . . . Douglas, of course, away at school . . .'

'Mrs Kendall . . . Aurora, Gregory . . . Mrs Kendall's other children too young . . .'

'And, of course, my brother-in-law, James Buchanan whom you have already met.'

'Good evening, Miss Dean.'

'Mr Buchanan.' An inclination of her smoothly brushed head which he returned.

'Oh, and do forgive me, this is our charming Miss Charlotte Gibson.'

'Miss Gibson.'

'Miss Dean.' With no more than the coolest nod Miss Gibson, who knew a nobody when she saw one and did not care for the competition with her own good looks this newcomer threatened, took James Buchanan's arm and led him away, reluctantly on his part, towards her hostess's conservatory, saying she had a fancy to see Mrs Buchanan's orchids which were well known to be the finest in the district.

The young people, especially the gentlemen, welcomed Lucy as though she were come from another species they had never before met, one which was enormously entertaining for, not caring a jot whether anyone might disapprove of her carelessly light-hearted behaviour, she flung herself into the festivities with the enthusiasm she showed at home, where nobody cared. She did a square dance with Job Gunson who, at eighteen, thought he was God's gift, being handsome as well as rich; an eightsome reel partnered by Frederick Mossop who, when the music stopped, told her she was the most beautiful creature he had ever met, and rippingly funny, which she thought he meant as a compliment. She even attempted the latest tango with Roger Askew. Did she know, he asked her breathlessly, that the German Kaiser had banned the dance, and the two-step, saying they were not 'proper', but Roger could see nothing wrong with either, could she, doing his best to appear older than his seventeen years.

There were lively polkas, the steps of which she remembered from Mama as soon as the music started and Gregory Kendall's boyish arms came eagerly about her. The St Bernard Waltz, the valeta and the lancers in succession, sharing her favours between Frederick Mossop, who liked to be called Freddy, he told her, Job and Lawrence Gunson, Roger Askew and fifteen-year-old Will Gunson, who had the impertinence and nerve of a fox, his infuriated brothers told him.

It was not until after supper that she was approached by Mr Buchanan, Mr James Buchanan, that is. She was surrounded by young men all clamouring to be allowed to fetch her another plate of mayonnaise of fowl, or perhaps tongue, or would she prefer raised game pie, for she certainly had a good appetite. In fact none of them had ever seen a girl enjoy her food as she did, they said, and it was a wonderful sight! She felt like howling with laughter, really she did, at the idea of someone simply enjoying their food being considered wonderful! But then half the things they said to her made no sense. Had she been up to London to see George Robey, 'The Prime Minister of Mirth' at the Hippodrome? No! Good heavens! But hadn't she heard that the old king, yes, King Edward that was, had loved the music-hall and went, apparently, to visit in secret, but of course now it was quite proper to go, even among the upper classes. She really must make a point of seeing him; no, not the king, the Prime Minister of Mirth, the next time she was there. Now would she care for more fruited jelly, or perhaps a meringue, ice-cream or a custard in a glass, while all about her the young ladies and their mamas whispered behind their hands, or their fans, that they had never seen a lady eat such enormous amounts, which was surely a sign of bad breeding. Franny Buchanan had vouched for her pedigree, saying she was of good family but really, would she act like she did, and eat like she did if her people were of the respectable class?

They seemed to make a path for him through their youthful masculine circle as he approached her, younger men showing respect for an older.

'Miss Dean.' His voice was quite without expression and his face showed none of the turmoil which seethed inside him. He had just spent an hour or more sitting beside Charlotte and her mama, Charlotte already preening in what was an annoyingly proprietorial way, listening to their description of the splendours of Paris and the fashion houses from where they had just returned after viewing the styles which were heralded for the spring. He had brought them supper from the magnificent buffet and a glass of champagne each with which to wash it down but as someone, Franny he suspected, put on a record of a slow and dreamy waltz he stood up abruptly. Charlotte smiled expectantly then her mouth dropped open when he asked her politely to excuse him and walked, bold as brass, across the shining floor to where Miss . . . Miss . . . whatever her name was, was sitting. Her face flushed with outrage and only her mama's warning hand on her arm stopped her from standing up and stamping her feet as she had done so often during her childhood.

'Miss Dean, as this is a waltz and therefore more suited to my old bones, may I take you away from your . . . admirers for five minutes? That is if you have had enough to eat?' One dark eyebrow rose questioningly though no smile warmed his face.

She was visibly startled. 'I'm sorry but I don't know how to waltz, Mr Buchanan. Besides, I'm—'

'Nonsense, Miss Dean, it's the simplest thing in the world. "One, two, three; one, two, three," and away you go.'

Without further ado he took her hand and almost pulled her from her chair and, short of making a small scene, she had no choice but to stand up and move into the centre of the room with him. They were the only couple on the floor.

The hubbub in the room ceased, for in every mind, except perhaps that of Miss Charlotte Gibson, was the thought that they really did make a handsome couple. Both tall with an excellent physique, his so completely male, hers so womanly. Both dark and graceful with a sort of dynamism between them which, though perhaps not evident to them, was clearly apparent to the onlookers.

'Now then, Miss Dean.' Their faces were almost level and this time he smiled, an incredible smile which lit his sombre face. His eyes were narrowed and his lips curled back across his startlingly white teeth. Lucy felt her heart do a little flip in her breast and her breath caught in her throat and she wondered giddily what on earth was wrong with her. 'I'm going to put one arm about your waist like this,' he went on. 'You put your left hand on my right shoulder and your right hand in my left.'

'I do know the position, Mr Buchanan,' she said coolly,

'I realise that, Miss Dean, having seen you dance with so many young men. I'm only telling you this so as not to startle you, you understand.' His eyes gleamed with mischief. 'Now'—when she was fitted, in her opinion, indecently close to his chest—'I shall move my left foot forward and you will move your right foot back.'

'I'm not a complete idiot, Mr Buchanan,' she hissed through clenched teeth, conscious of the hardness of his thigh just for a moment against hers. His male virility, which was nothing, *nothing* like that of the young men she had danced with tonight, made her feel decidedly peculiar. And why did he hold her so close, for heaven's sake . . .'

'I'm holding you close, Miss Dean, so that you can feel the rhythm of my body, if you'll forgive the impertinence, in time to the music and also where I am to lead you. Now then, let your feet move to the tempo of the music. It has, by the way, the foolish title of "Oh, Oh, Antonio", but nevertheless is wonderful to waltz to, don't you agree?'

Could he read her mind? she thought wildly as she stumbled and, had it not been for his firm hold on her, would have fallen. His breath fanned her right ear, for she kept her face averted from his and his gloved hand seemed to burn right through the back of Mama's silvery dress.

' "One, two, three; one, two, three," and turn . . . smoothly, Miss Dean.'

'I'm trying, Mr Buchanan.'

'No, you are bobbing up and down like a cork on a pond. Try to relax. I'm not about to press my embrace on you, delightful as it would be, Miss Dean.' His mouth was twitching. 'After all, we are attempting to waltz before a room full of people. There, let your shoulders go ... and turn. That's better, in fact that is much better. Now, if Franny will only put on the record again, or another like it, I will have you an expert within half an hour.'

He was a good dancer. Steady as a rock and yet light on his feet with a wonderful sense of rhythm, and to her amazement she found she could follow his steps quite easily and was even beginning to enjoy it. She didn't know what it was but there seemed to be some harmony linking them, a sense of shared timing, a graceful flow which soon had them drifting round the edges of the floor as though their feet were winged and they shared one flight. She didn't want it to stop and when, for the third time, Franny, at a small signal from James, again put on 'Oh, Oh, Antonio', she was content to continue their dreaming progress round the room.

'Oh, come on, Aunt Franny,' voices were protesting, 'Let's have something a bit more lively,' and it was with some reluctance that James Buchanan and Lucy Dean stepped away from one another as another two-step began. He bowed.

'That was perfection, Miss Dean,' he told her in a voice so soft no one but she could hear it. 'If only all young ladies had your grace and rhythm.'

'No, it was thanks to you, Mr Buchanan. Now I shall be able to go home and teach Margaret and Emily.' Her face had a strange unfocused quality about it as if she still dwelled in that enchanted world into which the lovely strains of the music and the shared delight of the waltz had spun her.

'Indeed you will,' smiling wryly, 'but for now, would you care to sit and drink a glass of champagne with me?'

'I'm not at all tired, Mr Buchanan. I find I could dance all night.'

'I'm sure you could, Miss Dean, but I would be glad of a chance to engage you in some idle conversation if you could bring yourself to put up with it.'

She frowned and he felt again that sensation which he had never known before he met Lucy Dean and which involved a curious movement of his heart, a quickening of his breath and something he could only call a bloody foolish weakening of his knees. She was so direct, an enchanting directness which he had always thought was not a part of the female character.

'What do you call idle conversation?' she asked him. 'I'm no good at this "small talk" they all seem to feel is so necessary at a party.'

'Oh, no, not small talk, just anything that takes your fancy, except fashion which I warn you I know nothing about,' though he'd heard enough about it in the last hour!

'That makes two of us, Mr Buchanan. In fact I seem to know nothing about anything that other young ladies find so fascinating. Not that I know what that is, you understand, so I suppose that's why.'

'What do you like, Miss Dean? What do you like to do?'

'I like pictures and I wish I had some.' Her tone was regretful, 'I enjoy the art exhibitions when they come locally and I love to read.'

'So do I. Now who is your favourite painter?'

'Oh, that's easy. I have no particular favourites among them but the French impressionists ... well, I could stand in front of Monet's *Woman with Umbrella* for hours on end.'

'I'm the same about Renoir's *Near the Lake*. Now what else pleases you?' he went on autocratically.

'I love walking and climbing as high as I can.'

'So do I. We have much in common, it seems.'

'Do you really like climbing?' She was clearly startled.

'I'm not quite so decrepit as you seem to think, Miss Dean. I often put on a pair of stout boots, a few sandwiches in my rucksack and climb up to ...'

'Where? Where? What is your favourite?' Her bright interest intoxicated him.

By this time he had manoeuvred her into a chair in a quiet corner of the room with a glass of champagne in her hand and, after warning her sternly, as though she were a child, not to drink it too quickly or it would go to her head, encouraged her to tell him all he longed to know about Lucy Dean.

'You tell me what you like to read first then I'll tell you where I like to climb. Is that a deal?'

She smiled then leaned back in her chair, putting her hands together and bringing them to her lips as she considered the question, staring out over the heads of the dancers, for by this time supper was over and a military two-step was being performed with more enthusiasm than grace. Franny Buchanan was always generous with her champagne and as Olivia Askew murmured to

86

Laura Kendall, there'd be tears before bedtime if Marion Mossop drank another drop. The young men, those dancing and those lounging about the room, constantly turned their heads in the direction of Lucy Dean and James Buchanan, wondering what a spiffing, fun-loving girl like Miss Dean was doing with an elderly gent like Mr Buchanan, or Uncle James as some of them knew him. She was talking nineteen to the dozen, but so seriously they really could not believe she was having a good time.

Should they rescue her? Job muttered to Roger, but James Buchanan was his mother's brother; of the next generation and it might be thought ill-mannered simply to go up to them and ask her to come and dance. Aunt Franny had put on a record of what was very new and called ragtime, again from the London show which was transforming the world of popular music, and everyone's feet were tapping, even those of the older guests.

'Mr Buchanan,' she was saying, 'I really have no one preference. There are so many I love. Jane Austen, of course, and Charlotte Brontë. I adore *David Copperfield* and Dumas's *The Count of Monte Christo* but ... yes, I think I must say Tolstoy's *Anna Karenina*. I know it is a story of adultery but how can one pass judgement on those sad lovers. Anna is so ... so ...'

'Rebellious, Miss Dean?' His lips curled up in what she was beginning to recognise as humour

'Oh, not just that. Courageous, maligned ...'

'Aah, maligned. You have some sympathy with her then, Miss Dean? Perhaps because she was married to an older man. A beautiful young woman ... ?'

Lucy found she was quite intrigued by this unusual man and also that she was enjoying their conversation enormously. It was the most sensible she had engaged in this night. The gentlemen seemed to concern themselves only with the fox-hunt they were to take part in the next day and the ladies what they were to wear at a charity ball to be held in Fellthwaite Assembly Rooms in a week or so.

She leaned forward confidentially and those watching held their breath, for it seemed she might put her hand on James Buchanan's knee.

'Oh, no, Mr Buchanan, I don't think that signifies. I don't think age counts if two people truly love one another.'

'You are a romantic, I think, Miss Dean.'

'Am I, Mr Buchanan?'

'Indeed you are and none the worse for it, I'd say.'

There was a gleam of something in James's velvet grey eyes which might have been a reflection from one of the many lamps that stood about the room, or it might have been satisfaction, but before Lucy could even wonder about it, Franny's voice broke into the small circle of agreement that had developed between Lucy Dean and James Buchanan, breaking the slender thread which had linked them together.

'Now then, James, I cannot allow you to commandeer Miss Dean any longer and don't glare at me like that,' a remark which bewildered Lucy and infuriated James. 'There are half a dozen young men dying to dance with her.'

'But does she want to dance with them, Franny?' James's voice was as smooth as silk but his eyes had narrowed and turned to the leaden grey of pewter.

'Now you know that's not how it works, James. Besides, there are more than a few young ladies who would be delighted to take a turn round the floor with you.'

Franny could see it in his eyes and the way his lips firmed that he was longing to say, 'Bugger the lot of them,' but he was a guest in her house and he knew his duty. He stood up reluctantly, conscious of a horde of eager, younger men at his back.

He bowed to Lucy. 'Perhaps the next waltz, Miss Dean, or would you like me to show you how to tango properly?' His look was severe as though she were badly in need of a lesson or two. Her own expression was bewildered but all she said was, 'Thank you, sir.'

*   *   *

They had all gone, Marion Mossop, as Olivia Askew had prophesied, tearfully begging Mrs Buchanan to believe that she had had the most wonderful time of her life. The young men were beseeching Miss Dean to tell them when they would dance with her again and would she consider coming with them on the fox-hunt tomorrow? They were to meet at the Fox in Chapel Stile and they would be overjoyed to see her.

They were nonplussed and suddenly speechless when she told them gravely that she attended her papa's services on Sunday.

Only James remained after standing with Alex and Franny to see her into the Vauxhall, to her great astonishment, his eyes dark as the night as they looked into hers.

89

'Until the next time, Miss Dean. I have yet to tell you what my favourite climb is and perhaps, if you are agreeable, we might do it together?'

'Oh, yes . . . of course . . . yes. Well, goodnight.'

They sat, the three of them, Alex, Franny and James, in Alex Buchanan's study before the warm glow of the applewood fire, sipping a whisky nightcap apiece, and it was quite five minutes before anyone spoke.

'So, James Buchanan, you realise, do you not, that you have lost all hope of winning the hand of the charming Charlotte?'

Franny, her shoes kicked off, her feet resting on the broad back of Alex's black and white English setter who lay, head on paws, before the fire, smiled roguishly through her glass at her brother-in-law.

He smiled back, a lazy, satisfied smile, and she thought how attractive he was and if he had not been her husband's cousin she would have done her feminine best to take him as a lover.

'Do you know, Franny, I find I can't care very much about that.'

'You made it pretty obvious, old chap.' Alex's voice was slow and deep. 'And what, if one might be so bold as to ask, are you to do about the luscious Lucy? You also made it clear you were . . .shall we say smitten by her charms, which I must say are quite splendid.'

'Now look here, Alex.' James's face had turned to thunder. 'I'll have no slurs cast on Miss Dean, nor sly innuendos regarding her charms.' His voice was menacing. 'What I am to do about her is my business and mine alone and—'

'Then you are to do something, James?' Franny

put in, her voice soft, her eyes narrowing, her expression one of keen interest.

'Again, that is my concern.'

'Which means you are,' Alex burst out incredulously, 'otherwise you'd deny it at once.'

'Will you two stop trying to make me say something which ... Goddammit, just because I spend a few minutes talking to a beautiful girl does not mean I am to ... to ...'

'Yes, to what?'

James sprang to his feet and the dog lifted his handsome head and looked at him reproachfully, then replaced it on his paws. His eyes swivelled from one person to another then came to rest adoringly, unwinkingly on his master.

'This is bloody ridiculous. I'm off,' James proclaimed. In his voice was a ring of bluster and yet uncertainty as though he were revealing too much of his inner thoughts; then, just as suddenly, he sat down again. Franny and her husband exchanged glances.

James sighed then took a steadying sip of his whisky before he resumed speaking.

'I suppose it will be all over Fellthwaite, Ambleside and Grasmere by morning what a fool James Buchanan made of himself over a pretty face, but you see, she's not just that to me. Granted she is a beautiful young woman ...' He paused and across his face flitted an expression Franny could only call fatuous, then, shaking himself as vigorously as a dog coming from water, as if he were throwing off some enchanted picture that was bemusing his mind, he continued, his voice soft.

'But she is not just beautiful. She has a mind of her own, unclogged with all the rubbish young ladies of the day seem to find appropriate.'

'We noticed that, lad. Calls a spade a bloody—'

'Alex,' Franny warned, but it seemed James had retreated again into some secret bewitched world where Lucy Dean had unwittingly thrust him and did not notice.

'She's bright and clever. Her brain is as sharp as that of any man . . .'

'Dear sweet Christ,' Alex muttered under his breath.

' . . .and given the chance she could become . . . well, anything she set her heart on. She's forthright, I grant you that. I call her honest. She's sensible, practical and, unlike many girls, has no airs and graces and false pride. She has a sense of humour and, if you'd seen her with her family you would know at once what love and loyalty she gives to them. She has lived in a cloistered world, even more so than most girls of her class, but she is not pedestrian. I have never met anyone like her.'

He lifted his head and glared as though to dare either one to argue with him.

'I know I have done Charlotte Gibson a grave injustice. I have given her and her parents reason to believe that I might be considered as a serious suitor. I suppose the whole district was aware of it and will call me a bastard of the first order for my ungentlemanlike behaviour but I can do nothing about it. I have offended them, I know I have, and if I could apologise I would but it would hardly do to go round there and say I'm sorry but I no longer wish to press my suit—what a stupid expression— since I now find I'm—'

He stopped speaking abruptly. There was a silence filled with awkwardness and Alex fidgeted, uncomfortable with his cousin's evident emotion.

Franny sat up, putting her feet to the ground. She drained her whisky glass then placed it carefully on the low table beside her and said quietly, 'What are you to do then, James? About Miss Dean, I mean? It seems there is something on your mind.'

'I will call on her father tomorrow . . . No, he will be busy, it being Sunday. On Monday then, I shall call and ask his permission to—hell's teeth, it sounds so bloody trite, stilted—to pay court to his daughter, and I'd be obliged if you'd keep it to yourselves for the moment.'

Alex sat up slowly, his face slack with shock. 'You mean to marry her? That gauche, unpolished child, that naïve, unworldly, unsuitable . . . Oh, she's lovely, I grant you that and no doubt your bed will be sweet with her in it, but, James, lad, she won't do. Not for you. You need a woman to run your house. Confound it, you can't mean to marry . . .'

'I do and if you say one more word against her I'll ram your teeth down your bloody throat.'

CHAPTER FIVE

The Reverend Edward Dean was surprised and not a little annoyed, since he was busy cataloguing some new butterflies when Elsie, clearly overwhelmed by the importance of the visitor in the hall, piped that there was a Mr Buchanan to see him.

'What does he want, Elsie?' the rector asked her

and she shook her head wonderingly, for would a fine gentleman like Mr Buchanan confide in kitchen maid Elsie Blount the reason for his visit.

'Nay, sir, that I couldn't say.'

'Is . . . is he alone?' though what that had to do with anything Elsie failed to see. He was a funny old stick and no mistake, was the rector. More like a lad than a grown man which was why Elsie was so at ease with him. He never shouted or made her feel stupid but spoke pleasantly, politely, almost as though Elsie were as good as he was but she never, and never would, take advantage of his goodness and kindness. She knew her place, did twelve year-old Elsie.

'Yes, sir, all alone. Them dogs of 'is is safely in't motor fastened wi' a lead ter't door 'andle. 'E's got top up an' all as it looks like rain.'

Failing to see the significance of this remark the reverend gentleman looked about him vaguely.

'Yer remember last time,' she prompted.

'Last time?'

'Aye, them dogs an' Thimble caused a right old rumpus. Made sure it don' 'appen again, Mr Buchanan 'as.'

'Mmm . . .well . . . I see,' though he didn't, Elsie recognised that.

'Is my daughter at home, Elsie?' he continued. 'Perhaps she could speak to Mr Buchanan.'

'No, sir, she an't childer've gone ter see old Mrs Seaton.' She nearly added, 'poor old soul' for a visit from the Dean family was like being invaded by the hordes of China. Not that Elsie knew anything about the hordes of China but she'd been in the nursery one day when Miss Lucy had told the children about them. ' 'Sides, 'e ses 'e wants ter see

94

thi' particular like.'

Edward Dean sighed. 'Show him in then, Elsie.'

Elsie sketched a curtsey. 'Rightio, sir. Will I fetch tea?'

'I suppose you'd better.'

Though November had just whistled in on a bitter wind straight from the North Pole, or so said Mrs Hutton, shivering by the kitchen fire, there was little warmth in the Reverend Dean's study. There were several pieces of coal in the grate flickering bravely against enormous odds, but there might as well have been no fire at all for all the heat it threw out, or so James thought as the rector waved him politely to a chair before it. Reverend Dean still held a sheaf of papers in his hand just as though the moment his visitor had gone he would at once resume whatever he had been doing and therefore it was not worth putting them away.

Tea arrived, hot certainly but so weak James was positive he could see the roses painted on the outside of the cup through the liquid. Nevertheless he drank it valiantly down. Neither he nor the rector were au fait with the customs, so important to the ladies, of calling on one another, of taking tea, or not taking tea, all the protocol which one generation passed down to another, and so they sipped and told one another what an extremely cold day it was and expressed the hope that the approaching winter would not be too fierce. It usually was, of course, up here in Lakeland, snow making its appearance soon after Christmas, or sometimes before, with great drifts reaching the eaves of the low cottages so that folk were snowed in for weeks on end.

Edward Dean did his best to be courteous,

wondering in his detached way what on earth had brought James Buchanan to his home again. It was nothing to do with his will. That was the first thing he had asked as he had shaken Mr Buchanan's hand, but no, that had been signed, witnessed and was all in order, Mr Buchanan assured him.

There was the clatter of feet on bare boards as someone ran upstairs singing a chorus of 'O God our help in ages past, which James supposed was appropriate considering whose home this was, then clattered down again. A door opened and a cheerful voice, possibly that of the skivvy who had let him in, proclaimed, 'I found it. It were in Master—' The rest of the sentence was cut off as the door banged to again. Even the servants in this house appeared to behave as ebulliently and with the same amount of noise as the family who resided here.

Edward Dean, his repertoire of small talk exhausted, began to fidget, doing his best not to let Mr Buchanan see his impatience to be back with his butterflies.

At last his visitor drew a deep breath, like a man about to dive head first into murky waters, and began. 'It was kind of you to see me without prior arrangement, Reverend Dean, but I felt I should speak to you first before approaching your daughter. It is customary, I believe, in the circumstances, and I would like to do this thing properly.' He drew in another deep breath and let it out gustily.

'This thing?' Clearly Edward Dean was mystified, not only by the content of Mr Buchanan's conversation but by his reference to his daughter.

'Yes. It's a matter of some delicacy and I hope you will bear with me.' He cleared his throat and scowled. 'I have never done this before, sir, so I beg you to forgive me if I seem somewhat precipitate.'

'Of course,' The rector smiled encouragingly though he had not the slightest idea what Mr Buchanan was getting at.

James steadied himself. He had come here on an honest mission, one not undertaken lightly and he wished to make a good show of himself. What he had to offer was worthy of any young lady's consideration. Without false modesty he knew himself, along with his cousins, Paul and Andrew, both still unmarried, to be an eligible man in the marriage market. There were a dozen young ladies in the district about Fellthwaite, Ambleside and Grasmere from whom he could pick a wife. He was a very wealthy man. He had a magnificent home, servants by the score and, not to put too fine a point on it, was endowed with reasonable good looks. In other words he was a good catch. He had property and businesses in many parts of the Lakeland and beyond. His forebears had given service to succeeding monarchs in the protection of the borders against the wild, marauding Scots and for this they had been rewarded and allowed to retain their rights as landowners, calling themselves Estatesmen, shortened to Statesmen. They were proud men, those who farmed in Cumberland and Westmoreland, true yeoman class since the days of Elizabeth. They were well-educated men for the most part, gaining degrees at the university of their choice, in engineering, the law and medicine since his cousin Paul had just qualified as a doctor.

'Is ... is Miss Dean at home, sir?' His voice

softened as he spoke her name.

'Oh, it's Lucy you want to see.' With great relief the rector stood up, his eyes already straying to the sheaf of papers in his hand.

'No, sir, no. It's about Lucy ... Miss Dean, that I'm here.' James's face which, in his dealings with men of business never gave away an inkling of his thoughts, remaining cool, self-controlled and smooth at all times, revealed his anxiety now. He felt somewhat foolish, which he didn't like and yet at the same time his heart raced and his throat was dry. He wondered why, since he had never suffered with nerves. It was a measure of the effect Lucy Dean had on him, he supposed, and the sooner this was settled the better he would like it.

'Aahh.' Reverend Dean sat down again slowly and a frown began to crease his face.

'Yes. This is a ... complex situation and one I'm confident you will treat with discretion. I appreciate that Miss Dean and I have only recently become acquainted but I ... my feelings for her are ... Sir, I would like to get things ... finalised as soon as possible.' He paused, then began again. 'I am a well-set-up man, sir, and I have the means to give a good life to the lady who becomes my wife. I'm thirty-four years old and I know Lucy ... Miss Dean is only eighteen or nineteen but I'm healthy and good for years yet so ...'

Edward gasped. 'You are saying you want to marry my daughter?' He fell back in his chair, every vestige of colour leaving his face. It was apparent that he was not only surprised but badly shocked.

'I do, sir. And may I add ...' James looked down at his hands which he had not realised were tightly clenched, then up again at the rector and in his

98

eyes was an expression the Reverend Dean instantly recognised. He had seen it twice before: in the lovely golden depths of those of his Evelyn, and in his own reflection in the mirror when he thought of her.

His colour came back and he smiled. 'Yes, Mr Buchanan?' His voice was very gentle.

'I have never said this before, sir. I have never felt like this before but . . . well . . .' God, why was he acting like some callow youth confessing his first love, and the truth was, that was how he felt. And yet it was not so, not really. He was a mature man. His feelings for Lucy, though so new, were strong, rooted deep, true and steady and enduring, and as a man he could only say so. First to her father, then to her. He took a deep breath.

'I . . . I have a high regard for your daughter, sir. I can give her far more than material things. She will be safe with me, and cared for. I will not part her from her family. She will, of course, live at Howethwaite,' he added hurriedly, the enchanting image of Lucy Dean—Lucy Buchanan—moving about his home, sleeping in his bed, temporarily silencing him, then he went on. 'But she can come here as often as she likes: every day if she wishes. Her family will not suffer. You will not suffer her loss, sir, for I give you my word—'

Edward Dean raised his hand, looking in surprise at the papers there as though wondering where they had come from, then he returned his kindly gaze to James.

'Mr Buchanan, Mr Buchanan, please, let us both stop and catch our breath. I will admit to you that it would give me the greatest pleasure to see my daughter, all my daughters, safely and happily married to a good man.'

James began to smile, thinking the battle won, his breath easing out on a great sigh of relief. He had the rector's approval and that was a great step in the wooing of Lucy Dean, but the reverend gentleman had not yet finished.

'But there is someone else who should be part of this ... these arrangements and that is Lucy herself.'

'Of course, but . . .'

'So until I have spoken to her . . .'

'Of course, sir, I understand that.'

A gust of wind rattled the windows and the curtains lifted dramatically and James, with that part of his brain not totally involved with his courtship of Lucy Dean, had time to speculate on the necessity of getting the frames fixed as soon as he and Lucy were married. A handful of sleety rain followed the wind, and smoke billowed from the chimney carrying particles of soot, which settled in the hearth. By God, the sooner he could get her out of this crumbling old rectory and settled in the warm comfort and luxury of his home the happier he would be. He had been reasonably warm when he entered the room but now his feet were solid blocks of ice and he had to stop himself from blowing into his cupped hands and flapping his arms like a duck about to fly.

There was a long and pregnant silence. The rector in his preoccupation had gone so far as to place his papers on the table next to him. He pulled at his lower lip as though deeply perplexed, staring into the fire which, if something wasn't done about it soon, would go out completely. James waited and at last Edward Dean looked up at him.

'Mr Buchanan, I can make no promises except to say that I will speak to Lucy first. She will . . . she has no idea . . . It will be a shock to her. She is very dear to me as she is to us all . . .'

'I appreciate that, sir.'

'But I cannot say what her answer will be.'

'But . . . do you approve of me as a prospective husband?' A thrill ran through him as he spoke the last word.

Edward Dean looked surprised. 'I cannot say that either, Mr Buchanan, since I barely know you. Oh, I am aware of your family, which is well respected in this area. You seem to be a . . a decent man, forgive me if I'm blunt. And you are certainly endowed with more than your share of life's fortune. You have treated me courteously and though, from what I hear, you have no need of it, you have honourable employment. But I am ignorant of your character, your nature. I know you are not a church-goer . . . no, oh, no, please'— holding up his hand as James would have interrupted—'that is of no concern to me. Some of the most devout can be hard family men and the opposite can apply. All that concerns me is Lucy's happiness. She is not an ordinary young woman, Mr Buchanan.'

'I realise that, sir.'

'She is very like her mother. Put her with a man who would not appreciate and understand her unique qualities and I do believe she would wither away like blossom on a branch. She needs to live in . . . warmth. Do you know what I am saying, Mr Buchanan?'

'Yes, sir, I do. Loving warmth.'

'Exactly.'

101

'She will be loved and cared for, sir. She is very
. . . dear to me.'

'I am beginning to believe you, Mr Buchanan.'

'Then may I . . . ?'

'You may try, Mr Buchanan, but if I see that
your attentions are not pleasing to her I will put a
stop to them. Is that fair?'

'It is, sir, and thank you. Now, if I may, I would
like a word with Miss Dean. No, please, sir. I only
mean to ask her, and perhaps Edward, or indeed
any of the children who would care to come, if they
would like to do some hill walking before the
winter truly sets in. Perhaps up to Loughrigg Fell
from Ambleside. Miss Dean did say she liked to
walk and climb.'

'Indeed she does, and if I'm not mistaken that is
Lucy and the children now. They have been sick
visiting.'

From a chilly peace the house seemed to
explode into a noise which at once gave the feeling
of warmth and movement as though those who
invaded it had brought their own heating system
with them. James could hear his own dogs barking
at the front of the house and was glad he had had
the foresight to leash them, for it seemed whenever
they encountered the Dean family their manners
deserted them.

'We're absolutely starving, Buffy,' he heard
young Edward bellow, just as though whoever it
was he was addressing were in Carlisle. 'Has Mrs
Hutton made those scones she promised?'

There was a murmuring which James did not
catch.

'Well, I could eat a dozen,' a younger voice
added, 'with strawberry jam and cream.'

102

'Fat chance of that, lad.'

'And don't be so greedy, Percy Dean,' a prim young girl's voice admonished him, probably that of . . . Emily, was that her name?

A faint scream sounded from the kitchen as the Dean children advanced on its occupants and another voice, a young woman's voice, told them to behave themselves or she'd tan the lot of them. There was much laughter at this remark followed by silence as a door banged to, though James was convinced he could hear the shrill tones of Thimble beyond it.

Suddenly the study door was flung open and Lucy Dean burst in with the force of a whirling dervish, glowing, red-cheeked, her polished chestnut hair tumbling about her neck and dangling a bright blue ribbon. She looked absolutely glorious, James had time to decide, shining with joy and good health, due no doubt to the brisk gallop she and the children had been forced into in order to beat the sleet which was now lashing against the windows, then she saw him and her jaw dropped, whether in amazement or dismay he could not tell. It was evident that she and her brothers and sisters must have come into the house through a back or side door or she would have seen his motor.

'Papa,' she had been just about to say but changed it to, 'Mr Buchanan, what on earth are you doing here? We weren't expecting you, were we?' she asked him accusingly.

James sprang to his feet as she entered the room, that stern look almost of disapproval darkening his face, and not for the first time Lucy wondered what she had done to displease him.

'No, Miss Dean, I was passing and took a chance on Reverend Dean being available. Just a small matter I wished to discuss with him but now I must get on, if you'll excuse me.'

Lucy looked enquiringly at her father but it seemed he was not about to explain and neither was Mr Buchanan.

'I see,' she said, though she obviously didn't.

'Will you see Mr Buchanan out, Lucy?' Papa asked her, making no attempt to take his guest's hand but nodding politely as he took his leave.

At the front door James hesitated. The hubbub in the kitchen continued, threaded with the shrill barking of the puppy and he wondered if there was ever peace and tranquillity in this house. It was all very well to be full of high spirits. It was one of the things about Lucy that drew him to her but the constant commotion would drive him mad, he told himself, and if he could manage it he would keep the visits of Lucy's family to his own home when they were married to the minimum. In the meanwhile there was still something he wanted to ask her.

'Miss Dean, do you remember at Mrs Buchanan's dance you told me you liked to climb?'

'Yes.' She was clearly puzzled.

'I was wondering whether you would like to attempt Sergeant Man with me tomorrow. If the weather is fine, of course,' he added hastily, 'and you are not otherwise engaged.'

Lucy, still looking puzzled, studied his face, noting once again that he seemed to find it hard to allow even the smallest smile to light his face. He was so serious, so stern, like a forbidding schoolmaster who was dealing with a recalcitrant

104

pupil. And yet his eyes were soft, like grey velvet, she thought, set so beautifully among thick brown lashes. They really were his best feature and, though he was probably not aware of it, revealed feelings which his stern face did not. Not that she recognised what those feelings were but they were obviously of a kindly nature.

She smiled, her sweetly shaped mouth, which looked as it had on the first day he met her, bee-stung with kisses, parting over her even white teeth.

'Yes, I would, Mr Buchanan. Thank you for asking me.'

'A pleasure, Miss Dean. Perhaps nine o'clock if that is not too early for you?'

'That would be splendid, Mr Buchanan.'

'Until then, Miss Dean.' He bowed, ran lightly down the steps, climbed into his motor car and roared away up the drive.

'Well now, Papa,' she said as she returned to the study. 'What was all that about? With Mr Buchanan, I mean? Not another legal matter? Surely you are not considering changing your will?'

'No, child, not my will, but something to which I must give a great deal of thought.'

She was astonished. 'Why, Papa, what can you and Mr Buchanan have discussed that causes you so much concern? We're ... we're not in trouble, are we?' Her expression turned to one of anxiety and her father smiled and held out his hand to take hers.

'No, dearest. No trouble, but a problem I must wrestle with for a day or two. I promise I'll discuss it with you then.'

*　　　*　　　*

105

James Buchanan was seriously dismayed and not a little put out to find not just Lucy waiting on the steps for him the next day but her brothers and sisters as well, not to mention the damned dog. But with his usual talent for hiding his feelings, whatever they might be, he politely helped them to cram themselves into the motor car, pushing aside poor Holmes and Watson who had had the back seat all to themselves. The two big dogs found, to their mortification and sad loss of dignity, that they must perch on the children's knees while the scrap called Thimble crawled over everybody, which nobody but James's dogs seemed to mind. Lucy sat next to James.

Their passage through the town excited much comment among the people who were that morning out and about in Ambleside. Well, you could hardly miss that enormous machine which James Buchanan drove at such terrifying speeds and when it was filled with singing children and barking dogs you would have to be deaf and blind not to notice. Who were they? You could see the open-mouthed wonder in the eyes of those who stood and stared as the Rolls-Royce thundered by, though the two ladies who were just about to enter a rather smart bow-fronted shop in Market Place knew exactly who was being driven by James Buchanan.

Charlotte and Mrs Gibson had made an early start that morning. It would be Charlotte's birthday in a week's time and she was to have a party to which James Buchanan was not invited, though others of his family were. Though her new evening gown had been made for her in Paris when she and her mama visited there, she had taken a fancy to see what Miss Medlock, the cleverest and most stylish dressmaker in Ambleside, had in stock. Miss Medlock dressed the ladies of the district who had not the wealth, or perhaps even the inclination, to travel to Paris for their clothes. Her silks and laces were superb, her taffetas glorious, her gold brocade, her fans and muffs and sheer, pale, silk stockings, her sashes and belts much in demand. Her broderie anglaise was of the highest quality, her bead fringes, her fur trimmings, her ropes of pearls, her gloves of kid, suede and silk, some short with two buttons, some long with twenty, her stoles and boas and parasols and indeed all her splendid merchandise was of the very best quality and much sought after by her customers. She employed two clever milliners besides her seamstresses, who made hats of every shape and size, in the latest styles, naturally, hats with wide, turned-up brims of beaver, plush, velvet and straw, toques of velvet, tam o' shanters and berets, juliet caps sequined for evening wear and bandeaux with or without feathers or plumes. Her millinery was as chic as the outfits she designed and made, and those who knew her and were dressed by her could not for the life of them understand why Miss Charlotte Gibson had to go to Paris to be clothed. Just to be able to say she did was the general consensus of opinion among the ladies, since Miss Medlock's creations were just as stylish.

Charlotte and her mother watched, like the rest, their mouths hanging open as the Rolls sped through Market Place. James raised his cap to them as he swung on to the Rydal road. The motor was travelling at some speed by the time it passed Armbroth Hall where Janet and Angus Gunson and their four sons lived. The song the occupants had chosen for some reason was 'Rule Britannia' and the sound of it rang out on the air even after the motor car had disappeared round the bend.

'Well, did you see that?' Mrs Gibson gasped unnecessarily, clutching her daughter's arm. 'It was that dreadful Dean girl and, one presumes, her brothers and sisters. What can James be thinking of, making a spectacle of himself in such a way? And to tip his cap at us, too, as if he didn't want us to miss him. As if we could. You would think a gentleman in his position would—'

'Be quiet, Mama.' Charlotte spoke through gritted teeth. 'There is no need to carry on about it.' Her face had turned bone white except for a streak of red temper high on each cheekbone, a sign her mother recognised with some trepidation.

'But, my dear, what is he doing consorting with that girl when he could have had the daughter of—'

'That's enough, Mama. Not another word.'

'But he has belittled you in the eyes of—'

'Mama, I swear if you say another word I shall strike you, right here in the middle of Ambleside. And let me add that what James Buchanan has done to me will not be forgotten.'

Mrs Gibson's face became even more bewildered. 'What on earth are you talking about, child?'

Charlotte's voice was vicious, 'I shall make it my business to see that he and that ... that woman suffer for humiliating me as they have done. I shall find out something; anything, I don't know what. There must be, there will be a secret one of them wishes to keep hidden. No, I don't know what, Mama,' as her mother would have begged her to

108

tell her what she meant. 'But I shall find it out, and, I don't care how long it takes, I shall humiliate them as James Buchanan has humiliated me. All our friends were . . . were aware of his interest in me and now . . . Dear God in heaven . . .'

'Charlotte, please darling, someone will hear you.' Mrs Gibson glanced round in anguish. She and Arthur had had a terrible time with their daughter ever since Franny Buchanan's dance. Tantrums, screams of tearful rage at being deserted by James for that shameless vulgarian, and in front of all their friends, too. She would not be treated like this, she had shrieked and her papa must drive over to Howethwaite and tell James so. In her mind, as it had been in others', it had been only a matter of time before James Buchanan would speak for her. A spring wedding, she had planned. A honeymoon in Italy. She would be Mrs James Buchanan, mistress of Howethwaite which, though not as grand as her parents' house, was old and venerable and at the same time filled with the luxurious comforts she had always known. Now it seemed that James's attention had been captured by the appallingly dressed, appallingly mannered daughter of a local rector, and to prove that it was to be taken seriously, by the rector and by James's family, he had just driven past for all the world to see with the rector's lot stuffed in the back of his motor car and the rector's daughter preening herself beside him. Charlotte had hoped that by omitting him from the guest list for her nineteenth birthday next week he would come to his senses; realise that he was being punished, cast out from the Gibson circle and, seeing the error of his ways, return penitent to throw himself on her mercy. She would make him grovel, then forgive him charmingly, and her plans for him would proceed. Now it seemed he did not care and she wanted to kick and scream and break something as she had done as a child.

'They will pay for this,' she hissed, taking her mother's arm with fingers which pinched cruelly and hurrying her towards the Salutation Inn corner where their carriage waited.

'But we have not done our shopping,' her hapless mother protested.

'Damn the shopping. I want to go home.'

Meanwhile, on the road beyond Ambleside, the Rolls-Royce, its occupants either singing or barking, continued steadily along the north side of Rydal Water where the birches, bright and delicate among the heavier foliage of beech and oak, larch and ash, lined the shores and inlets. Autumn colours fading now but still beyond description as the blueness of the sky and water merged. On past Grasmere Lake, through Town End where Dove Cottage stood and on to the village of Grasmere itself.

'Will she be able to manage it, d'you think, sir?' Edward asked presently. Even he, staunch devotee of the magnificent motor car and the wonders which lay beneath its bonnet, looked somewhat strained as he hung over Lucy's shoulder. He had wanted to sit beside Mr Buchanan, two motoring enthusiasts together, but Mr Buchanan had been most insistent that Lucy sat next to him, since he could not stand the thought of talking engines and miles per hour with a squirt like Edward all the way up to where they were to get out. Edward had sighed but took it in good part and he and the

110

others, with the three dogs, had no option but to cram themselves in behind.

'Manage what, Edward?' James was always patient.

'The climb to Goody Bridge, sir.'

'Oh, we shan't go that far, lad. I'll leave the motor in Grasmere and we'll set out from there.'

'It was a splendid day to be out, a clear day with the light spreading along the summit of Sergeant Man. Below them as they progressed through the waist-high valleys of autumn bracken they could see the brilliance of Rydal Water, a silvery calm as sunlight travelled across it. On wild days it would be rippled with fast eddies blown by the wind but today it was as gentle and soft as silk. It was edged with reeds, and groves of silver birch added magic to a scene already superlatively lovely and the intense green of the little pastures between created a mosaic of colour that beggared description. The waterfall which cascaded from Easedale Tarn, the run called Sour Milk Gill because of its similarity to sour milk as it scrambled down the mountain, thundered on their right, the spray from it misting about them and scattering them with diamond drops.

They paused at Easedale Tarn itself to give Percy a rest, sitting in quiet contemplation of the scene before them, their backs to the trunks of trees, comfortable in the softness and vivid, multicoloured carpet of the fallen leaves, the dappled surface of the peaceful tarn having almost a hypnotic effect on their bemused senses. A low and solitary rock pierced the glassy smoothness and standing on it was a heron, patient, motionless, silent as a sentinel, its yellow eye following the

111

movement of a brown trout in the water and James wondered out loud at seeing the bird so high on the fell. Even the dogs, which had raced madly hither and yon in a euphoria of delight, lay still, their tongues hanging from their panting mouths, their sides heaving.

'I'll put Holmes and Watson on a leash here. You take Holmes, Miss Dean, as he's the quieter of the two and the boy can take Watson. And I'll see to this little ruffian,' advancing on the unsuspecting Thimble.

'Why, Mr Buchanan? Why must they be leashed? There are no sheep hereabout,' Lucy protested as she reluctantly took Holmes's leash from him.

'Because I'm going to teach Thimble—God what a name,' shaking his head in mystified disbelief at whoever had christened him, 'some manners.'

Instantly Lucy bristled at the slur cast on the puppy's name. 'What's wrong with Thimble, may I ask? It was because he was so small that we called him that, and anyway, can it be more foolish than Holmes and Watson?'

James frowned, evidently not caring for her criticism. 'Perhaps you're right but that's not the issue here. The puppy must learn to walk to heel and there'd be no chance at the moment that he'd behave with my two capering about. Now don't look so woebegone, all of you. Anyone would think I was going to give him a thrashing. I promise I won't hurt him but I must be firm.'

It did not take Thimble long to become aware that he had met his match in James Buchanan. For the first ten minutes as they followed the rocky path up through the endless bracken beyond Belles

112

Knott, named the Matterhorn of Easedale because of its sharp peak, to the stretch of grass which lay below Codale Tarn, the dog pulled and pranced and whined to be free and each time James steadied him with a jerk and a sharp word.

'Oh, not so hard, Mr Buchanan,' Lucy begged, but he would not give in.

'Miss Dean, unless we persevere you will have a dog who will be a puppy all his life. He is not hurt, only infuriated at being made to do what he doesn't want to do. I'd be obliged if you'd drop behind so that he can't see you. When we get beyond the tarn I'll let him off.'

Thimble dragged along disconsolately after that, evidently deciding he might as well submit to it. All five Deans were vastly impressed but also relieved when Mr Buchanan decided that Thimble had had enough for one day but they were to continue with the lessons each day, he told them, with little hope that he would be obeyed, until the pup would walk beside them, even without his lead.

They all agreed that it was a grand day. Progress beyond Codale Tarn seemed to be barred by slanting tiers of rock but Mr Buchanan said that they would come very soon to a remarkable grassy shelf, wide as a road, running up from the foot of Lang Crag, affording a simple way to the easier ground above. Percy was tiring and when, at the summit marked by a stone cairn, they had eaten the simple lunch each had brought and had a rest, James packed his rucksack and rose to his feet. To their surprise he instructed the small boy to climb on to a waist-high rock. Percy, bewildered, did so, then, on being told arbitrarily to 'hop up, lad' found he was on Mr Buchanan's broad shoulders from where he had the best view of them all. They could just make out, turning in a slow circle, the high, shrouded peak of Skiddaw to the north, Helvellyn, High Street, Loughrigg Fell, Coniston Old Man, Scafell and High Raise, range upon range of rolling fells stretching out to the far horizons, vivid and silent except for the call of a flock of whooper swans spreading their wings across the waters of Rydal far below.

James and Lucy did not talk much, at least to each other. She could hear him pointing things out to Percy as he strode ahead of them, the child on his shoulders. Edward and the two girls, being strong, healthy, well nourished and used to exercise, did not tire easily, even the girls making nothing of their hampering, calf-length skirts though Emily was heard to say that when women got the vote, which could not be long now, she would ask them to pass a bill allowing females to wear breeches like their brothers.

Lucy studied the strong line of Mr Buchanan's jaw which was just visible beneath Percy's clinging hands. She could see the uplifted corner of his mouth and the lean plane of one cheek and, as he glanced down at the rocky littered path, carefully placing his feet, the long curve of his dark eyelashes.

His hair, which was uncovered since he had left his cap in the motor car, was a thick, untidy thatch of dark curls, not helped by Percy's careless handling of it. Strangely he didn't seem to mind and she mused on the two sides of his nature. He had been an undemanding companion, not exactly cheerful but patient and instructive, since he was a Dalesman born and bred and seemed to know

114

every rock and beck, every plant and bird and, what was most satisfying to Lucy, appeared to find the company of her brothers and sisters bearable.

They were a tired but satisfied group as they tumbled out of the Rolls at the front door of the rectory just as the light was beginning to fade. The sky was still luminous but the trees pressed close to the square, ugly house and James wondered how long it would take him to woo and wed Lucy Dean and get her away from these dismal surroundings.

'Will you come in, Mr Buchanan,' she was saying. 'Perhaps a hot drink?'

The others had gone in after thanking Mr Buchanan most profusely for a splendid day, calling to Mrs Hutton that they could eat a horse if she had one to spare, but Lucy lingered on the step. She had no idea of the lovely picture she made standing with the soft light of the newly lit lamps behind her. It outlined the slipping mass of her hair, forming a golden halo through which the light shone. It darkened her eyes, which were in shadow, to unfathomable depths and touched tenderly the strong line of her waist and hips.

'No, I'd best be off. Now mind what I told you about the pup. Every day on the leash.'

'Yes, Mr Buchanan,' she dimpled, and bobbed a curtsey.

'I want to see him walking to heel the ... the next time we meet.' Whenever that would be!

'Yes, Mr Buchanan, sir.'

'No shirking now. Remember what I told you.'

'Yes, sir, I will, sir.'

He was stern with her but she could see he was ready to smile. 'It's been a first-rate day, Miss Dean. Perhaps we might do it again.'

115

'I hope so, Mr Buchanan. The children did so enjoy it.'

'And you?'

'Of course. It was kind of you to take the time and trouble.'

He had been leaning on the bonnet of the motor, his arms crossed, watching the mass exodus of the children and Thimble, speaking firmly to his own dogs who would have followed. Now he moved slowly towards her and, she didn't know why, she felt tension move with him, almost an excitement which stirred in her as he looked up at her from the bottom of the steps.

'Perhaps next time,' he said quietly, and she felt the most incredible sensation of being drawn down the steps towards him. 'Perhaps we can do a more strenuous climb but it would mean we would have to do it just the two of us. I'm sure Edward could manage High Raise, which is what I propose, but I could not look after two of you. It would mean ropes and equipment, you see, for there are crags to be climbed. And it would have to be before winter sets in. What d'you say?'

He was asking her a very simple question which required a simple, 'yes, please' or 'no, thank you,' but there seemed to be something odd in his manner, the way he stood so casually, one foot on the bottom step, his hands in his jacket pockets, confident and easy and yet as tense as a tiger about to spring. She found herself to be quite intrigued by it, intrigued and confused and yet what was there to be confused about? She supposed it was because Mr Buchanan was taking so much trouble to be kind to her and her family and she couldn't imagine why. How many gentlemen would be willing to be cluttered up with children and dogs and all the paraphernalia that a day out with them involved? He had a kind heart, she told herself. He was a good man, if somewhat reserved, and yet so were other men in Fellthwaite but none had taken an interest in the Dean family as he was doing. Why wasn't he married? she wondered, the question, coming from nowhere, surprising her, an attractive and wealthy gentleman such as he. And why, for heaven's sake, was she dithering and vacillating over what was merely an invitation to go climbing with him? She had told him of her interest in the activity and, knowing she could not do it alone, or with the children, he was inviting her to accompany him since he was keen on it too.

'You seem to be hesitating, Miss Dean. Don't you trust me?' He began to frown.

At once she was full of contrition. 'Of course I do, Mr Buchanan. I was just wondering why . . .'

'Why what, Miss Dean?' His voice was expressionless.

'I would sooner put my trust in you than any man I know, Mr Buchanan,' she told him seriously, meaning it, 'and yes, I would love to come.'

They shook hands like men, hers warm and strong in his.

'Thank you again. I'll wait to hear from you then.' It was as though they were businessmen bidding one another farewell after a satisfactory deal had been struck and for a moment he was disconcerted. Then he recovered, for was this not what he wanted? Friendship to start with, then trust and a growing ease between them which would turn to something deeper.

'Soon, Miss Dean. It's November already and . . .

well, I'll call you.'

'Call me?' a questioning note in her voice. Her hand was still in his and he was more than happy to leave it there.

'Telephone you, if I may. I have several meetings this week—' He stopped speaking as she began to laugh. 'What?'

'We have no telephone, Mr Buchanan. We have no electricity, let alone a telephone. Surely you know that? And is that the thing to say? I'll call you! How extraordinary.'

For a moment he was nonplussed, as though the idea that in this day and age, since it was almost the end of 1913, there were houses still without the wonders of electricity, at least in his circle of acquaintances, was very novel. Then he shook his head at his own stupidity, smiling in wry amusement.

'I'll get in touch with you by carrier pigeon then.'

'Mr Buchanan, you do make me laugh. I'm so glad you make me laugh.' And on this note she took her hand from his and went indoors, laughing as she did so as though she spoke only the truth.

CHAPTER SIX

'He wishes to marry you, Lucy, and there is nothing wrong in that. His intentions are honourable. He spoke to me the other day and told me of his feelings. He has been a gentleman in all this and I respect him for it. He has been . . . a friend.'

'Yes, friends, that's what we are, Papa, but no more. We have met only on—what?—two or three

118

occasions, so how can he know that ... how can he have decided that ... that we should be married? That there is enough between us to ... to lead to a stronger feeling. I'm sure I've given him no encouragement to make him believe ... Good Lord, if I'd known, guessed, I would have ...'

'Why are you so angry, child? There is nothing to be angry about. He has done the proper thing. He is a decent man but if you cannot accept what he offers then he will leave you alone.'

'Oh, yes, Papa, that's what I want. To be left alone.'

'You do not wish to become his wife?'

Lucy looked horrified. 'Of course not. I don't want to be anybody's wife, not until I fall in love. And besides, Mr Buchanan is so ... old. I really cannot imagine why he has picked on me.'

She really couldn't see it. She really didn't know her own worth, her beauty, her sweetness, and her love of life that had drawn James Buchanan to her, her father realised, shaking his head. She was genuinely bewildered that he had chosen her, and it showed in her distraught manner.

'There must be dozens of girls who would be more suitable,' she went on desperately. 'You know what I'm like, Papa. Far too outspoken for folk like the Buchanans who demand of their women that they be demure and soft and without an opinion of their own.'

'Mrs Frances Buchanan doesn't strike me as being like that, dearest, and neither would you have to be.'

'Papa, do you want me to marry Mr Buchanan?' she asked him quietly.

'Only if it is right for you and only you know

119

that, Lucy.'

'Then that is the end of it. I don't wish to marry Mr Buchanan.'

Even to her papa it was very evident that Lucy, just by the way she said Mr Buchanan, not James Buchanan, nor yet James, was somehow insulted by James Buchanan's offer. She thought of him as a man of another generation. Someone who a person of her generation addressed by his surname with the prefix Mr in front of it. He had asked her to be his wife but the idea was not something she could even contemplate with any sort of composure. She was, in fact, quite appalled, just as though Bibby, or old Mr Henley from where Thimble had come, had had the presumption to imagine that Lucy Dean, who was eighteen years old, would consider him.

She was huddled in the depths of the sagging armchair which stood to one side of the fireplace in Edward Dean's study where Edward had summoned her. Her feet were tucked up beneath the hem of her skirt, her arms wrapped tightly about her knees. Her father sat opposite, grave and preoccupied. There was the usual sullen fire smouldering in the grate. Beyond the window the rain lashed down and the trees thrashed wildly in the accompanying wind, what old Bibby called a 'rheumatic' wind which cut through the valley, plaguing his old bones. He was at this moment huddled up to the kitchen fire, his knees almost in the flames, a pork pie in one hand and a glass of ale in the other, 'them bairns' safely tucked out of his way in the breakfast-room with Buffy Tyson in charge of them and their voracious appetites, playing some board game they favoured, and good riddance to them, cheeky little hooligans.

'Lucy, can I give you some advice,' her papa asked her hesitantly. Although he was hesitant, his usual vague manner was missing. It was his practice to drift pleasantly through the days, leaving everything to his eldest daughter who seemed to thrive on it, cheerfully taking on what should have been his responsibility, but this was different. She would never get another offer like this and in his floundering way he wanted her to realise it. He would not press her, naturally, nor belabour her on how advantageous her marriage to James Buchanan would be, not only to her but to her family, but perhaps if they talked it out she would come to realise herself how suitable it would be. She was loved. That, of course, was the most important factor. She would be safe and so would his other children, for James Buchanan was not the sort of man to see his wife's brothers and sisters wanting.

'Lucy,' he continued, 'I'm a firm believer in not making hasty decisions,' knowing as he spoke that he made none. I really think you should give this offer . . . yes, I know he hasn't made it yet,' as she looked up in surprise, 'but he will and I feel you should give it some consideration.'

'No, Papa, I cannot.'

'Why not, child? You will live in a way which is your due. You are . . .well, I know it sounds silly in this day and age, but you are a gentlewoman, Lucy. Your mama was a great lady and Mr Buchanan can give you so much. He will take care of you.'

Lucy propped her chin on her knees and stared stubbornly into the feeble blue and green flames of the fire.

'I can take care of myself, Papa. I'm no weak and

121

foolish maiden who needs a gentleman's arm if she steps out of doors. I'm strong and sensible. Besides, if I married it would interfere with . . . well, you might as well know, Papa, I am very interested in the Women's Social and Political Union. You know of it? Yes, of course you do. There is to be a branch in Ambleside and I wish to . . . to become involved.'

'Lucy, I'm not sure your mother would have approved.'

'Oh, Papa, no harm will come to me. I just feel that women have rights, just like men and I'm sure Mama would agree with me.'

'Well . . .'

'So now you see why I haven't time for marriage. I can look after myself . . .'

'I know that, dearest, but have you any idea how hard life could be if . . . well, I shall not say another word about it after this, I will not try to persuade you except to say that, of all people, I know the joy of a good marriage.'

Lucy turned to glare at him and he wondered why she was so horrified. 'Papa, it is not the same at all. You and Mama loved one another. How can you compare what you and she had with what Mr Buchanan and I would have if we married? I do not love him and I cannot marry a man I do not love.'

'Of course not, child.'

Her voice was very sure as she continued. 'Papa, it's no good. I have . . . I have enjoyed Mr Buchanan's company on the few occasions we have been together. For an older man he is quite . . . interesting. We found we had one or two things in common when we talked at Mrs Buchanan's dance and I admit he loves the fells as much as I do but that is no basis for a marriage. You must know that.

No, it is impossible. He is, I'm sure, a good man and will make some woman a splendid husband but I'm afraid it won't be me. He is not unpleasing to look at and, so they tell me, very rich and I'm sure he will have no trouble finding—'

'Lucy, you must not make light of Mr Buchanan's feelings for you in that way. You speak as though they were no more than a boy's passing fancy for a pretty girl. He struck me as being quite sincere and I feel that . . . should you refuse him he will not take it easily.'

Lucy looked contrite. 'I'm sorry, Papa, I did not mean to.'

'I know that, child, so let's speak of it no further. You are absolutely certain that . . . ?'

'I am, Papa.'

'Then we will say no more on the subject though I feel that not only will you lose Mr Buchanan's friendship but that of Mrs Buchanan who, I believe, has invited you to dine next week.'

'Yes, she has, Papa but—'

'There will be no more socialising with the Buchanans from now on. You realise that. It would put Mr James Buchanan in an impossible situation. Especially when it becomes known that you have refused him.'

Lucy looked distressed. 'Oh, no, surely not, Papa. I will tell no one if you don't and Mr Buchanan is hardly likely to . . .'

'Dearest, you know how servants talk.'

'But not ours, Papa, not ours.'

'Well, let us hope for the best.'

'And I don't care about going out into society, Papa. I find it does not matter to me in the least. I don't speak their language and they don't speak

123

mine.'

Edward Dean sighed. 'Well then, that is the end of the matter. There is just the question of speaking to Mr Buchanan, Lucy.' Her papa looked at her sadly. She returned his look, startled.

'Speaking to him? I don't understand, Papa.'

'You cannot believe that you can just leave him dangling without a yes or no, child. He has asked my permission to court you which I gave on the understanding that should you find his attentions unwelcome he would be ... informed and leave you alone.'

'Then ... you could do that for me, couldn't you, Papa?' she begged him anxiously, her face strained.

'Lucy, the man has behaved entirely properly. He has done exactly what he has said he would do. He has acted responsibly and you must do the same. He has dealt with both you and me courteously and must be treated in the same way. I shall let him know that you are aware of his interest and ask him to call when you can explain how you feel. It is only fair, Lucy.'

'Oh, Papa.' She found herself flinching away from the awkward picture of herself and Mr Buchanan in a room somewhere speaking of a marriage which she must refuse. She wanted to run away from it, forget she had ever met him, that all this had never happened. Go back to the relaxed and happy atmosphere of the carefree life she and her family had dwelled in over the years, but before she could do that she must speak to Mr Buchanan. Oh, dammit, why couldn't he have been satisfied with the way things were? Why did gentlemen always want ... other things, again shying away from what those other things might be. Was it

124

impossible for them to be merely friends with a member of the opposite sex? It seemed so and tomorrow or the next day she would be forced to tell him so and cast him from her life, she thought with a heavy heart as she slowly climbed the stairs to her own room. She needed to be alone for a little while to put all this chaos in her mind into some sort of order, though never before had she had the slightest inclination towards orderliness. She supposed she must prepare some words, those she believed a lady used when refusing a proposal of marriage from a gentleman, but really, that was not her style. She knew herself to be brutally frank and honest, hating deception, pretence and speciousness. Come right out with it, that was how she did things, but she could not be like that with Mr Buchanan. He was worth the truth and would want if from her, the truth that she did not love him in a way a woman loves a man.

A tap on the door cut into her reverie, telling her that her privacy was ended. It was Buffy and Lucy was not surprised, for Buffy had been her support, her friend in need, her critic, her conscience sometimes, ever since Mama had died. Unassuming but always there when she was needed. Sometimes it was no more than how to coax another pound of shin beef from the butcher whose bill was still unpaid, and at other times, like now, a crossroad in Lucy's life when she needed to speak of which path to take. Not that she was undecided about that. She had made up her mind and would not change it, but it might be helpful to talk it out with Buffy who had a good heart in her breast and a good head on her shoulders.

Buffy closed the door behind her, standing for a

moment to study the disconsolate figure in the chair before the empty grate. It was bitterly cold and though both women had automatically thrown a shawl about their shoulders as they mounted the stairs to the icy regions of the upper floor, they were shivering.

'Your papa asked me to come in case you needed ... something,' prepared to give whatever it might be without stint. Buffy limped across the bare wooden floor and sat down on the end of the bed, waiting.

Lucy sighed and frowned at the same time, looking down at her fingers which were twisting and twining about themselves. Buffy reached out and placed her own hand on Lucy's and at once the quiet calm which was Buffy Tyson's nature lapped itself about Lucy Dean.

'He wants to marry me, Buffy. Mr Buchanan.'

'Well, don't say it as though he'd asked you to commit murder, Lucy. A decent proposal of marriage is something most girls long for, and anyway, I'm not a bit surprised.'

Lucy looked up at her in amazement. 'You knew?'

It was written all over him, lass, for all to see. How he felt about you.'

'Well, I didn't see it. Why didn't I see it? Come to that, why didn't you warn me? I would have sent him away with a flea in his ear, I can tell you.'

'Why? It's not a crime for a man to fall in love and want to marry, Lucy. And why are you so mad at him?'

'I'm not ... mad with him, just disappointed.' Lucy jumped to her feet, throwing off Buffy's restraining hand and strode to the window, pulling her shawl more closely about her. Her breath misted the glass and she rubbed it with the corner of her shawl.

'It's getting worse,' she said absently, referring to the rain which pelted against the window.

'I can see that. The children are going wild being shut up in the schoolroom.'

'I might take them for a walk.'

'Don't be daft. You'll get soaked, and don't change the subject. We were talking about Mr Buchanan who seems to me to be a perfect gentleman and would make a splendid husband.'

'Yes, perfect. For some woman he would be perfect, Buffy, but not for me. He says and does all the right things but I hardly know him. I'm sure he has all the ... qualifications and I'm sure any woman would give her right arm for such a husband. I believe he has a ... a gentleness underneath that gruff exterior and yet he is strong. He shows a sort of arrogance which says that no one, man or woman, will ever be his master. He'll be no woman's puppet, Buffy.'

'Is that what you want then, Lucy? A puppet whose strings you can pull?'

'Don't be stupid, Buffy Tyson.' Lucy's voice was flat. 'When I marry it will be to a man I can respect. One who has all the qualities ...'

'You have just described in Mr Buchanan.'

'Oh, Buffy, leave me alone, please. I don't want to hurt him if he really does love me, which, by the way, he has shown no signs of doing, at least to me, but I have no choice. I don't love him. Besides, I couldn't possibly leave Papa and the children, and all of you. I am needed here and here I must stay.'

The rain, which had begun early that day, and

127

with a squally wind to help it, had begun to dash itself with increasing force, the wind howling directly at the back of the house. It became so heavy that by the end of the day a racing slick of water flowed like a small beck down each side of the house, cascading into the front garden and on to the lawn where it had begun to form a wind-tossed pool. The drumming of it on the roof could be heard distinctly even by those on the ground floor and Mrs Hutton moaned that she feared for the windows. They were rattly old things at the best of times but if this kept up she was convinced they would give way and the rain flood the house.

By morning, not having had a wink of sleep, she declared, she was even more fearful when she saw the amount of water that had collected about the house. It was still bucketing down, sweeping in a great impermeable curtain across Loughrigg and at the back of the house, the Hundreds, blotting out the high peaks until it seemed the very skies, black and surly, were pressing down on their heads. The fast-racing rainwater carried muck and mud, ripped out heather and gorse bushes and the bodies of many small fellside animals, depositing them in an appalling heap on the front lawn, and the water began to inch up the front steps of the house. Already at the back kitchen door Bibby had stacked bags of soil to prevent the kitchen from flooding, all the while bemoaning the fate of his 'veggies' which were under six inches of water and with no sign of it letting up. It was almost as dark as at midnight and the only one enjoying the spectacle was Edward who longed to get out in it, fight the elements, though with what in mind he was not awfully sure.

After his Trojan effort with the sandbags Bibby settled himself by the fire declaring that, 'Ah's gaan' nowhere an' the bloody 'ens'll 'ave ter fettle fer theirsenn.' He worked his bum more comfortably into Mrs Hutton's chair by the fire and that's where he stayed for the rest of the day and the night, toasting his toes and telling anyone who was interested that there were plenty more sandbags in the stable if they were needed for the back door. If it got up to the windows, well, there was nowt he could do about that so best not to get in a mish-mash about it.

The following day it had stopped and the tidal wave of rainwater had receded and, sorry in a way since he had enjoyed the rest, Bibby, with the help of them hooligans, began to clear up his garden. His grandson, a strong lad of thirteen who sometimes helped him out after school with heavy jobs, lent a hand. He was surprised, and so was Bibby, when a command came from the reverend that he wanted a note delivered at once to Mr Buchanan of Howethwaite.

He was at the rectory within an hour of the note being delivered.

'I came at once, sir.' His voice was eager, filled with hope, for the note had implied it was to do with Lucy. He had discarded his caped overcoat and knee-high rubber Wellington boots at the front door, handing them to an excited Elsie, for those in the kitchen had got wind, as servants do, that 'something was up'. Padding in his stockinged feet, he entered Edward Dean's study. They shook hands and Edward indicated that he should sit, appearing not to notice that his guest had no shoes on his feet.

It seemed, now that James was here and seated with as much comfort as the old chair and the meagre fire afforded, the rector did not know where to begin. It was a measure of his distress that he felt compelled to pick up the heavy brass poker and plunge it into the centre of the coals, for normally he would scarce have noticed if the fire was in or out.

He cleared his throat and passed his hand over his thinning grey hair, a picture of a man in some confusion and it was at this precise moment that the first small twist of doubt struck at James Buchanan's gut, though he did his best to ignore it, for the unthinkable was . . . unthinkable! He did his best to be patient while the rector hemmed and hawed and commented on the weather, hoping he had not had too tiresome a journey from Howethwaite until at last James could stand it no longer.

'You said you wanted to speak to me, sir. Is it about Miss Dean?'

Looking vastly relieved that the reason for James's visit had been so quickly reached, Edward Dean became calmer, then nodded his head.

'It is, my dear fellow. I spoke to her of our conversation.'

'And . . .' James leaned forward eagerly.

'She is waiting for you in the small parlour. You know where it is?'

'Yes, sir.' Before the two words were out of his mouth James was across the room and through the door.

Edward sighed sadly. So ardent, so joyful in his need at last to put before Lucy the gift of his love. His patience had been rewarded, it was written in

130

his face and now he was to speak the words, about his feelings, about marriage, about the happiness to come for himself and Edward's daughter.

Dear Lord, help him to bear the pain of his rejection, Edward prayed, his heart heavy for the man.

In the kitchen Mrs Hutton, Bibby and Elsie, who was filled with a great sense of her own importance, for had she not relieved Mr Buchanan of his coat and boots, debated on how long it would be before the wedding took place. They'd seen it coming, of course, they told one another, for no man took the trouble to be nice to a lady's brothers and sisters, as he had, unless it was serious. It would certainly take a burden from the rector's back, which was not strong at the best of times, to have a wealthy son-in-law and make a difference to them bairns who needed a bit of discipline.

'Throw another shovel of coal on't fire, Elsie,' Mrs Hutton instructed her handmaiden, in anticipation of better things to come.

The door to the room was ajar. James knocked softly and at Lucy's command, entered.

She was sitting, her head bowed as though in deep thought, by another of the Deans' lacklustre fires. She had a quilted shawl about her shoulders and he had time to gloat in his mind that soon, in the warm, fire-lit comfort of the rooms, every room at Howethwaite, she would no longer need such a thing.

She looked up as he entered, smiling, half smiling really, as though it were no more than her duty as a hostess to welcome him as a guest. He stood on the threshold and found his mind wandering from the images of her resting by his

131

warm fireside to the consideration of why she looked so pale by her own. Her flesh was always a creamy white with little colour except when there was excitement in the air, or during vigorous exercise, but now she looked strained with shadows beneath her eyes. Her soft mouth quivered and she took her full lower lip between her white teeth. She was so exquisite. In this one girl was the promise of all he desired. She breathed exhilaration into what he saw now had been a sterile life, stimulating not only his body, but his mind. She gave him energy, inspiration, hope, captivating his senses and he could scarcely believe that the moment had come to claim her.

'Miss Dean ... Lucy.' His voice had never been so warm, so soft, so loving, allowing her to hear for the first time the depth of his feelings for her.

'Mr Buchanan.' No more.

'Your father said ...'

'Yes, yes, I know. He told me ... I would have ... well, we could not ask you to come sooner ... the rain ...' Her voice trailed away.

'I'm here now. May I sit down?'

'Oh, of course. I'm sorry ... will you have tea?'

'I think not.'

'Very well. You managed the walk then?'

'As you see,' smiling at her, his eyes clouded with some buried emotion.

If only he would not smile that whimsical smile of his. If only he was not such a ... a good person, so decent and honourable. if only there was something nasty she could focus on, something to shore up her ebbing determination and let her get through this without weakening. Not that she would weaken. She knew without a shadow of

132

doubt that she could never marry this man, or any man while the children needed her, but she liked him and it was very difficult to hurt someone you liked deliberately. The expression on his face was unreadable and she knew he was making a decent effort to keep it neutral but his eyes, the grey of them pale as silver, not a cold silver but with a warmth in them, changing as she watched them, as they watched her, to pale misted smoke and they revealed exactly what James Buchanan wanted of her.

He took a deep breath. He supposed it was up to him to begin. Before she could answer he must ask the question so best get it over and then ... and then, by God, he'd kiss that paleness from her cheeks, remove that drooping frailty from her lips, bring her alive as he had dreamed of doing for weeks now. God almighty! Was that all it was? Weeks! He felt as though he had been in love with Lucy Dean for all his adult life.

'You know why I'm here, Lucy, don't you? Your father has explained ...'

'Oh, yes, Mr Buchanan, but ...'

'No, let me speak, then. Well ...' He took a deep breath and leaned forward in his chair so that they were almost knee to knee. He looked boyish in his haste to tell her of all that had been confined within him for so long. Ardent, and tense with his ardour, and excited too, like a lad about to have granted a youthful desire long denied him, compelling, oh, yes, and very attractive. The suave self-control of the mature man he was had melted away like mist before a breeze.

'Lucy, you know my feelings for you, don't you? No, let me finish. I've had a ... a deep regard for

133

you since we met in the wood. You have something in you that calls to something in me and though I don't fool myself that you feel the same way at this very moment, well . . . I think we would do very well together. I am a wealthy man. Not that I think that would matter to someone like you, but I could keep you and your family safe and . . .'

'Mr Buchanan, please don't . . .' Her cry was agonised.

James Buchanan frowned. 'Don't, Lucy, but I must. I must tell you of my feelings and, of course, though I doubt it concerns you, your father will want to know that I can keep you in comfort, even luxury. You will want for nothing.'

James Buchanan was an intensely reserved man who went to a great deal of trouble to hide his true feelings. He needed a wife and he thought Lucy Dean needed a husband, if only to see to that wild family of hers, but there was more, much more to him than that. He had, under the forbidding aloofness he showed to most, a heart capable of a great romantic love. Not romantic in the manner of a tuppeny novelette but a love which wanted to, and had, put a woman, this woman, into a secret place where only he could reach her. Not hide her away, God forbid, but have the knowledge that she was committed to him, in her mind, in her soul, in everything she was, as he would be committed to her. He had, almost without knowing it, wanted, needed a woman who could give this to him and he believed he had found it in Lucy Dean. She would make him a perfect wife and, by God, he would make the perfect husband for her.

'Mr Buchanan, please, don't go any further.'

'Lucy . . . ?'

'It will only make it worse for you when ... She was deeply distressed. 'You see ... I can't ... That's why I asked you to come to tell you ... I can't ...'

'Lucy,' he said again, his voice almost a whisper.

'It's out of the question, Mr Buchanan. I'm sorry.'

He must have misheard her. The words she had spoken were there, in his head where his brain recognised them but they made no sense. She had not understood. She had mistaken his meaning. She thought he was saying something else. She ... she ... Dear sweet Christ ... She sat there in her innocent sexuality, her eyes huge and dark with shock and ... and ... there was no sense to it.

Then, suddenly, there was. Then he heard them, her words of rejection and with them the hidden capability to love, to feel, to give, shrivelled and died inside him. He felt as though he had walked ... run ... full tilt into a brick wall that he had not previously noticed. A wall that had not been there a moment ago. He could actually feel its impact as it slammed him back in his chair and from a great distance he watched her hand rise and reach out to him in alarm. From somewhere far away, it must be up on Loughrigg Fell it was so far away, he heard her speak his name in what appeared to be anguish and she stood up as though she would cross to him.

'Mr Buchanan, I'm so sorry.' She was actually weeping though he couldn't think why. He didn't know where to hide from her. She had shattered his belief in himself, broken down the fortifications that all men have inside themselves so that he had not even a bit of blanket to pull up over himself in defence. He was defenceless. She had done it and

135

yet it was not her fault. It was his own. He had taken it for granted that a love as great as his must generate it in her, but now it was finished, and so was he. God, what power a woman has over a man, he remembered thinking as his mind fell into a mercifully numbed state.

But she must never know. She must never know the full ferocity of his agony. He must have some shred of dignity to get him through the next few minutes.

He stood up, his face as grey as the ash in the hearth, then turned jerkily, making for the door, making for the escape route which would get him away from her pity, from her compassionate tears which she was shedding because she had hurt him so. Where had that bloody girl put his coat and boots? He didn't know, nor care. He'd walk home without them if needs be.

Jesus ... oh, Jesus ... he couldn't just blunder about like this. He was a man who had asked a woman to marry him. No, he hadn't even done that. In her eagerness to have it over and him out of her sight she had refused him before he had even got the words out, but he must not let her see his pain and sense of rejection.

He turned back to her and his face, the expression on it and in his eyes so blank she shrank away from him. His smile was terrible, turning his face into one of those gargoyles which adorn old buildings.

'Well, I'll get off then.'

'Mr Buchanan ...'

'I don't think there's anything further to be said except I'd be glad of my coat and boots.'

'Of course, but, Mr Buchanan ... please ...

136

won't you . . .'

His voice was harsh, icy, excessively polite. I think not, Miss Dean.'

CHAPTER SEVEN

By the end of the week it was all over Fellthwaite and Ambleside and even further—the servants' grapevine saw to that—that James Buchanan, after toying with the affections of the rich and beautiful Miss Charlotte Gibson, and then discarding them, had been refused in his turn by Miss Lucy Dean. Well, it served him right was the general opinion, for you couldn't do that sort of thing and still call yourself a gentleman, could you? That kind of behaviour would always find its just deserts, and, by God, he'd got his. Two young ladies, both as lovely as the day, one rich and one exceedingly poor and because of the way he'd gone about things he'd ended up with neither. A well-respected man was James Buchanan, who'd made a right fool of himself and no mistake and there wasn't a man nor a woman, especially a woman, who didn't have a bit of a chortle. How are the mighty fallen, they told one another, for it was believed in the area that James Buchanan was a prideful man and this would bring him down a peg or two.

'He'll be mortified, Alex. Dear God, how is he going to show his face in society after this?' Franny Buchanan was genuinely distressed, for she had a soft spot for James which had nothing to do with the fact that he was Alex's cousin, though that counted too. Franny Buchanan had a soft spot for any man whom she considered might make a good lover. She loved her husband dearly but Frances was one of those women, and there are, of course, men the same, who are not satisfied with one partner. Since her marriage eight years ago, and even before, she had taken to her bed, or more precisely, a discreet bed of her choosing away from her home, many young men who took her fancy and she would have liked James to be one of them. She had never approached him or let it be known in any degree that she was available to him, since she knew the kind of man he was. His loyalty to Alex would have prevented him from taking up any offer she might have made to him and so she had made none. Nevertheless he was dear to her and though she had considered any alliance between him and the Dean girl would be disastrous from the start, for, in her opinion, he needed a more mature wife, a more discreet wife, a more conventional wife, she was aware that his suffering now would be a burden to him. He wouldn't allow it to show, naturally. How much wiser it would have been on his part to take the well-brought-up, well-trained Miss Charlotte Gibson, he was no doubt thinking. The same age as Lucy Dean but many years older in the sense of becoming a wife, a hostess, a mother to any children they might have, than the delightful and unconventional daughter of the Reverend Edward Dean.

'It's his own bloody fault, darling, and I for one have no sympathy for him,' her husband told her, taking his knife and fork to his breakfast sausages, bacon and mushroom. 'You and I both told him what a bloody fool he would make of himself but he wouldn't listen to us. D'you remember? After that dance of yours? Great God, she's no more than a child and it showed in her behaviour.'

'She's about the same age as Charlotte Gibson and you thought her a marvellous choice. But then she's worth a lot more than the Dean girl.' Though Franny agreed with him she still couldn't help but defend not only James but the lovely girl over whom he had lost his head.

'That has nothing to do with it, Franny. Charlotte would have been much more—'

'Yes, yes, I know.' Franny sighed irritably, watching her husband stoking up for the day, which always set her off on the wrong foot. She usually had breakfast in her room but today she was up early since she meant to call on James. Not that she expected to get anything out of him except a bitter demand to be left alone, but she must make him see that he could not hide away and nurse his hurt pride, which she expected played a large part in his disappointment. With Christmas coming and all its attendant parties and dances he must force himself to be a part of them, if only for the sake of all of them and to scotch any rumours that he had a broken heart, and she meant to tell him so.

She did her best. His clerk told her he was occupied when she strode into his offices in Church Street but, with that high-handed refusal to be dictated to which the gentry have, at least in the clerk's opinion, she swept past him and into James's rooms, telling him over her shoulder that she and Mr Buchanan would take coffee.

James was sitting in his high-backed chair apparently staring at the mostly horse-drawn traffic in the busy street beyond. She could see nothing of him except his arms resting on the arms of the chair, as he had his back to her, but even when she burst in on him he did not turn round. It was a dreary day, with low sullen clouds hanging greyly across the fells and even down to the rooftops of the town, but though the room was dark and chill there were no lamps lit, nor had a match been put to the fire laid in the grate.

'Good morning, James,' she said brightly, not yet having decided what her plan of action would be. A pretence that nothing untoward had happened? Casually cheerful perhaps? Sympathetic? Brisk, ordering him to pull himself together? Whatever it was she wasn't going to do it addressing the back of his head.

She was shocked when she walked round his desk and stood in front of him. It was a week now since word had filtered slyly through the community that James Buchanan had been rejected by Lucy Dean. Got his come-uppance, as they said, and it appeared from the expression on his face they were right. He was just as immaculate as always. A sparkling white shirt front gleamed beneath his double-breasted waistcoat and his well-tailored, dark grey business jacket. His trousers were of a dark grey pinstripe and his tie was black. He was freshly shaved. His hair was neatly brushed, though she noticed it needed trimming. Indeed he looked as he always did for a day's business. It was in his face that the change in him showed. The flesh was the colour of the underside of a mushroom, not exactly grey and not exactly brown but a mixture of the two and his eyes were set in liver-tinted hollows. The eyes themselves, in the fraction of a second before he realised she was there, were a dull pewter, dead and unseeing.

140

'James?' she said hesitantly as though unsure it really was him, though of course she knew it was and at once he looked up at her, then swung his chair to face the desk, straightening his back and lifting his head aristocratically. He reached for a pen and a sheaf of papers that lay on the desk and began to put a scribble or two on the top page.

'Franny,' he answered politely. 'To what do I owe the pleasure of your company at this time of the day? I was under the impression you liked to breakfast in bed and rise at your leisure. It must be something important to bring you out so early.' Despite his mild politeness the tension in him was very evident.

'Well, we haven't seen you for a week, none of us. It's not like you to be so reclusive so I told Alex I would pop in to ... Oh, dammit, James, why pretend? It's all over town that ... that you have been ... Oh, for God's sake, James, you know what I'm talking about. I just came to see—'

'To see what, Franny? If I was still in the land of the living? That I'd not slit my throat or my wrists or whatever it is rejected suitors do? Well, as you see, I am surviving and none the worse for the experience, though I can promise you it will never happen again, so I'd be much obliged if you'd push off and let me get on with my work. And I'd also be obliged if you would keep your nose out of my affairs. It's nothing to do with you or anyone.'

It was my concern when you wanted me to 'take up' the Dean girl. I believe that is the expression you used,' she cried hotly. 'Then you were very keen for me to stick my nose in.'

'That is finished and done with, as well you know so I'd be glad if you'd take yourself off to whatever

141

it is you do with yourself all day. I am no longer interested in . . . in . . .' It seemed he was unable to bring himself to speak Lucy Dean's name. 'It's over so kindly leave me alone.' He had never been a man for smiling a great deal but in his eyes had been a glint of humour, a certain softness, a glow of warmth, despite their colour, which said that he was a man with a heart. That was gone now, leaving a coldness, a distancing of himself from others, an inaccessible resolution which told Franny Buchanan, sadly, and indeed anyone who tried to get near him, that he was not to be approached and those who attempted it did so at their peril.

Franny studied him compassionately. He was holding on to his composure with the tips of his fingers, a man come close to a cliff edge, and it was taking all his strength to prevent himself from plunging over. Like most men who have never had a woman touch their heart, when it happens it is like a tornado that picks them up and whirls them along and, if they are not careful, smashes them down again with a force that can cause serious damage. Apparently he had never considered that Lucy Dean would not want him. All his adult life he had had women flocking to his side and he had come to believe that he had only to beckon and the one he wanted would smile and say, 'Yes, please'. Not only his heart had suffered but his pride, and he was defending himself savagely.

'James, you're not going to—'

'What I'm going to do is my affair. Certainly not yours or any other member of my family so kindly remember that and if anyone asks, which I'm sure they will, tell them to mind their own bloody business. And you can leave me out of any future

142

hospitality you intend to—'

'James, please, you surely don't mean to hide yourself away from now on. There are dozens of suitable girls who—'

'Stop it, Frances.' His voice was heavy with menace and for the first time a wave of colour washed beneath his skin. 'Don't say another word. just get out and leave me alone.'

'James . . .'

'I'm warning you. If you don't leave now I swear I'll make you leave with force. Go home and get on with—'

'But it will look so obvious if you suddenly stay away from the . . . Christmas will be here soon.'

'Sweet Jesus, d'you think I give a . . . a damn about that,' he snarled. 'Now take yourself off and leave me alone.'

*   *   *

November bludgeoned its way into December on a ferocious vortex of gales that swirled up and down the valleys and fells, tearing up trees by their very roots, whipping at the bracken and gorse with such force they could not keep a grip on the earth. The streets and gardens were littered with the flotsam for days and it was not until the middle of December that calm came and with the calm, the snow.

It began with a flurry of flakes floating on the grey air about lunchtime, then, as though to match the storms at the beginning of the month, swept in violent eddies across the invisible fell slopes. The light faded rapidly so that by mid-afternoon, as the slanting snowflakes thickened, it was almost as dark as full night, the storm enclosing the Dean

143

household in a solid and ferociously moving curtain. Nobody could move out of doors, not even to fetch the milk from the farm further up the lane, and Bibby declared they'd all have to drink their tea milkless since there was no way he was going out in this. Had Mrs Hutton seen the state of the yard, for God's sake, just as though Mrs Hutton were pressing him to go out in it. Window deep, the snow was and until it stopped they'd all have to stick indoors. As soon as he could he and them hooligans would be out there to clear it, he told her, placing himself, his pipe and his out-of-date copy of the *Fellthwaite Packet* in the chair by the fire and prepared himself most pleasurably to sit it out.

The children were shut up for two whole days and Mrs Hutton pronounced that if she had to go through it again with them children racing about the house, surging into her kitchen and out again in some game of their own making, shrieking and carrying on like them dervishes she'd heard were to be seen in some heathen part of the world, she'd hand in her notice. Why in God's name the reverend couldn't control them was a mystery to her. She knew what she'd do if they were hers, she told Bibby savagely in one of the lulls in the madness, and he'd give her a hand, he told her.

Christmas came and went, very much like all the other Christmases the Dean family had known since their mother died. Money, of course, was the biggest problem, but they managed a scrawny turkey, bought on Christmas Eve in the market, one of those picked over and rejected by careful housewives or housekeepers and Mrs Hutton mackled together a plum pudding, for if there was one thing they had plenty of it was plums. Miss Lucy, bless her heart, managed a small gift for every member of the household. Not the toy train Percy had beseeched Father Christmas to bring him, nor the handsome book on motor cars Edward had seen in the bookshop window in Ambleside, but, as Mrs Hutton tearfully said to Bibby, there was always plenty of love and fun to go round in the family.

'Aye, too much bloody fun,' he sniffed, as racing feet thundered over his head in a game of what Miss Lucy called Sardines.

Lucy was in Ambleside when she saw him. She was making her way to the corner of Church Street where it ran into Market Place with the intention of picking up a copy of the *Suffragette*. There was a young woman who sold them there and, though it cost a precious penny, Lucy managed to buy one now and again. The woman, no more than a girl really, worked in the office of a local gunpowder mill and was an ardent member of the Women's Social and Political Union and she and Lucy often discussed the enormous differences between the WSPU, as it was called, and the National Union of Women's Suffrage Society. The latter was all very well as far as it went but it did not go far enough in their opinion. It did not put up its fists and fight, not like the Women's Social and Political Union which Lucy longed to join. She was a firm believer in women's suffrage and had been a fanatical follower of the WSPU ever since she had been old enough to understand its aims. She entirely agreed with the war they waged on the government and if she hadn't the children and Papa to care for she'd be window-breaking, setting fires, marching,

145

demonstrating and hunger-striking with the rest. She wanted justice for all women, she told anyone who cared to listen, including Bibby who said he'd never heard such damned nonsense in his life and she should be ashamed of herself, a lady like her, wanting to get mixed up with a lot like that. What was wrong with it? she asked him hotly. She wanted equality with men under the law, and equal wages. There were 50,000 members of the National Union of Women's Suffrage Society and only 5,000 of the WSPU, but those 5,000 were doing more to further the cause in a few short years than the former had done in nearly fifty. Christabel Pankhurst who, last year, had advocated an even more violent policy of militancy, was her idol and her opinions on the infamous Cat and Mouse Act, passed only this year, drove them all mad in the kitchen at the rectory as she swept them along on tales of mass meetings, demonstrations, and legalised torture, which was, after all, only what the force-feeding of suffragettes in His Majesty's prisons could be called and which frightened Mrs Hutton and Elsie to death. Mad, they all were, in Mrs Hutton's opinion and the lot of them should be at home where they belonged.

He was walking towards her and for a ghastly moment she felt herself spin into panic, dithering on the possibility that she might dart into a convenient shop doorway and so avoid coming face to face with him, but he had obviously seen her. The sudden tightening of his mouth, the narrowing of his eyes as though he viewed her very person with loathing, the lifting of his proud head, all spoke of his bitter renunciation of any friendship there might have been between them and if he were not a gentleman he would have cut her dead. instead he raised his hat courteously and in a voice as cold as death said, 'Good morning, Miss Dean,' then passed on.

She found she was trembling without the faintest notion why, since she had done nothing wrong. It was not immoral, or illegal to refuse a gentleman's offer of marriage though she could see why Mr Buchanan might feel rebuffed by it. Well, rebuffed seemed a mild word when one put it in the context of the splendid Mr Buchanan and she supposed that he, perhaps more than many men, would take it hard to be turned down flat. She had known that one day they would come across one another again. Fellthwaite was a small town and Ambleside not much bigger, so it followed that though they would never meet in the home of a mutual friend since they had none, and certainly not at Grange House or any other home of the Buchanans, who had dropped her like a hot coal, this was bound to happen.

'You look very pale, Miss Dean,' said the young woman who was unsuccessfully doing her best to persuade the passers-by to purchase a copy of the *Suffragette*. Her name was Letty Hodgson and her family, respectable and frowning on her involvement with the women's suffrage movement, lived in a small house on the edge of Ambleside. But though her father threatened to give her a good hiding if she continued to go against his justified parental authority, Letty was undaunted, standing wherever there might be a crowd and calling out to all who would listen that the crimes against her sisters, those who were being ill-treated in His Majesty's prisons, should not go unpunished.

She and Lucy often exchanged a word and smile, sometimes a more lengthy conversation about Lucy's longing to do more for the cause.

'Well, if you want to give me a hand selling these newspapers, Miss Dean, I wouldn't mind,' Letty had said and Lucy had pondered on whether she might.

Today, as though the encounter with Mr Buchanan had stiffened her resolve, she didn't know why since her concerns were nothing to do with him, as she put her penny in Miss Hodgson's hand and took her copy of the *Suffragette*, she asked diffidently, 'Did you mean it when you told me you would like a hand selling your papers, Miss Hodgson?'

'Indeed I did, Miss Dean, and please, won't you call me Letty.' Though Letty Hodgson was not the lady Lucy was, since her father was not a gentleman like the Reverend Edward Dean, it seemed Letty saw nothing odd about two women who were, after all, longing to fight for the same cause, calling one another by their christian names,

Lucy bobbed her head smilingly, not shy nor even awkward but somewhat amazed at the unconventionality of Miss Hodgson.

'I'm . . . Lucy.'

'Well, Lucy, if you take half of these newspapers and walk up to the Salutation Inn there's a spot there where you'll catch those going in and out of the hotel, besides those passing by. And if anyone asks you you'll know what to say.'

'About . . .about what?' Lucy gulped as she took a small armful of the newspaper.

'About the cause, naturally. From what you've said to me you know as much about it as anyone I

148

know and if you can catch them without their men some of the women are interested.' Letty gave her a cheerful grin as she thrust a copy in the face of a bowler-hatted gentleman, begging him to buy one.

'Get out of my way, young woman, or I'll fetch a policeman,' he bristled, pushing both of them to one side.

'See what I mean? But don't be put off,' Letty told her.

'I'll try . . .'

'Perhaps when we've done you'd like to come to our place in Compston Street and meet the others. It's not much, just one small office but we call it our headquarters.'

'The . . . others?'

'Oh, yes. There's more than you and me engaged in this campaign, Lucy. Well, good luck. See you in half an hour or so.'

It was her voice, calling out in desperate but well-bred tones that drew the attention of James Buchanan to her as he made his way back to his own office via Market Place. There she was, dressed in an extremely shabby but well-pressed tweed walking costume of oatmeal and brown, the neck high, the waist neat and fitted over her womanly hips, the skirt just touching the tops of her black buttoned boots. On her head was a brown velvet tam o' shanter, clinging for dear life to the tumbling masses of her hair. The sun shone and was caught in its burnished depths and put a liquid gold in the deep brown of her eyes. In her arms was a bundle of newspapers with which she struggled as she was jostled here and there. She was attracting a great deal of attention since not only was she very beautiful, which drew the men to

149

her like flies to a honeypot, but it was well known that she was a rector's daughter and he could hear the remarks, some of them bordering on the offensive, about the appalling state of affairs when a lady should act as she was. They could perhaps understand the poorer class of girl, who after all knew no better, getting involved in such carryings-on but a lady and the daughter of the rector into the bargain! That seemed to make it worse.

Before James could even consider what he was doing, what it meant, or even how it looked, he had marched across the crowded road, narrowly missing the wheels of an enormous dray, pushed his way through the crowd of delighted men and taken her arm in a grip which, for a moment, terrified her. She was so hemmed about and so alarmed by her own inability to speak with a loud voice, let alone beg these people to buy a copy of her newspaper, she did not see him coming, and as the hand which had her arm in a bruising fist whisked her almost off her feet and beyond the crowd, she dropped her papers.

'Stop . . .' she shouted to whoever it was that held her. 'My newspapers.'

'Be damned to your newspapers, Miss Dean, and I'd be obliged if you'd pick up your feet and walk properly instead of dragging along like a bad-mannered child.'

She recognised him at last and was so astonished she allowed him to carry her several more yards before she began to struggle to detach his hand.

'Let go of me,' she hissed furiously, conscious of the stares of the people going by. 'What on earth do you think you're doing? You have no right . . .'

'Only the right of a gentleman assisting a lady to

recover her senses and her dignity, Great God, I've never seen—'

'Do you know, Mr Buchanan, I don't give a damn about your sensibilities and I'd be very glad if you would allow me to take care of mine. I . . . I am to become a member of the Women's Social and Political Union and as a member I am helping to sell our newspaper.' She said it with enormous pride. Her eyes were huge and burning with fervour and her cheeks were banners of bright carnation excitement. She had never felt so alive, her manner said, and though she had been overwhelmed outside the hotel she wouldn't be again. Oh, no! Now she knew what to expect. She'd speak up and tell them all, men and women, what their aims were, those of them who were members of the WSPU, since she meant to join as soon as possible. This very day, in fact. She didn't know what she might be found to do to help the cause, here so far from London or any of the major cities, but she and Letty and the others—the others, oh, Lord—could spread the word if nothing else. It was almost like being one of the disciples that Papa preached about from the pulpit, going among the people and telling them about the wonders that women's suffrage would bring.

That is if Mr Buchanan would leave go of her arm.

At last he did so, his face inscrutable, his eyes as dark and ominous as Lake Windermere on a stormy day. They were without expression, for he did not wish to reveal the awful truth which was that he had just discovered he still loved Lucy Dean with all his heart and soul and man's body and always would. Distance and time had not blunted it and he felt the despair racing through him, for what was he to do with the rest of his life without her in it. He had spent the last weeks becoming more and more reclusive, despite his family's pleas to come to this or that affair where he was certain there would be a dozen pretty young women paraded for his inspection. He could not face the idea of taking up Charlotte Gibson again, even if she would have him, which seemed doubtful for there was a rumour to the effect that his cousin Paul, young Doctor Paul who would need all the money he could lay his hands on to get himself a decent practice, was showing an interest in her. And she in him, it appeared.

'Well . . .' Lucy said, somewhat abashed by the strange look on Mr Buchanan's face, wondering why, now that he had totally disrupted her first attempt to help the cause, he just stood there with what she could only call an empty look on his face. She found she couldn't simply walk off, which was strange, but just as suddenly that familiar look of brooding bad temper smouldered in him, filling the emptiness and his words were biting.

'You'd best be off home, Miss Dean. Your father would not care to see you in such a predicament.'

'I am not in a predicament, Mr Buchanan.'

'Yes, you are, but that is your affair, as you said, and I'm sorry if I discommoded you in any way. I won't do it again. Good-day, Miss Dean.' Tipping his hat, he turned and walked away.

Letty was not there when she returned to the corner of Church Street, to Lucy's surprise. She waited for about fifteen minutes but Letty did not return. She wondered what to do. Should she try and find the WSPU headquarters in Compston

152

Street, which she knew comprised a long row of small terraced houses in one of which, presumably, the WSPU went about its business, or should she go home and come again tomorrow? She knew that Buffy, at least, would wonder where she had got to and she really must go and collect her bicycle which she had left propped against the side of a shop in Lake Road.

She was just about to walk away, deciding that perhaps it would be as well if she made her way home, when a male voice hailed her.

'Are thee t'lass what were with the one sellin' them there papers?' it asked.

She whirled about to confront a large gentleman whom she recognised. He had a bright red and cheerful face and had evidently just crossed the road from his fish shop on the corner, still wearing his soiled striped apron and a straw boater.

'Yes.' Her voice was hesitant since she wanted no more confrontations with angry members of the opposite sex.

'She's bin arrested.'

'Arrested!' Lucy was appalled, for what crime could decent Letty Hodgson commit that would put her in the hands of the law?

'Aye. Disturbin' the peace.'

'Disturbing the peace,' she repeated foolishly.

'That's right. Some chap didn't like 'er pushin' that there suffragette paper in 'is face so 'e fetched a constable.'

*   *   *

'I just don't know what to do, Buffy,' she agonised. 'Should I go to the police station and plead for

153

Letty? Ask them to let her go since she was doing no harm at all. I was there. I can vouch for her. I just can't bear to think of her in a . . . a cell. I wonder what the sentence is for? . . . What did the fish man say . . . breaking the peace? No, *disturbing* the peace. Heavens, it could have been me, for there was no peace on that corner by the Salutation Arms. Oh, Lord, poor Letty,' almost wringing her hands, 'what can I do to help her?'

'Nothing, and if you ask me you'd be better off leaving the whole thing alone. Your papa would have a fit if he knew what you had been doing. It's all very well believing in a cause like the WSPU does but to get caught up in such unlady-like behaviour is appalling.'

'Oh, Buffy, do shut up.'

'No, I will not. Your mama—'

Lucy's face became cold. 'Please be good enough to leave Mama out of this. I'm amazed at you, really I am. And you know my views on women's suffrage. In fact I believed you thought as I do.'

'I do, but not when it brings your name into disrepute. It will upset your papa, you know it will.'

Lucy's face crumpled. 'Oh, God, Buffy, I know it will. What on earth am I to do? I can't just leave poor Letty to rot in gaol.'

'She'll hardly do that, Lucy. Her family will be informed.'

'Dear God, that makes it worse,' Lucy wailed. 'Her father is set against it and said he'd give her a hiding if she continued.'

'I doubt that, Lucy. Now let's sleep on it. In the morning you can confess to your papa and if I know him he'll go down to the gaol with you and speak for her.'

CHAPTER EIGHT

There was no need after all for Lucy and Edward Dean to go down to the police station in Ambleside the following day, for a note was delivered to Lucy saying that Letty had been released the night before into her father's care. She was to appear at the Magistrates Court and would probably, as this was her first offence, be released with a caution.

'There you are, Lucy. You had no need to worry after all,' Buffy told her in great relief and was surprised and offended when Lucy turned on her like a tiger.

'No need to worry! Oh, I admit the immediate threat has been removed but I can't just ignore Miss Hodgson's predicament and get on with life as though she had never existed. I feel ... I feel as though she befriended me, trusted me. She went out of her way to let me know she had been released which was kind of her and so I feel I owe her ... well, something. Besides, I still have those copies of the *Suffragette* to sell,' which she had retrieved. She gnawed at her thumb, which she was wont to do when she had some problem that might take a bit of solving and her delicate eyebrows dipped in a frown.

'Lucy!' Buffy was outraged.

It was a bitterly cold January day, bright with a hard frost. The trees and shrubs beyond the frost-glazed window were outlined in silvery tracery against a pale pink sky as the sun struggled to get through the fine layer of mist. A great flock of rooks and starlings swooped across the lawn then up over the roof of the house before coming to rest in their hundreds on the white branches of the denuded trees. Robins, their red waistcoats brilliant against the dazzling rime, pecked at the grass but there was little of sustenance at this time of the year.

And yet in a sheltered corner of the garden, struggling for life between the roots of the great oak tree, were pale primrose, polyanthus, winter aconite and snowdrops. The usual weak fire flowered in the hearth of the Deans' small parlour and both girls were wrapped about with a shawl apiece, their hands encased in the woollen mittens Mrs Hutton turned out by the dozens of pairs. Each of the children wore them in the house and so did the Reverend Dean, for there was no worse fate than fingers ablaze with chilblains.

'Lucy! You're not trying to tell me that you mean to go and stand at that place again,' for Lucy had told her all about the altercation outside the Salutation.

'And why not, pray? If Miss Hodgson—Letty—is brave enough to do it then, as a member of the WSPU, which I mean to be, surely I can do the same. But I feel that I should, that I must go and visit her in her home first.' She turned a fierce glare on her friend and lifted her head defiantly as though challenging Buffy to argue with her. Buffy ignored the gesture.

'Oh, Lucy, you might make it worse for her with her father, not to mention your own. Could you not ... well, send Edward with the newspapers and a message. I feel you might get her into even worse trouble than she already is.'

'Not if I explain to Mr Hodgson that it was my

156

fault.'

'How on earth do you work that out, for heaven's sake?'

'Well, I was there when the gentleman became cross. Perhaps seeing two of us made him . . .'

'What absolute nonsense.' Buffy drew herself up to her full height, which came to about Lucy's shoulder blade, getting ready for a further battle, but Lucy was already striding towards the door.

'It's no good, Buffy. My mind's made up and no one can change it for me.'

Only your papa, Buffy thought sadly, but the Reverend Dean had kept to his bed this morning, saying he thought he was in for a cold and would stay there, at least for today, with two hot-water bottles and a supply of honey, glycerine and lemon mixed in hot water, taken up to him hourly by the faithful Elsie.

'I'm just going out for a half an hour, dearest,' Lucy told the watering eyes and red nose which peeped over the top of the piled-up blankets in her papa's bedroom. 'Oh dear, that's an awful cough, Papa,' as the Reverend Dean hacked harshly into the cold air. There was a fire burning in the grate— Lucy had insisted on it despite Papa's weak protestations that he was as warm as toast and she was to stop fussing—but it did little to warm the bare, chilly room. At least it gave the appearance of a bit of cheer, doing its best to flicker bravely.

'I really think we should send for the doctor, Papa,' she told him, anxiously putting a hand on his feverish brow, but he twitched away, saying in his mild way that he was perfectly all right and would she stop worrying and go and do her errand.

'Well, if you say so, but if you're no better when I

get back I shall send Edward to bring Doctor Hayward.'

'It was a bit tricky, Lucy found, cycling between the deep and frozen ruts of the lane down to Lake Road. Even there it was hazardous, for a thick layer of hoar frost gave no sign of melting in the weak sunshine, turning the surface into an ice rink. She skidded and slithered her way through Fellthwaite and on to Ambleside, her breath wisping away like smoke in the thin air. Her tam o' shanter wobbled precariously on the top of her roughly swept-up hair and her face, red as a poppy, was buried in her father's warm winter scarf. She called out to several tradesmen who were guiding their horse-drawn carts carefully along the treacherous road, and they all agreed with her that it was not a good day to be out.

By the simple expedient of knocking on several doors—and having one shut in her face when she told the woman who opened it who she wanted—she found the house in Compston Street in which the WSPU had their headquarters. Well, you had to laugh, said the bright-eyed girl who let her into the tiny room, the very idea of this, waving a thin airy arm above the table, two chairs and a chest of drawers, being the Ambleside division of the Women's Social and Political Union, though she thought the posters on the wall made it more exciting, didn't Miss Dean agree. One said, 'What women may be and yet not have the vote,' with five positions listed: mayor, nurse, mother, doctor or teacher and factory hand. Underneath was printed: 'What a man may have been and yet not lose the vote,' detailing convict, lunatic, proprietor of white slaves, unfit for service and drunkard. Another depicted a woman in knight's armour with the word justice on her breast. She was bearing a sword and a banner. There was a third, all of them done in the distinctive white, green and purple of the suffragist movement, of a woman holding aloft a newspaper on which the words 'Votes For Women' were printed. Lucy felt the tears come to the back of her throat, for it was all so splendid and brave, this one small room, or so it seemed, and the women who worked in it for the cause and if they would have her she would be proud to join them.

'Edwina Lawson's my name,' the slender young lady said, sticking out her hand, 'but everyone calls me Eddy. My father has the chemist shop on the corner.'

Lucy, slightly breathless, first from her ride, then from her exertions along Compston Street followed by Eddy's enthusiasm, grasped it ardently, for she had never met such . . . well, smiling to herself, she supposed Mrs Buchanan's lot would call them 'spiffing girls'! First Letty and now Eddy.

She explained why she had come and was relieved to hear that Letty had been released with a caution. Yes, her father had been absolutely livid— oh, do sit down—but that wouldn't stop Letty. She was used to arguments with her father, who threatened to throw her out if she didn't stop all this damnfool nonsense but so far he had not done so. Her own father, who was more liberal-minded, believing that women such as his sensible daughter, who had more intelligence than many men he knew, should be allowed the vote. Not until they were twenty-five, though, Eddy said cheerfully, but she supposed it was a start and better than nothing. Anyway, as long as it did not interfere with her duties in the shop he allowed her to continue her campaigning. Women were proving their strength in fund-raising, propaganda, organisation and publicity stunts, though as yet he had not been tested on that one, Eddy laughed. She had a few ideas up her sleeve if Miss Dean was interested. There were several occasions when they might make their presence felt, she told the open-mouthed visitor. The Rushbearing ceremony in May, for one, and the May Queen procession for another. Then there was the Grasmere Sports when she and several of the others meant to demonstrate in some way not yet decided that the Votes for Women movement was not confined to the big towns and cities.

'Letty means to have a dinner-hour meeting today at the gates of the factory where she works if you'd care to go along and listen to her, and only today we received a range of purple, white and green 'Votes for Women' merchandise which we shall sell with our newspapers. You know, of course, that green, white and purple are our colours, don't you? There are lovely sashes. Would you like one? That is if you're to join us. You could wear it when you take up your stand outside the Salutation,' eyeing the sheaf of newspapers still clutched in Lucy's hands, 'that is if you mean to . . .'

'Oh, yes . . . oh, yes, please, I do. I mean I really want to join. At least . . .' She bit her lip, for it seemed that the very first time—or did yesterday count as that?—she was to be asked to help she had to refuse. 'You see . . . my father's ill. My mama died when I was a girl and there is no one but me to look after the household. I have two brothers and two sisters younger than myself so you see . . .'

160

'Of course, Miss Dean.'

'Lucy.'

'Of course, Lucy, you go home and look after your father. It was good of you to come and enquire after Letty. I'll tell her you called and then, when you can, come again. There's always someone on duty and I can promise you we'll find some work for you to do.'

It was to be several weeks before Lucy could get down to Compston Street again. Her papa had a dangerous and weakening bout of pneumonia which kept him in his bed for over a fortnight, and then in his room, huddled over the poor fire which was all Lucy could afford, for another week. The prolonged coughing, so agonising it shook his thin frame like a sapling in a high wind, had strained his heart and the doctor, filled with compassion for the poor young lady who was already overworked and overwrought with the financial needs of her family, his bill among them, told her he would need a long rest with good nursing for several more weeks. He must on no account think of taking up his duties, not until the warmer weather came, and in this Lakeland climate of treacherous changeability, that could be any time up to May. Thank God for Buffy, was a constant cry on Lucy's lips, for she knew she would not have got through without her. Margaret, brave and uncomplaining, took turns to sit with Papa during the day but Lucy and Buffy shared the night vigils and they both smiled, when it seemed the Reverend Dean was on the mend, to see what scarecrows they had become.

'Oh, for a bit of sunshine on my face, Buffy, and a good long walk on the tops. I feel like some desiccated old crone who has not breathed fresh air

161

for weeks.'

'It's been weeks, Lucy, and if you want to go, you go. Your papa is sufficiently well to leave to Margaret and me. But promise me you will go up to the tops and not to that office in Ambleside. You know how I feel about that.'

'I promise.'

And so it was in the second week of February when the air was still crisp with frost and the ground hard and solidly frozen that, donning sturdy boots and tying herself about in a warm shawl, Lucy Dean set off to climb to the top of Loughrigg Fell. Loughrigg was one of the lesser heights of Lakeland but enough for Lucy to tackle on this first day out after being confined to her father's sickroom for so long. She decided on the ascent from Ambleside, riding there on her bicycle, leaving the children behind with the promise that they would all go the next week, or at least as soon as they were able to leave Papa alone with Buffy.

It was a climb of just over 1,000 feet and two and a half miles of walking. It was a glorious winter morning with the sun rising through a pink mist, delicately tinting the sky and the tops of the fells, which were still shrouded with a fine layer of snow. The trees were stark and black against the ethereal loveliness of the gradually awakening day and Lucy drew in deep breaths of it, filling her lungs which had for so long been thick with the smells of the sickroom. The sun turned to gold as it rose above High Street in the east, lighting the tip of Scafell Pike, the summit of England, and turning the waters of Windermere far below to a silent sheet of exquisite gold.

Her boots crackled against the frosted bracken

and stiff grasses, the sound snapping in the air like a dry twig broken across a man's knee. She paused just below the peak and turned to look back, her heart stirring painfully with the perfection of it, of this land she had come to love so well. The blue of the sky hurt her eyes and the glittering diamond symmetry of the frosted trees dazzled her heart and it was perhaps this which blinded her for a moment to the presence of the man who rose from a rock above her. He stood, etched against the sky, tall and dark and silent, forbidding as an eagle ascending from its nest and for a moment her heart jittered in her breast until she recognised him.

'Mr Buchanan, I did not see you there,' she said quietly, for it seemed a sacrilege to speak out loud in such a heavenly place.

'Miss Dean, I beg your pardon. I did not mean to alarm you. I'm just about to leave.' His face was set in lines which were quite unreadable and she wondered if anyone had ever got to know this man who could hide his emotions so cleverly. His expression said he was neither pleased nor displeased to see her. It was a matter of sublime indifference to him whether she stayed or went.

'Please, Mr Buchanan, don't let me drive you away.'

'Miss Dean, believe me, you could not do that if I wished to remain. Good morning.' He bowed coldly. He was not wearing a hat and the rays of the sun put streaks of chestnut in his dark hair and lit his velvet grey eyes to ice crystals. Somehow he managed to avoid looking at her and she wondered why he felt the need to do so since his every gesture, his aloof bearing, conveyed to her that he found her presence distasteful.

'Mr Buchanan, I . . . I have wondered . . .'

'Yes, Miss Dean?' Still turned away from her, he stopped, studying with what seemed to be great interest the fox head on the top of his walking stick.

'I regret . . . that is to say . . .'

'Please, Miss Dean, I beg of you, don't tell me of your regrets, for I don't wish to know of them.' His voice was harsh. 'What is in your mind, if it concerns . . . past indiscretions, is of no interest to me. I don't look back, only forward and I advise you to do the same.'

Without once turning to look at her he strode off, taking the path towards the Grasmere Cairn, his tall figure upright despite the slope of the land and she did not see the tremble which shook his frame nor the spasm of pain which twisted his face into what might have been a smile but was not.

She sighed then sank down on to the rock he had recently vacated, wondering why she felt so sorry that she and Mr Buchanan could not have parted friends, but then she supposed a gentleman's pride would not allow him, after being rejected as a husband, to be no more than a friend. She watched him until he disappeared beyond the bracken which ended at Loughrigg Terrace, taking the path which led him through the wood and on to Grasmere.

She did not know that he had her in his mind's eye all the way down through Deerbolts Wood. He could still see that shining look of innocence which was particularly hers, that look of bewilderment in her great brown eyes that she should have earned his dislike to such an extent that he could not bear to talk to her; how could she know that the exact opposite was true? And yet at the same time he

164

cursed the day he had ever set eyes on her, that never-to-be-forgotten day when he had been, for the last time, a man without care or heartache. He loved and wanted her still and in his despair at knowing he would never have her, when Alex and Franny Buchanan called on him that evening to make sure he had received his invitation to the best-publicised event of the Ambleside calendar and, more importantly, that he was to accept it, he received them with a mood little short of boorishness.

Mr and Mrs Arthur Gibson had been delighted to announce on 14 February—such a romantic day—that their daughter, their beautiful daughter Charlotte, was to marry Doctor Paul Buchanan. An engagement party was to be held at their home, Ravenscourt, and the élite of Ambleside society was invited, including Mr James Buchanan, whom Charlotte was determined must be made to see what he had so casually thrown away. She had not loved James Buchanan just as she did not love his cousin Paul but James had been the greater catch and she had the distinct feeling that her friends and her mother's friends believed that she was 'making do' with his cousin. She was resolute that they must be made to see that they were wrong. A great party in the enormous, glittering richness of her father's home would be the ideal way in which to demonstrate to them that this was a 'love match', that she had had a narrow escape when she gave up James in favour of Paul, and though she was well aware that she was being married for her money, she did not care. Paul Buchanan was of good family, a clever young man on his way up, and with the help of her father's money and her own vital talents as a hostess, she meant him to get to the very top. She'd show James Buchanan and that strumpet who'd had the effrontery to turn him down, though why that should matter she couldn't quite understand, even in her own devious mind.

'Well, old fellow,' Alex began, as Franny had instructed him, in a casual, not a word about the Dean girl sort of way, 'and how are you this cold evening? Well, I hope. Didn't see you at the fox-hunt yesterday. We missed you, didn't we, Franny?'

'Indeed we did, James. It was a damned good day. The hounds found the scent just after daybreak. I bet the beggar, with the hounds in pursuit, covered sixty miles. A rare cunning beast, that one.'

Fox-hunting in the fells is as much a necessity as a sport and bears little similarity to the colourful ritual which takes place further south. Few huntsmen wear the pink coat and black hat of the squirearchy, and to follow the hounds one requires, not a glossy, well-groomed hunter but a stout pair of boots and a stick, for fell packs are followed on foot. Most of the huntsmen are farmers but many of the local gentry looked on it as a day's sport and the Buchanans had always taken part for as long ago as any of them could remember.

James was sprawled in a deep armchair, a glass of brandy in one hand and a cigar in the other. His chin was sunk on his chest and he stared joylessly into the leaping fire with the same unconcern for the fox's doings as the two labradors at his feet. Alex and Franny exchanged a quick glance which asked what should be said next.

'Yes,' Alex went bumbling on, just as though James had answered him. 'Mind you, Franny and I didn't manage that, did we, old girl? Kept up until lunchtime then had a bite to eat in the—'

'It's no use, Alex, I'm not going and that's that. It's beyond me why you can't bloody well leave me alone. I'm bothering no one—'

'I don't know what you mean, James,' Franny cut in.

'Yes, you do. You're here to try and persuade me to go to this bloody do at the Gibsons for her and Paul. Well, if he wants to take her on, good luck to him, though I must admit I pity the poor sod.'

'James, it's family. You must go. Paul is your cousin and this is an important moment in his life. The Gibsons are influential.'

'Franny.' James's voice was very weary. I don't give a—for the Gibsons,' using a word of extreme obscenity.

'Here, steady on, laddie,' Alex protested. 'That's no way to speak in front of a lady.'

'No, I apologise, Franny. It was extremely bad manners and I'm sorry, but you see I am so bone weary of being pestered to "snap out of it", to "stop being so bloody sorry for myself", and similar expressions meant to bring me to my senses. But the thing is, I have not lost my senses. I just seem to have lost the ability to caper about and make a fool of myself as the rest of you do.'

'Now look here, James, that's enough. We didn't come here to be insulted.'

'Why did you come here, Alex? I can't for the life of me work out why it is so important to you that I give up this ... this rather pleasant quiet time I am enjoying and attend all the madcap things you get up to. I find I like staying at home.'

'Rubbish!' Franny's voice was curt. 'You were

167

always glad to come for dinner and to attend the madcap affairs, as you so quaintly put it, before that damn Dean girl got her hooks into you.'

'That's enough, Franny.' James sat up so abruptly he spilled his drink down his shirt front. His voice was heavy with menace and his eyes glittered in the firelight. Both dogs lifted their heads and turned their devoted eyes on him, alarmed at the tone of his voice, but he touched each one with his foot and they lay down again, shuffling about until they found the most comfortable position on the rich Indian rug.

'It's true, James, so don't deny it. She seems to have warped something in you and—'

'That's enough, I say.' James's voice thundered through the warm calm of his study and both dogs leaped to their feet. If you've had your say you had better leave. I shall send my congratulations to Paul and Miss Gibson but that's all and I'd be much obliged if you, and indeed the rest of the family, would leave me alone.'

'James, please, we worry about you . . .' Franny began but he cut her short with a peremptory gesture.

His voice had softened. 'Don't, Franny. My heart is not broken or anything as foolish as that. It's just that . . . well, I'm getting older and . . .'

'Fiddlesticks, James. You're in your prime and there are several young ladies who would be glad to prove it to you.'

'Franny, stop it. If I need a young lady then I'll find my own. Now the pair of you push off.'

*　　　*　　　*

Lucy didn't know what it was that woke her. There was no particular sound to disturb the absolute quiet. Thimble wasn't barking or the hens cackling, which they were in the habit of doing when disturbed, perhaps by a fox. In fact it was so still she could hear the fast beat of her own alarmed heart. The bed creaked as she shifted in it, then, reaching for her shawl she pulled it closely about her before getting out of bed. The floor was icy to her bare feet and in the starlight that shone through the uncurtained window she could see her own breath steam about her face. With shivering hands she struck a match and put it to the candle, then looked at the dainty fob watch which had belonged to her mother and her mother's mother before her. It was three thirty.

Well, something had wakened her and she'd not be able to get back to sleep until she found out what it was. She wouldn't be a bit surprised to find that it was Thimble after all, for he had a naughty habit of leaving his basket in the kitchen and scampering up the uncarpeted stairs to snuggle in with Percy and Edward, who shared a room and a bed in this cold weather, at the back of the house.

She was right. He raised his head apologetically, his eyes bright in the candlelight, his tail moving hopefully as he lay in blissful ecstasy between the two sleeping boys. She touched the dark hair of each of her brothers, then patted the dog, smiling her permission for him to stay.

In the large, icily cold bedroom at the front of the house the girls were twined about one another beneath a mound of bedclothes, their dark heads close together. Emily muttered in her sleep, then, as the candlelight fell on her, smiled and said

169

Thimble's name quite distinctly.

Her father's door was closed. She put her ear to it and was relieved to hear the quiet on the other side of it. That dreadful wheezing breath which had plagued him for weeks now had slowly eased and with the help of the honey, glycerine and lemon approved by the doctor, who liked the old remedies, he had been sleeping well.

A light sound at her back made her turn quickly and the candle almost blew out. It was Buffy, bundled as Lucy was in a shawl, but on her feet she had thoughtfully put a pair of the woollen socks Mrs Hutton turned out with the mittens.

'Is ... everything all right?' she whispered, placing a loving hand on Lucy's arm, a comforting hand as though already her instincts told her it would be needed.

'Oh, yes. All fast asleep. I don't know what woke me.'

'No, nor me. Is your papa ... Is he ...?'

'I haven't looked but I think I might just have a peep at him.'

'I'll come with you.'

'No. You wait here.'

But it was Buffy who held her up and Buffy who pleaded with her to be quiet, for her cries would frighten the children, she said, as they gazed into the open but dead eyes of the Reverend Edward Dean.

CHAPTER NINE

The funeral was not well attended. It was March now and a late but icy 'bottom wind' blew straight down between the fells from Siberia, or so the old folk told one another, and it was enough to keep them indoors. Most of the Reverend Dean's parishioners were elderly or even downright ancient. Besides which, he had not been what might be described as popular since he was, though a kindly man, somewhat inclined to be reserved. It was as though his mind were elsewhere and his sermons were vague and not to the taste of those who liked a bit more substance to their weekly admonishment to heed the word of the Lord. To make matters worse he came from down south, an 'offcomer' who had been given the living through his connections with the squire's family at Dalebarrow Hall and though a nice enough chap, not really one of them.

They made a pathetic little group, the reverend gentleman's family. All in black right down to the youngest, a boy of five or six, a passing farm labourer, whose old mam attended the Reverend Dean's church when she was able, reported to her when he returned for his dinner. The girl, his eldest, God only knew how she'd managed it, for it was well known the family was penniless and would be in worse plight when the new rector came, for where were they to go? The servants, one old man, one old woman and a lass of about twelve, stood at the graveside with them while the chap who, it was rumoured, was to take over the living, committed the body to the earth. None of them was crying, he told his mam when she asked, which was strange, for you'd have thought that the girls at least would have shed a tear, but they just stood close to one another, holding one another up, it seemed to him, white-faced and silent and when it was over and the parson had hurried off to something more important, they walked in a close-knit group up the path and through the trees to the rectory.

He was not to know, that inquisitive labourer, that Lucy Dean had managed decent mourning for her family by the simple expedient of throwing every outer garment they possessed into Mrs Hutton's enormous boiler, the one in which she did the weekly wash but to which black dye had been added. For a couple of days, while the dyed garments dried and were pressed ready for wearing, they stayed indoors, not even venturing into the garden, for Lucy was determined that every respect must be shown to her beloved father. The boys had black caps, but Mrs Hutton delved into her wardrobe and found several old black bonnets which, being a frugal woman, she had kept, 'Just in case' and on the day of the funeral, from the top of their heads to the tips of their black boots, they presented a picture of a family in deep and grievous sorrow, which was what they were.

It was a week later when they were visited by the squire's agent who, though he was filled with compassion for the frail and lovely girl who greeted him courteously and even asked him to take tea, was forced to inform her that the new rector would be taking up his post on the first day of next month and would Miss Dean, therefore, make arrangements to be out of the rectory by then.

'Of course, sir.' By her calm manner and perfectly controlled voice one would have thought she had several places to where she and her family might go, and perhaps she had, for surely there were relatives? But he didn't think so. Not from the gossip he'd heard about the estate. Both her parents had been only children, so it was said, and relatives were in short supply.

She was very quiet that evening as she sat with Buffy in the small parlour. Of course, they had all been quiet since her papa's death, and in the seclusion of their home they had wept together for him, despite the brave front they put on for the rest of the world to see. As Mrs Hutton said to Bibby, she'd never seen such fortitude, the poor lambs, and what was to become of them, that's what she'd like to know. Indeed, burying her face in her apron, to Elsie's great consternation, what was to become of them all, for who would want to employ an old woman in her sixties and a man even older. Their Elsie'd soon be fitted up, being young and, thanks to Mrs Hutton, well trained but where would her and Bibby go, tell her that if he could.

' 'Ere, 'oo are thi' callin' an old man,' Bibby cried in high dudgeon. 'Aah can still do a bloody good day's work wit' rest of 'em,' but he knew she was right. What he did in the garden of the rectory he did at his own pace, and when he felt like it. He was helped by his grandson and by them hooligans, for despite the way he went on about them they were good-hearted kids. True, he hadn't had a week's wages since he could remember but he lived snug across the yard in the rooms above the old stable and ate as well as royalty on the vegetables he himself grew. Mrs Hutton was a dab hand with a

173

spoon, a pan, a few herbs and that old oven in the kitchen and could make a grand meal out of a bit of mutton, making it taste like the tenderest cut of lamb. Aye, comfy he was and settled and where, like the rest of the family, was he going to fetch up now?

Lucy said the same thing to Buffy, though in different words.

'We have to be out of here by the month end, Buffy. Squire Forsythe's agent was very sorry but he had been sent to . . . let us know, he said. The new incumbent and his family, quite extensive, I believe, want to be in by the first of the month so it means we shall have to find somewhere else.'

'Yes, I see.' Buffy's heart quailed and she could feel it thump quite frantically against the black wool bodice of her mourning dress, but she held her head high and her back straight against the chair. She did her best, like Lucy had that afternoon when the agent called, to give the impression that there was nothing to be troubled about, that they would soon find a place of security, but within her desperation surged, as it did in Lucy, for where were four adults and five children—for what else could you call Elsie who Lucy would never abandon—to find a home and the wherewithal to support it and those who would live beneath its roof.

'I must find a home for the children, Buffy, you know that,' as though Buffy was giving her an argument. 'And then there's Mrs Hutton and Bibby and Elsie. They are my responsibility now, you understand that?'

'Yes. If there's anything . . . anything I can do. I'm a hard worker, you know that.'

174

'It was as though Buffy had not spoken. I have a week.' Her calmness was frightening and Buffy knew she was still in the black space into which her papa's death had thrown her and yet her mind was working clearly. It was up to her to find them a place of safety, she knew that, and Buffy's heart contracted in love and pity.

There was only one answer, of course, and they both knew it.

*   *   *

'There's a young lady to see you, sir.' Dimity Blamire was so excited she almost forgot to bob the customary curtsey which her position as housemaid to Mr Buchanan demanded. Not that he'd notice, not if she appeared without her cap and dressed in a feather boa, she thought, and when he peered round his newspaper at her she could see he hadn't really heard her. Not properly.

It was Dixon's day off and so, by the greatest good fortune, it had been Dimity who had answered the door. She was dressed in her afternoon uniform of a black cotton dress over which she wore a crisp white muslin bibbed apron which tied at the back of her waist in a huge bow, the ends of which fell to the hem of her floor-length skirt. On her head a pretty white muslin cap trembled and though Mrs Burns, the housekeeper, was very strict about such things, a tendril of dark and glossy hair escaped it and drifted on to her neck.

'What?' he muttered irritably. It was a Sunday and almost into April and though it was a fine day he had not thought it worth the trouble to dress

175

himself in his walking boots and outfit and get out on to the tops. He could hear through the half-opened window the sound of a chiff-chaff which had nested near the house and smell the wild daffodils and the great mass of golden catkin which hung about the willow tree near the pond, and something stirred in him. Something which had been dormant all winter but which somehow, more and more these days, he found he was inclined to let slip away since he had come to the conclusion it wasn't really worth the bother. He must make an effort, he kept telling himself, for he was fast becoming a recluse. Had it not been for his legal practice he believed he might not go out of the house at all. At first he had walked the fells for weeks, alone but for the company of his dogs, high above the 'intakes', roaming the heights with the hardy sheep, glad to be away from those who pitied him, and, he was inclined to think, laughed at him for his foolhardiness. It had been his only pleasure until, one day, he had met Lucy Dean on the peak of Loughrigg Fell and even that was now denied him.

Dimity waited, longing to nudge him into some sort of response. She was almost hopping from foot to foot in her eagerness to see the visitor in and get back to the kitchen to tell them who it was who now sat in the straight-backed chair in the hall and who had asked to see their master, but until he came from his reverie and told her what she was to do about it she could only hang here in a dither and wait. She knew who it was, of course.

'A young lady, sir.'

'What young lady, for God's sake? And what in hell's name does she want? Can't Mrs Burns see to her?'

'Oh, not that sort of young lady, sir. A real lady. To see you.' Dimity beamed her encouragement.

'What does she want?' James Buchanan's heart did a little flip as though some instinct told him who it was who was waiting to see him, but at the same time, encased in the ice put there months ago by Lucy Dean, it told him not to be such a bloody fool. Nevertheless he raised himself from the lounging position he had been in after his Sunday lunch, put the newspaper to one side and glared at the housemaid.

She was not daunted. 'I'm sure I couldn't say, sir.'

'Well go and ask her.'

Dimity was shocked. 'Oh, I couldn't do that, sir. She's a lady,' and as such not to be approached with such a rude question by a mere housemaid.

James steeled himself to ask the question, already guessing the answer, calling himself all kinds of fool, for his mouth had gone dry and his heart was banging quite furiously in his chest. He hated her for having this effect on him and his voice was almost a snarl.

'Who is she?'

'Miss Lucy Dean, sir.'

His heart did a somersault. 'Tell her I'm not at home.'

'But, sir, she particularly noticed the motor car on the drive and when she asked I said you—'

'You stupid girl. Well, you can just go and tell her to be on her way.'

'Oh, sir . . .' Dimity looked ready to weep now.

James Buchanan stood up and strode to the window with the savagery of an enraged tiger, looking out over the soft spring loveliness of his garden and in his heart he despised himself for his cowardice and for his treatment of the maidservant. He was afraid. He was afraid of Lucy Dean after all these months. He was afraid of the hurt and the loss of his pride, the loss of his dignity and the belief, which he knew was not so, that wherever he went people were pointing at him and calling him a fool. He couldn't bear to suffer it again. Twice he had seen her: in Ambleside on the day she had been selling newspapers for that damned suffragist movement, and then on the top of Loughrigg Fell when she had tried to engage him in conversation. He had nearly given in to her then. Her flower-like beauty combined with that enchanting grace, not just of figure but of spirit, had almost unmanned him. She had looked at him with honesty and candour, with the unexpected earthly common sense which her life with her father had given her and using every atom of strength he had he had turned his back on her, walked away from her and now she was here in his hall asking to see him and again he was afraid.

'Show her in,' he told the maid curtly.

James Buchanan's home, Howethwaite, stood with its back to the wind-ruffled waters of the River Brathay. It was a big house built 300 years ago, the original farmhouse scarce more than a huge kitchen with a scullery off and a bedroom or two above, but over the generations bits and pieces had been added here and there until it could now be called a manor house, unrecognisable as the building it had once been. There were still the original pantries, a dairy, a laundry, an enormous, modernised kitchen plus a butler's pantry and a housekeeper's sitting-room.

On the ground floor to one side of the wide, glass-panelled front door was an elegant drawing-room, big enough, once the carpets were carefully rolled back, in which to hold a dance. On the other side of the hall was a dining-room, well able to seat thirty or more guests, a small, pretty sitting-room at the back of the house for the mistress's use, a study for the master and a library complete with a billiard table.

On the first floor was a modern tiled bathroom and half a dozen large bedrooms stretching across into the extension put on by James's own father, joined together across the front by a wrought-iron balcony on to which the long bedroom windows opened. The second floor had another bathroom, as luxuriously appointed as that on the first floor and used when guests were in residence, and at the back of these and in the roof space, with dormer windows looking out over the back towards Colwith Woods, were the women servants' bedrooms. At the end of the extension James's mother had had built a delicately soaring glass conservatory which opened on to the side garden. The house was painted white and had a blue slate roof. The windows were flat and square, the whole presenting a picture of solid, enduring patience coupled with a serene and ageless beauty.

If Lucy was dazzled as she sat in the wide sunny hallway waiting to be summoned into the presence of James Buchanan, or shown the door, whichever he decided, she did not show it. She had lived for the whole of her life in what could only be described as spartan conditions. Her mother, though Lucy was not aware of it, had brought some

179

pretty pieces of furniture, a picture or two, some good crystal and Meissen chinaware to her marriage to Edward Dean but, over the years, to pay an enormously overdue butcher's bill, the servants' wages, to purchase warm, winter clothing for her growing children, these had found themselves in the salerooms and auction rooms of Buxton and Lucy had no recollection of their existence. She had become used to bare walls and empty fireplaces, uncarpeted wooden floors across which their boots snapped smartly, old chairs and wobbly legged tables, and the sudden explosion of colour and warmth and sunlight streaming through wide polished windows, the smell of fresh cut flowers overwhelmed her. She gazed at a portrait which hung above the fireplace of an exquisitely beautiful woman in a low-cut blue silk dress. She had hair the colour of the chestnuts she and the children gathered from the woods and her eyes were a pale velvet grey, reminding her of someone, though she could not bring to mind who it was.

'Will you come this way, miss,' the pretty little housemaid beseeched her, smiling and bobbing and doing her best not to appear too excited. She led Lucy along the hallway, turning left into another until she came to a doorway which stood open. She knocked on it, then stepped inside.

'Miss Dean, sir,' she announced importantly, then, at her master's thank you, scampered off as fast as her legs would carry her in the direction of the kitchen.

He was leaning with one arm along the mantelpiece, a cigar in his hand which, though she was not aware of it, trembled slightly. He was casually dressed, since he was not expecting

180

visitors, in a blue polo-necked jumper and a pair of dove grey breeches which showed off the athletic leanness of his figure. His knee boots were well polished. He himself was well shaved and he looked exactly what he was, a gentleman enjoying a lazy Sunday afternoon rest from the exigencies of business. The strain he had suffered over the past months did not show in his face. In fact he looked the picture of health with no care in the world beyond the annoying prospect of spending half an hour with an unwelcome visitor.

Lucy, still as a doe which scents danger but is incapable of avoiding it, stood hesitantly in the doorway and waited. She was like a black wand, slender and ready to sway in the path of any stray breeze, her face pale but composed and James felt the sad loveliness of her hit him hard in the chest, but nothing of it showed in his face.

'Miss Dean?' he asked enquiringly.

'Good afternoon, Mr Buchanan. It was good of you to see me.'

'Not at all.' His voice was polite, nothing more, and he glanced at his watch as though to show her he was not a man who had time to spend gossiping. 'May I offer you my condolences on the death of your father,' he asked her civilly. 'It must have been a grave shock to you.'

'It was.' Her eyes were steady but they became moist, soft golden brown pools of grief, the emotion in her difficult to contain.

He hardened his resolve, for this was not the time to weaken. He had not wanted to see her and the sooner she went the sooner he could get back—crawl back, some unwanted sneering thing inside him said—into the lonely life he had chosen for himself.

'Won't you sit down?' he asked her, for after all he was a gentleman and she was a lady, but his hostility was very evident and he hoped she could see it. He wondered what the devil she was doing here, hoping to God it was not for a handout, but his own knowledge of her told him Lucy Dean was not one to go begging.

'Thank you.' She swayed towards the chair he indicated and sank down, her back as stiff as a ramrod, her bonneted head ... Dear God, where had she got that monstrosity which covered her hair, drowning her white face with its huge old-fashioned brim and high crown. Somehow it made her seem all the more vulnerable and he swore under his breath at his own helplessness at being moved by her frailty.

'What can I do for you, Miss Dean?' he asked her brusquely, again looking at his watch, for he really did not think he could stand much more of this. Let her tell him what it was she had come for and be done with it. Whatever it was he would agree to it. A loan to tide her over. Jobs for her servants, who he was certain she could no longer keep. In fact where was she to live, now he gave it some thought, for the living had died with her father and ...

'I came to see if the kind offer you made me last year was still available, Mr Buchanan. If it is I find I ... would be willing to ... to take it up.' Her face had whitened even further as she spoke and even though she was seated, she swayed a little.

'Offer?' he asked dazedly. 'What offer?'

'I believe it was an offer of marriage, Mr Buchanan.' Her eyes gazed steadily somewhere over his shoulder, huge and somehow frightened and for a moment he felt compassion wash over him, for it had taken enormous courage on her part to come to him like this, then it was replaced by a savage anger and he had to whirl away from her in order to hide it. He wanted to crash his fist on the mantelpiece and swear obscenely, since it seemed she had come to offer him what he had asked for months ago. She was telling him that, distasteful as it was to her, for the sake of her family—oh, yes, it was that, there was no doubt of it—she was willing to sacrifice herself and take up the position, as if it were one of housekeeper or laundry maid, that she had turned down so rashly before Christmas.

Lucy sat impassively and waited. She felt very calm and yet inside her there was a small flutter of something she knew to be fear. Fear not of this man and what he would do to her, but that he might do nothing. That he might turn her out, tell her he was no longer interested and if he did she had no idea what she was to do next. There was always the poorhouse—was that what it was called?—she supposed, or perhaps she could go to the squire and beg a cottage on his estate. She and Buffy might get employment in service somewhere. Buffy was very clever with her needle, but then what was to happen to Mrs Hutton and Bibby and Elsie and who would take care of the children while she and Buffy . . . Dear Lord, dear Father in heaven, don't let him turn his face from me, let there be something remaining in him that is willing to forget what happened between us . . .

He turned slowly and she was amazed at the expression of amusement on his face. He was actually smiling as though at some absurdity. He drew on his cigar, the smoke swirling about his head as he blew it out, continuing to lounge indolently to the side of the leaping log fire. His dogs, now that she was seated and their master was happy about it, settled themselves at his feet. When he finally moved he had to step over them. He sauntered to the window and looked out over the garden, putting his head out and sniffing appreciatively, or so it seemed, at the spring fragrance that hung there. He had all the time in the world now, he appeared to be telling her, and whatever Lucy Dean had done to him she was about to pay for it. Still she waited impassively, her fate and that of her family in his hands.

'So, you have decided that my . . . attentions are welcome after all, is that it, Miss Dean? Now that you have nowhere else to turn, no other person in the world who can help you out of this dilemma your father's death has plunged you in,' cruelly ignoring the small distressed sound she made in the back of her throat, 'you have changed your mind and elected to, despite your aversion, become my wife?'

'If you are still interested, yes, Mr Buchanan.' Her voice in no way said she was humbled and he thought he had never before seen such bravery. She didn't love him, probably didn't even like him much. She hated the way his family lived, the conventions and rules, the etiquette that had to be observed in their strata of life, which was in direct contrast to the careless way she and her family had lived in the rectory, and yet she was ready to submit to it all, all that she despised, for the sake of her brothers and sisters, for there was no doubt in his mind that they would be part of the bargain.

184

'And what if I were to tell you that I am not, Miss Dean, what then? Would you trail round all the eligible bachelors of the district offering your very delectable self to anyone who will have you, or will you—'

'I would like an answer, Mr Buchanan. I am willing to marry you, and yes, it is for the sake of my family, for I can only be honest with you. I . . . I seem to have something you want.'

'Wanted, Miss Dean.' His voice was brutal and she winced.

'Very well, if that is the case I will waste no more of your time.' She rose to her feet and her hands went in a pathetic gesture to her comical bonnet, setting it straight. A wisp of her silken hair drifted from beneath the brim to her forehead, for the bonnet was far too big, and she brushed it away with a hand which was trembling violently. He wanted to go to her, put his arms about her, tell her she had nothing . . . nothing, ever, to worry about again. That he would look after her until his dying breath, and her bloody family, but he could not do it, of course. She had wounded him deeply, wounded his pride and his self-esteem, damaged his standing in the community and he could not forget it. It stood between him and what he felt for her and he was not willing to chance it again.

'Not so fast, Miss Dean.' His mouth curled at the corners and again she was astonished, for she knew it to be a satisfied smile that played there. And then it came to her. He was playing with her like a cat will play with a mouse, cuffing it almost affectionately as it makes a dash for safety, then pinning it down once more. A game the cat enjoyed, for it was its nature, but a sorry day for the

185

mouse, and she was cast in the role of mouse.

But her name was Lucy Dean. Destitute she might be but she was not about to allow this man to treat her like some . . . some street woman who had come to offer her wares, for a price. She had dealt with him fairly last year. She had been courteous, even distressed by her inability to accept him and she did not deserve his contempt, for that was what he was showing her.

'Mr Buchanan, I would be glad if you would stop this . . . this . . .'

'Yes, Miss Dean? This . . .'

'This charade. If you no longer wish to marry me then say so.'

'I do not say so, Miss Dean.' In his eyes was a hard glitter of ice, silver grey and quite dazzling, but it was not meant to allay her fears, she knew that.

Nevertheless, 'Then you do wish to marry me?'

'I did not say that either.' His face was smooth and amber-tinted, totally without expression and Lucy died a little, for where else was she to go from here? But again the pride and strength she had drawn about herself since her mother died and her father had retreated into his shell of grief came to her rescue. The bonnet rose and the ridiculous black feather on it bobbed. Her back was very straight as she made her way towards the door which the maid had closed behind her.

'I'm afraid I have wasted your time and my own, Mr Buchanan. I shall have to make further arrangements to protect my family and I have only until the end of the month to do it in, so I'll bid you good afternoon.'

'What other arrangements, Miss Dean?'

186

'That is my concern, Mr Buchanan. Now, if you will summon your maid I will—'

'Miss Dean, may I ask you what you intend to put into this . . . marriage? If it is to take place, that is?' His voice was like silk and she turned, bewildered.

'I'm not sure I understand.'

'Oh, I'm sure you do, Miss Dean. You know what a married woman has done to her each night in her husband's bed, surely? Does the . . . bargain include that?'

Her face changed from bone white to poppy red and her lips trembled but she did not hesitate. 'I will be your wife in every way that you need, Mr Buchanan. That is my part of the . . . bargain. Yours is that you will look after my brothers and sisters, until they are of an age to look after themselves. Would that be satisfactory?'

'Perfectly, Miss Dean. I will call on you tomorrow to make the arrangements.'

'Thank you, Mr Buchanan. Good afternoon.'

He was trembling so violently after she had gone he had to sit down in a chair or he would have fallen. His teeth clicked on the glass of brandy he had poured himself but in him was a tiny bud of hope which he had not known for many months.

CHAPTER TEN

Her voice was without expression as she spoke. 'We are to be married in three weeks' time.' She ignored Buffy's gasp of amazement. 'Mr Buchanan will arrange it all.'

187

'Not . . . not in your papa's church?'

For a moment the mask of calm on Lucy Dean's face slipped. 'Dear God, no! It is to be at St Mary's on the Kelsick Road.' The curious woodenness returned and she continued in a lifeless voice. 'Apparently Mr Buchanan's family worship there. He wants it to be . . . smart, the sort of wedding to which his family is accustomed. White, of course, for all young ladies of good family are married in white, with Emily and Margaret as bridesmaids. He thinks Edward would be old enough and a suitable choice to give me away and there will be a reception at Howethwaite afterwards. He asked me if I had any preference for a honeymoon. I said I didn't, but would leave it to him. I have never been anywhere, Buffy, so how could I choose? And we have no need to fear . . . eviction. Mr Buchanan will see to it. "Arrange to have your family and servants moved to Howethwaite in the next few days and you must stay with Franny." She is, well, you know who she is . . . until . . . Apparently she will know everything I will need in the way of . . . a trousseau. It seems I must have one. He will pay for it all.'

'Darling . . . darling . . .' The endearment was a measure of Buffy's deep distress, for she was an undemonstrative young woman. She and her mam had had no time for it in the fight for life they had known. Before her mam had lost hers there had been a deep affection between them, just as there was between her and Lucy Dean, but it was not her nature to make a show of it. Now, the unnatural numbness with which Lucy told her of the plans Mr Buchanan was to make for them all affected her deeply.

'I know I must marry some time, Buffy, and Mr

Buchanan is a ... he will be kind, I'm sure, and there are the children ... which explained it all. If she was alone, or just had Buffy to protect, they would be off somewhere, probably to London, to get a job, perhaps with the WSPU, and her life would be wonderfully exciting, worth while, special, but the slump of her shoulders said that it was not possible so she must make the best of it, which was all any woman in her position could do.

'He loves you, Lucy, I told you that months ago, and with time ...'

Lucy turned to her in surprise. They were sitting before the parlour fire which, to the servants' astonishment, had been banked up to enormous proportions. They were to do the same with their own in the kitchen, she had told them mysteriously, and they were not to worry about the future. It was all taken care of, as they would be taken care of, and though they trusted Miss Lucy with their lives, they were dubious, for what were they to make of that remark. Not worry about the future when their very home was to be taken over by another family at the month's end. What did she mean? What was to happen to them? Who was going to pay for the coal which, delightfully, burned halfway up the chimney, and the hamper, come from the local provision merchant, which had been delivered at the back door by a most polite, one might almost say servile messenger on a bicycle only an hour since. Meat pies and hams, chickens and eggs, though they had no need of those, a shoulder of lamb and a leg of pork, a whole salmon, in fact enough food to keep the Dean household for a week.

Yes, Miss Lucy had said vaguely, it had been

delivered to the right address and would Mrs Hutton prepare something for the children's tea. The children, fed for the last month on eggs and more eggs, on bread and jam, both of which Mrs Hutton made herself, on porridge, on dishes made up mostly of potatoes and vegetables, all delicious and cheap, had been ecstatic, only Margaret showing a dubious face, for where had it come from. She was the closest to Lucy in age and was a practical child. She knew that such things didn't grow on trees, as Mrs Hutton was wont to say, but for the moment she kept her counsel and allowed Edward and Emily and Percy to enjoy what some guardian angel had provided.

Now Lucy considered the strange statement Buffy had just made, considered it as though it were a puzzle someone had just presented her with, a small frown on her ashen face.

'I don't know what love is, Buffy, between a man and woman, that is. Oh, Mr Buchanan informed me that we would share a bed and I think I have some idea what he is to do to me in it . . .'

'Dear God, Lucy.'

'There is no use feeling sorry for me, Buffy. I have to face the fact that there is no other way open for me. He will pay for Edward and Percy to be properly educated, he said so. A governess for the girls. He is to come over tomorrow and explain it all to me. I am to be here at ten o'clock to receive him. I believe there are certain legalities . . .'

'Lucy, darling, I cannot bear to hear you talk like this, as if it were no more than deciding what the menu is to be for Sunday lunch.'

'To me it is no more than that, Buffy. Now I must go and . . . and break the glad news to the children. Edward, at least, will be pleased.'

'Edward?'

'To have a Rolls-Royce in the family, of course.'

* * *

'You're to marry the girl who turned you down last year and not only that you expect me to have her here, in my home, until you do. Well, all I can say is that you've a bloody nerve and I'm surprised at your lack of pride, James Buchanan, really I am. You know she has accepted you only because of her changed circumstances, and everyone in the valley will believe the same.'

James Buchanan's face was unreadable. 'It does not matter to me what anyone believes, Franny. Lucy Dean'—her name came easily to him now, Franny noticed—'is to be my wife and there is nothing that can change that.'

'You're off your rocker, old boy,' Alex growled, the first words he had spoken since the dreadful news had been broken to them. 'She'll be nothing but trouble.'

'Why is that, Alex?' James asked mildly enough. 'She will be my wife and as such will have a position to keep up. She will do as I tell her,' which is more than can be said for yours, he almost added.

'But why, old chap, for God's sake, why? What in hell's name has she got that a dozen much more suitable girls couldn't give you? Why this obsession with her? She has two arms and two legs and all that goes with—'

'Be careful, Alex, that you don't say too much. I am to marry her and no man will insult my wife.'

'Dear sweet Lord, I can't believe it.' Franny was

191

still grappling with the audacious request James had made of her to have the Dean girl in her home, to lead her through the ways of a society wedding, to see she did the correct thing, bought the right clothes, said the proper words to the proper people. She must be married from a decent address and what better than hers, he was telling her and yet, why not. It might be fun. She was always ready for something different, something perhaps the others might not agree with; besides which, she was between lovers at the moment and had nothing else to divert her. And though she had not really considered it in any great depth, she realised now that she had liked the girl. She had spunk, did Lucy Dean. You only had to see the way that old dodderer of a father she had, had acted. Dead now, of course, but when he was alive Edward Dean had had no life in him and it had been left to Lucy to bring up her family and run the household. But with him dead the small income, his living at the house which belonged to the squire, had died with him, which was why Lucy had accepted James's offer. The surprising thing to Franny was that he had made it again. For the past few months he had brooded morosely in his lovely home, refusing all invitations, snapping at her when she went to winkle him out, almost growing old before her eyes and yet here he was looking as he had always done. Attractive, debonair, a curl of humour at the corner of his undeniably sensual mouth, looking, she was inclined to think, like the cat that has just been offered a saucer of cream.

James watched her for a moment, then, smiling, walked to the window, satisfied, for her expression told him she would do it. His bride would come, a proper bride, a Buchanan bride, from this charming house. It would be seen as a mark of favour in the town and make Lucy's progress in his society so much easier. There was no one more suitable to help Lucy Dean through the difficulties that lay ahead of her than Franny Buchanan, whose position in society was assured. James was an influential man and his wife, when seen to be approved by the Buchanan clan, would find her way smoothed by the patronage of Mrs Alex Buchanan.

*   *   *

The worst moment, Lucy believed it firmly at the time since she had no way of looking into the future, was getting the children settled in their new home. The girls were tearful and bewildered, begging her not to leave them, and Percy declared that he would run away back home at the first opportunity.

'You can't, you silly beggar. The new rector will be there and his boy will be sleeping in your bed,' Edward told him ungraciously to hide his own fear of this new environment. He didn't know whether to be pleased or sorry that Lucy was to marry Mr Buchanan, and he was worried about the difference it would undoubtedly make to their lives. Would Lucy become a grand lady dressed in silks and furs, for he knew Mr Buchanan was very rich, or would she be as she had always been, fun-loving, carefree, ready to join in any game, most of them devised by herself? Would she still romp with Thimble and take them for long walks up on the fells or would Mr Buchanan take up all her time, stealing her

193

away from them? There was talk of going to school and how was Percy to deal with that, telling himself that Percy's welfare was at the forefront of his mind, not his own misgivings.

'Darlings, you know I will always be here for you, don't you? Though I shall be Mr Buchanan's wife I shall be, first and foremost, your sister. You are my first concern. We shall be together every day, I promise you, and apart from living in these rather luxurious surroundings, which you must admit are quite splendid, things will be exactly as they have always been.'

'Except for Papa,' Percy said gravely.

'Papa will always be with us, sweetheart. He and Mama are looking down on us now, watching over us.'

'But they're not here, Lucy,' Emily breathed, looking anxiously round the large, airy but unfamiliar room, flickering with firelight, which was to be theirs. Not a nursery, of course, for they were too old for that but a room in which they could keep their own things, play their own games, read, eat their meals and generally consider it to be theirs and theirs alone, Mr Buchanan had told them. Margaret and Emily were to have lessons here with a daily governess, a young lady by the name of Miss Bradley, who would be driven in from Ambleside and who would teach them all that a young lady of their class needed. A little geography, French, English composition, poetry, the Scriptures, history, some arithmetic, and, of course, all the artistic accomplishments such as drawing and painting.

Lucy had not liked the idea of her brothers and sisters eating here, at least not all the time, and as soon as she and Mr Buchanan were married she meant to discuss it with him. They were well mannered and could be trusted to dine with adults, at least Edward and Margaret, and she would not have them banished to the far reaches of the second floor where they were to live. Two of the bedrooms up here and the bathroom were to be used by them, Edward and Percy sleeping in one and Margaret and Emily the other. Not to share a bed as they had done at home—the rectory, she must remember that, the rectory was no longer their home—but having a bed each. The rooms were well furnished with thick, springy carpets on the floor, heavy velvet curtains at the windows to keep out the icy winds which often whistled down the valley and a good fire burning in the grate, for Mr Buchanan was inordinately generous, not just with her and the children, but with his own servants who, in many folks' opinion, were spoiled rotten.

'It will be all right, you wait and see,' she told them, trying to draw the four of them into her arms and it was a measure of Edward's insecurity that he allowed it. She had told them that Mrs Hutton and Bibby had been found a small cottage apiece in a corner of Mr Buchanan's grounds and they could go and visit them whenever they wanted. Wouldn't that be nice? And Elsie was only downstairs. She had been put to work in the kitchen which, it seemed to Lucy, was already over-staffed with six maids working in it, not to mention a cook, a housekeeper, a butler and God only knew how many more. But that was not her concern. She was to leave her family here, leave them in strange surroundings and be taken, driven by Mr Buchanan's chauffeur in the Rolls-Royce, to Mrs

195

Buchanan's house, Grange House, where she was to stay until the wedding but, she promised them as she kissed them a tearful farewell, she would be back first thing in the morning to see that they were all right. They were to be good and obey Buffy who was to look after them and sleep in the room next to Margaret and Emily's. They were to eat well and sleep well and not to worry, for she would always be here to protect them. Did they understand?

Gravely they said they did, coming to the top of the stairs with her and watching her all the way down, even Thimble who stood with his head on one side, evidently wondering what the devil was going on.

Mrs Buchanan put her in what she called the 'apricot room' which was very pretty, and very warm. It had evidently been decorated and furnished with Franny's impeccable taste, for it was all pale colours, apricot, green and sand, the furniture of rosewood so light and delicate Lucy was afraid to touch it. The pale green velvet curtains at the window were swathed and tied back with ribbons of silk and there were flowers everywhere, the fragrance a delight. Spring flowers but all the right shades of apricot, cream, peach and gold to match the décor. There were brushes and combs and mirrors lying on the dressing-table, exquisite in silver. Lucy had never seen anything so lovely, so feminine and for a moment the woman in her delighted in it, savouring the idea that this sort of comfort and warmth would for ever be hers. But there is a price to pay, a small, defiant voice said inside her and when she turned to Mrs Buchanan her face was as expressionless as it had been, except when she was with the children and Buffy, for the past week.

There was a bathroom next door, she was told, which she was, of course, to consider her own. Would this suit her then? Mrs Buchanan asked her, an ironic smile on her face, for had she not seen first hand the lack of comfort and warmth at the rectory. They dined at seven, she added, but if Lucy would like to come down earlier she and Alex would be . . .

'I would—if it's possible and not putting anyone to any trouble—I would like to eat here.'

'No, my dear, I'm afraid not. James was most particular that you should start as he means you to go on.'

'I am still in mourning for my father, Mrs Buchanan. Surely . . . ?'

'I'm sorry about that, Lucy, and I do wish you'd call me Franny, since we are soon to be . . . related, but James thinks—'

'Mrs Buchanan, please.'

'Is that all you have to wear, Lucy?' Franny viewed Lucy's shapeless black gown with some distaste, not at all softened by her appeal. It was Franny Buchanan's belief that when disaster struck you didn't just give in to it, you damn well took it by the throat and twisted it to suit yourself, and she was determined to see that James's bride, who she knew to be strong, did just that. She was sorry for the girl, but she was here for one purpose only and that was to be transformed into a bride fit for a Buchanan. Franny guessed that the dress was shapeless because of the weight Lucy had lost in the last weeks but that would soon be remedied and tomorrow she and the girl were to be taken to Miss Medlock's in Ambleside and there Lucy Dean was to be fitted out with a trousseau suitable for the young queen James evidently saw her to be. Everything she could possibly need from the skin out, for every possible occasion from the moment she got out of the bed she was to share with him until she got back into it, again with him. No expense was to be spared, he told Franny and if Lucy protested her protests were to be ignored. He wanted her to be the most elegantly gowned young matron Ambleside, Fellthwaite, Grasmere, indeed the whole of Lakeland had ever seen.

The first hitch, if you liked to call it that, occurred the very next morning. Lucy had dined with the Buchanans as she had been commanded. She ate a little of everything that was put before her, as young ladies of breeding were expected to, her manners faultless. She refused wine, drinking only water. She smiled only at the butler who served her, who was clearly startled, and at the footman who helped him. When spoken to she answered politely, but apart from that sat like a statue, staring ahead of her into the soft candlelight. There had been electricity installed at Grange House but Franny still liked to dine by candlelight and the effect was very lovely. Flowers and shining cutlery, flawlessly glinting crystalware, white damask tableware and Franny in a gown of quite stunning style, a scarlet chiffon so fine and clinging it was transparent and under it she wore a scarlet, fitted, tube-like underdress. There was a scattering of crystal beads at the neck and hem and her maid had cleverly arranged some in her hair so that it looked as though raindrops sparkled there, Her satin slippers had been dyed to match her gown and beside her husband, resplendent in his black and white dinner suit, the effect was dramatic.

Lucy scarcely noticed, nor was even aware of the contrast in herself to Franny Buchanan and would not have cared if she had. The young footman, when the butler was out of earshot, carried back tales to the kitchen of what a 'guy' she looked, and he only hoped when madam had finished with her she would look more presentable.

'You shut your mouth, you fool,' Cook hissed sharply, for she was a kindly soul who had heard something of the hardships the young miss had suffered.

'I was only saying . . .'

'Well, don't. See, help Agnes with them pans if you've nothing else to do.'

The table had only just been set in the breakfast-room and the food had certainly not been brought in when she appeared like a slender black ghost at the breakfast-room door asking for a piece of toast and a cup of tea. They were not to bother with anything else since she was going out.

'Going out, miss,' the same footman gasped, for it was well known, as is always the case in big houses with many servants, that she was to be driven into Ambleside to be fitted out with a new wardrobe.

'Yes.' Lucy sat down at the table and waited.

'But . . . well, miss . . .'

'Is there a problem?' she asked him distantly, not meaning to be haughty but anxious to get to Howethwaite to see how the children were. She had barely slept for worrying about them, though she had been warm and comfortable, and very clean after the bath the smiling little maid had drawn for her and the white lawn nightdress, persumably one of Mrs Buchanan's, she had been put in.

'No, but . . .'

'Yes?'

'Are you not to go into Ambleside, miss? The motor has been ordered for ten.' It was not yet eight o'clock.

'Yes, but that is later, I believe. I have an errand to do first.'

'An errand?'

'Yes.'

'But the motor is—'

'I shall not need the motor. I'll walk.'

'Walk, miss?'

Lucy stood up abruptly and the footman fell back. She looked so determined, her face set in harsh lines as though she had a problem of the utmost difficulty to solve. Should he run and fetch Mr Barrie, who was hardly out of bed himself yet? Short of physically tackling the young lady how was he to stop her just walking off and then what would madam do? Liked her own way, did madam, but then so did this one, it seemed, as she left the room, ran lightly up the stairs, coming down again struggling into an old black coat which his own mam would have been ashamed to be seen in.

'I won't be long,' she told him as he hung about at the foot of the stairs, still not having made up his mind whether to go for Mr Barrie or not.

'Very well, miss,' he said lamely before walking slowly up the hall to inform the rest of the servants that their guest had gone off—where, how the hell did he know?—without any breakfast.

The children were pathetically glad to see her.

200

The same pretty housemaid who had answered the door the last time let her in, her face a picture at the sight of who was on the doorstep, and as Lucy ran up the stairs she passed maidservants on their knees with their brushes or energetically polishing the banisters. They all watched her go with open-mouthed wonder.

She stayed for an hour, just long enough to have some breakfast with them and to listen to their tales of this or that wonder, or this and that problem, all of which she reassured them would soon be solved. Buffy was with them, comforting and familiar and, drawing Lucy to one side, she was able to tell her that they had slept well, for she had checked on them through the night, though the girls had slept in the same bed, as had the boys. Thimble, already bearing the instincts of a family dog, had also shared the night with them all, moving from one bed to another in his determination to protect 'his people' in these strange surroundings.

'They're fine, Lucy, really. You're not to worry. Don't forget both Mr Buchanan, and Mrs Buchanan at Grange House, have a telephone and I promise, though I don't know how I'll get the hang of the blooming thing, to telephone at the first sign of trouble. And you can telephone here if you want to speak to me or the children. Get the telephone number before you go. I'm sure Mr Buchanan won't mind.'

'Buffy, what would I do without you? You've set my mind at rest. I thank God for the day when Mama found you, and now I suppose I'd better go or Mrs Buchanan will be sending a search party out for me, though I'm sure she knows where I've gone.'

He was waiting at the foot of the stairs when she reluctantly left. His face had its usual stern, unsmiling countenance but there was something in his eyes which told her she was not to be chastised. A softness that he did his best to hide. She had no idea what it meant, for his mind was a closed book to her, but she sensed he was not displeased with her.

'They'll be all right, you know that, don't you, Lucy. They are your family and as such . . . they will want for nothing.'

'I must see them every day.' Her voice was abrupt. 'They have been with me; they miss me and are in a strange place and I must make sure they are . . . happy.'

'Will you be happy, Lucy?' he said with a suddenness which made her blink sharply. What on earth did he mean by that? Her mind was at rest that she had found a place of shelter and security for them. A home, good food, schooling and all the things her papa had never been able to give them. Except love, of course. He had given them, and her, that in abundance and she must take his place.

She said so and was bewildered by the strange feeling that some light that was flickering inside him had gone out. She didn't know what to make of it and if she did, could do nothing about it. She was prepared to keep her side of their bargain, as it seemed he was to keep his and that was all that mattered, surely?

'Of course, and now Baxter will run you back to Grange House. I have telephoned Mrs Buchanan to say you are here. She is waiting for you.'

'I can walk.'

'No, you can't, Lucy, and when you want to come here to see the children, or me, you must ask Mrs Buchanan's chauffeur to bring you. It is only correct. You cannot just saunter about.'

'You mean like Lucy Dean used to do,' she said bitterly.

'Exactly. Now, will you have some breakfast with me before you go?'

'No, thank you.'

It was as though she were telling him that she would take up her duties on the day they had specified, two weeks on Friday, 21 April, and not a moment sooner.

*　　*　　*

She made a beautiful bride, everyone agreed, even the Buchanans who were prepared to criticise her at every turn for what she had done to James. She wore the white her bridegroom had insisted upon, a dress of straight simplicity, silk net over chiffon which rested on her hips and hung in pleats to her ankle bone. On her hair, which Mrs Buchanan's maid had dressed back into a smooth bun was a juliet cap with a veil attached which fell at the front to her breast, but fluted, so that at the back it reached her calves. She carried a small posy of white rosebuds, freesias and baby's breath. Her brother did well. He was almost as tall as she was and in the grey morning coat and striped trousers his new brother-in-law had tricked him out in, he made a handsome foil for the fragile beauty of the woman he led down the aisle. At their backs were her sisters, both in white, simply dressed with tiny wreaths of rosebuds in their hair. Why was it, the congregation wondered, that they gave the impression of being a close family group to which no one else was admitted? Even her younger brother, a lad of about six, walked ahead of her, carrying her wedding ring on a velvet cushion. They appeared to be protecting her, the lovely floating bride, hemming her in, and when they reached James Buchanan seemed reluctant to stand aside for him.

They wept inconsolably, except for the elder boy, when she and James climbed into the Rolls-Royce which was to take them on the first part of their wedding trip, and so did the bride. They clung together in a most embarrassing way and had it not been for the little crippled girl who came to prise them apart they might have all been swept into the motor with James and his new wife. Not that James Buchanan was the sort of man to stand such nonsense, and it was seen that he spoke sharply to the new Mrs Buchanan. Her lovely head drooped and there were more than a few who remarked that it was not a very auspicious way to begin a marriage.

CHAPTER ELEVEN

At the end of May Lucy Buchanan had her nineteenth birthday and to celebrate it and to show her how much he valued her she was given an exquisite bracelet and necklace to match by her husband. The set had been specially made for her. Tiny pearls, two rows linked by a chain so fine it looked like a cobweb on which droplets of dewed pearls hung. He also gave instructions to his housekeeper that a party was to be held in his wife's honour at their home, Howethwaite, to which a hundred people, friends and relatives, were to be invited, since he wanted to show off his beautiful, elegantly dressed young wife.

Though they had been married for six weeks he continued to make love to her every night and sometimes in the morning as well. The new Mrs Buchanan had become accustomed to it, though she could not say she cared for it. It had been painful the first time, though she felt certain, how she did not know since she was ignorant of such things, that he had made a decent effort not to hurt her.

'Do you know what it is I am to do to you?' he had asked her that first night after she had spent half an hour sitting up in bed waiting for him.

'Oh, yes,' she had answered, anxious to have it over and done with so that she could turn away and go to sleep. She had expected an immediate assault in the dark, the lamps turned out, but he had left them on, sitting down on the edge of the bed and looking at her in the strangest way.

'You are the most beautiful thing I have ever seen.' His voice was musing and his hand lifted a tress of her long hair and put it to his face.

'Thank you,' she answered politely.

'So, here you are and you must be afraid.'

'Oh, no, I am not afraid, Mr Buchanan,' lying fiercely.

'So, you mean to be brave and suffer it without a word, is that it?'

'It seems I have no choice. Please, don't think me ungrateful since you have done all you said you would do. Now it is my turn to—'

'Is that how you see it, Lucy? Your turn to pay your dues?'

'Not at all,' but he knew she was not telling the truth. For a moment he felt the devastation creep over him, but then what else had he expected? In the past she had been more than honest with him so could he expect her to be anything else now. The ceremony today, though it had altered her status, had not altered her heart, which certainly did not belong to him.

'Come, let's be honest with each other. This is a . . . an arrangement which suits us both. You want security for your family. I want a wife, someone to run my home and entertain my guests, and naturally, soon, I hope, children.'

If he had expected a reaction he was disappointed. She sat straight-backed in the bed, not lounging in any way against the piled-up pillows, her face slightly averted.

'So, have you nothing to say in answer,' though what he hoped for he didn't know.

Suddenly she was angry. 'Oh, for God's sake get on with it, Mr Buchanan, or are you to chatter all night?'

He laughed out loud then, the first time she could remember him doing so. 'You're a rare bird, Lucy Dean, and you're right. I'm eager to see what I have bought . . . oh, yes, I know I have bought you, my darling, for the price of a home for your brothers and sisters you have sold yourself to me and so I'll have a look at what I've paid for.'

'I don't know what you mean,' she said coldly.

'Yes, you do, so off with that nightdress if you please.' He put the tips of his fingers on her shoulder and she flinched away but he took no notice, running them down her arm and back again to her neck, tracing the outline of her ear, aware all the time of the rigidity of her body but ignoring that too.

Lucy could feel the red-hot flush of embarrassment move to every part of her when, with what she did not recognise as an anxiety as great as hers, he lifted her arms above her head and drew her nightdress from her. She had regained a little weight in the few weeks before her wedding and her breasts were full and rounded, the nipples, rosy and flushed, standing proud. He had not even kissed her yet except for the chaste peck at the altar; now, slowly, he put his lips to hers, enfolding them, caressing them, parting them in some curious way, his tongue brushing against hers while his hands went to her breasts. She closed her eyes and held her breath, for she felt as though she were being devoured, by his mouth and by his hands and if she kept perfectly still and made no protest surely it would soon be over, this humiliation, but James Buchanan was a skilled lover and one who liked to please not only his own need but that of the woman to whom he made love, and he wanted more than anything to please his bride. He had shrugged out of the dressing-gown he wore and, to her horror, was clasping her naked body to his own, savouring her, with his mouth, his tongue, his fingers, which found every private part of her cringing body.

'This might be . . . painful,' he told her when at last some crescendo appeared to be approaching, and it was, for a moment later the pain of penetration lanced through her. His body was nailed to hers, shuddering in what must be agony, she had decided, only too glad when, at last, it seemed to be over.

'Don't be alarmed,' he told her, breathing hard. 'It will be easier next time. In fact I'm determined you shall like it. Now, go to sleep.' He put his arms about her possessively, one hand cupping her breast and at once fell into a deep sleep. She did her best not to mind, telling herself that she would get used to it, that it was what she had promised him, but if only she could ease herself away from him, put some space between his hard, warm male body and hers, which felt as though it had been tossed upon storm waters and thrown up on a rocky shore. Was this to happen every time they got into bed together and if so how was she to bear it? She knew that it was just a small part of marriage, that there would be many blessings to balance it, to make up for the indignities she had suffered tonight. She must dwell on them, not the crushing arm which lay across her body, the heavy breathing of a man beside her—the hand which, even in sleep, seemed to fondle her breast. She must remind herself of the grammar school in Ambleside which Edward was to attend and which she had won from Mr Buchanan who had wanted him to go away to a boarding school. The concession she had begged for Percy who was, in her opinion, too young for the grammar school and for the time being was to share Margaret and Emily's lessons. She must keep her exhausted mind on the warm, well-made clothing she had bought for them, pretty dresses for the girls, stout new boots for the boys, on the good and plentiful food they ate and the warmth and comfort in which they now lived. They were safe and she must be glad of it. The price she was paying was worth it. Mr Buchanan was right. It would get easier.

The party was not the success that James had hoped for and she knew it was her fault. She felt the hush fall on the room the moment she entered it on James's arm. Around her neck and on her wrist was the expensive birthday gift from her husband which they'd all heard about. She wore a gown of shimmering loveliness which clung to her magnificent, long-limbed, full-breasted body like a second skin. There were those among them who had the fanciful idea that she put them in mind of an Amazon queen. The gown was a simple sheath which, though it did not show either in her manner or James's, had been put on twice this evening, which was why they were a trifle late. Dimity, who was now her lady's maid, for Franny said she must have one, had been sent packing by her master, her face as red as a poppy, for she was well aware of what he had in mind for her beautiful mistress. An ice maiden she had looked like and James Buchanan had sworn that this time he would thaw her so that she would melt into his arms like the true woman he knew her to be but, once again, she had submitted willingly enough to him then calmly shrugged herself back into her gown, asking his help with the fastenings since she could hardly summon Dimity to do it again, she told him coolly.

Her guests looked at her critically and could find no fault, for there was no doubt she was a gorgeous young creature and, the gentlemen at least, wished they could be in James Buchanan's shoes, or rather his bed for a night or two.

There were not quite the hundred James had

envisaged but everyone who had been invited had come. They wouldn't miss this for the world, they told one another. The debut, so to speak, into society of the girl who had earned herself so much notoriety during the past few months. The girl who had turned her nose up at James Buchanan and then changed her mind!

The élite of Ambleside society was there. The Mossops with their son Frederick and their daughter Marion, remembering her, they gushed, from Franny Buchanan's dance where she had so enchanted them all. The Askews, with Rosalyn, Louise and Roger; the Kendalls with Aurora and Gregory, and the Grahams with their eldest, Rose. And standing somewhat aloofly, for they could not forget the slight to their daughter last year, the Gibsons, with Charlotte clinging possessively to the arm of her fiancé, soon to be husband, Doctor Paul Buchanan. A pleasant young man who, James was of the opinion, and had said so to Lucy, almost making her smile, would be eaten alive by Charlotte the moment she had him up the aisle.

There was Ben Buchanan, the eldest of the cousins and his comfortable wife, Joan, who could always be relied upon to be kind. Anne Mounsey and her prosperous farmer husband, Thomas and Christine Scott and her husband Douglas. Alex and Franny, Janet and Angus Gunson and Andrew Buchanan, who she was meeting for the first time, the only one still unattached, smiling wickedly into her eyes as he kissed her cheek, which, as a cousin, he was entitled to do, he told her, winking at James. For the first time Lucy felt a tremor of real warmth run through her.

Eight cousins, counting James, male and female,

who were descended from Alex and Christy Buchanan and there was not one among them who was not dark-haired and attractive as their grandparents had been, only the colour of their eyes differing, some a soft velvet grey come from their grandmother, others the vivid blue, a sapphire blue from their grandfather.

She had met them before, naturally, for Franny had given a family party when Lucy stayed with her prior to the wedding, but this was the first time they were to see her as Mrs James Buchanan, wife and hostess and how would she shape up, they were dying to know. The gentlemen bowed over her hand and the ladies smiled graciously, distantly kind, since she was related by marriage to them after all, treating her as though she were a miss from the schoolroom despite the magnificence of her white bosom which the low-cut gown showed off to advantage. They were inclined to be critical, at least the womenfolk were, for they had had high hopes of Charlotte Gibson who was one of them, or at least her mother was. They were all well dressed, the women, if not fashionably, then expensively so, the gentlemen in full evening dress consisting of a dinner jacket, single-breasted and unbuttoned as was the mode, a black bow tie, gleaming white shirt front, pleated, and a waistcoat with short points. They were drinking the latest cocktails mixed by Dixon, the Buchanan butler. A glass was pressed on Lucy and she tasted it, enjoying the pleasantly fizzing sensation that rushed to her head. She took another sip and was instantly disconcerted and not a little annoyed when her husband took it from her, murmuring that there was to be champagne later and she was not to drink cocktails since she was not used to them. A fruit juice for Mrs Buchanan, he told the hovering footman. He smiled pleasantly as he said it, sipping his own drink and looking round the somewhat astonished group who had witnessed the exchange.

It was as though a small imp, a wicked and angry imp, entered Lucy's brain, needling downwards and though it was not painful it was hot and rebellious, taking over and defying the grateful state of impassive obedience in which Lucy Buchanan had dwelled ever since she had known that her beloved family were to be safe. She had never been a girl, or young woman, to be dictated to, for she had been the virtual head of the Dean household ever since her mother died and all decisions made had been hers. Now, for almost two months she had done her best to please James Buchanan and his family, resolute in her determination to succeed. The imp said to hell with it!

'I think I could manage another, James,' she said, signalling to Dixon who, up to now, she had allowed to intimidate her. 'I'm hardly likely to become intoxicated on one, am I, or even two if I feel like it. After all, it is my birthday. My nineteenth so I can hardly be considered a child,' especially after what you do to me at least once a day, her flashing golden eyes said into his.

'I think not, my dear.' He was beginning to scowl and his eyes became icy grey slits of annoyance. 'These are very strong, made to Dixon's own recipe and will go at once to your head.'

'And why shouldn't they, James? As Lucy says, it is her nineteenth birthday and by God, it's a few years since any of us, at least this generation, had one of those.'

It was Franny, of course, a rebel herself and always willing to aid another. She took a small gold case from her bag, extracted a cigarette, allowed James to light it for her and inhaled deeply. She was wearing the most ravishing dress of gold chiffon studded with crystal beads and had a gold satin underdress beneath it caught at the ankle with narrow crystal insertions. It was very low cut, showing the swell of her small breasts almost to her nipples and Lucy, ready to laugh almost fondly at her rescuer, hoped to God they would not fall out. A long chiffon scarf with tasselled ends drifted about her bare shoulders. Her pale gold hair had a centre parting and was brushed into a heavy coil on her neck. About her forehead was a band of crystal set on gold satin. She was not a pretty woman but her style was such that no one noticed it. She was twenty-eight, childless, sophisticated and could be malicious if put out of countenance.

'Thank you, Franny, but I think I know how my wife should behave,' James began but Franny merely grinned audaciously at him and, taking Lucy by the arm, led her away to where Andrew stood leaning indolently against the wall, his eyes on Lucy's splendid bosom as they approached.

'Don't be so stuffy, James,' Franny said over her shoulder. 'You were young once yourself, or so they tell me.'

James Buchanan, with the gritty control which had been part of his nature for many years and which he was to perfect in the future, became even more rigid. He turned a tight smile on the group with him, then, bowing politely, showing none of the emotion which surged through him, begged to be excused for a moment.

She was flirted with by all the gentlemen, particularly Andrew who had no lady to restrain him, passing from one group to another and all the time sipping, first the cocktails and then the champagne which Dixon opened at a signal from James. He had her firmly by the arm again by then, his face inscrutable, his eyes as cold and dangerous as a snake's in his brown face and Franny was heard to say in an aside to her husband that the 'child' was in for it when they had all gone home.

But she couldn't help it. Franny just loved to stir things up a bit, to make trouble, even for someone of whom she was fond. To throw a live squib into a gathering which needed livening up and this, now that James had Lucy firmly anchored and drooping at his side, seemed to be proving to be one of those. They were having supper, a buffet supper set at small tables in the enormous drawing-room and afterwards there was to be dancing. There was a throb of conversation humming about the room and the tinkle of instruments as the small band set up in readiness. There was some laughter, especially from the corner where Andrew Buchanan and several other young ladies and gentlemen were sitting. Nevertheless from the table she was sharing with her husband, James and Lucy, Franny's voice could be heard by everyone in the room.

'And what is your opinion of the women's suffrage movement, Lucy? I believe you are interested in their cause?'

The result was electrifying. It was as though a hand had reached inside her and flicked on a switch, like one of those that were placed on the

214

wall beside the doorway of each room at Howethwaite and which so fascinated her. Her head came up, her slumped, bored shoulders squared and her eyes became a clear golden yellow, like a leopard's, the enlarged pupils black as sable. She turned with such force she knocked over a glass of champagne which Dixon leaped to retrieve but she did not even notice.

'My opinion,' she cried, a clarion call which silenced every voice in the room. 'My opinion is that they are quite marvellous, Mrs Buchanan ... er, Franny, as I'm sure is the opinion of every woman who has a brain to think with.' She glared about her as if defying them to deny it. 'The National Union of Women's Suffrage started it but it needs fighters to achieve our aims, like those in the Women's Social and Political Union which I long to join.'

Every face in the room turned expectantly to James, waiting breathlessly for his reaction to this staggering statement.

'We want equality and—'

'We? Mrs Buchanan?'

She did not know who spoke and she did not care, for here was something she could talk about at last. She was not interested in so much of the tinkling chatter which the women of James's society indulged in. They talked of people she did not know, plays she had not seen, books she had not read and places she had never visited. She would die for the cause, she told the frozen-faced and silent figures who sat or lounged about the room, just like Emily Wilding Davison who had thrown herself on to the racecourse at the Derby last June. She knew the suffragette movement did not meet with everyone's approval but surely . . .

Slowly she became aware of the vice-like grip on her arm, a grip so fierce she could feel the flow of blood to her hand become cut off and pins and needles attacked her fingers, and with it her torrent of words came to an end. By their silence and by the pain James was inflicting on her she was made to realise just how far she had gone to break every rule of society. The flush that washed her lovely face died down but she did not subside. Not her. Not the newly married Mrs James Buchanan, despite the appalled shock she saw in every face, at least those of the ladies, for the gentlemen were quite bowled over, wondering whether the enthusiasm she showed over this damn fool nonsense ever transferred itself into James's bed.

She tossed her head with a lofty gesture which brought a shower of curls tumbling in charming disarray about her ears, and grinned. 'Oh dear, I have set the cat among the pigeons, haven't I?'

His rage was quite killing when eventually it could be let out in the privacy of their bedroom.

'Get out,' he snarled at the terrified Dimity, who ran for her life, believing fearfully that her mistress would be sporting a black eye the next time she saw her. They had all heard in the kitchen about the show their young mistress had made of herself, spouting on about those dreadful women suffragettes, or so Mr Dixon had said, and the repercussions were just about to begin, it appeared. There'd be ructions the minute Dimity left the room but she daren't linger, not even to save her mistress, of whom she had become extremely fond. Oh, she did hope he wouldn't hit her!

'Now then, madam, what do you mean by

216

upsetting my guests ... your guests, with all that claptrap you spouted downstairs. I've never heard such bloody nonsense in my life and I'd be obliged if in future you'd keep it to yourself. Particularly when we have company.'

'I was asked a question and I answered it. Was I supposed to—'

'I'll be having words with that bloody woman tomorrow. This is all her fault.'

'That bloody woman, as you call her, has been extremely good to me and anyway, I was glad to be able to talk about something of real interest instead of that bloody rubbish.'

'And I'd be obliged if you would refrain from swearing. It is not becoming in a lady.'

'Dear God above!' She was as incensed as he was now. 'Why is it perfectly permissible for a man, a gentleman, to use the word 'bloody' and not—'

'You know perfectly well what the difference is.' James's face was expressionless, carved in amber-tinted stone but his eyes were wild, brilliant with a dangerous, frosted grey. He stood in the centre of their softly lit bedroom, his hands clenched into tight fists which pressed against the sides of his upper legs. He was self-assured, completely certain in his masculine world that he would have his own way, arrogantly believing that it was a wife's duty to do as her husband did, think as her husband thought, and the havoc that pounded inside him was not allowed to show.

'This is what the suffragette movement is all about, isn't it?' she said slowly, as though a light had just been shone on some tricky problem which had not been quite clear to her up to now. 'It is not just fighting for votes for women. It's for the rights of women. The right to be equal with men.'

'Don't be so bloody ridiculous, Lucy.'

'No, I cannot turn my back on it.'

'Turn your back on what, for Christ's sake?'

Her jaw clenched as tight as his fists and she turned away from him as though she were no longer concerned with his petty tyranny. This was the first time they had argued, fought over anything, for he had denied her nothing, even over the question of the boys' schooling. She was as shocked as he was by the bitterness of their quarrel but it was not in her to give up, and he was the same. Well, it made no difference. Already, after only a few weeks of marriage, she was bored to the point of tears by the domesticated routine she was supposed to take up as a young matron. She did not want to be consulted each day by Cook on her preference for this or that menu for dinner or luncheon. She was not concerned with whether the windows had been cleaned properly or the kitchen floor scrubbed, if that was supposed to interest her, so she totally ignored her duties as the mistress of the house, believing that between them, Mrs Burns the housekeeper, Mrs Bunting the cook, and Dixon the butler, could manage things far better without her interference. James had been well looked after for many years and it certainly didn't need her half-hearted and reluctant involvement to keep up their standards. The house was run like a well-oiled clock under their supervision. The meals were splendidly cooked and served promptly and her only concern was for Elsie, though she realised that it made things no better for the little scullery maid to have her constantly asking after her. She had even made the grave mistake of going into the kitchen and talking to her, questioning her on her duties, for the child was only twelve years old and had had a poor start in life. She knew she had made an error by the way Mrs Bunting drew herself up and took a stance of offended righteousness before her ovens; yes, *her* ovens, as this was *her* kitchen and not a place where the mistress of the house was expected to show herself.

She kept away after that, making discreet enquiries from Buffy who, slowly, for she was neither a servant, nor a member of the family, was finding her feet at Howethwaite. Buffy had made a friend of one of the housemaids, a girl of her own age, and, as Buffy described her, plain, sensible and discreet, and was able to report that Elsie was fine and dandy. Not that Fanny, as she was called, was prepared to pass on tittle-tattle from the kitchen, Buffy was made to understand.

Though Buffy was against it, Lucy would not hear of giving up the long talks she and Buffy had. She and Buffy had been friends for many years and Lucy was not prepared to give up that friendship, no matter what the change in their circumstances might be, she declared stoutly. Buffy had been her help and support through many bad times, she told her, and if Buffy wanted to see her, to come and sit in Lucy's drawing-room and talk to her, then she should, and if Lucy needed to go up to the schoolroom, as it was called, and chat with Buffy and the children, then she would and no one, not James, not society, not the somewhat disapproving servants, would stop her. By God, she said, it was a damn sight more entertaining than the chitter-chatter of the ladies who called on her in the way society ladies did, and the only thing that kept her sane.

She had been taken to task by James, who had been complained to by Miss Bradley, for going against her during lessons by whisking them and Percy away on a walk up to Stockghyll Force and on another bright May afternoon to the top of Wansfell Pike.

James had not been too hard on her, understanding that the lives of the Deans, all of them, which had been unfettered by authority for so long, were now vastly different, but she must realise that if they were to have any sense of discipline and the education that had been so lacking in their lives, then she must leave them alone during lessons. At the weekend they would all get in the Rolls-Royce and he would take them wherever they pleased, not realising in the newness and softness of his love, and the fulfilling of it, that it was precisely this they did not want. They did not want Mr Buchanan. They wanted Lucy and the old ways they had known before Papa died, and so did she.

She had tried to understand and be patient, but this with the suffragette movement was not something she was prepared to abandon.

She said so, and was alarmed by the savagery in his voice.

'I'm warning you, Lucy, this has got to stop. I will not have my guests insulted as you have done this evening. You are my wife and—'

'And so I'm to be allowed no opinion or views of my own.'

'Not if it means airing them at parties to people who don't want to hear them and are offended by them. D'you hear? You are to keep your beliefs about the damned suffragettes to yourself in future. Follow the example of the other ladies and talk about . . . well, whatever it is they talk about but the word suffragette is not to be mentioned in my presence again. Is that understood?'

He had forbidden her to speak of it again but not for a moment did it occur to him to forbid her to go to the suffragette headquarters in Compston Street.

CHAPTER TWELVE

The first Lucy heard of the trouble in Europe was at the WSPU headquarters in Compston Street where she intended to go as often as she could, which meant, of course, when she could get out of the house without some domestic trivia interfering with her plans. Some days, of course, when she could not avoid it, she was compelled, because of her position as the wife of James Buchanan, to visit Franny, or one of James's other female relatives on the interminable round of 'calling' which was the practice of ladies of their social class. They told one another they were only doing what they saw as their duty in shaping James's young and somewhat unconventional wife into the kind of lady they themselves were, putting themselves out in their efforts, for they felt they owed it to James. Often enough, during the period of what was known in their circle as 'afternoon calls' when the ladies were either called upon, or called on other ladies, they would be told that she was out. Simply that! Out! Dixon, his face managing to be expressionless and yet at the same time sorrowful, could not even say where she had gone when asked by Mrs Joan Buchanan, or Mrs Janet Gunson, or Mrs Anne Mounsey, for one minute she was there in her small sitting-room at the back of the house and the next, vanished and only she knew to where.

It was hard work, for plainly she was not interested in becoming 'one of them' but they struggled on, for surely, very soon, James would get her with child and she would be forced to confine herself to the suitable activities they themselves followed. It was known she was very fond of walking, or even fell climbing and had been seen once or twice on that ancient bicycle of hers in Ambleside, but where she ended up was anybody's guess. They would have been appalled if they had known.

They were delighted and quite astonished to see her at the headquarters of the WSPU in Compston Street.

'Lucy . . . oh, I beg your pardon, should I call you Mrs Buchanan now?' Letty cried, seemingly none the worse for her brush with the law. They had all heard of Lucy's splendid marriage and might she not now be, in her elevated position, different to the young girl who had offered her services several months ago?

'Lord, no! I'm only sorry I haven't been able to call sooner but . . . well, my father died, as perhaps you know. I . . . married Mr Buchanan and, naturally, have had to get my brothers and sisters settled in their new home, which took a while, but the fact that I'm married hasn't altered my interest in the suffragist movement. I'm still eager to help in any way I can so, if there's anything, anything at all . . .'

Her voice trailed away uncertainly as she became aware that she and Letty were not the only ones in the room. There appeared to be at least half a dozen other women, young women, crammed into the small space which was now furnished with not one but two tables, on one of which two of them were clacking away on rather ancient typewriters.

Or at least they had been until she walked into the room when every head turned to look at her. She was clad in the smart cycling outfit she now, as Mrs James Buchanan, could afford to buy. The short jacket was in a very fine, pale grey wool, the lapels edged in caramel and the ankle-length skirt had an inverted pleat down the centre of the back, the inside of which was lined again with caramel. The buttons fastening the jacket and those on the sleeve were covered in caramel-coloured satin. She wore a silk scarf at her neck and a small, caramel-coloured beret skewered by an unstable hatpin to her slipping hair. She looked quite enchanting, flushed and eager, and the women stared, mesmerised as most plain or ordinary women are by such loveliness.

She smiled shyly at each one, wondering why she should feel shy. Perhaps because this was so important to her, so new, so sacred almost and these young women already had a kind of mystique about them that made her at the same time feel envious and humble. They were working girls, the decent but plain clothes they wore told her that, probably from a farm or a factory. They appeared to be addressing envelopes and wrappers. One was carefully turning the handle of a machine with a roller which, as it revolved, printed some message on to a sheet of paper. There was a stack of newspapers piled at the end of the table where the girls were addressing envelopes, tied about with string which Letty had been about to cut and Lucy could see that it contained copies of the *Suffragette*, probably just come off the London train.

The last woman, a bit older than the rest, very obviously came from a different background. Though she was painfully thin, gaunt even, and though she smiled politely, her manner was uncertain and her movements weak as she reached for a pile of envelopes which the other girls had addressed. It was her clothing, obviously expensive and well made, if ill-fitting, and a certain manner the other girls lacked that told Lucy she was a lady. The daughter of a gentleman in fact. When she smiled at her Lucy saw that one of her teeth was broken.

'We're always glad of help, Lucy, and believe me there is always something to be done. Those handbills, for instance. The ones Connie is printing. They need to be handed out by the weekend. Outside the railway station at Windermere is a good spot and at the gates outside the grounds after the football match on Saturday. In fact anywhere there's to be a crowd. Connie and Isobel, this is Isobel,' indicating a tall, ginger-haired girl with a mass of freckles across her nose who looked up from the envelopes and smiled again at Lucy, 'and that's Connie,' nodding at the young girl on the printing machine who bobbed her head at the elegant Mrs Buchanan, 'will go up to Windermere and to Bowness, but Edwina, she's not here by the way since she was needed in her father's shop. I believe you met her the last time you were here. Well, she's looking for some help at the match at Grasmere. It's only a couple of local teams but there'll be a big turnout and wherever there's a crowd we aim to be there. And there's to be a procession in Fellthwaite in a week's time, something to do with a Rose Queen, Sunday school, you know the sort of thing and there's bound to be a good crowd.'

'This Saturday, you say?' Lucy's face creased with anxiety and she wondered how on earth she was possibly to elude her husband on a Saturday, a day on which he expected her to be home to entertain him, and also and more importantly, the day Miss Bradley did not come for lessons and Edward was home from school. The children would be looking forward to spending some time with her, which was really not a problem since they would think it no end of fun passing out the propaganda handbills, but escaping from James might be more difficult.

Her glance wandered round the office as though looking for illumination. There had been shelves put up since last she was here and they were stacked with books, of what sort she didn't know. To the pale brown wall there had been added a notice-board on which dozens of pieces of paper were pinned, including a map of the area. It seemed the Ambleside branch of the WSPU was getting organised. There was even a small fire flickering in the grate and on the wall, added to the posters she had noticed the last time she was here, was one of Christabel Pankhurst and above the mantelpiece a framed photograph of Emmeline Pankhurst.

'But first, before you decide, won't you speak to Anne?' Letty put her hand on the pale young woman's shoulder and in the gesture was pride and awe, some tribute she seemed to be paying her, and a deep affection. 'Anne is up here to recuperate. She has just been released from prison.'

There was a deep and reverent silence and for the first time Lucy noticed the small purple, white and green brooch pinned to the young woman's lapel, shaped like a broad arrow, which proclaimed she had been imprisoned for her beliefs.

'She needs some rest and the sort of food that will give her back her strength, don't you, Anne, and so we are proud to look after her. She is staying with Edwina and is supposed to remain in bed until lunchtime but she insists on coming over here.'

'Please, Letty, don't go on so. I'm feeling much better and besides, I'm only sitting here sorting envelopes.' Anne laughed, and as she did so Lucy could see that her mouth was half healed at the corners as though she had suffered some injury. She turned to Lucy and held out her hand. 'I'm Anne Longman and it's a pleasure to meet you, Mrs Buchanan.'

'Lucy, please.' Lucy was ready to kneel down and pay homage to this woman whose body had been violated in the cause for other women. She felt a great need sweep over her to break down and weep for her suffering. For what Lucy saw as her nobility of purpose and for her cheerfulness and fortitude in the face of it. Would she, Lucy, be able to laugh and carry on with her life if she had been subjected to the indignities, no, the cruelties which had been imposed on Anne Longman? She hoped so, that is if she was ever allowed to fight for the cause, which seemed unlikely in the state of marriage that now tied her down.

'Oh, Miss Longman—'

'It's Mrs, Lucy, and please, call me Anne.'

'Mrs!' Lucy gasped. 'Does your husband not object to your involvement in the movement?'

'No, he doesn't. I'm one of those fortunate women whose husband does not think women have second-class brains. He is an active member of the Men's League for Women's Suffrage and supports us one hundred per cent in our fight.'

'When ... what ... where ...' Lucy was longing to hear more but she felt she could not pry into the obviously painful experience Anne Longman had suffered, but it seemed that Anne was, if not happy to tell her, then felt she owed it to them.

'I was involved in the riot, as they called it, at the Constitution Hill gate of Buckingham Palace. We were attempting to get our deputation in to the king with a petition but he refused to see us, so we marched on the gates. Our object was to demand votes for women and to protest against the torture inflicted on us in prison. We were met by ranks of the police, both mounted and on foot, who brutally ill-used us, and I mean in a sexual way, Lucy.' Her voice was quiet and detached as though she were telling them of some happening on the other side of the world which had not affected her in any way.

Connie, who could have been no more than seventeen, had begun to weep silently.

'Dear God ...'

'He did not come to our aid, Lucy. Mrs Pankhurst tried to but an inspector carried her bodily away to a waiting motor car, taking her off

227

to Holloway. We tried to climb the gates of the palace but the police were too strong for us. Sixty-six of us, and two men, were arrested. We refused to give our names and so we were allotted numbers when we came before the magistrate at Bow Street. I was number thirty-six,' she said simply. 'We were dragged and kicked and . . .well, eventually bound over. I received a month's hard labour and, when I refused food and water I was . . . forcibly fed. That's where I got this broken tooth.' She smiled to show them and reached for another bundle of envelopes while the other young women, who, they told themselves, would die for the cause that was so important to them, wondered if they could be as stoic, as calm, as accepting of what was almost rape.

'Mrs Longman . . . Anne, if there's anything I can do. . .' to help you, to help the brave women who fought alongside you, to help this cause which had become almost holy to her, Lucy wanted to say but her throat was clogged with suppressed tears and she wondered despairingly if she was ever to be of service to them if the smallest thing was to reduce her to tears. Not that what Anne Longman had suffered was small, nor her recounting of it, but it seemed to Lucy that to be of any help, to be the sort of woman the movement needed, you had to bury all emotion and go coolly to war; was Lucy Buchanan capable of that with her tendency to feel so desperately the sympathy which, though worth while, clouded the mind which had to be clear?

'My dear, we all want to help and only a few weeks ago I would have encouraged you, all of you,' looking round the silently respectful circle of young women, 'to march, to break windows, to set fires and do any kind of damage, to property, not to people or animals, you understand, that would move our campaign forward, but I think we are going to have to put aside our struggle in what could be a greater struggle for mankind.'

Lucy looked about her at the faces of the other young women to see if they had understood Anne Longman's last remark but it seemed they were as bewildered as she was. Give up the struggle! Give up the struggle, she seemed to be saying, and after all she had suffered in its cause! What on earth could she mean? But Mrs Longman placidly continued to put the envelopes in neat piles, apparently the only work they would allow her to do.

'Mrs Longman . . . Anne,' Letty began, her plain face creased into lines of worry, for surely poor Mrs Longman must be deranged. Had she suffered more in prison than was shown on the surface? Beside her broken tooth, her torn mouth and the damage to her lungs and heart which five periods in gaol had caused, was her mind broken, too?

Anne Longman sighed and looked up at them. 'I'm not saying you must shut down at once, for it might not come to it but it seems likely, or so my husband and men he is acquainted with are saying. I know you are planning a meeting at—where was it?—Millan's Park, a week on Saturday, and that you are hoping to have a well-known speaker. No, I'm not about to say her name lest it get about and she is arrested, but I think it likely it will be the last.'

'The last?' It seemed they could not get to grips with what she was saying, let alone what she meant by it and again she sighed.

229

'You will have heard of the assassination of the Archduke Franz Ferdinand last month, will you not?'

Yes, they all nodded their heads in agreement but what, in heaven's name, was that to do with the WSPU, their young, anxious expressions asked. None of them was well educated, not even Lucy, for her education had been sketchy at best. They could, of course, read and write, but the details of what went on outside their small world, unless it was to do with the WSPU, did not greatly concern them.

'That shot was considered a challenge to Austro-Hungary's position as the ruler of Bosnia.'

'Bosnia?' one of them whispered in a total state of stupor.

'Yes. It is a challenge to its prestige as one of the Great Powers and there will be repercussions.'

'Repercussions?' It was as though they could, in their lack of understanding, only repeat whatever Anne Longman said.

'Yes, military repercussions. Relations between France and Germany are not good and now this Balkan unrest has exacerbated the situation. It is the belief of gentlemen with whom my husband is associated, and indeed in the world of business, that that shot fired in Sarajevo will be the first to ring round the world. There are, of course, many instabilities in European society, far too many to enumerate here, but when they erupt, as it seems they are about to do, there will be war.'

'War, between who?'

It did not seem to matter who asked the question.

'A European war in which Britain will be

involved, but come, we must not cross the bridge until we come to it, as they say. Let us hope it will blow over and in the meanwhile we women must continue our fight. Pass out your handbills, send your letters, have your meeting next week and pray that I am wrong.'

*   *   *

The children were so excited she was afraid it would be noticed by the servants, or even by James on the Friday evening before the Saturday she and Edwina were to bicycle to Grasmere to the football match.

'But what are we going to do there?' Percy, who had never been to a football match in his life, whispered in a voice that might have been heard in the next room. 'And why is it a secret?'

How could she tell them that if James heard about the expedition he would put a stop to it, probably confine them, and herself, to the house and her efforts to help the WSPU would be seriously impeded. Already she knew that her visits to Compston Street were risky, for he could put a stop to those as well if he found out from his cousins that his wife was very rarely where she was supposed to be.

She and James had settled into a polite but somewhat uneasy routine in those first weeks of their marriage. James was an early riser, sometimes leaving their bed at six in the morning so that she was allowed a blissful couple of hours without his dominating male invasion of it and he spent many of his evenings in his study with what appeared to be a mountain of paperwork in front of him. She

231

was still awkward and uncertain in his nightly embraces which were often prolonged and, on his part, accompanied by the most astonishing heaving and groaning, but she found if she lay still and let her mind drift off to some pleasant place, perhaps the top of Loughrigg Fell, or even to the office in Compston Street, she could accommodate him without any undue stress.

Not once did it occur to her that her performance, or rather lack of it, might not suit her husband.

'I know women aren't supposed to like it, ladies, that is, but I had hoped that ... with time you might learn at least to hide your distaste,' he said brusquely to her one night as he rolled away from her submissive body.

She was astonished, sitting up in bed to stare down at him, her naked body shielded by the mass of her tumbled hair. She looked quite glorious, her flesh flushed and rosy, though she was as untouched by what had just happened as a virgin. James felt his heart constrict with his love for her. He had been tolerant, knowing that what he did, no matter how much care he took to please her, did not touch the core of her, that sweet centre of a woman which comes alive when a man loves her. He had accepted her stoicism, believing that if he was patient, one night when it was over she would not turn away with a small sigh of relief as she did now but would cling to him, stretching languorously in the aftermath. One night he would awaken that slumbering sexuality which he was certain lived within her. He was painstaking in his effort to please her body, to please her unawakened heart, to please the woman in her with

232

his caresses, his hidden love which she knew nothing about. Surely, even if she did not love him with her emotions her ripe young body would instinctively respond to his, but so far the best he could hope for was that she would not yawn as she turned away from him. It was becoming too much for him. He sometimes thought he would leave her alone, sleep in another bed, find a mistress to slake his thirst which never seemed satisfied but then, how would she conceive a child which he hoped might turn her to him, bind her to him.

'I don't understand you, James,' she said to him now. 'Am I not . . . not more than happy to . . . to make love in our bed?'

'Is that what it is?'

'What d'you mean?' She was clearly perplexed.

'I mean, Mrs Buchanan, that what we do in this bed has nothing to do with love.' He lay on his back, his arm across his face, his hard, muscled body spreadeagled, one knee slightly bent. He was a fine-bodied man and she had become used to him and to his nakedness, but for one inexplicable moment she had a strange feeling that she wanted to . . . to lean over him, to put a hand to his face, to remove his arm from it and see what he was hiding underneath. Then it was gone, that feeling, and indignation came to take its place.

'I have not deceived you, if that's what you're saying, James. I have never professed to love you, nor you me. It seemed that it was a marriage of convenience. Convenient to us both. Have you changed your mind? Though if you have I don't see what we can do about it.

'No.'

'Well then, we must go on as we are. If there is . . .

233

well, something you wish me to do . . . more than I do now . . . in bed, I mean,' ducking her head in some embarrassment, 'then please tell me.'

'And you'll see what you can do to gratify me, is that it?'

'Well . . . yes.'

'Thank you, my dear, that is most generous of you but really, don't trouble yourself. It is of no consequence.'

'Well, then . . .'

He rose suddenly and strode across the room to the fireplace where he kept a box of cigars. Taking one from it he lit it, leaning indolently in his nakedness against the mantelpiece, then, reaching for the silk dressing-gown which he had flung over the chair, he shrugged into it. His face was shadowed though a lamp was lit beside the bed, for he would not make love in the dark like some peasant, he had told her, and she could not read the expression in it.

'I'm not tired,' he said abruptly. His efforts had not only not satisfied him, he was telling her, they had not wearied him. 'I'll go downstairs for a while.'

She sighed and shrugged as he left the room.

And so, like conspirators in a plot that was to change the world as most knew it, she and the children were able to creep down the back stairs the next day disturbing no one except young Elsie who was on her knees at the kitchen fire raking out the ashes. She started violently as they giggled their way into the kitchen, leaping to her feet and spilling them on Ivy Bunting's rag rug on which no feet but Ivy's were ever allowed to rest. Ivy's chair, the rockers of which just touched its edge and

234

where Ivy 'took the weight off her tootsies', rocked vigorously as though Ivy had just sunk into it and Elsie squeaked in alarm.

'Oh, miss, you didn't half give me a turn. I thought it were Mrs Burns, though she'd not be about at this time of the morning.'

Lucy put her finger to her lips. 'Ssh, Elsie, not another word,' though there was no one yet up to hear another word. 'We're ... we're off on an adventure so not a whisper about seeing us, d'you hear?'

'We're going to a football match, Elsie,' Percy told her excitedly, doing his best to hold the squirming little body of Thimble who, though nearly a year older than when James Buchanan had first set eyes on him, was still just as daft.

'A football match!' Elsie's eyes were round as saucers. 'Eeh, well, I never ...'

'But you're not to tell anyone, Elsie,' Edward, who had been given instructions on his part of the day's proceedings, informed her importantly.

'What time's kick-off then?' for it was barely six fifteen in the morning.

'Oh, not for hours yet but there's a lot still to be done.'

'I see,' though Elsie clearly didn't.

Mass football matches between Lakeland villages were a common custom and the annual battle between the Rovers and the Wanderers was to take place on a wide stretch of ground on the shore of Grasmere Lake.

They were quite a little procession, she and Edwina, whom they had picked up in Ambleside, Edward and Margaret, Emily and Percy on their brand-new machines. At least she and the children

235

were on new bicycles, for with his characteristic generosity, or was it indifference, James had told her to go ahead and buy them something decent since he was ashamed of the contraptions Bibby and Edward had so ingeniously put together. Edward's had a big basket on the front where Thimble, for all the world like a guide directing his party, sat and stared ahead of them.

They arrived in time to sit with the rest of the crowd and eat the picnic which, the night before, Buffy had prepared for them, having been let in on the plans, though she could not agree with them, and telling the servants that there was to be a picnic the next day. It was not a lie. She just was not to divulge where it was to take place.

The match was in full swing when they began to move about the noisy crowd handing out the handbills on which was printed 'Votes for Women' and in smaller letters the information that there would be a suffrage meeting and demonstration next Saturday at Millan's Park, Ambleside, at which a well-known suffragette was to speak. The men, for there were very few women interested in the free-for-all which the match rapidly turned into, took the handbills without looking at them, most of them stuffing them in their pockets, peering round the two women and, strangely, the children who handed them out, for they were blocking their view.

'Votes for women,' Edwina cried above the uproar and Lucy, taking courage from her, did the same and even Margaret took up the cry.

'Nay, tha'should be ashamed,' one man retorted, 'a little lass like thee. Get 'ome ter tha' mam.'

'She's in heaven,' Margaret answered shortly, to the man's discomfort, moving on to the next

236

outstretched hand. The men were quite flabbergasted by the sight of pretty little girls like her and Emily passing out the leaflets and were inclined to take them before they were aware of what they were.

'Votes for women,' Lucy shouted, taking no notice of the pushing and shoving that was beginning to take place and when she fell into the mud that the struggling players had churned up she took the first hand to reach out to help her.

She looked up into the appalled face of Ben Buchanan.

CHAPTER THIRTEEN

'I don't hold with it and I never will,' Ivy Bunting declared stoutly to her crony, Maud Burns. I don't hold with what them suffragette women get up to and I reckon they deserve to be behind bars, but to see the young mistress dragged by the scruff of her neck ...'

'Oh, hardly, Mrs Bunting.'

'As near as makes no difference, Mrs Burns. Up all them stairs, Dixon said, and her tripping up on each one and begging him to stop and let her get her breath and them children all crying, especially them little ones and that damn dog yapping its daft head off. Dixon said—'

'Mrs Bunting, this is really none of our business and besides ... Mrs Burns nodded her dignified head imperceptibly in the direction of the kitchen maids who were standing about clutching mixing bowls and saucepans, spoons and baking pans, their mouths agape, excited by the commotion though as yet they were not sure what it was all about. They had been busy at the tasks Mrs Bunting had set them in preparation for Mr and Mrs Buchanan's dinner when it all started.

Actually, if they were to be accurate, it had started at breakfast-time when it was discovered that not only Mrs Buchanan, but the children had mysteriously disappeared. Gone on a picnic, their companion—what else could you call her since she did no work in the house?—Miss Tyson said when asked by Mr Buchanan, who was in a right paddy, according to Bridie, his face as black as thunder and on it an expression which boded ill for their mistress. There was a whisper, a very quiet whisper since Mrs Burns didn't care for gossip, that the master had not spent the night where he usually spent it, which was in the mistress's bed, so what were they to make of that, they asked one another, in whispers, of course, and when young Elsie, who got on with her work and rarely offered an opinion about anything, reared up and told them to mind their own business they could not have been more surprised if the kitchen cat had spoken.

'"On a picnic?" says the master, glaring at Miss Tyson as if it were all her fault,' so said Bridie who was in the schoolroom at the time seeing to the coal scuttle. '"Where on a picnic and why wasn't I told about it?" says himself, and "I'm sure I don't know, sir," says Miss Tyson. "It is not my place to inform you of Mrs Buchanan's whereabouts," she says, bold as brass. "Is that so?" says the master. "Well, in future see to it that you make it your business." "I can't do that, sir. I'm sure if Mrs Buchanan wished you to know she would have told you."'

'Glory be to God,' said Bridie to the fascinated group of open-mouthed maidservants, smoothing her snowy white apron over her ample hips. She was all puffed up with a sense of her own importance at being the bearer of such exciting news. 'Didn't I think the master was goin' to land her one, him looking so wild, so he was, but I've got to hand it to her she stood up to him, the spalpeen, and didn't he storm out o' there like the divil himself was after him.'

Cook came upon them then, huddled in the scullery where none of them but Elsie should have been, and gave them the rounds of the kitchen, and since then they had hardly been able to get on with their work, constantly looking towards the kitchen door which led into the hall as they waited for news, wondering where Mrs Buchanan and those imps had got to.

Oh, yes, after being quiet and somewhat fearful at first in the home their sister's marriage had transferred them to, Mr Buchanan's new family had become imps again, reverting to their usual natures which was to be cheerful, noisy, teasing, always under your feet and invading the kitchens whenever they felt like it, begging for Mrs Bunting's chocolate shortbreads which, they said, were the best they had ever tasted. That Percy was a grand little lad, full of mischief, inquisitive and good-natured, and now that he had settled himself in, the pet of them all. The little girls were more subdued, but with lovely manners and willing to hold a conversation with any of them, seeing no difference between the servants and themselves, which Mrs Burns didn't like, of course. Master

239

Edward was at school during the week and they hadn't really got to know him as well as the other three but at the weekend he often led his brother and sisters into some devilish prank or other which would involve a great deal of noise, laughter, usually muck and often water, like the time they dammed the stream which ran at the back of the house. It had overflowed into the rockery, causing havoc and tormenting Clapcott, the gardener, into threatening to give his notice in at once. They built 'dens' where they shouldn't out of the wood he was sawing and chopping into neat piles for the winter fires, invading the mounds of branches and rubbish that he had stored after pruning ready to be turned into compost, for there was nothing ever wasted in his garden. They were harmless, the tricks they got up to, but sometimes Mr Buchanan, who was not used to such noise and exuberance, was heard to remonstrate with them, asking could they not find some quieter, less destructive pastime, because if they couldn't he could certainly find one for them. Perhaps a book in the schoolroom which was out of hearing of his study and had Edward done his homework? But they looked at him as though he were mad for suggesting such a thing on a lovely day like this and so did Mrs Buchanan. Even his own well-behaved dogs had got out of hand, racing round the garden in a barking circle of madness, no doubt spurred on by that Thimble, who even Mr Buchanan despaired of and who was as undisciplined as the children. Edward had discovered some great adventure books in Mr Buchanan's library, read apparently by Mr Buchanan as a boy, though Edward found it hard to visualise such a thing, boys' tales that were good,

240

patriotic yarns. One was *With Roberts to Pretoria*, by G. A. Henty, which he and the others, under his direction, of course, played out in the gardens and woods surrounding Howethwaite. They were all cast in the roles of the brave heroes in the book, even the dogs, and the hullabaloo when the natives' uprising was in progress was enough to waken the dead, Mrs Bunting said faintly. And then, naturally, when the heroes and natives were hungry, for didn't adventures give you a tremendous appetite, they were inclined to invade her kitchen on the lookout for 'rations'.

At other times it was the Boxer Rebellion in China with Edward as the brave Sir Claude MacDonald who had held the garrison at Pekin for fifty-five days, with Percy as his trusty captain and the girls, their hair in pigtails, as the dastardly Chinese. There was the Relief of Ladysmith, in which battalions of the Border Regiment, stationed at Carlisle, took part. They were events that happened over ten years ago but they still thrilled small boys the length and breadth of the land with their daring and excitement and the greatness of the British, which they were proud to be.

Was it any wonder then that Mr Buchanan shut himself up in his study with the door closed and strict orders that he was not to be disturbed, which was probably why he didn't miss them until the morning was well on. The empty chair at the breakfast table in which Mrs Buchanan usually sat was not commented upon and Dimity had her own theory about that. She had not seen Mr Buchanan leave his wife's bedroom the night before, nor Mrs Buchanan's escape this morning but it didn't need a detective to realise that only one body had slept in their marriage bed!

The arrival of Mr Buchanan, Mr Ben Buchanan, in his dashing blue, Prince Henry Vauxhall, the motor car overflowing with what seemed to be a dozen children, plus Mrs Buchanan, brought their Mr Buchanan to the wide front door where he elbowed Dixon aside as though he were no more than the gardener's lad. Mrs Buchanan looked as though she'd been dragged through a hedge backwards and then across a muddy field, Win, the parlour maid reported. Win had just been about to tackle the dining-room table ready for dinner when the motor car drew up and, hoping Mr Dixon wouldn't spot her, she hung around in the dining-room doorway to see what was to happen next.

It was plain Mr Buchanan was so stunned he didn't know what to say, but only for a moment or two, then his voice rang out, carrying to the far corners of the house, the garden and even into the bit of woodland where Clapcott and Bertie, who was his lad and learning the trade, lifted their heads from the wood they were peacefully sawing and stared at one another in amazement.

'What the bloody hell's this?' James Buchanan roared and for the space of a second, perhaps two, Lucy felt her heart falter in her breast. Then Emily began to cry broken-heartedly since Mr Buchanan was an imperious figure who did no more than nod when she happened to pass him on the stairs and she was frightened by the sheer volume of his bellow. It was hard to recall sometimes that day when he had taken them all up on to the fells, carrying Percy on his shoulders, telling them about the plants in the verge, the birds in the sky, smiling a little as though he were enjoying it as much as they had done. That was before he and Lucy were married, of course, so perhaps that was where the difference lay, though she didn't understand why.

Lucy drew her protectively to her side. 'There's no need to yell, James,' she told him calmly. It can all be explained but first I must get out of these clothes.'

'Never mind that, woman. Where in hell have you been in that dress? You look as though you've taken part in a rugby scrum.'

'In a way, I have, James, but can we not discuss this in private?' she asked him patiently, dabbing with her little lace handkerchief at the mud on her dress, fruitlessly as it happened.

James ignored her. 'Ben,' turning to his cousin, 'can you explain to me what my wife is doing in your motor car on a Saturday afternoon with her gown, which I'm sure wasn't cheap and which I'm also sure I paid for, totally ruined?'

'Oh, no, James, it can be sponged clean and—'

'Will you stop babbling, Lucy, and explain to me what has happened to you?'

'I will if you'll let me—'

'I . . . I found her in Grasmere, old chap,' Ben interrupted, looking uncomfortable as though somehow it might be his fault but he felt so bloody sorry for James who, against all their advice, had taken this young, independent and strong-minded woman as his wife. He would never forget his sense of shock and outrage when he saw who it was who was handing out those damned suffragette handbills, and she wasn't even *his* wife! And then to fall so ignominiously in front of Frank Askew and Edwin Kendall who, like himself, were keen on watching the Lakeland village football matches,

243

and naturally it would be all round the district by morning that the newest member of his family was showing them up once more. The party when she had been so forceful about women's rights had not been forgotten!

James whirled about, his hand to his forehead, then, spotting Win in the doorway of the dining-room, snarled at her to get back to her duties, ready to vent his spleen on whoever got trapped in his line of vision. This wasn't a bloody peep show, he told her as she scuttled away, and would someone stop that bloody dog from barking or he'd have the thing shot.

At once Percy joined his sister, exploding into tears, wailing in terror, clutching the excited Thimble to his chest and dripping enormous tears into his fur. Margaret was trembling, leaning against Lucy, who was doing her best to hold her family in her arms and Edward, braving the lion who roared on the step, moved forward courageously, somewhat in the manner of Roberts of Pretoria.

'There is no need to shout at Lucy, Mr Buchanan. We have done no wrong. My sister, as a member of the Women's Social and Political Union, was passing out handbills, and we were helping her. It is not against the law.'

'Is it not? You know the law then, do you, lad? Have you heard of disturbing the peace which is an offence for which the offender can be given a prison sentence? But you see that is not the issue here, though that is bad enough. Your sister is also my wife and she knows my views on suffragism. She also knows that, as my wife—'

'But, sir—'

'Damn you, don't interrupt me when I'm speaking.'

'I was only going to say—'

'I would be much obliged if you would say nothing. Take your brother and sisters up to your rooms and stay there until I send for you.'

'Stop it, James. How dare you speak to Edward like that.' Lucy's face was brilliant with anger and her eyes had narrowed to pure slits of gold, venomous as a lioness whose cubs are in danger. It is not his fault. If there is any fault it is mine but I won't admit even to that. I was merely—'

'Hell and damnation, woman, will you be quiet? Can you not see that you are no longer Miss Lucy Dean whose father allowed her to do as she pleased. You are Mrs James Buchanan, a woman of some standing in the community since you are my wife. We are an old, respected family and I will not have you cavorting about the countryside as you did before you married me.'

'And I rue the day I did that.'

He stood there as though he had been struck by a bolt of lightning. Every drop of colour drained from his face and for a second Lucy felt remorse race through her, since she did not mean it. She was not unhappy with James, since he was good to her and the children, if aloof. He gave nothing of himself, his inner self, to any of them, not even her and only for those few moments in their bed when he totally lost control was he not in cool command of himself. He did not care what she spent, on the house if she fancied anything new, he told her, on her clothes which, as his wife, must be tasteful and expensive, on the children—which was the best of all—new shoes, bicycles, pretty dresses for the girls,

245

books and toys and games, and he did his best to accustom himself to the uproar which often invaded his previously quiet home. Even Thimble was tolerated in the schoolroom where he was learning to lie peacefully on a rug until the children were free to romp with him, and in Percy or Edward's bedroom at night. His own dogs were not allowed upstairs, sleeping in a tumble of legs and tails at the foot of the stairs where he and Lucy left them at night, waiting for him when he came down to breakfast. He had made many concessions to accommodate her family, many compromises and she would always be eternally grateful to him.

'I'm sorry,' she whispered into the dreadful silence. 'I didn't mean . . .'

As fast as it had left the blood rushed back into James's face, even seeming to leak into his fine grey eyes, but he had himself clamped tightly, his lips, which had been inclined to snarl in temper, folded into a rigid line of restraint. He spoke through them almost as though they were stitched together.

'Thank you, Ben, I'm much obliged to you. Give my regards to Joan.' Ben was dismissed and he knew it and what's more was glad to go.

'Right, old chap. Perhaps we'll see you for dinner one evening?'

'I'm sure you will.'

Ben climbed awkwardly into his motor car and it was plain he was not quite sure whether he should bid farewell to Lucy but he decided against it in the circumstances. He drove off quickly, leaving the tense, frightened group huddled in a protective circle about one another and up on the step his cousin James who, he told Joan later, he was sure

246

meant to beat the living daylights out of his beautiful young wife.

Then, 'You heard what I said, Edward. Take your brother—'

'Please, James, don't punish them. They only did what I asked them to do. They are not to blame.'

'Will you allow me to speak, madam. You and I will have this out in private but they cannot just hang about here while we do so. I am not about to punish them as I am perfectly well aware that whatever it was they did you put them up to it.'

'Oh, yes,' she told him eagerly, 'so please—'

'Then they will go upstairs now.'

'May I not . . .'

'You may not.'

'But what about our bicycles? They were left . . .'

'They will be collected.'

Without another word James moved down the steps and took her arm, just above the elbow. She did her best to resist, to cling to her brothers and sisters as though still wanting to protect them against whatever it was James was to do to them, but he was too strong for her, dragging her up the steps and into the hallway where they followed in a pathetic straggle. Dixon still hovered there lest he be needed. He had not been dismissed by his master, after all, and besides, Mrs. Burns and Mrs Bunting would be agog to hear what had happened. He would not deign to speak to the maidservants, of course, or even Fallows, the footman, but they would all know about this within the hour.

'Please, James, there is no need . .

'It seems there is every need, Lucy,' he told her as she pulled back from him but he continued his steady progress up the stairs where she was forced to follow him, tripping on the hem of her ruined gown until even Dixon felt sorry for her in her humiliation.

The door to their bedroom closed with a crash and the children, continuing to weep as though their hearts were broken, gazed up the stairs. Not until Miss Tyson limped hurriedly down to collect them did they move.

James released her arm the moment they were alone. He walked to the window and stared out sightlessly but not by the flicker of an eyelash or a tremble to his voice did he allow her to see the pain she had inflicted on him with her admission that she was sorry she had married him. It had been as though she had viciously thrust a serrated knife into his heart and then, for good measure, turned it round in the wound. He felt as though he were bleeding to death inside. He had always known that she did not love him but their life since their marriage had been relatively pleasant, and she was his. He lived on hope that one day, he would be hers. Now that they were alone the madness had left him and he wanted to turn and plead with her not to go against him but he must not. He must be strong, upright, dignified, the master of this house and of her. He loved her with a devastation that was crippling him but he must draw back from it or he would go insane.

He leaned for a moment more against the window, his hands on the windowsill, then turned to her, his composure complete. He was almost undone once more, for she stood with her back to the door, her hand on the door handle as though ready for a quick getaway should he turn violent, but her golden eyes were fixed on him with a defiance which told him he had really not won a victory here today.

Nevertheless he must let her know that this with the suffragette movement could not go on.

'You must stop this, you know that, don't you?'

'Stop what?' Her eyes held his steadily.

'Don't pretend, Lucy. You know what I mean. As my wife you cannot associate with these women and their movement.'

'Why not? There is nothing immoral in it. It is something in which I believe. I always have done and you knew that when you married me.'

'I must confess it did not enter my head that you would become a member. I did not even know that there was a branch in this area. Nevertheless, you must finish with it. I do not believe, like a vast number of other men, that women should have the vote.'

'Why not, for God's sake? What are you afraid of? That we will take over the government?'

'Now you are being ridiculous, which just proves my case that women should—'

'I won't give it up, James. The moment you go out of this house I shall cycle down to Ambleside and do whatever they ask me to do, whatever I am able to do.'

'No, Lucy, you will not.'

'How will you stop me?'

'I will stop you, believe me. There are the children . . .'

She looked at him, aghast. 'You would blackmail me with my own brothers and sisters? You would stoop so low?'

'I will do whatever I have to, my dear. So, now, will you dress yourself for dinner.'

'James, I beseech you . . .'

'No, don't.'

'I won't be—'

'Yes, you will, Lucy. I am the master in this house and my word is the word that is obeyed.'

'Damn you to hell, James Buchanan. I hope God strikes you dead and that you rot there for eternity.'

'I probably shall, my dear. Now, shall we get ready for dinner?'

*   *   *

No one knew what went on in the bedroom the master and mistress shared but it was as though whatever it was had been accepted by them both, for they came down to dinner together in full evening dress, though it was noticed the mistress's face still bore signs of strain. Her gown was of barley-coloured georgette, which was the very newest fabric of the year, a beautifully draped but very simple style in which she looked quite glorious. She wore no jewellery and her long, creamy neck was graceful, the stalk on which her lovely head swayed as she nodded smilingly to Dixon and Fallows. The bodice of the gown was cut very low and Dixon noticed that she had a gauzy scarf tucked about her shoulders and into the neckline which rather spoiled the effect. The master must have insisted on it, he whispered later to Mrs Burns and Mrs Bunting, for he swore it would have revealed more of her . . . ahem . . . bosom than was modest.

He was right, for when he turned from the sideboard where he was serving the first course he nearly dropped the plate of Dover soles *à la crème* in her lap. She had removed the scarf, flinging it to the back of her chair with a movement of pure defiance. Though the master's lips tightened, he said nothing.

* * *

On the following Saturday, the day on which Lucy had planned to go to the rally that was to be held in Millan's Park in Ambleside and where a notable member of the movement was to speak, among others, she was prevented from doing so by the fact that this was the day on which Miss Charlotte Gibson was to marry Doctor Paul Buchanan. Even she, despite the defiance she had flung in James's face the week before, could not refuse to go since this was a member of the family who was to be married. Besides, she had the feeling James would simply have taken her arm as he had done last week and dragged her there.

Charlotte Gibson looked simply magnificent in her wedding gown which must have cost the earth, the lady guests whispered to one another. Her bridegroom, who was as handsome as all the Buchanans, seemed somewhat unnecessary beside her as she bowed from a carriage drawn by four white horses, as they drove away from the church where the bells pealed out to let the world know that Miss Charlotte Gibson had herself a husband at last. The wedding breakfast was meant to overwhelm and overawe the guests, some of whom were of the nobility, and it did that all right, spread out in a marquee on the lawn at Ravenscourt. There were silver trays overflowing with champagne, mountains of confectionery, a wedding cake weighing at least a ton, Franny whispered to Lucy, making her laugh, the whole spectacle decorated with sprays of white roses and white and silver satin ribbon. The ladies were elegant in their wedding finery of georgette and silk, satin and velvet, on their heads enormous flower gardens of roses of pink and white. Parasols twirled, as the weather was kind and the sun shone from a cloudless blue sky, and all Lucy could think of was the rally at Millan's Park, of Letty and Eddy, of Connie and Isobel and Betty, and of Anne Longman who was, if she was strong enough to speak, to tell the massed crowds what she had suffered in prison.

But instead there was Charlotte, Mrs Paul Buchanan, a plain gold ring on one hand given her by her husband and a diamond cluster on the other, given her by her father. She circled among her guests with quite royal composure, stopping even to speak to the James Buchanans, allowing her triumphant gaze to travel up and down Lucy Buchanan as though she were surprised to see her in such an unbecoming outfit. She would show them, her gaze seemed to say. She would be the most successful young hostess in the district and if Lucy thought she had caught the most eligible bachelor in Ambleside, Charlotte meant to show her that she was mistaken.

She was surprised and more than a little peeved when Mrs James Buchanan turned away in total disinterest, even stifling a small yawn. A yawn Charlotte Buchanan would not forget!

CHAPTER FOURTEEN

'Is there going to be a war, James?' Lucy asked her husband on 29 July 1914.

They were eating breakfast, just the two of them, for this was not one of the days when he allowed the children to eat with them.

He had been quieter than usual since the conflict which had erupted on the day Ben brought her home from Grasmere, more distant, less inclined to engage her in conversation at mealtimes and sometimes she thought he forgot she was even there, as now, surprised when she spoke. The question of her brothers and sisters and their banishment to the schoolroom for meals had been one that had been a thorn in her side from the day she and James were married, but just recently, ever since the fierce dissension over her involvement with the suffrage movement, she had kept what she liked to call 'her head down', reluctant to arouse more disharmony between them. When she had suggested that, perhaps on a Saturday when the children had no lessons, they might all breakfast together, he appeared to be amenable to the idea, providing they were well behaved and didn't chatter. After all, they had to learn to take their meals with adults at some time in their lives, but it was not a success. The girls and Percy were intimidated by him, and Edward resentful, for he could not forgive Mr Buchanan's treatment of his sister on that fateful day. They were so silent James told them that unless they had something to say they might be excused.

They had fled like rabbits let out of a cage and so far Lucy had not repeated the experiment.

He glanced up from the newspaper he was reading and regarded her as though he were wondering if she was capable of understanding even if he explained it to her.

'I am aware that there is some trouble—in the Balkans, is it?—and that hostilities have been threatened for weeks,' she continued. 'Yesterday the Austrians declared war on Serbia, so what does that mean?'

If he was surprised that she had such a grasp of the situation he did not show it. He put his paper down and looked at her in that cool, quizzical way he had, a look that seemed to ask some question though he himself did not know what it might be. He sighed, unaware that he had done so, and certainly not attributing it to the deep sadness that welled up in him whenever he looked at this beautiful, intelligent young woman he had married. He knew that she had again been to the WSPU headquarters which he had learned was in Compston Street, but only once, presumably to tell them that she could no longer help them, since her husband was forcing her to give it up by threatening her with some retaliation to her brothers and sisters. Not that she would tell them this. She was too loyal, even to him, and he was filled with sorrow that he had been forced to act as he had. He had had no choice, he knew that. The wife of a Buchanan could not go round acting like some shop girl or factory worker, displaying herself in public, holding herself open to public ridicule and humiliation. Oh, he knew that there were many ladies, real ladies with titles, who championed the cause, but he was appalled that their husbands allowed it.

She looked quite glorious. Breakfast was a casual meal at the weekends and they were both dressed in the casual country clothes that were customary among their class. Franny Buchanan had persuaded her to learn to ride and, finding to her surprise that she enjoyed it and what's more was good at it, she had had a stylish outfit made which was not at all what James's family thought was suitable. She refused absolutely to wear the shapeless apron skirt over breeches which was considered suitable, or the divided skirt which was the fashion, for ladies at any rate. She wore what he himself wore, specially made breeches with flaring wings and vigorously polished chestnut brown riding boots. As a concession to her sex and James's dignity, she had agreed to wear a slightly longer well-fitted tweed jacket, and a stunning little bowler hat. Before she went to the stable she was to have her hair smoothed into a net snood by Dimity so for the moment it was loose about her face and shoulders, falling down her back to the seat of the chair. Her jacket was flung carelessly on another chair and her breasts strained, nipples hard and proud as cherry stones, against the fine silk of her shirt. James had made love to her last night, and again this morning, for no matter what she thought of it, he could not get enough of her long and lovely body, but even so he could feel his own breeches becoming extremely uncomfortable as she leaned across the table for another slice of toast. He wondered, and not for the first time, why, in all these months, she had not conceived. God above, he had played his part, and so, he supposed, had she, opening herself to him willingly whenever he asked it of her, but in the three months since their marriage he had not got her with child.

It seemed he was making some decision, his face thoughtful, his eyes looking at something only he could see, then he spoke.

'I think there is, Lucy. Only a week ago the Austrians sent an ultimatum to Serbia demanding that anti-Austrian propaganda should be banned in Serbia and that the man behind the assassination of Archduke Franz Ferdinand be found and arrested. Well, to put it simply, there were disagreements too numerous to mention and yesterday the Austrians declared war on Serbia.'

'But how is that to affect us, and the rest of Europe?'

'That remains to be seen, but I'm afraid it will be like a row of dominoes, one toppling another, country after country until we are all involved.'

James was right. The next day, 30 July, Russia mobilised. Sir Edward Grey, who was the British Foreign Secretary, asked both France and Germany if they would observe Belgium's neutrality, to which France answered in the affirmative. The Germans remained silent and the Belgians ordered that mobilisation should begin the following day. On 1 August it was France's turn.

Bank holiday Monday, 3 August, was hot and still, and in England crowds of holidaymakers sweltered under a shimmering haze of sunshine which reddened their skins and peeled their noses, in blissful ignorance of the fact that Germany had declared war on France. The following day German forces marched into Belgium. The British issued mobilisation orders and the British

Ambassador in Berlin told the Chancellor that unless Germany withdrew its troops by midnight their countries would be at war with one another.

The Germans did not withdraw. It was war.

Six days later on 10 August the government released all suffragette prisoners on the understanding that there would be no more violence.

Despite what her husband might say, that day Lucy walked into Ambleside, making her way to the WSPU headquarters in Compston Street. She had read the news in James's copy of *The Times* but the report had said little else and she was eager to get more details.

She took the path through the small wood at the back of Howethwaite, dressed in her stout walking boots and a dark green gaberdine divided skirt that was easy to stride out in. Her shirt was cream, a crisp lawn with a high neck and a pleated front. The sleeves were long and narrow and she unbuttoned the cuffs and pushed them up her arm, leaving them bare to the elbow. Around her waist was a broad leather belt, narrowing it even further and displaying her graceful, womanly hips.

Leaves were already beginning to fall, drifting in slow spirals to rest on the mossy ground as they waited for winter, but the great beech trees were still heavy with foliage. She gazed up into the great limbs spread above her head and the layer upon layer of the branches cast a deep shade over her bare head. She carried her hat, a straw boater which she would put on when she reached the town. She could hear the musical sound of running water, purling and trilling from the beck that ran towards the river at the back of the house. Crossing

257

the bridge that spanned the river, she continued up Clappergate until she reached the town, forgetting to pull down her sleeves and put on her boater, turning heads as she strode out, and drawing comments from one passer-by to another that James Buchanan's wife was still as unconventional as when she had been the Reverend Edward Dean's daughter!

She found Letty and Edwina industriously packing up the contents of the small room in which Lucy had hoped to achieve such great things in her own fight for the cause. The small printing press, the typewriters, all were consigned to cardboard boxes and the papers and books and posters were stacked in neat piles awaiting their turn. Already the room in which so much emotion had been aroused, emotions of hope and determination and unswerving dedication to the cause, looked strangely lifeless and Lucy supposed sadly that there were hundreds of such rooms and offices up and down the country, setting aside their own fight to take part in the much bigger one that was at hand.

'Aah, Lucy, there you are,' Letty said somewhat distantly, for none of them had completely understood why she had so suddenly dropped the work for which she appeared to have so much enthusiasm. 'Come to help?'

Lucy sensed the mockery but ignored it. She knew Letty had been disappointed in her and would have given a lot to explain that it was not her doing but she felt Letty would not sympathise so she let it go.

'I came to find out what's going to happen, Letty.'

'You mean to the movement? Well, as you can see we are disbanding this branch and obeying orders to take up war work and war relief work. Those who persecuted us now need our support and so Emmeline and Christabel have stopped campaigning for the vote and intend to throw themselves into anti-German propaganda and recruiting women war workers for the Home Front.' She lifted a box and threw it furiously into a corner as though she would dearly love to do the same with Emmeline and Christabel!

'What does that mean?'

'It means that women are to take over jobs to free the men who are to fight.'

'To fight?'

'Dear God, Lucy, are you not aware that already the BEF, the British Expeditionary Force, has sailed for France? Yesterday, in fact, and as far as we know could already be fighting. They are going to need women to be nurses, ambulance drivers, women for munitions and . . .'

'How do you know all this?' Lucy gasped.

Letty clicked her tongue in exasperation, pushing Lucy to one side and reaching for a pile of handbills, handbills which would no longer be passed out wherever a crowd massed.

'It doesn't take a great deal of imagination, Lucy, to know that where battles are, men will be wounded. As soon as this is packed up Eddy and I are off to volunteer.'

'Volunteer?' Lucy felt she was involved in some strange play in which everyone but her knew their lines.

So far Edwina had not spoken but now she turned a grave look on Lucy. 'We were sorry when

259

you said you felt you could no longer support us earlier in the year but ... well, we realised how difficult it must have been for you, having a husband and a family, but surely Mr Buchanan would not object to your doing some kind of war work. That is what Letty and I mean to do. Nursing. We are to go to the General Hospital in Carlisle tomorrow where we are to begin our training. They're taking us as paid probationers since neither Letty nor I can afford to work for nothing as the VADs do.'

'VADs?'

'Voluntary Aid Detachment. They're organised by the Red Cross and the Order of St John and, as you might imagine, they are recruiting girls from middle and upper-crust families.' She pulled a face, not of derision but of acceptance. 'As neither Letty nor I come from that sort of background, the sort of background where our families can support us, we must train as nurses. We've already been interviewed and as we're both over twenty-one we are to begin immediately.'

There was a deep silence except for the rustle of paper and the click of their heels across the wooden floor as Letty and Edwina got on with their task of closing down the Ambleside branch of the WSPU. There was a firm resolve about them, a calmness that Lucy envied, a certainty that come what may they were to be a part of this fight the British people had on their hands and she wished with all her heart that she could do the same. Throw off the restraints that bound her, not just to James who was her husband and who, in the eyes of his world, owned her, but the responsibilities of Edward and Percy, Margaret and Emily, but it was not possible. She had a duty to them, laid upon her by her mother, and then her father, and she could not abandon them, no matter how well cared for they might be without her, and take a train with Letty and Edwina to what she knew would be the greatest experience of her life. She was not even sure that, had she not had her brothers and sisters, a woman could just march off to war without the permission of her husband. There might be some law forbidding it and so what was she to do?

'What can I do?' she asked the two busy young women who really had no time for her now. They turned to look at her, kindly, as they might a child who has offered to side the table, or help with the washing-up and she knew they thought her helpless, hopeless even. But as they considered her thoughtfully, like two grown-ups faced with a difficult child, she felt an unshakeable belief enter her heart, a sureness, a fixity of purpose that seemed to tell her that there was something she, Lucy Buchanan, could do, something that might not be as demanding as Letty and Edwina's new cause but which would fulfil this call to arms that was sweeping the country.

'I'll find something,' she told them firmly. 'I don't know what but I'll find something. I wish you luck, both of you, and when the war is won, we will get on with the battle we are putting aside for the time being. We can't let fifty years of fighting for universal suffrage go to waste, can we?'

YOUR KING AND COUNTRY NEED YOU

A CALL TO ARMS

An addition of 10,000 men to the Regular Army is immediately necessary in the grave National Emergency. Lord Kitchener is confident that this appeal will be at once responded to by all who have the safety of the Empire at heart.

So said the posters which began to appear several days after war was declared. The response was overwhelming. Recruiting offices all over the country were at once deluged with volunteers and by the end of the month 750,000 young men from every walk of life had joined up. Many of those who volunteered were to become officers, receiving their commissions on the strength of certificates granted by the Officer Training Corps of the public schools and universities they had attended. One of these was Andrew Buchanan; another was his cousin, Doctor Paul Buchanan.

The retreat from Mons, as they were beginning to call it following their defeat on 23 August, came when the BEF fell back south, suffering heavy casualties and pursued by the Germans.

The Battle of Le Cateau was next followed in October by the first Battle of Ypres but it seemed the Allied Forces were in a race to the sea and the German troops could not be stopped.

'I wish I could go,' Edward told them all gloomily day after day as the news of the retreat was reported in the newspaper, his attitude saying that, given the chance, he could turn the fortunes of the BEF right round in no time.

'So do I,' added Percy stoutly and they were both openmouthed with admiration when Bertie Clapcott, who, it appeared, had enlisted on the quiet since he was only seventeen and knew his dad would have stopped him, received an envelope with OHMS on it telling him to report to the Drill Hall in Penrith the next day.

' 'Ere, this is a nice how-d'you-do, an' no mistake,' Clapcott was reported to have said and as for Mrs. Clapcott, it seemed she had ranted and raved and threatened to 'stop his gallop if Clapcott didn't', whatever it cost her, but it did no good. Bertie took the train to Penrith with a dozen other cheering, excited young men, the first to go from the district, but certainly not the last. Over the next weeks it began to be noticeable that young men were fast disappearing from the district, their places being taken by women. Farmers were stunned when young women in breeches and smocks and broad-brimmed hats turned up to work on their land. Land-girls, they called themselves and they weren't the only ones. It was coming to something, one old chap said indignantly, when that Mrs Owen took over her husband's job as gravedigger when he went away to the front. It wasn't right and proper, and he wasn't having some woman digging his grave, which he expected to be put in any day now, the way things were going.

Lucy was at Franny's when the idea came to her, neat, not exactly planned down to the last detail, but an idea none the less.

It was almost the end of November and the casualties from the front were beginning to flood the hospitals all over the country. Almost 90,000 men and officers had been killed or wounded since the beginning of the war and the lists in *The Times* grew day by day. The ladies still carried on the custom of calling despite the war. Well, standards had to be kept up, hadn't they and besides, it was

263

convenient to use the time not just for calling on one another but to do something for the war effort. Rolling bandages seemed to be something they might be good at, at least until they were informed by Joan Buchanan, who had a friend with a husband at the War Office and so should know what was needed, what else they might pursue. Comforts for the troops, perhaps, knitting socks and scarves and those strange things soldiers wore on their heads in the cold weather. Not that any of them had ever knitted a line in their lives. A bit of fine embroidery was all they had been taught but they were willing to try if someone would just show them how.

Mrs Charlotte Buchanan was there that day, resplendent in an outfit her husband had certainly not bought her, the last to come out of Paris, she was devastated to tell them, where she and Paul had spent their honeymoon. Where, would they tell her, was she to buy her clothes if she could not get to Paris and her clever French couturier? She knew that Miss Medlock was gifted, casting a supercilious glance over the oufits of her new relatives by marriage, particularly Lucy Buchanan who had on her riding breeches, a woollen jumper and what looked like a checked jacket of her husband's. She'd decided to ride over, she had told them all, ignoring their shocked faces which she did more and more these days, pleasing herself, her expression seemed to say. She and Jacob, who was groom at Howethwaite, were to put her brothers and sisters up on the ponies James had bought them, since she had been a good girl over the WSPU, he had told her, though she did not mention this last, and she must dash off soon, for

264

lessons in the schoolroom would be over and they would be expecting her.

Charlotte smoothed down the lustrous silk of her afternoon gown, her hand caressing the lovely garment, her smile of self-satisfaction very evident, then, for want of something better to do, proceeded to admire the diamonds sparkling on her fingers. Her devastation over the cessation of visits to Paris for her wardrobe did not seem to stretch to her husband's decision to become an army doctor, nor the fact that he was to leave a week on Friday for a military hospital in London and then on to the front, she told them casually.

'Dear God, he kept that quiet,' Franny said, blowing smoke through her nostrils, then leaning forward to tap the ash from her cigarette into the cut-crystal ashtray.

'Oh, he seems to want to be 'in on it', as they say and as a patriotic wife how can I object? I certainly don't want one of those hussies to accost him in the street with a white feather.'

'So you'd rather he risked his life?'

'What can I do, Lucy? It is his decision.'

'But he can be 'in on it' by remaining in this country and treating the casualties in a military hospital.'

Charlotte shrugged as though to say what was a wife to do.

'Aren't you afraid for him, Charlotte?' Lucy asked her curiously, for she really did not think she had ever known a more heartless, thoughtless, mindless young woman. She had taken a liking to Paul, the youngest of the Buchanan cousins. He was often at family affairs where she sought him out to speak to him, for he was diffident and shy.

As James had predicted, his beautiful and rich young wife totally dominated him and she wondered whether it was this that had prompted him to volunteer for active service.

'Oh, not at all. He will be well behind the front line, after all. They are desperately in need of doctors, so I believe.'

Charlotte held the strip of bandage with which she had been fiddling for the past half-hour as though even that simple task were beyond her well-bred, undomesticated fingers. She gave Lucy the condescending and imperious look which she turned on her servants in the house her father had bought her and Paul as a wedding present.

'Mmm, and can you wonder when you see the casualty lists?' Franny retorted shortly, evidently agreeing with Lucy about the lack of feeling in Charlotte Buchanan. 'They're also short of nurses, stretcher-bearers and ambulance drivers. In fact, I'm thinking of going myself. I can drive a car so I'm damn sure I can drive an arnbulance.'

They all turned to stare at her in horror, Anne and Joan, Janet and Christine and Charlotte, speechless and frozen into poses of open-mouthed disbelief, all, that is, except Lucy who smiled at Franny with great affection.

'Oh, Franny, how wonderful.'

'Never mind being wonderful, you silly girl,' Joan declared. 'I've never heard of anything so foolish in my life. Good God, Franny, you're nearly thirty and . . .'

'What's being nearly thirty got to do with it, Joan?' Franny's voice and face were frosty. 'Anyway, it's nearly twenty-nine and if I feel like a little adventure then that's my business. I've

266

applied to the Red Cross and been accepted. I have to do a course in first aid and motor mechanics, would you believe, but I can see no problem there.'

'Problem! What about your husband? Does he not count as a problem?'

'It's because of Alex that I'm going. He's too old for active duty but he's been offered a post in ... high places. They were delighted with the offer of his services and expertise and so he is to go up to London by the month's end. We're taking a house there so that when I can get home from France he'll be with me.'

Franny turned a defiant look on them all and lit another cigarette while they continued to gape at her with growing consternation, all except Lucy who leaned forward to take her hand.

'I admire you, Franny. I think you're marvellous and I only wish to God there was something I could do. James is adamant—' She broke off, aware that she was saying too much to these women who believed, as she did, that matters concerning one's husband were not discussed with others.

Franny patted her hand soothingly, for she knew full well how James hemmed his young wife about with rules and conventions. She often wondered that Lucy put up with it, for if anyone was a fighter it was Lucy Buchanan. She had given in meekly about the WSPU which had amazed Franny but then, who knew what passed between husband and wife.

'Something will turn up, Lucy, you'll see. Something you can do at home. Who knows ...'

It was then that the idea came to Lucy, as certainly, as surely as the feeling that had come over her when Letty and Edwina had told her they

267

were off to Carlisle to be nurses. The WSPU must be put away for the duration of the war, and who knew how long that would be, but until then she must find something to occupy her, something worth while, a challenge to her mind and heart and soul which were stagnating in the life she led now.

And now she knew what it was to be.

She couldn't wait to get home. Her mare, which she had called Rose because she was so pretty, was brought round to the front steps from the stable and as the ladies watched her in obvious dismay, for what were they to make of the girl, she leaped into the saddle and, putting her heels to Rose's side, raced off down the drive towards the open gateway.

'I do believe if the gate had been closed she would have jumped it,' Joan remarked disapprovingly.

'I believe she would, Joan, and where was she off to in such a hurry? I don't know, girls today . . .'

She left Rose by the front steps, her reins adangle, calling for Dixon to send for Jacob and was the master in?

'Indeed he is, madam. He's in the study.' She was surprised by the look of gratification on Dixon's face. Though he did his job to perfection, Dixon's face had never been known to display anything more than total inexcitability in all the time she had known him, but now he seemed to be . . . what? . . . suppressing some emotion with the greatest difficulty, but she had no time to discover what was bothering him, if anything was.

She could barely contain her exhilaration as she flung open the door, hurling herself into the room with something like the enthusiasm she had once shown at her father's house.

'James ... oh, James, I've just come from Franny's and while I was there I had this wonderful idea. It needs your approval, of course, but ... but ...'

She did not immediately recognise the figure which rose from the fireside chair, a tall, erect, quiet figure of a soldier. A soldier in the uniform of an officer and when she did she was bewildered by the swooping anguish that struck at her heart.

CHAPTER FIFTEEN

James Buchanan told himself that he had volunteered for patriotic reasons but he knew in his heart it was not true. He had volunteered simply to get away from his beautiful young wife.

He could pinpoint the exact moment when he had recognised what was in his heart and what he was to do about it. He had come home unexpectedly and, still then with the hope that had flowered when she agreed to marry him, finding her not in her sitting-room had gone to look for her in the place where he realised she was most likely to be. He had opened the door of the schoolroom; it had been a cold day at the beginning of October, and a generous fire burned in the grate and there she was in an armchair in front of it, Percy and Thimble on her lap as she read them a story. It was *The Jungle Book* by Rudyard Kipling. The others were there, Edward building something at the table, Emily busy with a doll's house he did not remember seeing before, Margaret and the maid,

Buffy, as Lucy called her, both sewing what looked like baby garments.

They had all looked up as he stood for a moment in the doorway and in a way that shrivelled something inside him, the life went out of the room. But what went straight to the core of him like an arrow from a bow was the way in which Lucy's face, so warm and flushed and radiant as she rested her cheek on Percy's curls and read the story, altered, the coldness that settled in her eyes as they looked questioningly into his.

His heart, and he loathed himself for saying it since it sounded like some trashy novel and not the thinking of a mature man, right then and there knew it could stand no more of the pain of her indifference and, as they all waited politely for him to say what he had come to say, and leave, his decision was made. He was forced into accepting the finality of it. It was not that he meant to go to war and get himself killed. Nothing dramatic like that. It just seemed a perfect escape route from this appalling sadness she had brought into his life and one that would be accepted by her, by his family, by the community, since what more natural than that a man should go and fight for his country. His law practice would still be there when he came back—if he did—and his wealth from his many investments, from the Emmerson Gunpowder Works and the Buchanan Copper Mines would still continue to come in. Probably doubled if the demand for gunpowder continued to grow. Lucy and her family, his home, with her in it, would go on as before, those under Howethwaite's roof cared for while he was away.

The strange thing was he had begun to believe

she was settling down, if not to her married state, then to the life he had given her at Howethwaite. She appeared to be contented. The servants had taken to her, for though she allowed no liberties, she was fair and honest and let them get on with their work without undue interference from her. Mrs Bunting continued to cook meals she chose to cook since she was an expert, Lucy told her, and needed no prodding from her, meaning herself. She would be guided by her, she told the cook, when it came to dinner parties which, though she did not care for herself, she had come to accept she must give as part of her 'bargain'. Mrs Burns was in charge of the female servants and Mr Dixon the males and, as they had been at Howethwaite a long time as housekeeper and butler, knew the routine of caring for the house and serving the Buchanans in a way she never would. She was not domesticated, she told James right at the beginning but she could tell when a table top had not been dusted or a window polished, which, God forbid, should ever happen at Howethwaite.

Her delight in what she could give her family had been evident from the start and her gratitude to him was constantly acknowledged. She never failed to thank him warmly for the allowance he had made her, more money in a week than she had seen in a year at the rectory, and what it allowed her to do for the children. Edward was showing a great interest in mathematics, science and the growing technology of motor cars and flying machines, and was doing well at school. In the spring Percy was to start at the same grammar school. He had accepted Howethwaite as his home and the servants as part of his family and they had

271

taken a real shine to him, quite enjoying the new excitement four children generated in the house. The girls were growing up, Margaret as lovely as Lucy, inclined to be quieter but seemingly content with Emily and Miss Tyson as a companion. He knew Lucy spent a lot of time with them, particularly now as they were learning to ride as she had done, and the house seemed to wrap itself about them, cradling them as it had cradled many generations of Buchanans. It was as though the ghosts of those past children, himself among them, were glad to see the rooms filled again with shouts of laughter, the barking of dogs, the arguments, the racket boys make and in the middle of it all moved Lucy, his love, safe and established in her position as his wife and mistress of Howethwaite, content with her lot, if not with him.

He had just come from his tailor in Ambleside where his uniform had been especially made for him. He looked well in the khaki, the gleaming riding boots, the polished shoulder strap and belt, the leather holster in which was a revolver, but he had intended to take the lot off before she came home. His peaked cap with the badge of his regiment on the front lay on a side table. He supposed he should not have put the uniform on in the first place but the tailor had wanted to make absolutely sure that Mr Buchanan, Captain Buchanan, was as well turned out in war as he was in peace. James had been impatient to get home so he had not bothered to change back into his civilian clothes, roaring back through Ambleside in the Rolls and within the hour he was certain that every inhabitant would know that James Buchanan had answered his country's call to arms.

He didn't know why but he had intended telling her later that night, perhaps after he had made love to her for what might be the last time. He had not told her before because quite simply he could not stand the thought of days of seeing her happily moving about their home despite his imminent departure, since she was too honest to pretend it mattered to her. He was to take the train tomorrow for the training camp.

It was two weeks now since he had travelled to Carlisle to enlist in a battalion of the Border Regiment, his certificate granted by the Officer Training Corps of the school he had attended, sixteen years ago now, entitling him to a commission. In that time he had watched her, looking for some sign that might give him hope that she would perhaps be sorry to see him go, but there was none. He was not awfully sure what he expected, since she did not even know he was going. She had been exactly as she always was. Polite, ready to chat across the dinner table if he wished, willing in their bed, but as distant as the brilliance of a star in the firmament. He knew he had turned her against him when he had refused her permission to join the WSPU and particularly in the way he had enforced his refusal. He realised now that it had been outrageous to threaten her sisters and brothers, and, truth to tell, he had no idea how he would have carried it out. It had been a blind, hitting out with the only weapon he had against her, for he knew without a shadow of a doubt that if she had been alone, without responsibilities, she would have told him to go to hell. Well, be honest, she wouldn't have married him in the first place!

She might have run into a brick wall, or an invisible glass window, she stopped so suddenly. For a second something passed across her face; he didn't see it and if he had it is doubtful he would have recognised it. Lucy herself didn't know what it was that struck her so forcibly, but so swiftly come and gone it might never have happened.

'James?' she said questioningly, as though she couldn't quite believe it was really him.

'The same.' He smoothed down his jacket and tried to smile jauntily, for if she laughed he wanted to be ready for it.

'James, what have you done?'

'I should have thought that was pretty obvious, Lucy.'

'But I don't understand.'

'What don't you understand?'

'Why you've enlisted. You had no need to.'

'An old codger like me, you mean? I know what's in your mind, Lucy, so there is no need to protest. I am a married man of almost thirty-five and conscription will be a while coming.'

'Oh, it will all be over soon, James, or so they are saying and will not come to that.'

'Do you really believe that. Lucy?' He turned away from her and walked to the window and she had a moment to study his tall, athletic figure which the uniform fitted so admirably, displaying the hard lines of his body beneath it. He certainly did look very attractive, she thought detachedly. He had even had his troublesome thatch of hair cut short and it lay brushed smoothly to his head. His skin was suntanned still, for she knew he went walking up on the hills and the sun and the wind had put a good colour to his face. He did not turn as he spoke.

'Will you be all right on your own, Lucy?' he asked her, his voice detached and cool. 'I mean looking after things here until ... until I come back.'

'Of course I will, James. Don't worry about us,' she answered cheerfully, little realising what she was doing to him. 'We shall manage. There are many women all over the country who are to be left when their husbands go to war. Charlotte for one.' And if a nincompoop like Charlotte Buchanan can manage then I certainly can, her voice seemed to say scornfully.

'Yes, I heard that Paul was to go. And Alex is to take up a highfalutin' post in London. Andrew has joined the same regiment as me and is to travel with me tomorrow so the whole business will be on Ben's shoulders. He told me that Joan is determined to give him a hand, God help him.'

'No, I think Joan will make a fine second-in-command. Pity she can't go into the army, she'd have the war organised in a week.'

He turned back to her and smiled, the usual distant look of preoccupation on his face, his eyes clear and cool.

There was a catch in her voice as she spoke. 'You've heard that Franny is determined to go to France and be an ambulance driver?'

He sighed. 'Yes, but then Alex has no control over her whatsoever, more's the pity. But I must admit if anyone can do it, Franny can.'

'And that only leaves me,' she went on breathlessly.

His face tightened imperceptibly, but she saw it, for by now she had begun to read her husband's

275

expressions, at least those he allowed her to see.

'Yes?' he asked quietly.

'May I put something to you, James?' she begged eagerly. 'It's an idea I had . . .well, I went down to the WSPU. I know I shouldn't but I wanted to find out what was to happen. you know that we are giving up our fight for now . . .'

'We . . . ?'

'I cannot give it up in my heart, James, surely you know that. Though I have not been to Compston Street since you . . . you told me not to, I am still a believer, but that is getting away from what I was going to tell you. Two of the girls were there, clearing up, and they told me they are to go to Carlisle to train as nurses.'

His face hardened and he straightened his back and shoulders as he stood away from the window. About his mouth a thin white line appeared as he compressed his lips and his eyes grew cold and grey as frost on a pool.

'Oh, don't worry,' she said, seeing it, 'I am not fool enough to think I could go.'

'Though you would if you had not your family?'

She hesitated and her own eyes grew bleak. 'Yes.'

'Even if I told you not to?'

'Yes. I'm sorry, James, but it is not to come to that. What I want to do is . . . they are already overflowing, the hospitals, I mean, with our casualties from the front, and I've heard that the government would be glad of any help it can get in the way of accommodation. Now, I'm sure we could convert Howethwaite, with your permission, of course, into such a place and then I could help. Oh, I so want to help, James, and this is the only

276

way I can think of, and still remain at home where my responsibilities lie.'

There was a deep silence. Lucy's face was pink and her lovely golden eyes glowed with fervour as she looked into her husband's unreadable face. She had thrown her bowler hat on to a chair and pulled off the snood in which her mass of hair was stuffed. It fell all about her, rich and rippling, the light firing copper glints from it. Her lips were like poppies, parted over her perfect white teeth and she gazed at him beseechingly, her heart exposed, for she wanted this and only he could give it to her.

He could feel the distaste rise in him but he fought it down. Howethwaite invaded by strangers. His lovely home where he had lived all his life, where his ancestors had lived, stripped of the beautiful things his parents and grandparents had gathered about them. Wounded men lying in every room, the smell of infection, death perhaps, and in the midst of it this woman whom he loved beyond reason and from whom he was running away, possibly to his own death.

'James, don't deny this to me, please. Women all over the country are going to be doing jobs to free their men to fight. Did you know that Mr Owen the gravedigger has gone and that his wife is taking his place, and that there is to be a lady chemist at Lawson's? Now I cannot take over your work and would not want to but I think I would be a good nurse. I would not be a proper nurse, of course,' she added hastily as he frowned. 'A nurse's aid, I think they call it, but it would give me the opportunity to help in this war. Please, James . . . please.'

'What about the children and the servants?'

'Oh, I have been thinking about that all the way from Franny's.' Her face was alight with enthusiasm and he wanted to take her in his arms and crush her to him, tell her he could not bear the thought of other men having her compassion when she had none for him. Kiss her into subjection, into a submissive wife who would willingly stay at home and wait for him to come back home to her. He wanted to remember her in this deep comfort he had given her, just as she had been for the past seven months, not moving about a crowded ward in a white uniform smelling of disinfectant, putting the hands which had never, ever touched him unless forced to in the sexual act on other men.

'Well?' he demanded shortly.

'I would turn the dining-room, the drawing-room and the conservatory into hospital wards. We could probably get at least twenty beds in each one. My sitting-room could be made into an operating room or whatever they call it and your study—'

'Not my study, Lucy. Let's have that understood.'

'Very well, some rooms at the back of the house could be turned into small bedrooms for the nurses and doctors, and the children and I would have the upstairs floor. The servants' bedrooms would not be touched though there will be empty ones if needed. The spare bedroom would be my sitting-room and—'

'You have it all arranged, it seems,' he interrupted coldly.

'Yes. If you will allow it.'

'And the servants? How are they to manage all this extra work?'

She sighed sadly. 'I'm afraid some of them won't

be here much longer, James. You know that Fallows and Tom Baxter are to go, don't you?'

'Yes, Tom is going to put the Rolls up for the duration and I have a feeling the horses will be commandeered for service.'

'Yes, I'd heard.' Her face was sad, for she had enjoyed the few months of riding she had known and had grown fond of Rose. Perhaps the children's ponies would be spared but then Jacob, who was in his fifties, would be all that was needed to see to them.

'And three of the maidservants have been told that there is money to be made in munitions, besides which they also want to help the war effort, so there will be room and to spare. Whoever is left can help Mrs Bunting and I'm sure the War Office will send staff to look after their wounded.'

He made love to her that night with a tenderness and a passion he had never shown before. It was as though, knowing it might be for the last time, he drew from her, and from himself, some instinctive emotion which let him forget the past and the future and be James Buchanan simply loving his wife. He did not speak as he drew her close, drifting over her with barely any sensation, moving so slowly and feelingly she could sense something in him that had never been there before. His hands seemed to float about her body, soft as down, but ready to be hard with male sexuality. He cupped her buttocks, pulling her in to him and for the first time she was surprised by the sweet flickering which began somewhere in the pit of her stomach, a flickering which was ready to flare into a bright fire. He smoothed her back and she had the feeling that he had gone somewhere else though his hard body remained close to hers. Her breath drew in on a deep sound, almost a moan and her hips, of their own volition, pressed against his. Her breath was soft against his throat, getting faster and faster and when the explosion occurred somewhere inside herself she heard her own voice call out a name that was unintelligible.

For the first time she did not want him to turn away from her as he usually did. Her body was filled with the most delightful sensations, feelings, needs, stirrings which made her want to sigh and stretch like the tabby in the stable yard when the sun fell on her, but with James's back firmly presented to her as it always was she felt she could not. She had not the faintest idea what had happened to her and James appeared to be totally unconcerned with it, so what was she to do? She could not question him about it, could she, since it might be something he did not care to talk about, but really, it had been quite delightful and she wished she had the courage to touch his shoulder and ask if they might do it again!

Sighing, she turned on to her side and within minutes was sound in the sleep a well-satisfied female knows after lovemaking.

James stared into the darkness and his soul knew the meaning of the depths of hell. Tomorrow he was to take his life and remove it from this woman, this woman who had for the first time responded to him, who had gone with him to the far places of the enchanted love he had longed for, but it was too late. She had met him, woman to man, equal in their desire for one another and he did not know why. Nor, to be honest, did he care now, for it was all too late.

*   *   *

They kissed on the front steps, more for convention's sake than anything, a brief touch of their lips, for the servants were watching and waiting to say goodbye to their master, Mrs Bunting with her apron to her eyes, Dixon dignified but obviously moved and Mrs Burns keeping a stern eye on the maidservants who would, she was sure, lose total control and weep over one another with great enjoyment. He shook hands with them all gravely, his face shuttered so that not one of them could see what was in his heart.

'Good luck, sir, good luck.'

'You'll not be long away, I'm sure, sir. We'll soon have them Huns on the run.' This from Clapcott whose Bertie was at that mysterious place called the front, wherever it was.

'I'm sure we will, Clapcott.'

He crouched to fondle his dogs' heads, looking deep into their intelligent eyes and Holmes whimpered mournfully as though he knew what was to come.

Mr Andrew, Captain Andrew, had driven over from Yewdale Park, where he had said goodbye to his parents, in his dashing little sports car which made Edward's eyes pop out on stalks, and was to drive them both to the railway station in Windermere. He would leave the motor there to be picked up by his mother's chauffeur. Edward longed to say *he* would pick it up right willingly, for he knew how to drive now but, glumly, he knew he would not be allowed. They stood in a line, the Dean family, Lucy with her arm across Percy's

281

shoulders, smiling with all the appearance of a group bidding farewell to a guest who they would see within the week, ready to dash back indoors and resume whatever they had been doing before he interrupted it.

Andrew's kiss, and the one he received back from Lucy, had been warmer than his, and Andrew's arms had held her for a moment too long, but then Andrew was known for a charming rogue and a ladies' man.

'I'll look after him for you, Lucy,' he shouted, waving his hand as they roared down the drive. They were never to see Andrew again.

*   *   *

By Christmas the house had been inspected and found to be suitable for the needs of thirty or so wounded men. The equipment, thirty-six iron beds and everything else that would be required for the nursing of wounded soldiers had been delivered by the year's end. New Year's Day found Lucy and Buffy, alongside Gertie and Elsie, the only maids still in service at Howethwaite, scrubbing floors with buckets of water into which carbolic acid had been added. Even the walls had to be disinfected to the Hospital Board's high standard ready for the first arrivals which, they were promised, would be soon but it was not until after the Battle of Neuve Chapelle on 10 March that they arrived.

Lucy would never forget that day. She had felt a strange restlessness, a need to be about something and yet everything that could be done, was done. She had fiddled with the crisp white sheets that were tucked like envelopes on each waiting bed and studied the 'wards' to see how she could make them more comfortable for the soldiers. She was wrapped around in one of the capacious aprons she had taken to wearing and which she had borrowed from Mrs Bunting, much to Mrs Bunting's disapproval.

'You don't want to be wearing that thing, madam,' Cook remonstrated with her, for Mrs Buchanan was a lady, despite her efforts with the scrub bucket, and ladies did not wear aprons all day long.

'I never know when I might have to do some dirty job, Cook.'

'Well, if you do you just send for Gertie or Elsie, madam. They can do any dirty job that needs doing.'

She could not settle to anything, wondering why, and so, throwing a warm cloak over her apron, for it was still cold despite being April, she had gone for a walk. She had received one of James's strange letters that morning, written on Good Friday, which spoke of giving the men a holiday that day and of a service by a visiting clergy in a field. They had sung hymns, he told her, and would she thank Mrs Bunting for the splendid food parcel she had sent. The men had been most appreciative, especially of the chocolate shortbreads, and the shirts Lucy had forwarded were most welcome but could she manage a few cigarettes? It was short, formal, as though he were writing to the rector's wife thanking her for her kindness. Not a word about the children, or Howethwaite, and certainly not about her.

It was in her pocket as she took the road towards Grasmere. At the Knoll she left the road, striding out across the rough pasture until she came to the river. Spring was always later arriving in Lakeland than the rest of the country and it was still cold; nevertheless she took off her boots and stockings and stepped into the shallow water, gasping with shock as the icy water bit into her flesh. On the far side she dried her feet on the hem of her skirt and put on her boots, then began the steady climb through the trees until she came to a clearing where the sun struck and spring flowers were in full bloom. Wood anemones and primrose and violets, as shy and lovely as only they could be, lifting their faces to the sunshine. A yellow Brimstone butterfly hung in the sheltered air and for a moment her papa was there beside her. She could hear his voice, gentle, as he had been, and a great longing for him came over her.

She sat for almost half an hour, dwelling on the past as she looked down at Rydal Water, the sun touching it with such brilliance it hurt her eyes. It was as smooth and soft-looking as silk but even as she admired its beauty the surface of the water changed, ruffling as a breeze caught it, lapping to the edges of the lake, distorting the mirrored reflection of the trees which grew around it. She thought about James and Andrew and Paul, all in France now, and of the other young men who had come, khaki-clad, to say goodbye to her. Job Gunson, Janet's eldest son, nineteen, a boy still, but wild to get over there before it ended. Frederick Mossop, Roger Askew, Gregory Kendall who had all danced with her at Franny Buchanan's party, so long ago and yet it was only yesterday. And Franny herself, roaring off defiantly in her little car, as eager as they were to get to the front.

Dear Franny, abrasive and outspoken, a troublemaker some would call her but willing to be her friend if she wanted it.

For the last four months nothing much seemed to have happened at the front and those at home had begun to wonder why their boys were out there at all. The last Battle of Ypres had taken place in November, weighted down with mud and casualties, but Ypres had not fallen.

It was not until March that it had been reported that, following a massive bombardment, General Haig's 1st Army had attacked the village of Neuve Chapelle. British casualties were about 13,000, it was said, and a telephone message to the newly converted hospital at Howethwaite of impending arrivals had come through two days ago.

A convoy of ambulances was rolling up the drive as she came through the gate, and she began to run.

CHAPTER SIXTEEN

As the weeks passed she wondered what she had done with her time before Howethwaite opened its door to the flood of casualties which seemed to flow, via the clearing hospitals in the south, into her care. That was how she thought of it though her part in it was, as yet, very small. Her care! She was caring for the sick and the wounded and it was as though God had given her, at last, the very job she had been designed to perform.

She wasn't in charge, of course, far from it, and she had to take orders from Sister Colyford who had at first treated Lucy as she would any society lady who was acting out the part of Florence Nightingale, which, in Sister's opinion, many were doing. Playing at it. Dressing up in well-tailored nurses' uniforms and sitting about holding the hands of officers, those not too badly wounded to be objectionable, naturally. Like Mrs Buchanan's cousin-in-law, for instance!

There were no officers at Howethwaite but nevertheless Mrs Charlotte Buchanan came over in her papa's motor, a splendidly elegant chauffeur-driven Mercedes which was, in many enthusiasts' opinion, the best car in the world, dressed in an immaculately tailored, enormously expensive and beautifully fitted nurse's uniform the like of which Sister Colyford had never in her life seen. Their Mrs Buchanan met her at the door.

'Charlotte, this is a surprise, a welcome one, let me tell you, for a helping hand is always welcome. You have come to help, I take it, and may I say how charming you look in your uniform.' The touch of irony in Lucy's voice was not lost on Sister Colyford though it went right past Mrs Charlotte Buchanan.

'Thank you, Lucy. I thought, with my husband at the front and all these poor boys . . .' She actually put a wisp of handkerchief to her eyes. 'Well, I consider it my duty to help those who have been unfortunate enough to . . . I'm sure you know what I mean.'

'I do indeed, Charlotte, and you could not have come at a more opportune time. We are expecting Doctor Yates at any moment. An emergency operation so the stillroom, which has been converted into an operating theatre, must be scrubbed down with carbolic. Pennington and I'—

286

indicating a tall VAD who was armed with a bucket and an ominous-looking scrubbing brush—'are just about to start. We would be grateful for a bit of help.'

Charlotte smiled and inside her, where it still rankled that Lucy Dean had taken the man Charlotte Gibson had earmarked for herself, that small growth of malevolence that had been festering for almost two years increased a fraction.

'Scrub . . .' Her voice rose in horror. 'I thought perhaps . . . flowers or writing letters. I'm not sure Paul would want me to scrub the . . . the operating theatre.' Her voice grew stronger. 'In fact, it is not the kind of work I am used to at all.'

If she had ever done any work in her life, Sister Colyford, who was pretending to be busy with the post which had just been delivered, thought with amusement.

'Well, Private Andrews in the conservatory was asking if someone could write a letter for him to his mother. He lost both his hands when a land-mine blew up, you see, and, of course, if you could stay on and feed him at lunchtime we would be eternally grateful. Any help we can get, from anyone, is most welcome.'

Charlotte had turned the somewhat peculiar colour of dirty flour as every vestige of the rosy flush she usually wore drained from her face, then it hardened and she drew herself up in stiff rage. She was not only insulted to be asked to consort with a private, a man from the underclasses, but one with no hands and she would not forget it. She was a lady and ladies could not be expected to do what working women did. They were not brought up to it and when her father heard of this it would

287

be woe betide the unladylike wife of James Buchanan who was, after all, nothing more than a ...a... Well, she didn't know how to describe her standing there with that odd smile on her face, that smile which she had begun to recognise as contempt. She would not forget this, she swore it, nor the insult James had paid her by marrying this woman instead of her.

But she had not done yet. She had come over to Howethwaite for a purpose other than to offer her services to Lucy Buchanan. In fact, that was secondary to the real reason. An excuse, if you like, to call on Lucy legitimately without seeming too obvious. She had come to hurt her, to 'get her own back', though she would not describe it as such to anyone but herself, for past insults, or if not insults, then grievances.

'By the way,' she said, her voice gloating. I had a letter from my husband this morning. He has some leave and will be home next week. It seems James has a week too but, as I'm sure you must know, since the journey is so difficult he has decided to spend it in Paris. I'll bring Paul over to see you and perhaps give you some news of James.'

She turned on her heels and flounced triumphantly, there was no other word for it, down the steps, calling for Giles, the chauffeur, who had wandered across the lawn to have a word with one or two of the wounded lads who were sitting in the garden.

Mrs Buchanan put out her hand—Sister Colyford and the VAD both saw it—and put it on the door handle but neither of them noticed that she gripped it so hard her knuckles turned white.

Mrs Buchanan's other female relatives were not

quite so forthright. Mrs Gunson and Mrs. Mounsey and Mrs Scott came over, not dressed as Mrs Charlotte Buchanan had been, but prepared to help out in some genteel manner, since the hospital was a Buchanan contribution to the war effort and they felt they owed it to Lucy. They were prepared to sit with a soldier, read to him or perhaps play some board game to take his mind off his suffering. They would, of course, have been happier to associate with an officer as all their menfolk were of that rank but, since there was none, they would make the sacrifice. After all, they were accustomed to speaking to gardeners and footmen and so on, giving them orders, so it should not be too difficult to hold a conversation with a non-commissioned soldier. Ask him about his family and life before the war, if Sister knew what they meant. Yes, Sister knew exactly what they meant and she supposed it might perk up a badly wounded chap to speak of his wife or his mother and home.

Sister Colyford soon found that Mrs Buchanan and her companion, Miss Tyson, were not like the other ladies and so she began to treat them as though they were probationer nurses, answering the hundreds of questions they put to her and allowing them small but responsible duties, recognising their trustworthiness.

Before Howethwaite could be considered to be a hospital in the true sense of the word there had been acres of floor to be scrubbed, miles of skirting board to be attacked with a small brush and carbolic soap, windows to be polished to a high gleam, as though they weren't already spotless, a somewhat offended Mrs Burns retorted acidly, the kitchen converted into one that could cope with preparing meals for over fifty people and it was she and Buffy, with the help of two girls from Ambleside, who had done it, apart from the kitchen, of course. That had been arranged by the medical authorities. Howethwaite hospital, as the locals were now proudly calling it, as though they had had a hand in its creation, was to be run like any other military hospital. Because of its size there was no resident doctor; they had to share the services of Doctor Yates who moved between three other establishments in the area similar to Howethwaite, one of them a converted church hall which took only convalescent cases. He was summoned wherever he was needed in an emergency but the experienced nursing staff were more than able to take over the running of the wards and to nurse the soldiers who were in their care. There was no matron since Sister Colyford was a nurse with twenty years' experience, and under her were four fully trained nurses and three VADs. Lucy and Buffy were called nurses' aids by the others and were expected to perform any onerous or dirty job they did not themselves care to do. It was frustrating at first to be given orders by a seventeen-year-old girl who, because she possessed a first aid certificate was considered superior to her and Buffy, but they were learning all the time, standing at the elbow of Nurse Cartwright or Nurse Bickerstaffe while dressings were done, injections given, and wounds cleaned, and even, when Sergeant Collins's injured leg became gangrenous, standing with a bucket in the makeshift operating theatre to receive the amputated leg!

It was at the end of May, several weeks after their second intake of wounded had arrived which now meant they were full, that Lucy found herself lying on the floor of the sluice-room which she had just scrubbed. It had once been Dixon's pantry where he had decanted wine, supervised the cleaning of the silver and glassware and plate, and performed the important task of dealing with bills from the wine merchant and generally overseeing the running of the house. His work had been drastically cut when his master went away, for entertaining on the scale of before the war was practically non-existent, and now he shared Mrs Burns's small sitting-room next to the kitchen.

The war and the subsequent departure of so many of the servants to the call of their country in its hour of need had brought out of retirement two of Lucy's old servants, and glad to help they were, they said, especially Bibby who, he told them all, was sick to death of sitting on his bum and twiddling his thumbs all day. Mrs. Hutton, still with plenty of work left in her, though she had enjoyed the rest, she told Miss Lucy, bless her, trudged over every day from her small cottage beyond the greenhouses to give a hand in the kitchen. She couldn't do heavy work, she told them, but if she could sit down to it there were many jobs, once done by Win or Fanny or Bridie, she could manage nicely. Shelling peas for the patients' dinner, for instance, preparing the veg, mixing and stirring and generally giving Mrs Bunting a hand, for feeding thirty-six wounded soldiers and seven nurses, not to mention the family, three times a day took a bit of doing. There was many an argument between Mrs Hutton and Cook over the finer points of producing gravy or making an arrowroot blancmange that the poor wounded chaps in the wards could cope with, but on the whole they got on well enough.

Old Bibby had received a new lease on life when he was called upon, or rather pleaded with, to give a hand to Clapcott who sadly missed the services of his Bertie. The government was asking for flower gardens and lawns to be turned over to the growing of vegetables and though Bibby's back was not what it was, or so he was fond of telling them at frequent intervals, he picked up his spade and tackled the job with some enthusiasm, not taking orders, mind, for wasn't he a competent gardener in his own right, but, like Mrs Hutton, glad to be doing something for the war effort.

She didn't know how she'd got on the floor. She was alone and she thanked God for it, since if one of the others had found her there would have been no end of a fuss. She knew she was working harder than she had ever worked in her life. She fell into her bed every night, descending into a stunned sleep so vast and depthless she had a job to drag herself out of it in the morning but she knew deep inside her where she firmly refused to look that it was not tiredness that had made her faint. It might have added to it but the true reason was the life growing inside her, the life James had left behind when he drove away last November. She had buried the knowledge, wrapping herself in her capacious apron which would have hid the fact that she was carrying twins it was so roomy and, knowing they would try to stop her from this work which she loved so passionately, she had ignored every symptom that told her she was pregnant.

She picked up the pail full of reeking dressings which she had brought into the sluice—when?—

perhaps fifteen minutes ago, she couldn't be sure, ramming it upside down hard into the rubbish bin which was already half full, then moved carefully to the steriliser, putting her feet down with the precision of a marching soldier. It was as though she had to concentrate hard on keeping her balance, keeping her head clear, her back straight, an untroubled smile on her face, for she meant to hide her condition for as long as she could. She knew nothing about babies, before or after they were born since Buffy had performed the more unpleasant tasks of bringing up Percy. This one meant very little to her only in as much as it might prevent her, or at least force Sister Colyford into preventing her, from carrying on with her nursing. She had felt some movement inside the growing swell of her belly and, not knowing what it implied, deliberately ignored it. She felt well. She had never ailed a day in her life and she wasn't about to start now, just when she was doing something important, so the baby must await its turn! It was almost into June so she supposed she must be six months pregnant. It was also apparent to her that had she still been wearing the stylish clothes she wore before the hospital opened, she could not have got away with it. As it was, under her apron, she had to leave her skirt gaping with a big safety pin holding it in place.

She walked slowly along the bright hallway towards the open front door, pausing at the top of the ramp which had been laid for the easy movement of wheelchairs and stretchers, conscious of many eyes on her. Some of the men were well enough to be pushed outside into the garden in long, flat, wickerwork stretchers on wheels. They were recovering from the dreadful wounds they had suffered in the trenches at the Battle of Neuve Chapelle in March and would, some of them, be well enough soon to return to the front. They were part of the deluge of 100,000 soldiers wounded in the first few months of the war and had been shuttled along a casualty line beginning at the front with basic first aid performed by the Royal Army Medical Corps; to clearing stations a few miles behind the front line where they had received emergency medical treatment, were put in ambulances which took them to the ambulance trains and on to one of the military hospitals. The more seriously injured were shipped home. These men at Howethwaite had been in a hospital down south but when the second Battle of Ypres had brought another 60,000 casualties pouring into wards already at bursting point, these 'old' casualties, half healed and not in such desperate need of nursing, were sent to hospitals further afield.

Half a dozen of them lay in the shade beneath the trees, their wheeled beds in a precise line, for Sister Colyford liked things tidy, the dappled sunshine giving their thin, suffering faces a veneer of health. One or two sat in wheelchairs and, at a small table, four were playing some card game. In the midst of them was her family, for she had decided from the start that she could not forbid them to mix with these soldiers who were so pitifully grateful for any little attention, particularly from a pretty girl. Margaret was reading to them, *Robinson Crusoe* which many of them had never heard of. They were ordinary working men, plumbers and postmen and clerks who had answered their country's call and look where it had bloody landed them, they were inclined to think. Already the gloss of high ideals and fervent patriotism had worn off, tarnished by what they had suffered and seen others suffer and Lucy was aware that none of them wanted to get better and go back to war.

Thimble was lolling on Corporal Holden's knee, his tongue hanging from his mouth in the heat, his eyes screwed up in ecstasy as the corporal's hand caressed his rough head.

Thimble was in heaven with the fuss he got from all the soldiers, many of whom had a dog at home just like him, they said wistfully. James's dogs sprawled at the corporal's feet.

Emily, listening to the story, was resting her head against the knee of a soldier older than the rest, a quiet, fatherly chap with a full moustache and a pipe between his teeth. He was Sergeant Collins whose leg they had cut off and who was to go home to his own little girl soon, thank God. Emily was making a daisy chain, and on the grass Percy practised handstands with great enthusiasm, entertaining the men who, Lucy was positive, gained a certain healing from their contact with the children. Only Edward was missing, but soon he would come cycling furiously up the drive from school to talk to whoever would listen to him about motor cars or aeroplanes or some other mechanical marvel.

Though they had been watching the soft, girlish beauty of Margaret Dean as her voice murmured the story, in unison their eyes turned to Mrs Buchanan as she came down the ramp. Miss Margaret was a treat to look at, they would all have agreed had they discussed it, and was as sweet-natured as an angel, longing to help ease their pain, you could tell, but Mrs Buchanan was something they could not describe, some wordless thing that dwells inside all men who have a dream, a fantasy of the woman they will love, and as she approached there was a deep collective sigh from a dozen male throats. Not that they would aspire to think of Mrs Buchanan in that way, for she was so far above any of them it almost felt like blasphemy. Each of them had some small story to tell—not that they did, for it was precious to them—of Mrs Buchanan's face bending over them, perhaps in the dark of night and how she knew she was needed was a mystery to them, but there she would be, a hand to your brow, smoothing back your hair like your mam used to when you had a nightmare and by God, they had plenty of those.

'Who wants a cup of tea?' she asked cheerfully, walking towards them in that kind of swaying manner that mesmerised them. There was a blooming about her recently, a lovely flush, a gloss of good health, but they were simple men, simple soldiers who, most of them, being young, knew nothing of women and they did not speculate on the reason. She was married to an officer who was at the front, a soldier like themselves, and so they treated her tenderly, respectfully and with great affection. Most of them were half in love with her, and Sister Colyford said privately to Nurse Bickerstaffe that she attributed some of the more spectacular recoveries on the wards to the almost madonna-like beauty and care she gave to them.

'Pity she can't be a full-time nurse, for she's a natural.'

Cups of tea were wheeled out on a trolley and handed round by Margaret and Emily, while from the drive Edward shouted a greeting, standing up to cycle in order to put more pressure on the pedals and get there the sooner.

Behind him, but cycling much more slowly, came the telegram boy.

*   *   *

She was to be ashamed later of her sense of deep relief that the yellow envelope the boy held out was addressed not to her but to Mr F. Clapcott. She was conscious of the awful silence about her, for these men were well aware what the telegram boy and his envelope meant to their families at home. The poor lad was detested and yet he was only doing his duty, as she must do hers.

They watched her walk away, her head high, and softly Margaret began to weep for she had seen the name on the envelope. Private George, called Georgie by the others, put out a hand and took Margaret's in his, patting it clumsily as her head bent on her tears.

'What is it?' Percy demanded shrilly, afraid, though he didn't know what of. 'What's happened? Who's the telegram for?' He had just done a perfect handstand, walking for at least a yard on his hands before toppling over, and he was irritated that no one seemed to have seen it. Edward knelt down beside him and put a brotherly arm about him and all the while Emily continued to make her daisy chain, for this was the first time the war had struck personally at them and they must find a way through it.

297

'Give me the book, lass,' Sergeant Collins said quietly to Margaret. 'I'll read it fer a bit. There, there, lass, don't fret. See, come and sit close ter me an' us'll find out what that there Man Friday's got up to. But before yer do, pour us another cuppa, there's a good lass,' and Margaret was comforted by the simple task and the kind heart of a soldier who had witnessed more things than any man should be asked to witness, but still had compassion for the pain of a young girl.

Clapcott was turning over the soil at the side of the house where, to his sorrow, he had been forced to sacrifice the lawn into which he had put nearly thirty years of his life. It had been a grand lawn, like bloody velvet what with all his coddling of it and he was saying so to Bibby and Licky Thripp who, as odd-job man with not a lot to do now, helped out wherever he was put.

'I've fed that lawn better then me own babby,' he was saying, stopping a moment to relight his pipe and for a moment Lucy wanted to throw the telegram away. She didn't know what was in the envelope; perhaps Bertie was wounded or a prisoner of war, or even missing, which would give them all a bit of hope but something inside her seemed to say she knew this was not so. Just at this precise moment, to Clapcott his son was still alive, still the cheerful lad who had grinned impishly and marched off to war saying he wanted to see a bit of the world before he settled down like his dad, and now where was he? Dear Lord, spare Clapcott and Mrs Clapcott, who are part of this family, the pain of . . . Oh, dear, dear God . . .

He turned and was about to smile and nod, for they were all fond of their master's lovely wife, when he saw what was in her hand. She didn't realise she was doing it but she was holding the hated envelope away from her, towards him, and she watched as the life drained away from his face in terror. Bertie was Clapcott and Mrs Clapcott's only child.

Bibby and Licky Thripp moved away respectfully and both removed their caps as though already they knew they were in the presence of death.

'I'm sorry, Mr Clapcott,' Lucy said helplessly, holding out the envelope, but Clapcott began to shake his head as though in denial that it was for him, refusing to take it while further down the row they were digging Bibby and Licky sighed pityingly.

'Eeh, Mrs Buchanan,' the gardener moaned, 'eeh, I can't . . .'

'Would you like me to open it for you, Mr Clapcott?' She put a gentle hand on his arm, stroking it a little, her lovely, white-capped head bending towards him, her face filled with compassion.

'Aye, would thi', lass?'

When she had told him his son was dead, killed in action, she put her strong young arms about his bowed shoulders and held him, weeping with him as she led him towards the cottage where Mrs Clapcott was baking him an apple pie for his tea in cheerful ignorance of what was to come.

*   *   *

They couldn't believe it, really they couldn't, they told one another in the kitchen. Not that cheeky little lad who Mrs Bunting, Mrs Burns and Dixon had known from birth. He was a little tyke and no mistake, but sweet-tempered and honest and since he left school a good worker beside his poor pa. What were they to do, the Clapcotts; they must go over at once, one of them, to see if they could help, but it seemed the mistress was there and would stay as long as she was needed. She'd looked real bonny these last few weeks, which was daft really, for she'd always been bonny, and her tender pity for the men in her care had amazed them all. They'd thought the master had made a mistake when he married a girl of eighteen and brought her and all them children back to Howethwaite but would you look at them now, especially her, a family they were proud to serve. She'd proved times she was worth anyone's respect and affection and if anyone could help them poor Clapcotts it was her.

She came home just after midnight, her face calm but as grey as the ash in the kitchen fire. They'd not gone to bed, for it was as though they'd lost one of their own family and there had been frequent outbreaks of weeping, from Dimity who'd often been teased by the cheeky young lad, from Elsie who had had hopes of Bertie though she'd not let on and who couldn't seem to come to terms with the realisation that she'd never see him again. She had cried noisily on Mrs Bunting's deep bosom, setting Dimity off. Dimity had a sweetheart at the front, a handsome lad who had been groom to old Mr Harry Buchanan from Oak Bank and Bertie's death had finally brought the awareness that he, like Bertie, might never come home and if he did, perhaps he might be in the state some of those poor chaps at the front of the house were in. Dimity didn't do much 'maiding' these days, since Mrs Buchanan never went anywhere to need it.

Her hair, which she kept threatening to cut, was brushed each morning by Dimity, who insisted on it, and pulled back into a neat coil under her nurse's kerchief, a sort of square which was wrapped tightly about her head with the points down her back.

She was exhausted and so she was careless.

'I'll come up with you, madame,' Dimity told her sympathetically. 'A nice bath's what you need and when you've had it straight into bed with some warm milk.'

'Oh, Dimity, I really . . .'

'No, madam, I mean it. Now come along, up them stairs and off with that apron and I'll run your bath.'

She was unfastening the broad ribbons that held the apron round her waist even before she reached the door which led out into the hall. She was stunned with sorrow for the Clapcotts who had finally fallen into an uneasy sleep, and with her own aching tiredness. She held the apron in her hand as she turned to say goodnight to the servants, who were themselves on the move now she had returned, and her profile was silhouetted against the light from the hall.

For a second or two she wondered what was wrong with them, all staring in consternation, then, when Mrs Bunting began to smile, a smile of such joy it lit up her kindly face, she knew what she had done. Her hands went defensively to her belly where the child kicked, unconcerned with the world's woes but she said nothing.

Mrs Bunting did though. 'They say as one life goes another comes to take its place. God bless poor Bertie and God bless this new 'un.'

CHAPTER SEVENTEEN

They drove her wild with their protective solicitude, not only the servants who now considered her to be their exclusive property, for was she not to bear a child, a Buchanan child, the first in the house since the master himself had been born thirty-five years ago, but the nurses and patients as well. To the afflicted soldiers it was as though, in this world of madness that was killing and maiming human beings in their hundreds of thousands, the coming of a new life, which, now that they knew about it, they could see growing almost before their eyes, gave them a sense of continuation, of the bountiful goodness of Mother Nature who had nothing to do with the carnage at the front. Mrs Buchanan, in her new role of mother-to-be, was an image they carried into sleep, an image which in some way took them back to their own childhood and their own mother who was the comfort and blessing given to children. They were like children again, some of them, in their pain, calling out for 'Mam' in their delirium or sleep, and Mrs Buchanan, though it was said she was only twenty, was everyone's mother in her new role.

She fought it like a tiger, the restrictions they tried to put on her.

'You cannot possibly continue your duties on the wards, Mrs Buchanan,' Sister Colyford told her in that imperious tone which frightened VADs and nurses alike, as Lucy had known she would which was why she had kept her condition hidden.

'And why not? I am aware that I must no longer lift heavy buckets.'

'Or heavy men, my dear. You are in your sixth month.'

'I know that, Sister, but that does not mean I am an invalid. There are many tasks I can still perform and, believe me, you nor anyone else will stop me. This is my house and I shall do in it exactly as I wish.'

Lucy straightened her back and squared her chin and shoulders, the movement thrusting forward the bulge of her child. She still wore Cook's enormous apron over her nurse's uniform but her pregnancy was very obvious and those who had worked with her for all these months, especially Sister Colyford who should, as a trained nurse, have known better, were amazed that they had missed it. Of course she carried herself so well, so gracefully, and she was tall and womanly with splendid breasts and hips, like a young Juno, and so it was perhaps not to be wondered at, but that made no difference to Sister Colyford.

'And these are my wards and my patients and I will not have you here among them. They will be embarrassed.'

'So, none of them have seen a pregnant woman before, Sister, is that what you're saying and will shriek and faint away as spinsters did in Victorian times? I refuse absolutely to be kept from them and anything I am still capable of doing for them, I will do.'

They were both strong-willed women and everyone on the wards,—the soldiers betting on the outcome with Mrs Buchanan winning hands down—in the gardens and the kitchen could hear them going hammer and tongs, though Sister Colyford, for the sake of her dignity, was doing her best to remain calm. Lucy had no such scruples.

'I knew this would happen the moment you found out.'

'And none too soon, if I may say so, Mrs Buchanan. Do you want to harm the child?'

'Of course not, but if I am careful . . .'

'Perhaps your husband might have something to say on the matter. This is, after all, his child too.'

For the fraction of a second an expression of doubt, doubt and something else that Sister could not put a name to, slipped across Mrs Buchanan's mutinous face and her eyes clouded.

Ever since Charlotte had told her that James had chosen to spend his leave in Paris rather than come home, Lucy had brooded on what it might mean. She could not say it distressed her, since she knew that she and James were both aware that they were not as other husbands and wives were. They had struck a bargain over a year ago and she had more than kept her side of it, as he had. She was to bear his child which she supposed would please him and she had also supposed, in one of her infrequent letters, she should have told him about it, but she had been afraid that if she did the very thing that was happening now would be forced upon her.

And yet she was sorry in a strange way that he had not taken his leave here, in the home where he had been born, where he had grown from childhood to manhood and she hoped it was not because of her. Why he should avoid her, if that was what he was doing, she couldn't imagine, and she decided she was being silly to think so, but it

304

had unsettled her, upset her in a way, for it would have been ... What? What would it have been? She didn't know what she meant, where her thoughts were going, only that they were not happy ones.

'Mrs Buchanan, may I have your word that you will do as I ask?' Sister Colyford was saying. 'It is my responsibility to look after these men and if you should ... have an accident you know how it would upset them. They have a high regard for you, you know that?'

There was a catch in Lucy's voice as she answered. 'And I have a high regard for them, Sister Colyford, which is why I would like your permission to—'

'No, Mrs Buchanan, I cannot.'

'I was just about to say may I still continue to ... nurse them, not physical nursing but ... something that will help them to recover. It might be only helping them to tie their ties in the morning but I must feel I am ... Please, Sister, don't ban me from the wards.'

'Mrs Buchanan, as long as you promise not to do more than tie a tie, read a letter or a book, arrange flowers ...'

'In other words what all the other so-called society women are doing?' Lucy's voice was low and bitter but she knew she must have regard for this woman's position and also the wellbeing of the patients. If she was to take a tumble and lose the child it would put some of them back in their recovery, she knew that. There was a new illness, although some in the War Office did not call it that, to which the medical people gave the name of 'shell shock'. Men whose nerves had been pounded into

305

insensibility by the continual noise of the barrage that apparently went on and on for hours before they went 'over the top'—they were all learning the jargon the Tommies brought back from the front—and it was this along with the constant fear in which they lived that was driving some men to the brink of madness. They had one such in a separate ward, a small room at the back of the house since his cries disturbed the others. He had not been seriously wounded, a piece of shrapnel in his calf that had been successfully removed, but it was his mental state that gave cause for alarm. He must be tiptoed round, for any sudden noise, a door banging, the barking of James's dogs, sent him off into what Mrs Bunting called 'the screaming abdabs' which gave her the creeps, really it did, poor lad. He even slept under his bed and it was soldiers like him who must not be distressed.

'Nevertheless, Mrs Buchanan, will you promise me, until your child is born, that you will take no unnecessary risks. I will not ban you from the wards but if anyone reports to me, and they will all, staff and patients alike, be watching you like hawks, that you are not keeping your promise I will take steps to have you removed.'

If Sister was in high dudgeon over what she saw as sheer irresponsibility on Mrs Buchanan's part, the Buchanan ladies, who came over the moment the servants' grapevine revealed the news, were speechless and totally baffled, they told her, by her foolish negligence. Charlotte was to come later with Paul—had she heard that he was home on leave?—and would, no doubt, add her disapproval to theirs and they were, of course, quite sure she was to give this all up and leave it to the professionals. What would James say if he knew that she was still nursing, and then there were the men who were not gentlemen after all and it was not proper that the wife of one who was, a pregnant wife, should be continuing to mix with them and on and on until at last, standing up and sticking out her stomach for them all to see, she told them they must excuse her since she was tired and if they were to see Charlotte would they beg her to come on another day since she did not feel up to any more visits.

They left, somewhat put out, for they had not told her half of what they had intended telling her. After all, they all had borne a child and it seemed to them she was badly in need of their advice.

Lucy stood at the window and stared out into the thin drizzle that had started overnight. The garden was empty except for Licky Thripp who walked across the lawn on some private business of his own. She had seen him earlier with Mr Clapcott, who had resumed his duties as soon as he could, leaving Bertie's grieving mother in the care of her sister from Birmingham. He needed to be doing something, he had told Lucy, and his sister-in-law was a kind soul and would look after Mrs Clapcott as well, if not better than he could. It was all he could do to manage his own grief, just yet at any rate, and Mrs Clapcott was even worse.

Lucy sighed deeply, watching some blackbirds having a good wash in a puddle of water beneath the window. Their wings flapped, their heads bobbed and their feathers were wet and spiky. The rainwater flew about in a mad arc and the birds were totally unaware of the man standing under the gnarled oak tree that crouched at the gate leading into the vegetable garden. It was a soldier by the look of it, simply standing under the dripping spread of the tree watching the birds, as still as an animal trapped by a predator, cornered and terrified and unable to escape.

Lucy narrowed her eyes and peered at the figure through the rain, which was coming down faster now, dashing against the window of her sitting-room and running in growing rivulets. Who on earth among the wounded men was capable of walking round from the front of the house, where the wards were situated, to the back and why had no one noticed him? He had no overcoat on and she could see that the blue hospital uniform the men wore was darkening with rain.

Suddenly she recognised who it was. Swiftly she reached for her old cloak which she kept handy in her sitting-room and, throwing it about her shoulders, opened the French windows that led on to a small terrace lined with pots of herbaceous flowers. There were steps leading down to the lawn, which was next on the agenda for the growing of vegetables, and though she was quiet as she moved across the sodden grass she knew he had seen her by the sudden tightening of his body and the tic which developed in his pale cheek as she drew near. He took a step backwards, then another until his back was pressed against the trunk of the tree, putting out his hands as though to ward off some unimaginable horror and Lucy's heart moved with pity.

'It's only me, Rory,' she said quietly. 'I saw you watching the birds. I was too. They make a comical sight, don't they? But it's awfully wet out here. Why don't you come into my sitting-room and we'll have some tea. I don't know about you but I'm ready for one. My husband's cousins' wives—heavens, what a mouthful—have just left and I feel like a wrung-out rag. They are full of good advice on what I should or shouldn't do. You know I'm to have a baby, don't you?'

His gaze fell slowly to her swelling stomach and she saw him relax, the awful rigidity of his tall, slender body slipping away. His shoulders slumped and his hands fell to his sides. He moved away from the tree trunk, just one small step, but Lucy was encouraged to take one to meet him. He did not seem to mind.

Rory Cameron was an unusual soldier in as much as he did not come from the working-class background of the other enlisted men. He was what was known as 'officer material', for he had been educated at a well-known public school and had gone on to Cambridge. His family had an old and respected name. His father was a wealthy man from somewhere in Surrey, a stockbroker, and it had been hoped that Rory would go into the family firm but the war had put a stop to all that. Lucy had never actually talked to him, except to soothe him when his nightmares came, but she knew he had the drawling, well-bred accent of the privileged class into which he had been born. He had the appearance of a thoroughbred horse among a herd of sturdy work ponies, with an athlete's build, tall but pared down to the bone, a long, lean body without substance and a face that was almost too handsome. Had it not been totally and undeniably male it might have been described as beautiful. His hair was a pale silver blond, thick and heavy and his eyes were the deep blue of a cornflower.

'Will you come with me, Rory?' She smiled and was rewarded with a further relaxing of his muscles. 'I would be glad of your arm across this wet grass, if you wouldn't mind,' she went on, shamelessly exploiting her condition and at once his gentleman's manners, which had been bred in him since the nursery, prodded him into immediate action.

'Of course, Mrs Buchanan,' he said, almost leaping out from beneath the tree and smiling in return. Her condition did not seem to embarrass him, rather the opposite, for it overshadowed his own fears and gave him, for that small period of time, a crutch on which to lean. Not that he leaned on Lucy, far from it, he almost carried her across the grass, saying, in a solicitous voice, 'Now mind where you put your feet, Mrs Buchanan. It is really quite hazardous and those steps are covered with moss. Let me get the door. No, don't leave go of my arm just yet,' until at last he had her where he wanted her, which was in her armchair by the fire, her cloak carefully hanging over a chair back.

'Is that comfortable?' he begged her to tell him. 'Would you like to take off your shoes? They look wet to me,' and before she knew what he was about he knelt at her feet and with gentle hands undid the buttons on her stout shoes and drew them off her feet. He placed them by the fender, then sat back and grinned up at her.

It was like a miracle, a transformation, the merry twinkle in his lovely blue eyes, the creases in his cheeks where, in the past, he had done a great deal of laughing, the white perfection of his teeth in a face that was tinted now with colour.

'Rory, you make a better nurse than I did and I

shall tell Sister Colyford that if ever she needs a hand, you're her man.'

'Dear Lord, she'd reduce me to jelly the moment she came into the ward. I've heard her.' His voice rose to a light falsetto. ' "Nurse Bickerstaffe, why is that soldier lolling on his bed and as for the casters, they are a disgrace and I'd be obliged if you would straighten them at once." But I must admit she does her best with me and I'm not easy to deal with.'

It was said with total ease and candour and if Lucy had not seen for herself the dreadful shaking, the blankets under his bed where he hid from the nightmares, heard him cry out a name which sounded like 'Mama' she would not have believed this was the same man.

'Ring the bell, will you, Rory, and we'll have tea.' He did so and when Elsie, who had been promoted to the dizzy heights of parlour maid by the desertion of Win and Fanny and Bridie, popped her frilled cap round the door, she couldn't believe her eyes. There was Miss Lucy relaxed and smiling in her armchair, her belly out to here—this sotto voce to Cook so as not to offend Mr Dixon's sensibilities—and the soldier, the mad soldier, sitting on the floor at her feet.

'Tea, please, Elsie,' she was told, 'and will you ask Mrs Bunting if she could rustle up some of her chocolate shortbreads. I'm sure Private Cameron would love to taste one, wouldn't you, Private? Let me tell you they are the most wonderful biscuit you have ever tasted.'

'I bet they're not as good as the ones my mother's cook used to make. I can remember when we were children, my brothers and me, stealing them off the wire tray where Cook had put them to cool. We didn't half get a wigging, I can tell you. ',

'I couldn't believe it, really I couldn't,' Elsie declared in an awed voice. 'There he was, as happy as Larry, chatting away to the mistress and no sign of his shakes or anything. Eeh, that Miss Lucy,' she continued in a fond voice, 'she could get round anyone, her.'

He stayed with her for an hour and when Sister put her head round the door to see if Mrs Buchanan had seen him he told her to 'Bugger off, Sister, there's a dear,' with an impish smile on his face that took any insult out of his words.

'Well,' Lucy said later to Buffy, 'I might not be able to give Sergeant Collins a hand with his stump or help Nurse Bickerstaffe with rounds but I seem to have got through to poor Private Cameron.' She smiled with enormous satisfaction, believing in her naïvety that just one little chat with her had cured him of his shell shock.

She heard him yelling for someone to 'get your bloody head down unless you want the thing shot off', a couple of hours later, followed by Sister's firm tread as she hurried to his room with an injection. Lucy followed her, waiting until she knew the injection had taken effect. He was asleep, drugged and motionless, but his face had the marks of tears and she felt that compassion that she seemed to have in such overflowing abundance for these men who, most of them, would have to go back to the hell that had sent them here.

He spent a part of each day with her from then on, feeling, it seemed, that she needed his arm to go the smallest distance. He did not mix well with the other men, not because of the difference in their class but because of the difference in their injuries. His were not visible. His mind had been damaged and that didn't show as their wounds showed and though they were sympathetic since they had gone through exactly what he had and knew what he had suffered, they had not reached that fine line between sanity and madness which had affected him.

When Lucy walked in the garden or through the woods he went with her, guarding her every step and she had not the heart to stop him, feeling that here, at last, she was doing some good, giving him a reason for his very existence at that dreadful moment in his young life.

It was a lovely day towards the end of July and the heady scent of the roses, which Clapcott nurtured with the deep concern he gave to any growing thing, drifted over the roof from the front of the house to the back where she was walking in the shade. Her step was slow and heavy now, for she was near her time, and he followed her hesitantly, on his face an expression of great concern.

'I hadn't seen you on the ward today, Mrs Buchanan. I wondered whether you were ... unwell.' Quite naturally he took her hands and held them out to the side, looking down with great gentleness to her swollen belly. 'It won't be long now, will it? I asked Sister and after a lot of waffling, as though she did not think it quite proper for a gentleman to ask after the health of an expectant mother, she told me that there were only two weeks to go now. I had hoped to see the baby but I ... I may not be here.'

She looked astounded and her hands clutched

313

his tightly. 'Not here?'

'No, they say I am recovered and so I am to go back.' A shadow crossed his face but he managed to grin. 'I am better, I know that and I believe I have you to thank for it.'

She looked even more astounded. 'Me!'

He led her to a quiet corner of the garden which, as yet, had not been dug up for vegetables. There was a seat there, an old wooden bench which was in need of painting and with great care he helped her down on to it. He flinched as Thimble came tearing round the corner, not barking but going somewhere at great speed, but he remained calm.

Somewhere they could hear the sound of the children laughing and she knew they were messing about with an old perambulator which had been dug out of the attic and in which, presumably, James had been trundled about as a baby. It would do fine for the new little 'un, Licky Thripp had told her earnestly but Mrs Burns had been horrified, for the thought of putting 'their' baby in such an ancient contraption was not to be considered. Instead the children had taken it over, Edward informing them that he meant to put a motor on it if he could save up enough money and didn't they think a motorised perambulator would be enormous fun. James's dogs were barking, as they did now at every show of excitement and Lucy wondered idly what he would say when he got home. They were as wild and undisciplined as Thimble was but, she told herself, they had a great deal more fun.

'I felt . . . improved after that day we talked in your parlour, Mrs Buchanan, though I have had relapses. But these few weeks with you and the

314

thought of the new life. Christ, I hope you don't think me indelicate, but it has given me something. I don't know how to explain it, Mrs Buchanan.'

'Dear God, Rory, can you not call me Lucy after all this time.'

He flushed like a boy. 'May I?'

'Of course you may.'

'There was something I wanted to ask you. A great favour. You see I have come to ... well ...' He managed a boyish grin. 'I wondered if you would mind if I wrote to you, from the front, I mean. Oh, I write to my parents and they write to me but my father cannot forgive me for not taking a commission.'

'Why didn't you?'

'I wanted to fight the war the men fought. I know that sounds highfalutin', even pompous, but I felt the need to ... get away from the things my father thought so important.' He grinned. 'I was always a rebel, Lucy, doing the opposite to what was considered proper, so I enlisted on the day war was declared and my father has never forgiven me for it. That is why he has not been to see me here. Not a son who was cowardly and could not face up to his responsibilities. I have three brothers, all officers in a swank Surrey regiment, but ...' He looked down at his hands which were gripping one another in what seemed to be an agony of embarrassment, but she knew it was not that which had him in such turmoil. She put hers out and covered his and at once they stopped twisting about one another and relaxed. His fingers entwined with hers and she could feel her strength flowing into him and he smiled.

'There, you see what you do to me. One touch
315

and you cure me of my bloody jitters. I wish I could put you in my pocket and take you back with me. You know, don't you? You know that I love you.'

'Yes, I know, Rory.'

'Do you . . . mind?'

'It is something every woman should treasure, the offering of a man's love.'

'But it can come to nothing.'

'No, Rory, but I would like it if you wrote to me. We have become friends and one does not like to lose touch with friends.'

'Will you write back?'

'Yes.'

'Promise.'

'I promise.'

*   *   *

Somehow all the men knew the exact moment that Mrs Buchanan's pains began and among the married men who had children there was much conjecture as to how long her labour would be.

'My old woman was two bloody days wi' 'er first,' one offered, lugubriously, lighting a Woodbine and dragging the smoke deep into his lungs.

'Nay, don't say that. Poor lass. I wish . . .' another said wistfully and they all knew what he wanted to say. There was not one among them who would not have suffered their own injuries all over again if it saved the lovely Mrs Buchanan her pain.

''Appen it'll be quick. She's a big strong lass.'

''Appen.'

*   *   *

316

Lucy lay with her legs apart and her knees up, the mound of her belly jutting up so high she could barely see over it. She swore through gritted teeth that she would never go through this again, She had never felt so humiliated in her life, for Doctor Yates, who had been on duty at the time, had his nose almost inside her. And as if this wasn't bad enough she was suffering the most appalling pains which came at frequent intervals to tear her apart with a ferocity that appalled her. When would the damn child come, for goodness sake? She had been in labour quite long enough for several babies to be born and here was this old fool telling her, 'Bear down ... push ... push now, there's a good girl,' when every movement was torture. She was splitting apart and this had been going on for hours now and she didn't think she could take much more.

She said so weakly. Sweat stung her eyes and ran into her hair and someone—was it Buffy?—ran a damp cloth round her face.

'You're doing very well, my dear. When the next pain starts take a big breath and push.'

'It's all right for you,' she managed on anguished breath, but doing as she was told, trying to get rid of the round and heavy rock that was jammed inside her. It was breaking her open, tearing her tender flesh, wave after wave of pain until, with a surge which she was convinced was her life's blood, the rock slipped out and it became not a rock but a baby's head and she let out a long sigh of relief. The doctor was smiling with great satisfaction as though it had all been down to him and Buffy began to make foolish cooing sounds as the child was wrapped about in a towel and put in her arms.

317

She didn't feel like asking what it was.

'Well done, Mrs Buchanan,' Lucy heard Nurse Bickerstaffe say before she slipped into a lovely sleep which she hoped would last for at least a week. She deserved it!

They could none of them sleep that night, telling one another it was the heat, or the pain of their injuries, or that bloody dog barking its fool head off in the stable, though they all knew it was none of these things. When dawn broke, and Nurse Bickerstaffe bustled down to tell them that Mrs Buchanan had a beautiful baby girl, the cheer could be heard in the kitchen where the servants were keeping their own vigil.

There was champagne that day, the day Alice Buchanan was born, the day Rory Cameron was driven away and the day that Captain James Buchanan was promoted to major, though he did not celebrate with champagne. He did not celebrate at all.

CHAPTER EIGHTEEN

Lucy Buchanan wrote dutifully to her husband to tell him of his new daughter, saying in the letter that she hoped it would not be too long before they met, he and Alice. Did he like the name? She was sorry not to have conferred with him on the choice but Alice had been her grandmother's name and Christina, which was Alice's second name, had been his grandmother's. She made no apology for not writing more often; this was her first letter since telling him he was to be a father three months

318

ago. Alice was quite beautiful, she said, dark with pale grey eyes like his and not a scrap of trouble and the children adored her.

She did not mention that the soldiers did too.

'I don't hold with it,' Mrs Bunting told anyone who would listen to her, even Mrs Buchanan who she thought had lost her mind, the daft things she did. What Mrs Bunting didn't hold with she was not afraid to disclose. 'Them poor men I feel sorry for, I really do, but to let them have a hold of that poor little mite is more than I can bear to think of and I'm shocked and disappointed in the mistress. And that there Sister ought to know better an' all. All them bandages and what-not an' that poor chap wi' only his eyes showin'. Eeh, I've a good mind ter write ter the master.'

When Mrs Bunting was upset, as now, she reverted to the speech of her childhood, which had taken place in Bolton.

'Fancy, babby not even a month old and 'er passed round like a parcel from bed ter bed.' She shook her grey head in bewilderment and Mrs Burns patted her arm comfortingly, entirely in agreement with her. They had been overjoyed at the birth of Miss Alice and amazed at the splendid and speedy recovery of the mistress. Too speedy in their opinion and that of the other Buchanan ladies who were on her doorstep the very day the baby was born, ready with their advice and opinions on the upbringing of this newest addition to the Buchanan clan. Even the old people, the remaining grandparents, though not of Alice, of course, Mr Harry and Mr Job and their wives, all as spry as week-old lambs, Mr Harry, at sixty-nine, and Mr Job, a year younger, did her the honour of paying

319

her a visit, since this was, after all, James's first child. They poked the baby and told one another that she was the spit of old Alex, their father, and yet she had their mother's eyes. A real Buchanan and no mistake.

Lucy was not quite sure how she felt about Alice. She was glad she had arrived because it meant that she, Lucy, could resume her duties on the wards. She was keen to be involved with every aspect of nursing, not only on the three wards but in the operating theatre, she told Sister Colyford, and now that she was herself again, meaning without the burden she had dragged about with her all those weeks, she intended doing just that. She hoped to find a capable girl to look after Alice, which would leave her free to get on with her hospital work.

But when the time came she found, for some reason, she couldn't just give Alice over to another woman. It was strange really, for she had not expected this placid little scrap who had been put immediately into the family cradle, the one in which even Alex Buchanan, Alice's great-great-grandfather had slept, to attach herself so firmly to something in Lucy which she had not known existed. On Sister Colyford's advice, Sister Colyford having come from a large working-class family which thought such things to be entirely normal, she fed the infant herself, finding she had plenty of milk and quite enjoying the silent communion, except for the small grunting sounds of pleasure which came from Alice, growing between her and her daughter. Alice was left in the schoolroom with Margaret and Emily and Miss Bradley when Lucy was on the wards with instructions that they were to come for her at once if an emergency arose. She slept in her cradle or simply lay watching her own pink fists waving in the air and at the slightest sign of boredom on her part Margaret, Emily and Miss Bradley quarrelled over whose turn it was to pick her up.

Percy had started going to school with Edward now, both of them riding their bicycles along the country lanes and into Ambleside. He missed Thimble, he said, but otherwise it wasn't too bad. There was a splendid chap called Dickinson the same age as he was; oh, yes, they all called one another by their surnames. He was Dean Minor, of course, and he and Dickinson got on like a house on fire; in fact, if Lucy was agreeable and would telephone Dickinson's mother, he would like to have his new friend over to tea one day. That's if Lucy could pick Dickinson up, for Dickinson's father was at the front and his mother didn't drive their motor which was put away, like Mr Buchanan's Rolls, until the end of the war.

'But I can't drive either, darling,' she told him, holding him in her lap before the fire. He was seven years old now but still liked a cuddle, though she was careful not to do it before the others, for his dignity might be damaged.

'You could learn, Luce.'

'Why can't Mrs Dickinson learn then?'

'Oh, she's too old, but I bet you'd have the hang of it in no time. Edward'd teach you.'

'Edward?'

'Oh, yes, you know he's been able to drive for ages, only he's not old enough yet.'

The seed of the idea had been put into her head and it began to take root and grow. She could be found in the garage now and again, circling the Rolls-Royce which was carefully wrapped up in tarpaulin, a thoughtful expression on her face. She was not sure about Edward but she was sure there would be someone who could teach her.

*   *   *

Alice was eight weeks old when James came home on leave, almost a year after he had left.

Lucy was helping to dress the leg wound of a young private, no more than eighteen she was certain, who was doing his best not to scream out loud as Nurse Bickerstaffe, a pair of forceps in her hand, swabbed out the deep and appalling hole in his leg. It ran from his knee down to his ankle, probably two inches deep, and the nurse, who had to be brutal to clean it with the lysol, kept on murmuring like a litany, 'Not much more, old chap, soon be over, old chap,' while the young soldier clung to Lucy's hands, his eyes fearful holes in the ghastly grey of his agonised face, his gaze never moving from hers. There was a smell coming from the wound, a smell familiar to all those who treated these dreadfully injured men. After all these months Lucy could recognise gangrene when she smelled it and saw it and it lay deep in the young soldier's leg where cutting could not reach.

'Don't let 'em tekk it off, Mrs Buchanan,' he hissed through teeth which were clamped together so tightly the bones of his jaw stood out, white and rigid. Lucy bent over him, ready to gather him into her arms if necessary. She had a perfume, something James had given her in the early days of their marriage and she wore it on the ward, for she

322

knew it pleased the men who knew only the smell of lysol and carbolic and all the other aromas of sickness which could not be prevented. Her hair, which she bound back with her nurse's kerchief, despite the pins and combs Dimity tucked into it, still had a tendency to slip out in curling tendrils, to Sister's disapproval, and now one drifted across the boy's face, touching his cheek and he relaxed and smiled through his agony.

It was this that met James Buchanan's eyes as he stepped slowly into the hall and looked into what had once been his elegant drawing-room.

Along both walls, and even in a line down the centre of the enormous room were beds, each one filled with a bandaged man. Arms, legs on pulleys controlled with a mass of wires, heads that were totally encased in white, hands, faces with slits from which eyes peered and mouths gaped, and when he turned and looked into what had been the dining-room it was the same. The beds were close together with only a locker standing between each one and along the windowsills beneath each window stood a mass of flowers in vases and somehow he knew they were his wife's doing. Some of the lockers had a photograph standing on them: a family group, a wife, a sweetheart. There were trolleys draped in white gauze on which were kidney-shaped dishes, instruments, bottles of disinfectant, pads of dressings, cotton wool and hypodermic needles in disinfectant. The wide doors at the far end of the drawing-room opened on to the conservatory, through which even more beds could be seen and from it came the sound of a gramophone playing the soldiers' favourite song of the moment.

'It's a long way to Tipperary, It's a long way to go . . .' warbled a female voice, but from the conservatory, apparently unaware that they could be overheard, several male voices parodied.

That's the wrong way to
tickle Mary,
That's the wrong way,
you know . . .

There were several wheelchairs in which blue-uniformed soldiers sat, some with one leg, some with none, and in the midst of it was his lovely wife who had haunted his dreams and filled his heart with pain and rejection for two years now.

He had been slightly wounded at the Battle of Loos which had begun on 25 September. There had been heavy casualties at Neuve Chapelle earlier in the year and the disaster at Gallipoli had decimated not only British troops but those from Australia and New Zealand; but those in command, who must know what they were doing, or so the men in the trenches said with deep irony, began the attack at Loos on the 25th. The infantry had scrambled out of their trenches and headed across no-man's land in a haze of gas and smoke, gas which was later to turn on their own men, and it was then that the bullet went cleanly through James's upper arm and knocked him out of the battle. He had walked back to the casualty clearing station with scores of other walking wounded, carrying one young lad on his back and repeatedly telling the others to get on their bloody feet and follow him. His wound was clean, the bullet having gone right through, and as he had not been in contact with the filth through which his men staggered, it was easy to treat.

'Aren't you due some leave, Major Buchanan?' his commanding officer asked him and when he said he was, he was told to get on the convoy and take himself off until his arm had healed. He had come from London where most of the hospital trains arrived and, still with the convoy of wounded, had been brought north, since the hospitals in the south were no longer able to take any more casualties. The ambulances were gathered on the drive behind him.

An orderly pushed him unceremoniously aside, calling out to the nurse who stood beside Lucy that there was a fresh batch of wounded for her, though fresh was hardly the word to describe them for they had come straight from the trenches and had been on the move for several days.

At once other nurses appeared, led by an older one in a frilled cap and a small cape which evidently denoted her rank as a sister.

'How many, Corporal?' Her manner was brisk and not at all disconcerted.

''Ow many can yer take, Sister? We got abaht thirty, I reckon. I'm to share 'em out among the three 'ospitals up 'ere.'

The sister turned to Lucy and said crisply, 'Can you manage any more beds, Mrs Buchanan? I know the authorities delivered some a few weeks ago for emergencies but . . .'

'They're in the tack-room, Sister. I'll get some help and fetch them over. The mattresses are stored in my sitting-room upstairs. They can be put . . . let me see . . .' James saw his wife look round her, her eyes narrowed in concentration. 'We could

325

put some in the hallway and a couple at the end of the conservatory. Say about a dozen.'

'Very well, bring in a dozen, Corporal, and put their stretchers down wherever you can find a space. The beds will be ready for them in half an hour. Is there a doctor with them?'

'There is, Sister, an' 'e ses 'e knows these parts. Name of Buchanan.'

The dozen men, who had appalling untreated wounds, apart from the bit of rough first aid they had received at the clearing stations, were dumped on the floors with the mud and filth of Flanders still on them. One was screaming but the rest were grey and silent, deep in shock. Not for several hours did Lucy and James Buchanan take stock of one another in the quiet back reaches of her parlour. They had passed one another a dozen times in the sorting out of the men and the treating of their wounds, for James was soon caught up in the drama and could not stand idly by and watch those slips of girls, the VADs and his own wife, tussle with stretchers and heavy men who had to have their stinking uniforms cut from their damaged bodies. He had been helping Paul on the journey, Doctor Paul Buchanan, who was to return immediately to the war zone when he had delivered his broken cargo.

'Go and have a bath and spend an hour with Charlotte, man,' James had told him. 'And that's an order.' And as Paul was a captain and James a major he had smiled, kissed Lucy and left, for by this time Doctor Yates had arrived. With the increasing number of wounded pouring into the hospitals about Ambleside and Windermere there were now three doctors, all elderly men brought out of retirement but better than nothing, and they had had to learn fast the treatment of wounds that they had never, in their entire medical careers, expected ever to see.

'Well, Lucy, you seem to be keeping busy,' were the first words her husband spoke directly to her. 'I'm surprised you have the time with a new baby to care for.'

On the attack from the first, though it was not so much attack as a form of defence, for he could not seem to get his bearings around this lovely, calm, madonna-like woman who he had noticed, even in the madness of the past few hours, every man in every bed followed with his eyes. Though he would have given ten years of his life to put his arms around her and lay his weary head on her breast, it did not show in his expressionless face. His manner was cold, though inside the beating of his heart was so loud and fast he was certain she would see the movement of it beneath the stained jacket of his uniform.

'Oh, James, have you nothing else to say to me after all this time?' she asked him sadly.

'Such as what, Lucy? I knew, of course, that Howethwaite was a hospital now but I had no idea you were so totally involved in it. May I ask where my daughter is? In whose care have you put her while you play Florence Nightingale to these men?'

It had appalled him to see her continue treating the young soldier whom she had been holding when he had entered the ward. That alone had driven him to the point where he could have torn her from the bedside and struck the man who lay in it but, naturally, he had not done so, but later, when the first wild rush was over, he had watched

327

her place maggots, a hateful mass of wriggling maggots, into the open wound on the soldier's leg, his own stomach ready to heave and yet she had done it calmly, holding the boy's hand when it was done, brushing back his fair hair and telling him that if she could help it he would not lose his leg.

'They . . . they won't fall into the bed, will they, Mrs Buchanan?' the boy asked valiantly.

'No, Freddy, they won't do that. They will eat the badness from your leg and then it will heal. Now go to sleep.'

'I know you can't stay with me, Mrs Buchanan, not with all this lot to see to,' restlessly tossing his feverish head upon the pillow, 'but will you come and . . . see me, later?'

'I promise, Freddy.'

'You promise too much, Mrs Buchanan,' he heard the sister say to her as she passed. 'You can't be with them all, all the time.'

'I can do my best, Sister. As we all do.'

Now she spoke to him in the quiet voice, the calm and soothing voice she had developed over many months of dealing with fractious men.

'Alice is with the girls and Miss Bradley, James. Would you like to come up now and see her? She is ready for her feed so I must go.'

'Her feed?' His shuttered face revealed none of the antipathy he felt at the thought of some infant at his wife's breast, at that lovely rosy nipple, the white, full flesh which had given him so much delight.

'Yes, I am nursing her myself so you see she is not totally neglected. Perhaps you would like to inspect her for damage?'

'I think a bath first, if such a thing can be had,'

for the thought of his daughter gave him no pleasure and he was in no rush to make her acquaintance. He was not fond of small infants and this one, though it belonged to him and to Lucy, was surely the same as all others. He could not seem to care overmuch, though he knew he should, but over the last months his mind had begun to shut itself off to so many things—sights, sounds, smells, emotions, fears that he had to endure—and so, like many other soldiers, he put them from him, or at least did his best to put them from him in order to get from one day to the next without going completely mad.

'Of course, I'll get Dixon to—'

For the first time he showed some signs of pleasure. 'Dixon. Good God, is he still going?'

'Of course, what did you think had happened to him? That I had turned him out because we no longer give dinner parties?' Her voice was sharp. 'Some of the maids have gone. Munitions, but Mrs Bunting and Mrs Burns will be delighted to see you.'

There was the sound of frantic barking coming from the back of the house and James lifted his head eagerly.

'Holmes and Watson. I must go and greet them or they will wake the dead with their row.'

'Yes, though I warn you they are not quite so well behaved as they were. Thimble's bad manners have rubbed off on them and not the other way around.'

'I'll soon knock them into shape.'

'How long will you be home?' They were like two polite acquaintances, thrown together after a long interval, their faces averted from one another, their thoughts hidden.

'Oh, a couple of days, I suppose,' though he actually had a week.

As he was about to leave the room, his face warm with anticipation at the thought of greeting old friends, his dogs, his servants, all of whom meant more to him than she did, she asked him casually, 'Why did you not come home in the summer? Charlotte told me you had gone to Paris. Paul was here for a few days . . .'

'That was why. I would have spent too much time travelling.' He kept his back to her, his voice casual as though it mattered to neither of them.

'Paul seemed to find it convenient.'

'Well, perhaps he was sure of a—' he broke off, aware that he was about to show something of himself that he preferred her not to see.

'Yes?'

'Nothing. Now, I'll have a bath and then if you would send one of the servants to let me know when it is . . . convenient for me to see the child. When you have finished your . . . her . . . meal.'

'I wouldn't object if you were to come while she is nursing. She is your child, James, and I am your wife.'

'So she is, and so you are. Nevertheless, please let me know a time that would be suitable to you.'

He left the room and from the garden she heard the high-pitched excited barking of his dogs, frantic with joy. They had sensed his presence in the house but had been kept from him; now, in a frenzy of love, they were leaping up at him until, as she watched, they brought him down. He was laughing, his face creased and merry, his groans of remonstrance having not the slightest effect on

330

them. All over the grass they romped and when, at last, he went across to the kitchen door and disappeared inside they howled dismally, flopping down in a great heap of misery.

She sighed, a long-drawn-out sigh which spoke of her own misery, for how was she to treat this husband who had come home from the war with what looked like hatred of her in his heart? She didn't know why. Surely it was not simply because she was nursing? Before he became a soldier they had rubbed along, not in the way married people did, at least not like her mama and papa had done but it had seemed to satisfy James. Now, for some hidden reason he was treating her as though she had seriously offended him and she didn't know why.

Taking off the square of her nurse's cap and undoing the top buttons of her uniform, she moved slowly up the stairs to the first floor. She opened the door of her bedroom where, she supposed, she and James would sleep together tonight. She threw her cap on the bed with her stained apron then turned and walked out again, moving towards the stairs that led up to the children's rooms.

Edward and Percy were still at school but Margaret, Emily and Miss Bradley were sitting cosily round the fire. Miss Bradley had taught both girls to knit and they were engaged on long khaki scarfs that would wrap many times round the neck of some soldier at the front. Winter was coming and they would be glad of them, they had been told. They were making up a sort of a parcel of socks, mufflers and mittens, with thumbs only, though Miss Bradley was knitting the socks and mittens since they needed four needles and the

331

girls weren't up to that standard yet. Buffy was helping, though she was not as good with knitting needles as she was with a sewing needle.

She was nursing Alice, her plain freckled face soft and loving as she crowed over the baby in her arms. She had helped, like Lucy, with the influx of wounded soldiers and there had been blood and filth on her apron but she and Lucy made it a point to change before they came to the schoolroom. The baby's head was pressed close to Buffy's breast and the silver grey eyes in her face, so like her father's, stared up in sharp concentration, then with a sort of jerk, she smiled, putting her whole body into it.

'Look, oh, do look, she just smiled. For the first time she actually smiled. She's kept it for the day her father comes home. The little darling. Oh, Lucy, just wait until Mr Buchanan sees her. Can he help but love her?'

Lucy did not answer but took her daughter from Buffy. She opened her bodice and put the child's open mouth to her nipple where Alice latched on with great eagerness. The girls watched for a moment but, used to the sight of their sister and niece, resumed their industrious and laboured tussle with the needles and wool.

He came an hour later. She had sent Buffy, an astonished Buffy, she could see, to tell Mr Buchanan that he might come up now, just as though he had to have an appointment, Buffy said later to Miss Bradley, with whom she had struck up a friendship.

The baby was in her cradle, sunk in the deep and infant sleep that comes after feeding. She lay on her back in the pretty white lawn nightgown Buffy had made and embroidered for her, her arms flung up above her head, since no one had told Lucy that young babies should be wrapped like a parcel before they were put into a cradle. If the Mrs Buchanans could have got to her there was no doubt they would have been horrified at what they would have seen as Lucy Buchanan's careless handling of James's daughter. She had not even been christened yet and her, meaning Lucy, a rector's daughter.

There was pink ribbon threaded through the yoke of Alice's nightdress and about the cuff. She had been bathed and her dark hair lay in a fat, glossy curl from her forehead, across the pulsing fontanelle to the crown and in swirls about her ears and neck. She had the soft button nose and the pouting rosebud lips of the new baby and her satin cheeks were pink with health. Her dark eyebrows arched delicately over her closed eyes which had the long fine eyelashes he himself had as a child. Unlike his wife, he fell in love with his daughter the moment he set eyes on her.

'Well,' Lucy said ungraciously, expecting some criticism. 'Does she suit?'

James was frozen to the strip of carpet which lay beside the cradle. His gaze never wavered, his eyes as frozen in their sockets as the rest of his body. Had someone asked him to speak he could not have done so, for the vulnerability of the child moved him to such depths of protective love he was totally overwhelmed. He had not expected it. The child's breathing was light and she snuffled as air passed through her small nasal passages and James Buchanan was enchanted.

Without thought, without asking for permission,

he leaned down and with careful hands picked her up and settled her to his chest in the crook of his arm. He had changed into flannels and a clean, white, open-necked shirt and his daughter turned her face towards him and sighed in deep satisfaction and he could feel the tears begin to form at the back of his throat. She was his. This lovely child was his. To her he would give his love, the great swell of love that his wife did not want. Now, now he had something to bring him back to Howethwaite, something to get him through the horror of what was waiting for him out there in Flanders. This tiny child would bring him home.

They all stared at him in amazement, the two girls open-mouthed, for Mr Buchanan had never seemed to them, who were children, to be interested in children. Of course, Alice was his daughter which probably made a difference but would you look at him, sitting down in the chair Buffy hastily vacated, one leg bent and crossed over the other knee, Alice comfortably resting in the crook of his arm and on his face an expression none of them had ever seen before. Thimble came up to him, willing to be friends, though he seemed to remember harsh words from this man and he put out his hand to fondle the dog's head.

'Should the dog be up here?' he asked his wife idly, never taking his eyes from his daughter's face.

'They . . . they all come up, James. The children are used to them and so Alice . . . well, I thought she must get used to them too.'

'Of course.'

They sat for five minutes, all of them exchanging glances of total bemusement as Alice's father touched her cheek and her eyebrows and seemed in no hurry to put her back in her cradle.

'You all go about your business,' he said at last. 'I'll stay here for a while.'

'Well . . .' They looked at one another and shrugged, wondering what to do in this unprecedented moment of wonderment. Then, Lucy, with a gesture of compassionate understanding, for had she not seen the healing process her daughter worked on them when the soldiers downstairs held her for a precious moment, put her fingers to her lips and with a silent nod of her head, drew them all from the room, leaving James and Alice Buchanan alone.

CHAPTER NINETEEN

James had intended staying two days at the most. He had meant to give Paul a hand on his journey up north with the wounded, and, for the sake of how it looked and to give the impression that he was like any other officer on a spot of leave with his family, depart for the front as soon as he was able. He would go to London, get lost in the mad frenzy of soldiers on leave from France, perhaps get himself a woman, get drunk, see *Chu Chin Chow* which was all the rage in London, eat at all the best restaurants and night-clubs and generally have a bloody good time until it was time for him to go back to the hell of the Western Front.

Alice Buchanan altered all that.

He made them smile, even the soldiers watching him from their beds in the conservatory which had a good view of the gardens, as he wheeled his

335

daughter in her brand-new perambulator about the front lawns of Howethwaite, proud as punch and ready to show her to anyone he met. Licky Thripp told them in the kitchen he'd never seen 'owt like it. By gum, he'd got six bairns of his own, all grown up now and two of the lads at the front and he'd been fond of them. Well, a father was, wasn't he, but that there master of theirs took the bloody cake, if Mrs Burns would pardon his language. Queer as Dick's hatband, 'e was, but then perhaps that was what war did to you. Made you cling to what was at home and he certainly clung to that babby, by crikey.

' 'E stopped me by t' wall side o't river. Scrafflin' about in that there lupin bed waitin' for 'er ter wake up, 'e said. Wanted ter show 'er t' ducks, would yer believe, an' 'er no more 'n eight weeks old. "Look at 'er, Licky," 'e ses ter me, "in't she t' most beautiful child you've ever clapped eyes on an' watch her smile. They say she first did it on t' day I come home," 'e ses, 'an' I'm prepared to believe it. She never stops now, Licky, 'cept when she's asleep.' Aye, she were a right smiler now, an' no mistake, an' 'appen she did it fer't first time day 'e come 'ome but it was a bit of a facer ter see t'master what rarely did more than nod in yer direction, draggin' yer over to peer under th'ood o't baby carriage.'

'I think it's lovely,' Elsie declared stoutly, vigorously stirring the huge pan of vegetable soup she and Cook were preparing for the soldiers' meal. Elsie had come on a pace since she was the skinny little maid of all work who had answered the door at the rectory two years ago. She was fourteen and with the weight she had gained due to Cook's constant admonishment to 'eat up, lass, there's not a pick on you,' and the confidence which had come with her new position she was ready to tackle any suspected criticism of her master who had made all this wonderful change in her possible. Him and Miss Lucy, of course. She was still maid of all work, they all were, mucking in wherever it was necessary. There was nothing to be gained by Dimity arguing that she was a lady's maid and therefore it was beneath her to scrub out the sluice or polish the windows, nor in Gertie, who had been a parlour maid, refusing to do other than parlour maid's work. There was a war on and things were different and with the wards and the extra cooking it was a case of whoever was available, did it!

James was still home when Douglas Askew, and Janet and Angus Gunson's second son, Lawrence, came to say goodbye and at the same time get first-hand news of what it was like at the front, for that was where they were off, they said. They were wild with excitement and very conscious of the splendid officers' uniforms they both wore. Would Uncle James tell them about it? Lawrence's brother Job, who had been one of the first to go, was a real spoilsport, having nothing to say on the matter when he came home on leave and Freddy Mossop was the same. Roger Askew had been wounded in the recent Battle of Loos, they didn't know how badly, their young schoolboy faces gravely serious for a moment, and Greg Kendall was a prisoner of war, had they heard?

Uncle James was as uncommunicative on the subject as every other soldier they had spoken to and they left with no premonition of what was ahead of them. They averted their eyes from the unlucky chaps in the dining- and drawing-rooms, not because they were unfeeling but they could not visualise that anything like this could happen to them.

'Mrs Buchanan, will you get out of my wards and go and spend some time with your husband,' Sister Colyford said to her in an exasperated tone on the third day of Major Buchanan's leave. There he was, marching about the place with his baby daughter, either in her perambulator, or held gently, protectively against his chest, his dogs close at his heels and really, Mrs Buchanan should be with him. A week's leave was very short and, yes, they could manage without her for a few days and she was to stop arguing.

It was one of those glorious autumn days when the world seems to stand still for a moment, reluctant to let go of summer and head into winter, gathering to itself for a brief day, perhaps the last, all the glories of the year. A warm, delicious calm and sweet peace brooded over the house, broken only by the voices of the children who had gone blackberrying along the hedgerows that bordered the woods at the back of the house and the sound of one of the ponies whickering from the paddock. Clapcott and Licky were picking apples and there was to be apple and blackberry pie for dinner, Cook had promised, when the master, Miss Alice asleep in the crook of his arm, wandered into the kitchen to show her off.

Lucy found him there, sitting at the kitchen table watching Elsie make pastry, peaceful and relaxed in a way she had never seen him before. She could not get over the way he was with the baby and said so a dozen times a day to Buffy, who was still her only confidante. She herself had found that as the days went by her love for her child, which had been of an uncertain nature to start with, became stronger, the bond tightening until she longed, at many times during the day, to run upstairs for a moment just to hold her in her arms. She couldn't imagine her life without Alice now but that feeling had not come spontaneously. It had crept up on her stealthily, multiplying, giving her a deep sense of fulfilment and joy she could not have imagined. Now, James felt the same, she knew he did, but his feelings, his love had surged at once into his heart. From the very minute he had seen his daughter, there it had been, whole, complete, unending, and it had amazed and yet at the same time delighted her. She did not love him, she knew that, but now his daughter would and it gave her a sense of repayment, of a debt paid that through all the years to come, through her, he would know the love of his child.

'Sister says I'm to have a day off, James.' Her voice was diffident. There it is. If you wish for my company, I am yours, she seemed to be telling him, but if he didn't she would go away again and leave him to his deep contemplation of Alice Buchanan.

'Well, and what had you in mind, Lucy? A walk on the hills, perhaps, but I warn you I am not leaving my daughter behind.'

They all turned to stare at him, Elsie and Cook, Mrs Burns and Dixon, who had been studying the master's wine cellar with a view to tonight's dinner. Dimity held a spoon from which cream dripped, since there must be cream with blackberry and apple pie and the richness of it dripped on to Cook's clean floor where the kitchen cat immediately set to with its rough and greedy tongue.

'Here, mind what you're doing with that cream, my girl.' Cook was first to come out of her tranced state. The idea of walking on the hills with that babby and her no more than eight weeks old filled her with horror, just like when them soldiers with their terrible wounds were allowed to nurse the little mite, but who was she to argue, though her face said she'd like to.

The mistress laughed. 'On the hills. That sounds wonderful, James. I haven't been up there for weeks. Well, since before Alice was born and it's the perfect day for it; but I don't see how we can take Alice.'

Cook relaxed and turned back to her oven but she might have known the master wouldn't be overruled.

'Why not? It's dry and warm and if Jacob and I were to put our heads together I'm sure we could find something in the tack-room, some harness, or a nose band or two that could be mackled together to make a carrying contraption. Like a rucksack I could put on my back.'

Well! What next! They were to put that precious child in a rucksack and tug her about like some bit of climbing equipment. Cook stirred her gravy so hard it slopped over the side of the roasting dish in which the juices of the roast lamb had been combined with the cabbage water.

'Well, I suppose that would be all right, providing it doesn't rain.'

'We could take an umbrella.'

'And a picnic.'

'With a bottle of wine.'

'And James . . .'

'Yes?'

He turned to look up at her, the smile he had been bestowing on his daughter still there with a bit left over for his wife.

'Can we get the Rolls out? I want to learn to drive.'

They made a right pair and it did all the men a power of good to see their Mrs Buchanan, with her officer husband and their baby daughter, setting out for the day in the major's splendid Rolls-Royce which had been uncovered, brought out, the engine turning over as sweetly as though it had been used only the day before, given a quick polish, and filled up with a can of petrol Tom Baxter had put away for a special occasion.

The most astounding thing, beside all the other astounding things, was the sight of Mrs Buchanan in a pair of her husband's trousers with the legs stuffed into a pair of sturdy climbing boots. At least they supposed them to be her husband's, for she was tall, almost as tall as he was and where else would she have got them? Eeh, she was a right one, was Mrs Buchanan, they told one another admiringly. Holding the trousers up was a leather belt round her waist which was now back to the size it had been before the baby. She wore a shirt of some fine material with a jumper slung round her shoulders and as she climbed into the motor she turned and waved to them, laughing, her hair already all over the place and there was not one man there who would not have given ten years of his life to change places with Major Buchanan. The baby was settled on her lap, the two big black dogs were settled on the back seat, the major started the engine and with a fine flourish the beautiful Rolls-Royce Silver Ghost thundered off up the drive.

They were to motor to White Moss, a spot where Grasmere Lake and Rydal Water met, not far but just long enough to turn the engine over, James told her, which would do it the world of good. They would park there and on the way back he would give her a brief driving lesson. There was nothing much on the road and she might as well plunge right in. It was no good chugging up and down the drive. If she was to learn she must do it on a proper road. And she was not to think that when she could drive she would be allowed to dash hither and yon because she wouldn't. The shortage of petrol would put paid to that but he agreed that in an emergency—meaning naturally, to do with Alice—it might be wise to have some means of transport.

They had decided in the brief preparation for the outing that to climb as far as Elterwater would be far enough, at least with the baby. That was when Lucy had put it to him that she would be more comfortable and *safer*, which was of paramount importance with Alice, if she was to wear trousers.

He was pulling his own corduroy breeches on at the time and he turned to stare at her in astonishment. For a moment he hopped about comically and Lucy wanted to laugh but she knew she mustn't. Alice was lying in the middle of their bed, her arms waving vigorously, her eyes fixed on a shaft of reflected sunlight which lay across the ceiling. She gave a gurgle, or was it just wind, but whatever it was it distracted her father from what her mother was saying and he leaned over her, fastening his breeches round his lean waist.

'James?'

'Did you hear that?' he asked, totally bewitched by this tiny creature who, a few days ago, he had never met.

'Yes, now what about the trousers? You have some old flannels in the wardrobe and I'm sure they'd fit me.'

'Would they?'

'Mmm, so you don't mind?'

'Not at all,' his indifference to whatever Lucy Buchanan did totally obscured by what Alice Buchanan did.

It worked quite wonderfully well, the harness, and Alice seemed to find it all quite acceptable, nodding off to sleep on her father's back as they climbed up through the bracken which was beginning to turn from the deepest green to the brown of autumn. The heather, which was a dense purple coverlet in the summer, was changing to umber and burned yellow. Sheep called and a dog fetching them in streaked across their path as it answered the shepherd's whistle. Rock ledges, fan-shaped screes, black rocks and the green pasture contrasted sharply in the brilliant sunshine and a warbling beck tumbled past, rowan-shaded, on its way to the lake. They stopped for a moment, shading their eyes to look across the land, the harsh fell land which undulated fiercely, range after range, as far as they could see, before vanishing into the heat haze on the horizon.

They didn't talk much. She mentioned that Charlotte Buchanan was to have a child in the spring, apparently conceived on Paul's last leave.

'God almighty, don't tell me he actually

persuaded her to lie down and open her legs?' He grunted in disbelief then turned to share her shout of laughter, for he had never joked with her before, especially a crude sort of a joke which a husband would not normally tell his wife.

'That's all the men think of, did you know that?' He grinned at her.

'I don't believe it. How do you know?'

'Well, apart from being a man I have to censor their letters. One chap wrote to his wife . . . Good God, I should not be telling you this . . . It's not decent.'

'Oh, do go on, James. I'm not the ignorant rector's daughter you knew two years ago, you know.'

'No, you're not,' eyeing her rounded buttocks appreciatively. 'Well, he told her to get a good look at the floor because when he got home all she would see was the ceiling!'

For a moment she looked at him, at the deep, velvet grey of his eyes which were glowing with laughter then she began herself, listening as his voice and hers echoed about the hills.

She saw her husband sigh in contentment and within her was the hope that he would carry this, this beauty, the companionship they had so unexpectedly found, this love of his child who he was introducing to his land, back to the trenches with him. She, of all people, knew what he lived through. The tension of trench warfare, the terror of mutilation and death, the unceasing din of the artillery which could completely unhinge the sturdiest of minds. She had lived through it with soldiers who were in her care and who babbled ceaselessly in their nightmares of pals blown to smithereens before their eyes and other things that she did her best to forget, as they did.

They came at last to the small, gem-like lake of Elterwater, set among hummocks of enchanting trees, surrounded, but not forbiddingly so, by the mightier fells. Larch and birch and the crumpled deep yellow leaves of the oak to sit on and while Alice slept in the nest of her mother's jumper and her father's jacket James and Lucy ate the small pork pies, the hefty ham sandwiches, for a man likes something to get his teeth into, Mrs Bunting said, the almond cakes and chocolate shortcakes that the master had loved from childhood, all washed down with a bottle of dry white wine of Dixon's choosing. James drank most of it, for as Lucy said with studied casualness, she must feed Alice and they didn't want the child to be tipsy.

She hesitated when the time came, remembering James's command to fetch him when she had finished nursing but that was before he met Alice, and since then he had made love to his wife four times in their deep bed. He had seen her naked, fondled the breasts from which Alice gained her sustenance, put his own mouth to the nipple where Alice's had been, so was she now to turn prudish?

Holding the baby in the crook of her arm she bared her breast and at once Alice snuffled on to the nipple, her little mouth working ten to the dozen, milk dribbling from the corner of her mouth and for ten minutes, and then another ten on the other breast, James Buchanan watched his wife and child and it was not the child who captured his full attention. Alice was changed and put down in her little bed where she at once fell into a deep sleep under the watchful protection of the dogs, who knew their duty to this new, puppy-like creature, and when Lucy looked up to smile at James his eyes met hers with an intensity that made her heart skip a beat and her mouth dry up. A spark warmed her, like an arc of electricity from him to her, a touching of something inside her which was disconcerting but not unpleasant and when he reached out to her and took her hand she did not resist. Her shirt was still partially unbuttoned and her breast was only half covered and with his other hand he began to undo the rest, exposing it. His finger reached to touch her nipple. It was rosy, still damp from the child's sucking but at his touch it peaked and hardened at once. He looked up into her face, one dark eyebrow arched questioningly. He smiled and in her chest and throat something lurched in the most astonishing way. Her flesh shivered in delighted anticipation and without conscious thought her mouth reached for his.

He undressed her and then she undressed him, wordlessly, as though each was somehow aware that this might be something important to them and they were afraid to shatter it with the wrong words. Let their bodies speak, and their eyes. Hers had turned to an unusual light colour, golden brown, like amber in crystal, almost yellow as passion began to rise in her under her husband's sure hands.

For a moment she drew back, her hands pressing against his naked chest and at once he stopped, for this was not the first time James Buchanan had made love to his wife during his leave and she had responded as she had always done in the first months of their marriage, which was to be totally acquiescent, willing, but no more.

346

'I don't want a child, James,' she gasped, for the last time she had felt like this, her body answering his with a strength which matched his, Alice had been conceived.

'You won't have a child, my love, I promise you,' and under the deep blue bowl of the Lakeland sky, with the sheep bleating and the curlews calling and their child asleep beside them, James and Lucy took one another to a place of warmth and excitement and cherishing, and in his hard embrace their explosion of pleasure came at the same time.

When it was over she sat up, lifting her strong young arms above her head, her hands lifting her tumbled hair from the nape of her neck, arching her back, displaying herself for her husband's pleasure, and for her own. He turned her face to him and looked deep into her eyes and saw something there, he didn't know what, but whatever it was it made his heart sing with joy and hope.

He took her out without Alice on the following day, which was still warm and dry, letting her drive the Rolls up as far as Keswick, along the winding road in the valley bottom, below the towering heights of Helvellyn, which had a crown of low clouds, ragged and uneasy, and James forecast that the spell of warm summer-like weather would be over soon. They had tea in Keswick, again not speaking much but easy in one another's company, their eyes meeting, smiling, and Lucy wondered at this side of James that she had never seen before. He was allowing her to look into him, to see him, to know the sum and substance of the man who was James Buchanan, trusting her in a way that delighted her. Could it all be because of Alice? she wondered and was surprised when the thought sent a small frisson of disappointment through her.

On the way back they were jolted out of the almost dream-like state the day had wrapped them in by the sight of the gunpowder carts on their way to Windermere railway station from the Emmerson Gunpowder Works. There were twelve of them with a certain distance between each one in case of accident. The drivers walked beside them as a precaution but on the way back they were allowed to ride the empty carts. The procession, to which the last driver warned them they must not come too close, held them up for nearly an hour and when they got home there was a stream of servants, soldiers, nurses and even the children to tell her in a reproving tone that Alice was awake and crying for her tea. He raced up the stairs with her towards the sound of the indignant wailing which came from the top of the house, as flustered as she was to get the child to her breast, smiling in guilty relief at each other as they shared Alice's enjoyment. He knelt at her feet watching these two human beings whom he loved more than life itself, his lean face softened with emotion. His hand touched the curls on Alice's head, gently smoothing them back, then went to Lucy's wind-tossed, glossy mane and doing the same.

It was a Sunday and tomorrow he was to leave. The christening of Alice Christina Buchanan was to take place at the church of St Mary's in Ambleside where Lucy and James were married and for the first time since before the war the Buchanan family were gathered together and for the first time, in some amazing way, Lucy felt them to be *her* family.

Only Alex and Franny were missing and, of course, the young men of the family who were at the front. Charlotte was there looking exceedingly smart in a concealing gown the clever Miss Medlock had fashioned for her, though she was barely three months pregnant. She took full advantage of it though, clinging to some male arm throughout the afternoon, barely looking at Alice and certainly not holding her, since there was a possibility that the child might be sick on her. Paul had returned to the front the day after he had delivered his wounded, probably glad to do so, Lucy privately believed, since he would get no welcome from the self-absorbed woman he had married.

Janet Gunson and her husband Angus came, both with that strained and anxious look of those who had boys over in France, trying to talk to James, wanting to be reassured that Job, who had been home on leave but was totally uncommunicative, and Lawrence, who was really only a baby, his mother said, would be safe.

Ben and Joan, whose own lads were too young for soldiers, thank God. Anne and Thomas Mounsey who had all girls, again thanking the Lord though they had been disappointed not to get a boy. Perhaps it was as well, they now had told one another, and Christine and Douglas Scott, again with young children. The old people were driven over, bringing a magnificent silver christening cup which had been in the family for generations and which was to be held by Alice until the next baby was born, Mr Harry inclined to poke Charlotte Buchanan in the stomach and ask her why she was lolling about like an invalid.

They all exclaimed on the infant beauty of Alice Christina, passing her from one to the other in her lovely Buchanan christening gown. They were crowded into Lucy's upstairs sitting-room, for there was nowhere else to put them, perched on chairs that had been brought from here and there, marvelling over the behaviour of James towards his new daughter, telling one another that if they hadn't seen it with their own eyes, they wouldn't have believed the way he was acting, when there was knock on the door and Dimity peeped in.

'Oh, madam ... oh, madam,' she whispered, grief-stricken to be the one to deliver the loathsome yellow envelope that she held in her hand.

The silence in the room was total except for the murmuring of the child who was held in old Mrs Buchanan's arms, anxiously being watched by her doting father. Only Charlotte Buchanan seemed curiously unconcerned.

'Who . . . ?' someone said in a hoarse voice.

'Oh, God, Angus, I can't bear it.'

James moved forward and took the envelope from Dimity's hand and she scuttled away as though she could not bear to hear what the envelope contained. He glanced at it, his colour draining away, his eyes turning in compassion to old Mr Job and his wife, Mary.

'It's for you; they must have sent it over from . . .'

Job Buchanan's voice was harsh and his wife began to cry the slow tears of the elderly, for they knew who it was, while, leaning in her husband's arms, Janet Gunson's breath left her body in a great sigh of relief.

'Open it, lad, would you?'

350

It told them that Captain Andrew Buchanan, dashing, laughing, impertinent Andrew Buchanan, had died of wounds received in the service of his country.

James left the next day. The flesh wound in his arm had healed enough to satisfy Sister Colyford who pronounced him, sadly, fit for active service. He walked slowly down the drive with his right arm round his wife's shoulders and his child in the crook of his left and all those who watched sighed for the sadness of his going.

CHAPTER TWENTY

Charlotte Buchanan listlessly crumbled a piece of toast, on her face an expression with which her parents and the servants at Ravenscourt, her parents' home, were very familiar. It meant that something that she wanted to happen hadn't happened, or something she didn't want to happen, had. She wanted something and so far whatever it was had not been given to her; there was nothing more certain, as they all knew, than that she would move heaven and earth to get it.

Charlotte was staying with her parents at the present moment, the present moment having stretched from the day her husband 'abandoned' her, marching off to war which he had no need to do since he was a married man, to this day in December a year later.

And then, of course, there was this baby, the bearing of which she couldn't possibly manage on her own in that big house her papa had given her and Paul as a wedding present. No one could expect her to, surely, and though she was aware that other women coped on their own with their men gone to war she had always had her papa to look after her and had no intention of changing that situation just because she had a husband.

Where had it all gone, she often brooded, her lovely bright dream of being the perfect hostess, the smartest, most fashionable young matron in the district and the answer was it had been blown away by the winds of this stupid war, the reason for which she couldn't imagine and didn't care to know anyway. And to top it all she had had to suffer the indignity of Paul insisting on doing 'that' on his last leave, putting her in this appalling condition and she would never forgive him.

She could remember her wedding night with a clarity which never diminished, and her horror and shock, when he had intimated to her what he wished to do in the double bed in the smart Paris hotel where they had honeymooned, would never leave her. Take off her nightdress, he had demanded, as he had taken off his dressing-gown, standing before her totally naked with some great, thick, throbbing spear standing out from between his hairy legs and which he intended sticking into her. She had wanted to scream and hit out at him, the beastly man who was now her husband, but instead she had hissed that if he came an inch nearer she would get up, get dressed and take the boat and train back to Ambleside. He was to sleep elsewhere, she didn't care where but it was not in her bed.

Paul Buchanan, a gentle man who liked peace and tranquillity, wondered why he had allowed himself to be married to this selfish, heartless creature with the magnificent body of a woman and the mind of a petulant child. She had been indulged from birth by her doting parents and, having been thwarted in her attempt to marry his cousin James, who, he smiled sadly to himself, would not have been denied her bed on his wedding night, had swooped on him with the avarice and speed of an eagle. He was not a wealthy man since he had no head for business like his father, his uncles and cousins, and the small income that came from the few shares he had in the Emmerson Gunpowder Factory was certainly not enough to keep him until he established a practice in the area. He was honest enough to admit to himself that that was why he had married Charlotte, though, of course, the idea of getting into bed with her and having that splendid body at his disposal had been a further incentive.

His wife was still a virgin when he enlisted four months after their marriage, which was probably why he did it. They lived in their newly built and magnificently furnished home, which she had grandly named Buchanan Hall as though expecting a dynasty to come in the next generations, Charlotte settling down with great expectations of being a wife, in name only if she had anything to do with it, and hostess. She gave dinner parties and tennis parties, croquet parties and dances, swathing through Ambleside society as she had always imagined herself doing until suddenly, there was no society there to entertain. Wives, oh, yes, daughters, school friends, her female cousins by marriage, but who wanted strictly female company or that of elderly gentlemen and youths, too old and too young for the army whither the rest of the male population had gone. Even her servants deserted her, parlour maids running off to higher pay and shorter hours in munitions, her butler enlisting, along with her chauffeur and gardener.

'Mama, can I come home for a little while?' she had beseeched her mother, tears in her beautiful eyes. 'It's so lonely at the Hall without Paul,' and her mother, who had no idea of the state of affairs between her daughter and her son-in-law, agreed at once.

'Of course you can, darling. It will be quite like old times,' her mother had gushed.

'It's lovely to have you here, sweetheart,' her besotted father said at every meal, for he had missed her idle gossip, her childish chitter-chatter at the table, her lovely wheedling when she particularly wanted something from him.

Paul Buchanan, who had seen things and suffered things he would not care to describe to anyone, let alone his empty-headed wife, got into bed with her as he had always wanted to on his first leave. Though he had tried to be gentle, her strugglings and whispered commands to stop this filth at once, whispered since she did not want her parents to hear the disgusting noise Paul was making, turned the encounter into what he could only describe as rape and which she swore would never happen again. To be fair, with perhaps another man, an experienced man who would have known what to do with her, she might have been different, but that one night in her husband's bed, and the consequences of it, a child to be born in the spring, turned her mind from petty resentments to a bitter determination to get even with the woman

354

who had stolen the only man Charlotte believed could have made her happy. That was how she saw it. Though it was her husband who had taken her against her will and made her pregnant, in a twisted way she turned it round until it was the fault of that bitch James had married

It was nearly Christmas and she was six months pregnant and if she could have destroyed the life inside her without danger to herself or harming her reputation as the leader of society she meant to be when the damned war was over, she would have done, but she couldn't and so she gritted her teeth and let her parents cosset and coddle her, pet her and spoil her as they had always done, while waiting for the child to be born.

She looked hideous, she knew she did, huge and bloated and totally unable to wear any of the lovely clothes she had had transferred from Buchanan Hall to her parents' home. She was ashamed to be seen in public because not only did she look quite appalling with her swollen body and puffy face but because people would know that she and Paul had performed the obscene act which had made her like this. She had not been out anywhere except to droop round the garden of Ravenscourt since the christening of that brat of Lucy and James's. That event which had ended with such drama, she supposed she might even say tragedy, for she had been quite taken with Andrew Buchanan who had always flirted with her and admired her with his eyes which she had enjoyed. The christening party had made her all the more determined to find some way to make Lucy Buchanan suffer for what she had done to Charlotte. She had seen the way James looked at his wife, they all did, recognising it for what it was even if his wife didn't, and his devotion to his daughter, which was the most astonishing thing they'd ever seen, they told one another, and it boded well for the marriage when James finally came home, they all agreed. Not if she'd anything to do with it, she thought viciously, eaten up with jealous envy.

'Papa,' she said now, turning an angelic smile on her father.

'Yes, poppet.' Arthur Gibson looked up from the Times and turned his fond gaze on his daughter, wondering for the thousandth time how in hell he and Edith had got this exquisite creature who was their daughter. Edith was pleasant looking, he supposed, but then he'd not married her for her looks but for the wealth which had come with her from her father. He himself was not exactly ugly, but this child of his was like some exotic flower growing among the pretty but very ordinary blooms in a cottage garden. She turned heads wherever she went with her fair loveliness, the splendour of her full-breasted figure, which stunned the male sex to open-mouthed awe and the female to open-mouthed envy. Oh, he knew she was a handful, she always had been, but she'd only to look at him as she was doing now with those glorious eyes of hers and he could deny her nothing. He had been furious when his son-in-law enlisted, deserting Arthur's lovely Charlotte, Paul's wife of no more than a few months and he had told him so, but secretly he had been delighted when Charlotte had come home to stay for a while and he'd be sorry when her husband returned from the front. He was looking forward to having a grandchild—at least the bugger had done something right—and would
356

make sure his lass had all the support she needed during her pregnancy and when the time came for the birth.

'D'you know anyone at the War Office, Papa?' she asked him innocently, popping a piece of buttered toast into her mouth.

'The War Office?' He laughed and put down the newspaper, wondering what the hell was in her pretty head now.

'Mmm. You have so many contacts I just thought you might.'

He looked from her to his bewildered wife then back to Charlotte again, his expression asking Edith if she had any idea what the child was getting at because he certainly didn't. The War Office, indeed. Was it to be something to do with her husband? Did she want him to pull a few strings, which he could certainly do, and get Paul Buchanan back from the base hospital in France where he was stationed?

'What makes you ask, darling? Is it to do with Paul?'

'Oh, no, Papa.' A faint look of distaste passed across her face. 'I . . . well, I have been hearing the strangest stories; rumours, I suppose you'd call them, not that I believe them, of course, but I was wondering . . .'

'Rumours? About what?' Her father's voice was sharp.

She picked at the piece of toast on her plate. She was trying to eat as little as possible in the hope that not only would it perhaps starve the baby, making it smaller and, it had been whispered to her by her maid, easier to deliver, but prevent herself from putting on more weight.

357

'I hardly like to ... it is so fantastic it can't be true but, well, it's about Lucy Buchanan.'

Edith Gibson looked up quickly from the good breakfast she was tucking into. She and Arthur liked to start the day right with a breakfast of bacon and eggs, sausage and tomatoes and mushrooms. She came from a family who rode to hounds in the winter, shot grouse and partridge in season, were keen on tennis and sporting parties, and you had to have a sound constitution to do these things so a decent breakfast was essential.

She looked keenly at her daughter and her mind went back to the day, two years ago now, when she and Charlotte had been in Ambleside and James Buchanan, with the Dean family clustered round him in his motor car, had roared by, all singing at the top of their voices. Well, perhaps James had not been singing, for he was not that sort of a man, but the rest had, Lucy Dean and her sisters and brothers. Charlotte had been seized by a fury so violent Edith had had to restrain her from rushing after the Rolls-Royce and screaming what her mother knew to be her jealousy for all the world to see.

They will pay for this. Those had been Charlotte's very words but surely she had not meant ... She could not possibly still be harbouring ... Not after all this time ... no, it was not possible. She was well aware that her daughter liked to get her own way, and always got it, for how could any parent deny this lovely child, this lovely child who was sweetness herself, when she was not thwarted! She had always been difficult to handle, having hysterics to the point where she and Arthur had been afraid for her health, which was why they had given in to her

358

since she was an infant.

'Lucy Buchanan?'

'Yes. It is really very silly but she is rumoured to have formed an attachment for . . . one of the soldiers in her care. I was told by—'

'Great God, what a thing to say. One of the soldiers in her care! Why, they are only ordinary working men, not even officers,' as though, had they been this would have made it palatable.

'I know, that's what I said . . .'

'Who told you this, child?' Her father's voice was threatening, not towards her, naturally, but towards the person who had put such a nasty thought in his daughter's head.

Charlotte's expression turned truculent. She was not used to having her word questioned, especially by her father. She had not expected him to ask where she had her information from and if she had to tell him that it was from a servant who was friendly with a servant who knew someone who worked at Howethwaite and had reported the story of the 'idiot' who had been in Lucy Buchanan's care, when she was pregnant with James's child too, she knew her papa would not like it.

She did what she always did. The tears that she could command at will brimmed to her eyes and at once her mother and father both stood up and rushed to her side. She must not be upset, they told her, not in her precious condition and her papa was sorry he had taken such a firm tone but really, it hardly seemed the sort of . . .

'Perhaps we could find out who he was, Papa, that was why I was asking you about the War Office,' she sobbed against her papa's chest, 'and that should tell us whether the talk is ridiculous or not.' She did not explain why and nobody asked.

The two parlour maids, who were too old for war work and had been serving breakfast, exchanged glances. She was a troublemaker was Miss Charlotte Gibson and had been the bane of their lives ever since she was born, which was how long they had served the Gibson family, but this was the end, really it was. To accuse Mrs James Buchanan, who, it was reported, was a saint, giving of herself night and day to those poor wounded soldiers up at Howethwaite, of having an affair with one of them, was . . . well, of course, they were not to know what went on up there and perhaps . . . Mr Buchanan was away and there was no one to . . . and she was known to be unconventional, had been right from the start, if the stories they had been told were true. They found it hard to believe, their exchanged glances and lifted eyebrows said, but still, was there smoke without fire?

'I'll find out who he is, darling, and that will put paid to this nasty rumour. Old Reggie Withers owes me a favour for that surplus deal I put him on to. He'll have the lists, whatever they are . . .' Arthur said vaguely, patting his little girl's shoulder and begging her not to cry. He couldn't bear to see her cry, he told her, watching as she was led away by her mother who thought a rest on the bed was called for and perhaps her forehead rubbed with cologne.

'The chap's name was Rory Cameron, Private Rory Cameron,' he told his daughter a few days later. 'A shell shock case, apparently, but he's back in the trenches now. Still unstable, his record reports. Reggie says he comes from a good family in Surrey with a mother who has landed connections, and he can't imagine why the damn fool refused a commission but . . .'

'Yes?' his daughter said, leaning forward eagerly.

'He has left a document which says that on his death he wants a certain Mrs Lucy Buchanan to be informed.'

*   *   *

Lucy missed James and she was astonished by it. After all, she barely knew him. He had been Mr Buchanan to her for a long time, though she had persuaded herself to call him James. He had been a stranger sitting at the dinner table night after night, polite, sometimes even charming. A tyrant, she had believed him to be, even cruel when he had refused her permission to join the WSPU and threatened her family with some dire consequence if she disobeyed. A hard male body in her bed, demanding her submission and something more, which she had not understood then, but she did now. Oh, yes, smiling secretly to herself, she did now. A generous man who carelessly told her to spend what she liked on her family. A generous man with his money but not with himself. A humorous man, she had believed, though it was a side of himself he had not allowed to reveal itself to her very often.

But he had been none of these things and yet all of them during the few days they had spent together with their daughter and she had been strangely delighted with it, and with him. He had made her laugh. He had made her slumbering body come alive. He had been gentle and rough in his lovemaking, and tender and humble in his

361

gratitude for the lovely child she had given him. His pain at leaving, not just Alice, but herself, had been very evident. What a complex man he was, with so many facets to his nature, most of which she thought were still buried within him.

His letters came regularly, week after week, telling her not of his love, for he knew it was too soon for that, but of his love and pride in his daughter. She must promise to write as often as she could, he implored her though he knew she was busy. Would she send him photographs of Alice? Buy herself a decent camera, a Kodak or a Brownie and record every phase in her development, her every mood. He could hardly stand the thought that he was to forgo so much of her growing-up. He missed her so, she was his precious scrap and any woman with more insight into the ways of a man's love for a woman would have recognised at once that James Buchanan, though he loved and missed his child, was not speaking of her when he poured out his heart in his letters. He and his men ate well, he wrote, when they could but it was bully beef stew mostly, bread and cheese and jam, and sometimes even butter. They had an ounce of cold ham for their breakfast, a mug of tea and half a loaf, but if she could include some chocolate, Oxo cubes, peppermint drops, Camp cocoa, and writing paper and envelopes in her parcels they would be very welcome. It was very cold now, he wrote to her and he'd be glad of that thick woollen underwear he wore for climbing in the winter and she was to tell Margaret that her scarf and mittens, the technique of which she had mastered, were superb. He was billeted at a farm, he couldn't say where, but it was very comfortable.

She was so glad, she wrote back, imagining him in a clean bed and getting some fresh farm food, and he hadn't the heart to tell her that when they were not in the front line he and his men lived with the farm animals, sleeping in straw. Both armies were firmly entrenched for the winter and it seemed stalemate had been reached. He didn't know when he would get leave, but the photographs she sent him of Alice were wonderful and did she think she could get someone to take one of herself, perhaps with Alice, and send it out to him. He couldn't believe Alice was sitting up already but then he'd known from the start that their daughter was quite exceptional.

*   *   *

She first noticed the odd behaviour of the shopkeepers in Ambleside, and even one or two of the shoppers, just after Christmas. They all knew her now. She was not only the wife of one of the most prominent men in the town, but a man who was fighting for his country in France. She was also the woman who had opened the hospital of which they were so proud, if not a nurse, then a nurse's aid and what she did for those young men was to be greatly admired. They liked to nod and smile at her as she passed, gratified when she smiled back, which she always did for she was a gracious young woman. She didn't often drive the Rolls-Royce, for petrol was very short and when there was any shopping to be done she rode in on her bicycle, often taking Margaret with her. Margaret was growing up, at almost fifteen, ready to become a young woman, longing to help on the wards, which

Lucy had promised she would think about when she was fifteen.

They had just dismounted, leaning their bicycles against the side of the chemist's shop when two ladies, both of them known to her by sight, after a start of what looked like embarrassment, tipped their noses in the air and walked past her as though she didn't exist. They continued up the street past the chemist's window, pausing to look into the draper's next door where they turned to look at her, their heads together. When they saw her staring at them in amazement they hurried on as though afraid she might accost them.

'Well, what's got into those two?' she asked Margaret but Margaret had noticed nothing untoward, for she did not know the ladies concerned.

Lucy shrugged and pushing open the door of the chemist's shop went inside.

'Good morning, Mr Lawson,' she said to the elderly gentleman behind the counter. 'Have you heard from Edwina recently? I believe you told me that she was to go to France. How brave of her. Has she gone yet?' She smiled her lovely warm smile, eager for news of the friend she had made in the WSPU.

'Not as yet, Mrs Buchanan,' Mr Lawson said stiffly.

'But she is well?' She raised her eyebrows enquiringly, wondering what was the matter with everyone today. Those two women looked as though they had a pole up their backs and now Mr Lawson had his mouth buttoned so tight he could barely speak.

'Thank you, yes.'

'Is anything the matter, Mr Lawson?' she asked him, wondering why he was avoiding her gaze. He was normally full of Edwina's exploits in the nursing field where she had done so well, but today he passed her her purchases and gave her her change with barely a nod of acknowledgement.

'Not a thing, Mrs Buchanan.' And that was that as far as Mr Lawson was concerned. He had been polite but no more. Mrs Buchanan was a customer and customers must be treated civilly but if the rumour which was being whispered and which had even reached the church where he was a sidesman were true he had no wish to be more than that.

They did their shopping. Wool for more socks and scarves and mittens. A length of material for nightdresses for Alice who was growing so fast they couldn't keep up with her. A bag of pear drops for Cook and some tobacco for Mr Clapcott. Only small items, for the rations for the men and staff were delivered by the army. Several times Lucy was conscious of sly looks and whispers though most of the people to whom she spoke did reply.

She was surprised when she got home to find a note from Charlotte Buchanan begging her to go round and take tea with her if she could spare the time. She was so bored and, naturally, in her condition she couldn't go out but she had had a letter from Paul and James was mentioned in it and she also thought that Lucy might like to hear a bit of news Charlotte had of a friend of Lucy's.

A friend of hers? Was it perhaps Franny who wrote now and again in that laconic way she had, making light, even fun of what Lucy was sure was a difficult and dangerous job, but then why would Franny write to Charlotte whom Lucy knew she couldn't abide, calling her a silly simpering child without a thought in her head that was not put there by someone else.

She didn't want to go so to make the outing more congenial she drove to Ravenscourt, where, apparently, Charlotte was staying with her parents until after the birth of her child. She didn't quite trust this invitation, she didn't know why. She did know that Charlotte was no particular friend of hers though she had no idea why she thought so. There had always been this feeling of antipathy, of undercurrents that ran deep and hidden in Charlotte which was strange when one considered the shallow nature of the woman who had married the nicest Buchanan of them all, in Lucy's opinion. Nicest in the best sense, that is. Kind, sensitive, thoughtful, so unobtrusive that it took a while to recognise and appreciate his quiet charm, Paul was far too good for her and she shuddered to think of him living the rest of his life with such a woman.

'Will you come this way, Mrs Buchanan,' the Gibsons' pompous butler said, leading her from the overheated hallway, which was rich with pictures and ornaments and the expensive folderols Arthur Gibson liked to exhibit to show off his wealth, into a drawing-room which was even warmer and there was Charlotte reclining on a velvet-covered chaise-longue, cushions at her back, the colour of her full gown exactly toning with the colour of the velvet.

'Oh, Lucy, there you are. Do come in,' she trilled with the false sincerity that told Lucy she disliked Lucy as much as Lucy disliked Charlotte, so what on earth was she doing here?

'Send in some tea, Edwards, and please, Lucy, do sit down by the fire. I would ask you to take off your hat but I see you're not wearing one. Is it . . .windy outside?' her eyes straying to Lucy's tangled hair.

'No, it's just that I came in the motor. I had the top down,' Lucy answered shortly, wondering how much of this she could stand.

'Really, at this time of the year?'

'I like to feel the wind. Now then, what is it you wanted to see me about?' indicating that if Charlotte had time on her hands she certainly did not.

'Well, I hardly know where to begin.' Charlotte's voice was silky and for some reason Lucy felt the hairs on the back of her neck rise.

CHAPTER TWENTY-ONE

Lucy drove home in a state of dazed confusion, unable to shake off a feeling of impending disaster, though of what sort she couldn't put into words, unable to make head nor tail of her own emotions which were so mixed up she felt she would have to have an hour or so on her own somewhere to unravel them. Her first thought had been for James. With this sweet, slow blooming of something between them which she was not prepared to risk, a tentative softness, a tenderness even, which she knew was as precious to James as it was to her, she was aware that she must find some way to break it to him before someone else did, probably Charlotte herself.

One thing was certain, she had made a bitter enemy this day.

She barely remembered the journey home, winding her way through the main street of Ambleside, along Clappergate and over Skelwith Bridge, turning into the gates of Howethwaite without recognising how she got there. There were several ambulatory wounded in the garden, most on crutches, making a brave effort of stumbling about the gravel paths, and others in wheelchairs pushed by the VADs, getting some good air into their lungs, as Sister Colyford was fond of saying. Doctor Yates's Cowley motor car, his choice of colour never failing to amaze her, a vivid scarlet, was parked at the front steps and she wondered who it was that needed his attention. Perhaps the young private who was so ill with the dysentery that was sapping what little strength he had, not to mention the stomach wound he had suffered when a sniper's bullet got him, he was not expected to live through the day. Eighteen years old, poor lad, and kept calling piteously for his mother. She had been fetched from Manchester and sat by his bedside holding his hand, murmuring over and over again in her broad northern accent, 'Theer, theer, lad, theer, theer, Mam's 'ere,' and he had quietened, so perhaps there was a chance for him.

She parked the Rolls in the garage, shutting the big doors behind her then turned and sniffed the air, she didn't know why. There was just a strange feel to it, a sort of waiting, a hushed expectancy that she knew from experience heralded snow. The clouds, heavy and grey, sat ominously low on Loughrigg Fell and the image of James strengthened in her mind. These hills and dales and uplands were what symbolised her husband more keenly than anything else, for she knew how he loved it all. It was his heritage, the feeling for it come from generations of Buchanans and Emmersons and all those before them. She had had a letter from him only this morning written several weeks ago, saying the weather was cold enough to freeze the ... well, he had quipped, he wouldn't tell her what part of his person might be affected but she had smiled, for by now she was beginning to recognise the sharp humour, the sense of the ridiculous which James had kept so well hidden from her. It was as though he trusted her, which was a curious thing to say, with a private side of him no one else knew and it pleased her. They were going down the line, he told her, and he had put on the good warm underwear she had sent him, since there would probably be a lot of hanging about in this war which seemed to have come to a full stop with the winter weather. He did not elaborate and she knew there were many aspects of his life as a soldier which he, and all the rest of them, officers and Tommies alike, shared with no one but each other.

There was nobody about in the hall. Through the open doorway of the ward she could see Doctor Yates bending over the bed of the young soldier and the rest of the wounded were quiet, as though suspecting they were in the presence of death. The soldier's mother had her head bent over the face of her child, stroking back his hair and occasionally kissing his brow as Lucy did when she was soothing Alice. Her heart constricted in compassion for the boy's pain and the mother's sorrow and she wondered furiously when this bloody war would be over and they could all resume the peace and content which surely all God's creatures were

369

entitled to. She felt like dropping to her knees and breathing a prayer for them all, right here on the bottom step of the stairs and she was troubled suddenly by thoughts of her father. He had brought them all up to pray to God, to attend church and to help the afflicted, and since she had come to Howethwaite she had only attended to the latter. Dear Papa, would that suffice? she asked him gently and her heart was soothed, for she thought it might.

Those on the ward did not notice her so she continued quietly up the stairs to the sanctuary of her own room. There was a small fire, for they were not short of fuel, so taking off her warm winter coat and throwing it on to the bed, she sank into the chair, leaning forward, her chin cupped in her hands, her elbows on her knees, staring sightlessly into the flames.

Charlotte had taken her time, drawing out for as long as she could, Lucy was well aware, her enjoyment of the moment. Paul was well and had spent Christmas, at which time he had a few days' leave, in a château behind the lines, she had prattled. She seemed to be totally unaware of exactly where her husband might be. France, Flanders, they were all the same to her. The only place she knew in France was Paris because that was where she and Mama bought their clothes. Paul had told her the name of the place but she couldn't quite recall. Had James mentioned it? They had spent only an hour or so together, she babbled on, for as Paul was arriving for his few days' rest, James was just leaving. Wasn't it a shame that they could not have spent more time together, just as though they were holidaying on the continent, which was a fashionable thing to do and their paths had crossed. How strange that James had not mentioned it, she couldn't resist saying as though her husband never kept anything from her.

'My letters were held up over Christmas,' Lucy answered curtly, ready to tell Lucy to damn well get on with whatever it was she was drivelling on about, girding her loins, so to speak, ready for the blow she was by now convinced Charlotte was to aim at her.

'And then there is the news that a school friend of mine has just become engaged . . .'

'What?' Lucy was caught off guard by the sudden change of direction the conversation had taken.

'Oh, I'm sure you've heard me speak of Joanna Clarkson,' Charlotte said archly, sipping her tea from the fragile bone china teacup, the tea service of which the Gibsons had especially made for them with what looked like a coat of arms painted upon it. She had not moved once since the tea tray was brought in, her legs, crossed at the ankles, stretched out on the chaise-longue before her.

'I can't say I have,' Lucy answered shortly.

'I went to school with her and when she wrote to tell me she had become engaged to Aubrey Blane, Captain Aubrey Blane of the 1st Battalion, the Surrey Regiment, I immediately thought of that poor young soldier you nursed last year. Wasn't he in a Surrey regiment?'

Lucy felt the shiver begin somewhere inside her. She wasn't sure exactly where but it rippled outwards, touching her skin with feathers of alarm. She could feel the fine hairs on her arms lift and she put her cup and saucer down very carefully before she answered.

'I'm not at all sure I know.'

'Oh, yes, there was quite a lot of talk about him in Ambleside since he was the first case of . . . do they call it shell shock? . . . that had been reported.'

'I was not aware that his case was known about in Ambleside.' Lucy's voice was stiff with suppressed fury. 'And I fail to see what it has to do with anyone, apart from the medical staff at Howethwaite. Besides which he was cured and has since returned to the front.'

'So Joanna tells me.'

'What in hell's name has it to do with this Joanna, whoever she is?' Lucy felt her control slipping but Charlotte merely smiled.

'She had it from Aubrey who is in the same regiment, you see. The soldier, I believe she called him Rory Cameron, comes from a decent family, but then, I suppose you know that, don't you.'

'What has this to do with anything, Charlotte?' Lucy's voice was filled with contempt. 'He was nursed at Howethwaite and then went back to the trenches. As far as the hospital was concerned that was the end of it and why your friend and her fiancé are bandying his name about as if he had something to be ashamed of, I can't imagine. He was wounded, a wounded soldier who was put in our care.'

'Oh, quite, but I believe, or so Joanna tells me, he formed an attachment for some lady round here and—'

'Your friend Joanna seems to know a hell of a lot about . . . about this soldier and where she gets her information . . .'

'There is no need to be offensive, Lucy. I am just

telling you . . .'

'What are you telling me, Charlotte?'

'That he is corresponding with some lady, some woman . . . whatever, in these parts, a lady of whom he is very fond and I just wondered if you knew who it could be? Was he visited by anyone while he was with you?'

'Charlotte, really! I am not prepared to sit here and discuss a perfectly decent young soldier who your friend happens to—'

'Apparently he is still having these . . . attacks, or so Aubrey told Joanna. They seem to think he is merely trying to get out of the trenches by any means he can. A cowardly—'

'He is not a coward. He is afraid, like they all are but he still remains to do his duty, which is not the action of a coward and anyway, how does Aubrey come by this information? About the letter-writing, I mean.'

'That's what I'm telling you. When he goes off his head, which he apparently does with great frequency, Corporal Cameron'—there was a sneer in Charlotte's voice on the word "corporal"— 'babbles about the woman, calling for her. And then, naturally, Aubrey, being his captain, has the job of censoring his letters and . . .'

'And, of course, you and Joanna having found out what that name is, you had me over to tea to tell me all about it.'

'Well, it does seem strange.'

'There is nothing strange about it, Charlotte.' Lucy rose to her feet with great dignity, turning to look for her coat but Edwards had removed it.' I do correspond with Rory Cameron but there is nothing in my letters that my husband couldn't

373

read.' She did not tell Charlotte that the same could not be said about Rory's letters to her, but then she probably knew that anyway, They were filled with his love for her, every line and page a joyous enchantment overflowing from his heart. As long as he could write to her, describe to her his feelings, have the hope and rapture of her letters, her thoughts, her friendship it was enough for him to get through each day. He loved to hear about Alice. It kept him sane, or as sane as any other soldier in the insane world in which some of them managed to survive. He knew she would never be his, never. She was married to a fine officer and had a child but the letters, that bond her letters created, gave him a reason to go on, to cling to life and when it was all over ... well, that was something none of them could visualise.

'So James knows about the corporal then? He knows you exchange letters with a man in the ranks.'

'Dear God, Charlotte, what in hell's name has his rank got to do with it? Are you saying that if he were an officer it would be quite proper to correspond with him? I've never heard such nonsense in my life, so I'll be going. I'd be glad if you would ring the bell and ask that butler of yours for my coat. We're extremely busy at the moment.'

'How brave you are, Lucy.' Charlotte smiled slyly. 'I'm sure I couldn't do what you do and I'm sure Paul wouldn't want me to. After all, there are women to do these—'

'Shall I tell you something, Charlotte? I don't give a damn what you think of me, brave or otherwise and I've thought for a long time, in fact, ever since he married you, how sorry I am for Paul.

374

And how this child of yours will fare with you for a mother doesn't bear thinking about. No, don't bother with the butler. I'll find my own way out.'

* * *

Lucy was surprised and delighted when, having been brought from the ward where she had been dressing the leg wound of a cheeky-faced and impudent young soldier from Liverpool because she had a visitor, she found that visitor was Franny Buchanan.

'Dear God, what a bloody get-up,' were Franny's first words as she grinned at Lucy's astonished expression, but nevertheless her embrace was warm and affectionate. 'Mind you, mine's not much better,' looking down ruefully at the drab skirt and tunic she had on. It was dusty and stained, worn at the cuffs and collar but Franny wore it as though it were a designer gown from Paris, her head proudly set on her shoulders, her back straight. Her hair had been cut short in the newest style but Lucy had the feeling she had not done it to be fashionable but to be tidy without trouble.

'When did you get home? Is Alex with you? Where are you staying, surely not up at Grange House?' which had been taken over as an officers' convalescent home for those fleeing the Zeppelin raids in London. Lucy's words fell over one another in her eagerness to speak.

'No, darling, not at Grange House. I thought I might beg a bed from you. It's that or the mother-in-law and I don't think I could manage even one night with old Phyllis. I'll go round. Is the Rolls still in action? Oh, good, I'll do the rounds and visit the relatives then I'm off back to London. Alex will be expecting me tomorrow or the day after at the latest and I've only got a week's leave. The first I've had since I went, I might add. Now, what about you? You don't look too good. Dear Lord, we're all working ourselves into an early grave but you ... what is it? Not James?'

'No. Come upstairs into my bedroom. I've no sitting-room now, I'm afraid. There are patients in every corner and apart from the children's rooms we have all had to make sacrifices.'

'The children, and the child? I'm looking forward to meeting this paragon who, so everybody tells me, has tamed James Buchanan. He tells me she is—'

'You've seen him?' Lucy clutched at Franny's arm, almost overbalancing her as they walked up the stairs. 'When? When did you see him?'

'Ah-ha, do I detect something in the lady that was lacking on her wedding day? Why this sudden urgent need to hear about the man you married simply to gain a home for your brothers and sisters? Don't tell me that perhaps your feelings have become warmer?'

'Don't tease me, Franny. Have you seen him recently?'

'Yes, I have and he's ... well, but, darling, won't you give me a couple of hours. I'm dead beat and if I don't sleep I shall simply fall over and drop into an unconscious state at your feet.'

'Of course, and perhaps a bath?'

'Lucy, if you asked me at this moment to choose between the crown jewels and a bath, the bath would be it. If you could see what we have to put up with in France ...' She stopped suddenly and her face closed up. She put her hand through Lucy's arm as they walked along the broad landing. 'As though what we have to put up with is important.' Her voice was bitter. 'Those poor blokes . . . well, you will have seen them here, I'm sure.' She sighed raggedly, running her hand over her short cap of curls. Her face was strained now that she had stopped smiling, a curious grey colour, the tiredness seeping from her so that she drooped against Lucy's shoulder.

Within fifteen minutes she was bathed and, wearing one or Lucy's nightgowns, asleep like one dead in Lucy's bed.

It was almost midnight when she woke. Lucy had just come off the evening shift and was exhausted herself but she curled up in the armchair before the fire and, dozing a little, waited for Franny to wake. She knew there was something Franny had come here to say to her. Franny was not so fond of her relatives that she would come all the way from London to Lakeland just to look them up. She had travelled for hours on a slow train filled with troops, soldiers with the mud and filth of France still on them, desperate to get home for a few precious days, young men no longer young as Franny was no longer young. Lucy could not have said why that thought came to her but it was in Franny's face. Not lines or wrinkles but a certain detachment, an unwillingness to be involved in anything but the job in hand. Lucy could only think of the word *crippled* though Franny was unmarked. She had appeared to be mentally drained and Lucy knew, who had seen it in men in her care, that in the eighteen months since the war began Franny had met death so often, seen bodies torn, bloody, mutilated, gassed, burned, blinded, and to survive it was turning in on herself, holding herself aloof from life itself. It was how it was affecting them all, those who suffered it.

They talked quietly. They went up to the nursery and peeped at the beautiful Alice Buchanan, like a rosy cupid with the bloom of babyhood on her rounded cheeks and her eyelashes, so like James', curled tight on her sleeping eyes. Franny admired her politely, saying it was no wonder that James loved her so, then withdrew from the room.

'So, my dear,' she said at last, 'what's this I hear about you and one of the soldiers in your care? I don't believe a word of it, of course, so don't look so alarmed. I know you and one of your chief assets is your honesty which wouldn't allow you to cheat on James, but there is something . . .'

'Dear sweet Jesus, what have you heard?' Lucy was aghast, though she had been expecting something of the sort. 'I knew you'd come to tell me something dreadful and I thought—'

She stopped as though a fist had been driven into her stomach, expelling all the air from her body and every vestige of colour drained from her face. She put out a blind hand and Franny took it with great compassion.

'He . . . knows, doesn't he?' Lucy whispered, her voice stricken with a savage pain which came at her from nowhere. 'He's sent you.'

'No, you should know better than that, darling. That's not James's style at all. He doesn't even know I'm here. I had the devil's own job to get out of him what was wrong. He looked appalling. I've seen him a time or two since he was home on leave and if he'd been a woman I would have said he

378

positively glowed. Daft, isn't it, but that's how he was. In the middle of all that horror, he was calm, patient, unhurried, as though he had something inside him that was protecting him from it all. The men—his men—looked to him for support and leadership. They loved him, Lucy, because he gave them something they could not find themselves. Jesus . . .' She bent her head and Lucy thought she was weeping but when she lifted it again she was dry-eyed. 'He's lost that. I saw it at once and asked him . . . He wouldn't tell me at first. Said to mind my own bloody business, you know how he is, but I got it out of him. He'd had a letter from a 'well-wisher', a bloody well-wisher. Can you believe there are people so evil in this world? To take a soldier's sanity, his peace of mind when it's all he has to cling to. To tell a man fighting for his life that his wife is unfaithful to him. Who would do such a thing? Who? I can't believe it.'

'Oh, I can,' Lucy said softly. 'I know exactly who sent that letter. I was going to write to him myself.'

'Lucy!'

'No, not to speak to him of an affair but to . . . to tell him that I was writing to a soldier. I only knew that it was common knowledge—that others were aware of it—today. Charlotte Buchanan has a friend who's . . . Oh, God, Franny, it's a long story. I nursed him, you see, Rory Cameron. Shell shock. He seemed to find some peace with me and so Sister Colyford said I was to spend as much time with him as I could. Quite simply, he fell in love with me.'

'Who wouldn't, my dear?' Franny took Lucy's ice-cold hand in hers, then reached to smooth back her hair in a gesture that could only be called maternal.

'I was so sorry for him, Franny. He was a boy, no more, gone straight from university like so many of them to the trenches and he just couldn't take it. But he survived and was sent back. He begged me to write and I knew that if I didn't he would go out of his mind for ever or he would run away and be brought back as a deserter and shot. So I wrote. My letters were those of a friend to a friend, I swear it. I spoke of Alice. Great God in heaven, I was pregnant when he was here and on the day he left Alice was born so how in hell . . .' She began to laugh harshly and Franny shushed her, stroking her trembling hands.

'You and James were . . . lovers when he . . .'

'Oh, yes, we were. I had hopes and I think he did that when he came home . . . We don't write love letters, I don't know why.'

'Seeing that you love one another?'

There was a long and agonising silence and Franny watched as the truth slipped tenderly into Lucy Buchanan's confused mind, clearing it, warming it, burning away the last shredded mist of indecision.

She sighed, almost hopelessly. 'Yes.'

'Then you must write and tell him. Not just of this correspondence with Rory, but that you love him. You must give him back that magic something which kept him *and* his company from going under. This war is going to last a long time, darling, a hell of a long time and anything you, or any woman, can give to her man to keep him alive, to give him something to fight for, such as coming home to you, must be given without stint. I've seen it over there, darling, and . . .'

Franny's face crumpled and that devilish cheek that had driven her female relatives to distraction was gone without trace. She had always had a charm of spirit, a streak of defiance against authority, against convention, against the rules that governed her society and though they all loved her they all sighed with exasperation when she did outrageous things like buying a motor car and wearing the only knickerbockers seen in Ambleside. She had marched away to war like the men of her family, her head high, her grin wide, her expectations of a bit of 'fun' in the dull world in which she had up to then lived showing in her seething determination to do her bit. And it would be fun! Driving an ambulance! Well, hadn't she always loved motoring? Hadn't she always loved the unexpected, despised safety, but even her great capacity for bearing a burden had not prepared her for the suffering she had witnessed in her search for adventure.

'I shouldn't speak of it, not to you who have a man you love there but it is quite appalling, Lucy. Even when they're not fighting Germans they're fighting the cold, the mud in which a horse can sink without trace, the lice and rats, the dysentery, the sheer bloody boredom of waiting for something to happen and when it does the terror that comes with it. That Rory of yours—I'm sorry, I don't mean that how it sounds—is not the only one who is going off his head. Most of them cope somehow but it is with the help of men like James. Now James is . . . Dear God, Lucy, you must write to him and explain. About this Rory, I mean. He needs to know you are . . . well, I wasn't going to tell you this but whoever wrote that letter to him implied that . . . Alice might not be his.'

Lucy moaned deep in the back of her throat, putting her hand to her mouth as though to keep some dreadful sound inside her. She was shaking so much she seemed in imminent danger of collapsing, the horror of what Franny was saying sending her thoughts into a series of disjointed images which flew about so quickly she could not get a grip on any one. Charlotte's simpering face . . . she must have already written to James even before she summoned Lucy to . . . Mr Lawson, so that was why he was so . . . and those women, people she knew in Ambleside . . . sideways looks . . . she understood it all now. It had been . . . someone had spread it round. James, James, how could you believe? After that last time, up on the fells, the magical bond that had bound them together . . . She couldn't stand it, she couldn't go back to the way they were before. If she could only see him, go to France and see his face as she explained.

'Darling, don't look so tragic.'

'Franny, it is tragic and I don't know how to put it right. What am I to do? What am I to say to him? And in a letter which is so impersonal? Dear God, I can't stand it, the thought of what he must have in his mind. I haven't heard . . .no, that's not true, I had a letter this morning but it was written weeks ago, before Christmas and nothing since. That is why, because someone . . .'

'That damned Charlotte.'

'It might not be her, Franny,' she said, trying to be fair. 'I've had some funny looks recently whenever I've gone into Ambleside. Now I know why.'

'Perhaps, but I'm damned sure it was Charlotte

382

who wrote to James.'

'But why? What have I ever done to her to make her do such a thing?' Lucy's voice was anguished and she leaned forward in her chair, her arms about herself as though she were in great pain.

'She's never forgiven him for preferring you to her and she's never forgiven you for taking him. She had him, or so she thought, firmly in her grasp, and I must admit we all believed he would marry her. But then he saw you and that was it. He's loved you from the first moment he saw you. You know that?'

'No, I didn't. I thought it was a marriage of convenience for both of us.'

'And you've discovered that it wasn't?'

'Yes.'

'Hell and damnation, I'd like to go over to the Gibson house and smash Charlotte's bloody perfect teeth down her bloody perfect throat.'

'Can I hold your coat while you do it?'

*   *   *

Mrs Burns tutted irritably as she watched Elsie struggle with a great load of brightly shining copper saucepans, one piled on top of the other in such a totter she was having a great deal of trouble containing them.

'Girl, what have I told you, time after time, what I tell you all but will you listen, no, you will not. Lazy man's load, my mother used to call it. Take half of them to the shelf and then come back for the other half. And don't take all day about it. I want them ice-cream moulds rinsed and—'

'I only washed them this morning, Mrs Burns.'

383

'Don't back-chat me, girl. I don't care if you washed them two minutes ago, I want them rinsed and wiped with a dry cloth. Yes, all of them. You know how those lads like my ice-cream and Sister says it goes down a treat for them what can't fancy much.'

Elsie had to admit that the ice-creams, when set and turned out into the little fancy dishes Cook used to serve them, did look right pretty. Cook was clever that way. She made each one so that you'd swear they were real lemons, real apricots or apples or strawberries in a delicate pile, each fruit the exact shade nature meant it to be and the soldiers loved them.

She sighed, not because Mrs Burns had given her the rounds of the kitchen but because the atmosphere in the house, in the back and in the front, had changed dramatically since the New Year had come in. Of course, the war was dreadful and the columns of figures in the newspapers of the dead and wounded were dreadful too, but despite that they had all felt there was hope and optimism in the air, a feeling that they were sharing in the suffering of the men and doing their best to ease it. And that hope had been created by their mistress, fostered by her, nurtured along with her cheerful determination that they were all to do their best until the master came home.

It was very different now. Miss Lucy crept about like a stricken animal, haunting the front step for the sight of the postman and the letter from Major Buchanan that never came. No one knew why, that was the mystery of it. He was not wounded or dead, or Miss Lucy would have been told about it, but for reasons best known to himself the master had stopped writing and the light of life had gone from Miss Lucy's eyes like a candle blown out.

CHAPTER TWENTY-TWO

Lucy moved through the days like an automaton, doing what she had done for the past eighteen months but with no trace now of the spirit of resolution that had urged her to set up and run a hospital for non-commissioned men. Except when she was on the wards. Then she was the same as she had always been with the wounded men in her care, dedicated, patient, compassionate, encouraging, giving one hundred per cent of herself, day or night, so much so that Sister Colyford had a word or two to say about it.

'You must leave something for the others to do, Mrs Buchanan. You cannot be with the patients twenty-four hours day and night. That's why we have rosters and shifts. Nurse Cartwright tells me you sat by the bedside of Private Hardacre late into the night when you should have been asleep. It was not your shift and it may cause resentment in the other nurses if you interfere.'

She had been summoned to the cubby-hole at the end of the passage leading from the side entrance of the house, the one Sister called her office and which had once served as a store-room for wellington boots, walking sticks, cricket bats, tennis racquets, umbrellas and mackintoshes and all the paraphernalia of the outdoor pursuits of the Buchanans, and then the Deans. The miscellany had been whisked away to the large cupboard on the first landing, a walk-in linen cupboard and so crammed, every time the cupboard door was opened, falling out into a heap across the carpet, to the deep annoyance of whoever opened it. But they were so short of space, with rooms being cleared to accommodate the wounded any little convenient area, convenient for the nursing of them, that is, was pounced upon and this was one of them. The shelves were filled with bottles and jars and against the window was a small desk behind which Sister Colyford sat when she needed privacy to speak to one of her staff, such as now.

'I don't interfere, Sister. Frank's wound had just been irrigated and you know how agonising that can be. He knew he was to go through the whole painful process in three hours' time and quite frankly he was in such a state of dread I felt I could not leave him. Nurse Cartwright was very busy with the new intake and both Jones and Pennington were rushed off their feet. I was in no one's way and Frank became calmer.'

'And that is another thing, Mrs Buchanan.' Sister lifted her double chin, beneath which ribbons were tied and her dainty frilled cap bobbed. There was a neat pile of folders on her desk in which were the records of the new intake and Sister moved them determinedly from the left to the right as though to emphasise her need for order. Sister did not like to have her authority questioned. It was not that she was heartless but she ran the wards in the only way they could be run, and still function, and that was with a strict routine. She could not have people hanging about who were not performing some task, unless, of course, they were visitors come to see the wounded men, and there were not many of those

386

since Ambleside was a long way from the places most of these young men called home.

'Yes, Sister?' Mrs Buchanan asked patiently. She was very quiet these days was Mrs Buchanan. Gone was that lovely laugh which the men listened for and instead was the smile, just as beautiful but so sad it broke your heart, it really did, but just the same Sister must do her duty.

'You cannot call these men by their christian names, Mrs Buchanan. We must have order. They are still in the army despite being wounded and it is protocol to call them by their rank and surname.'

'Sister, I don't wish to be rude, but bugger protocol.'

'Mrs Buchanan!'

'I'm sorry, that was uncalled for, but you see I cannot believe that to address a man by his surname can do him any good at all. It gives them a sense of identity to be called by their first names. They are human beings who are suffering, weary for their homes and their families who do call them by their christian names and if it helps them just a little bit to hear them then I shall continue to say them. They respond, Sister, to a small gesture of familiarity. It seems to give them a feeling that they are perhaps being addressed by their mother or sister or wife, or at least a friend and not the company sergeant-major. They are men again, not just soldiers when they hear their names. Oh, I know they call each other by their christian name, or a nickname most likely, but just the same I believe that what I do is helpful in the healing process.'

Lucy had been just about to go on duty and she was dressed in the immaculate white uniform, high-necked and calf-length, the snowy apron and handkerchief nurse's cap which bound back her hair. Her face was flushed with indignation and a resolve not to be turned from what she believed was an intrinsic part of nursing, personal contact with the patient. They were always pathetically pleased to be given that extra bit of attention, reaching to the hand she held out to them, their faces smoothing, the grey lines of suffering leaving them for a moment as they warmed themselves under her smile. She could not give it up and her raised jaw and tight-lipped expression said so.

'I cannot treat them as though they were nothing but a gangrene leg or a stomach wound, Sister. They are young men, and some not so young who are equally vulnerable.'

'Mrs Buchanan, if you will not obey me I shall be forced to put the wards out of bounds. if you defy my orders . . . oh, my dear . . .'

Suddenly Sister Colyford leaned forward and, putting out her hands across the desk top, took Lucy's, holding them firmly when Lucy would have pulled away.' I know that something . . . I don't wish to pry but one can't help hearing gossip; rumours about this and that and I know you have had some . . . My dear, I don't know how to put this, but you cannot let your personal life control your professional work. These men rely on you, on us all and if you refuse to follow the rules made by myself and the doctor, then you will become ill and be of use to no one. You are not a trained nurse but you are the best nurse's aid I have ever known. You have a way with the patients that seems to reassure them when they are in distress.'

Where had she heard this before and who had

been speaking, and about whom? The question went through her aching head and when the answer came to her the pain became worse, crashing over her eyes, round the back and into the nape of her neck with sickening force. Franny. Franny talking about James and the men in his company. He was—or had been until his faith and trust in her had been destroyed—he had been like that, just as Sister was describing and it was her fault that it had been shattered by some ill-wisher. Charlotte Buchanan, she was sure of it, though she could not bring herself to face her with it, for what would be the good. The damage was done. But it was Lucy Buchanan who had caused it in the first place by becoming too friendly with one of her own patients and, pitying him, had continued the friendship even when he had left her care. James's feelings for her had been too fragile to stand the blow and he had believed it, believed that there was more to it than friendship and that was almost the hardest thing to bear. Though she had written and explained what had taken place; how her feelings for the patient had been nothing but those of friendship and pity, James had not answered. He had just stopped writing. It was as though he had died, killed by shellfire, rifle fire, fire itself, mustard gas or any one of the dozens of horrors that the men in her care babbled about in their nightmares. Oh, she knew all about them. She had relived them time and time again holding the hand of a delirious man who spewed them over her like some putrescent matter but she could not deny them the relief it gave them. She lived with it, slept with it, worked with it until she thought it might drive her mad, not because of what it would do to her but because she knew exactly what it could do to James and the taut ferocity of her grief almost overwhelmed her. How was it that she had not known? she asked herself in the bitter depths of the sleepless night. How was it that she had loved James Buchanan and not known? How could it happen?

Even Franny could not help her. She had promised when she got back to France to try and find James and tell him of Lucy's feelings, of her terror that, thinking he had been deceived, he might become careless, rash, indifferent to bullets and shells and whizz-bangs. She had sent snaps of Alice and some of herself with Alice, willing to blackmail him emotionally into responding, but it seemed he was inclined to believe that perhaps the child was not his, and he had told Franny to sod off and leave him alone. Not a word for Lucy. No message, just an empty nothing as though she were not even worth denying, let alone answering.

'Thank you, Sister, I'll try, but you see, whenever a man calls out for someone it makes me feel better if I can believe that . . . should my husband . . . if he were wounded, there might be someone . . . a nurse who could hold his hand and comfort him a little. I do it for . . . not just for the men but for their wives and mothers who can't be with them. Dear God, I'm sorry, Sister,' as she began to weep, broken at last on the terrible image of James wounded as these men were wounded.

Sister Colyford did not ask her to stay away from the wards after that. If she was on duty and she saw Mrs Buchanan's slender figure leaning over a soldier who wept for his mother or called for 'Annie' or 'Flo', she did not interfere, for she knew Mrs Buchanan was working through this appalling thing that had come upon her in the only way she knew how.

The snows which had fallen early in January had cleared sufficiently to allow her to take the children for long walks through the woods and up on to the lower slopes of the fells. Taking the three dogs, she would put Alice in the harness James and Jacob had devised and, wrapping the children up in warm clothing, take them on the tramp, going as far as the untouched snowline where they stopped to breathe in the breathtaking beauty of the white, shadowed hills which rose up before them. Every tree stood sharp as ebony against the pale blue of the sky, their branches heavy with the patina of glittering ivory. The snow was pure, with no mark save that of the dainty paws of a fox which had come this way earlier. Below the snowline the shadows cast by the mountains were a deep purple in which ferns, bracken and gorse, not dead but withered, stood frozen in pearl and silver.

They were mesmerised for a moment but they were children, made for fun and merriment and soon the virginal snow was trampled as they threw snowballs for the dogs and even attempted a small snowman. Alice, who could just about sit up unaided now, watched, ready with her slow, baby chuckle, but soon deciding she wanted to join in this wonderful game, struggling in Lucy's confining arms until Lucy took off her jacket and sat her down on it, letting her scoop handfuls of clean snow which she promptly put in her mouth.

Lucy found a sheltered spot, and keeping her eye on Alice sat with her back against a snow-speckled rock watching the shadows of the clouds form a shifting pattern on the white hills. They

391

seemed to hang in formation like sheep on parade, fat and fluffy, each waiting its turn to be off and Lucy moved back in time to that other day, in another world, when the sun was hot on two naked bodies who bonded together in love. James, her heart agonised, James! Why was I so blind? Why didn't I know that you loved me? It took Franny to open my eyes, to dash away all the stupid nothingness from my mind so that the clear shining light might be let in. A dozen things should have told her she anguished, but then she was not in love with him then and her heart took no notice. She was conscious that Margaret watched her, for her sister was fifteen now and though still a child in many ways was sensitive to the sadness in Lucy. She came now, leaving the others shrieking joyously in the snow, a child no longer, sitting beside Lucy, taking her hand, letting her know that though she was not awfully sure what was causing her such deep sorrow, Margaret was willing in any way she could to ease it.

Lucy confided in no one but Buffy. After the children were in bed and she was not on night duty, she and Buffy would sit before the fire in the homely comfort of the schoolroom and for hours, when she should have been sleeping, Lucy would talk, pouring out her sense of anguished loss and love for the man who, not believing—and who could blame him after the indifference she had shown him?—that she truly loved him had turned away from the dream, the hope they had begun to build together. At least, that was what she thought they had done on his last leave. Begun to weave a dream, to make small plans, if only in their minds, for the future. She had believed that something tender had taken root and was ready to blossom but Charlotte Buchanan, with the destructive hand of a spoiled child, had destroyed it, and she could not bear it.

'Even if I could see him, explain exactly how it came about, the friendship with Rory, I mean, I still cannot help but feel that ... that if his love had been as truly strong as Franny seems to believe, he would have been prepared to ... well, at least give me the benefit of the doubt, Buffy. He's known me for nearly three years and not once in all that time have I been dishonest with him. He never told me that he loved me, you see.'

Her eyes were grown so huge they devoured the rest of her face and Buffy leaned forward, her own face harrowed by Lucy's pain. She had always known her friend was capable of a deep and abiding love. That some day there would be a man who would see it, know its worth, take it and give it back and now it had happened, that man and that love, only to be crushed in the havoc that was consuming the world.

'It will be over soon, Lucy, or so they say, and then James will be home and you can let him see the truth of it in your eyes. He has only to look at you, see what is in your heart and he will realise how unthinkable it is.' Buffy tried to console her, knowing even as she said the words that they were no more than glass bubbles which would shatter at the slightest touch.

In January the First Military Service Bill introduced conscription for single men and those on the ward cheered, for it was about time those buggers who sat about at home got a taste of what they had suffered. They had heard of the young men who sat all day in the cafés of London, sipping coffee, smoking and playing dominoes while they had been sitting in rainwater up to their arses, slipping in the mud which could get you if you fell off the duckboard, crouching in minute dugouts which were little less than useless if a bloody whizz-bang decided it was your turn.

In February, 21 February, the tragic Battle of Verdun began. Verdun! 'A place of execution' it was later called and that was what it was, for the Germans believed that if they could kill as many French soldiers as possible with their artillery they would break France's will to fight. Wholesale slaughter, it was reported as, and that was just what it was. Over the whole of the front, it was reported, to a depth of many kilometres the dance of dust and smoke and debris was scattered while thousands of French soldiers bent their backs to the storm, clinging together at the bottom of holes, most of which were no better than scratches in the ground. Dante's Hell, they were calling it, the sacrifice of nearly a million soldiers in one battle when it ended in December.

The men on the wards were quiet that day when the newspapers came through, for hadn't they been there themselves.

In May there occurred the first and last great engagement between the British and German fleets and although the British fleet suffered serious losses the German High Seas Fleet never faced them again.

On 23 June the British army began shelling the German lines along the Somme and it was said that the sound of the massive bombardment could be heard across the Channel in England.

At 7.30 on a clear, sunny and pleasant morning on the first day of July, the bombardment stopped. There followed a moment's silence then waves of British divisions went over the top. James Buchanan, Rory Cameron, Aubrey Blane, Job Gunson, Lawrence Gunson and Roger Askew were among them.

'Follow the flash,' they were told, for each soldier had a tin disc on his back, glittering in the sunshine, to show their own guns where they were. 'Follow the flash,' they were told, but within seconds it was hopeless, for those at the front, all the young officers, were picked off like flies, disappearing in the dust and smoke so that there was no flash to follow. Soldiers who had been given orders to take a certain position marched into fierce machine-gun fire, falling in rows almost as though they were on parade. It became impossible to go forward without stepping on the dead and wounded, many of whom were mates and who were not only lying everywhere but were beginning to pile up, one on top of the other in hideous walls of suffering.

A field of craters formed in the strip of land between the two armies' trenches and soon they too were filled, not only with wounded men but with those who were terrified to leave their small safety and go on into the enemy's withering machine-gun fire.

The crater nearest to the enemy line where soldiers had not yet reached had only two men in it. The different battalions had been rehearsed on training grounds in the back areas of the trenches until every soldier in every battalion knew his part and exactly where he should be but the confusion, the smoke, the dust, the noise disoriented many and they just marched blindly forward, following the man ahead until he fell, then settling their sights on another. Often it was a soldier from another company.

One of the men in the crater was badly wounded. His uniform below his waist was soaked with his blood and his face, beneath the mud that coated it, was a dirty grey. It was impossible to tell his rank and what did it matter? They were all comrades in this hell on earth, two small parts in the 60,000 casualties that were estimated that day.

'Where are you hit?' the first soldier asked.

'God knows,' the second one answered, laughing weakly. 'Somewhere below the neck, I suppose, since I'm still conscious.'

'I'll have a look, old chap. Do you hurt in any particular place?' which was a bloody daft question when you saw the state of the poor sod's legs.

'Nowhere, that's the bloody—if you'll pardon the pun—worry.'

Shells thundered overhead from the German trenches and machine-gun fire rattled, the sound like the angry staccato swarm of bees disturbed from their hive, but nobody seemed inclined to join them in the precarious bit of safety they shared. There was water in the bottom of the crater and they both slid into it, the wounded man held firmly in the arms of the other. They both took a sip of water from one water bottle but it set the wounded man to coughing and still the blood pumped from him.

'Let me get this dressing on you. I thinks it's your thigh that got it,' which was an understatement if ever there was one, and putting a dressing on what was left of him would serve no purpose except to make him feel something was being done. As gently as he could the second soldier pressed the dressing on to the gaping wounds of his fallen comrade, hoping to staunch the flow of blood. 'As soon as there's a chance, which I'm afraid means when it's dark, we'll get the hell out of here, old chap. I suppose we should be going forward but to me that doesn't make sense.'

'Nor me, neither. What is it the lads say, 'the higher, the fewer' meaning brains, and whoever thought up this fiasco must have none at all,'

His companion laughed harshly. 'I hadn't heard that one but it's the bloody truth.'

Darkness did not come early for this was just past midsummer but when it did, gritting his teeth to stop himself from screaming as he was moved, the wounded soldier allowed his companion to hoist him on to his back and edge up to the lip of the crater. They both peered over the top, like two bloody moles, one whispered to the other, then, standing up with one on the back of the other, they began to stumble towards the British lines, falling a dozen times over the bodies, some of them still moaning, of those who had gone down earlier in the battle.

'Nearly there, lad,' the one carrying the wounded man gasped, and then the world blew up in his face and he fell into a hole as black and as deep as the crater they had just left.

The first news reaching British civilians about the battle was encouraging. Newspaper headlines declared 'Great Day on the Somme', 'Kitchener's Boys Make Good' and 'Swift British Advance', but gradually the truth, the real truth became known.

Within a few days the rolls of honour, the lists of deaths and casualties began appearing in local and national newspapers. Among those listed as dead were Job Gunson, Lawrence Gunson and Roger Askew. It was learned that in just a few minutes whole towns in the country had been decimated. It took two years for us to get here and ten minutes to finish us off,' one private from a 'Pals' battalion was reported as saying.

Trainloads of wounded men began to arrive from across the Channel and on 5 July one of these came to rest at Windermere station where a line of ambulances waited to take them to the three hospitals in the area. One of those to receive them was Howethwaite.

They knew they were coming, for they had been warned by headquarters to be ready but nothing had prepared them, even such experienced stalwarts as Sister Colyford, for the horror of what they found on the stretchers in the back of the ambulances. Lucy just had time to shriek to Buffy, who had come out on to the steps with Margaret to give a hand, 'Get the children back to the schoolroom and keep them there, for God's sake, Buffy,' and then it began.

They had known it was bad, for if 'our boys' were being sent as far north as this what in God's name was it like in the south, but nothing, *nothing* had prepared them for the contents of the ambulances which lined the road from Ambleside waiting to turn into the gates of Howethwaite. They parked wherever they could find a space, jostling among the flower urns which Clapcott had planted with his usual display of geraniums and white lobelia and when there was no more room simply lifting the stretchers out and placing them on the gravel drive or the lawn, driving away to leave space for the next vehicle. On each stretcher was a soldier, some still and dreadfully silent, others tossing and mumbling, moaning, many of them, a collection of khaki rags, each one with a rough, blood-soaked dressing slapped on it in one spot or another. Not fresh blood but blood that had dried and clotted and was covered with filth and flies and mud and whatever nasty matter had been picked up and clung to them on the long journey from the trenches to the north of England. Orderlies shouted, harassed and so distressed by what they were being forced to do to this broken flotsam, they wanted to smash something. They had seen some sights in the last two years, they told one another, but this beat the bloody cake and what in hell's name was going on 'up there', meaning the War Office, when they allowed such things to happen to poor, decent, hardworking blokes like these. They were not conscripted men, but volunteers who had answered the call of their country and it was a crying shame that they should have had this done to them. They hastily scrutinised the labels that were tied to each man, those that were red telling them that the soldier must be attended to at once, which was a laugh really when you considered how long the poor sods had been on the road.

They all helped to carry them in, even Clapcott and Licky Thripp, Mrs Burns and Mrs Bunting, Dixon and Elsie and Gertie and Jacob, for it was beyond the power of the nurses and the one doctor—though they had been promised another—to ease the men from the ambulances, or the gravel path and on to the hastily erected camp beds which stood wherever there was an empty space.

The men were, for the most part, quiet, for they were all deep in shock but there was an odd sound, a kind of sibilant rustling drifting on the warm, sunshine-filled air, and Lucy realised with stunned shock that it came from dozens of throats, lungs gasping for breath through the agony, the almost silent moans and retching of men who could endure no more but knew they must. She could feel the bile rise to her throat and she tried to draw shallow breaths, for the stink of war was appalling. Though by now she was used to wounds and even gangrene, her eyes slithered from the blood and bone of a wound that had come unwrapped. The men she had attended to in the past had been cleaned up when they got to her, strapped with pure white bandages, resting in white-sheeted beds. These men were not like that.

Her head began to spin and her stomach had a strong desire to spew forth what Sister had made them all eat before the men had arrived.

'You don't know how long it might be before you have a meal so get some of Cook's good soup inside you and you'll come to no harm.'

Cook's good soup was heaving violently inside her and for a moment she knew she was going to faint but Sister's voice snapped in her ear, telling her there were two soldiers lying on one stretcher. Don't ask her why, she didn't know, but the orderlies had told her they wouldn't be parted and had put them at the foot of the stairs. Would she go and have a quick look at them. She had been told they were alive but who could tell. Already several had been taken discreetly round to the back of the house and laid out in the stables ready for interment. Come along, Mrs Buchanan, she admonished, looking at Lucy's bone white face, this is no time for squeamishness.

Mrs Bunting was there, sitting on the bottom step of the staircase, her face wet with tears, begging to be told why she couldn't give these ... well, there were a few who would enjoy a nice cup of tea, surely, but that there Sister had said no and she thought it was wicked to deny them it. There was nothing like a nice cup of tea to pick a body up, then, realising the irony of a cup of tea helping these poor lads, she burst into tears, reaching for Elsie.

'Nay, Mrs Bunting, I'm needed here,' Elsie told her sternly, reaching out a gentle hand to uncover the faces of the two men who lay side by side on one stretcher. A bit of khaki blanket was wrapped about them, hiding what wounds they might have, though Lucy could see blood seeping from the end of the stretcher on to the black and white tiles which had been discovered when the carpet was taken up.

The head of one was wrapped about in what had once been a clean bandage though by now it was foul with mud, days old, and the residue of blood from what must be a head wound.

The other was Rory Cameron, unconscious, with several days' stubble on his face. It was unmarked, young and boyish, but unmarked.

'We'll take the one with the head wound, Mrs Buchanan,' the sharp voice of Nurse Bickerstaffe told her. 'We'll lift him on to this stretcher and then you can help me and Pennington to carry him into the operating theatre.'

She had been kneeling at Rory's side but it was as though, deep in shock as she was, some instinct got her on her feet and with Elsie and herself at the shoulders and Nurse Bickerstaffe and Nurse Pennington at his feet, they lifted the soldier on to a spare stretcher. His head lolled and he moaned beneath his bandages. He had had his arm round Rory Cameron and now, as they moved him, his hand fell limply from the stretcher and on the little finger was a signet ring Lucy had seen many times.

It belonged to James Buchanan.

CHAPTER TWENTY-THREE

There were dogs howling somewhere, a sound that seemed strangely familiar to him though he didn't know why. He didn't know anything really, and that was a bit worrying but there was nothing he could do about it except lie here on the bed and wait. He'd nothing else to do, had he, except wait patiently for the gentle hand that he knew was on its way. It was the only thing, that and her voice, that stood between him and the deep hole of blackness into which he was terrified to fall. In that hole which he had begun to recognise as sleep, or perhaps a state of unconsciousness, he was nothing, just a speck that floated mindlessly in space with no dreams or thoughts or memories, except one, and it terrified him, but when her hand touched him it gave him an identity of sorts and he felt calmed.

He could hear her progress up the ward.

'Andy, you're looking better. What, you've had a letter from Mavis? Well, that explains it. No wonder you've that grin on you. You look like a Cheshire cat. I'll be along presently to write your answer.

'Jack, did you sleep well? I know Sister was going to give you something ... good, good. Yes, I'll bring her in as soon as she wakes up but I warn you she's trying to walk and is a bit of a handful.

'Sid, let me hold your hand for a moment. I know, I know, the pain is dreadful but your mother will be here today, had you forgotten? She'll make you feel better. It will be better soon, I promise you. Yes, I'll slip back as soon as I can.'

He could not hear the soldiers' answers, just a murmur mingling with her compassionate voice. A clock ticked nearby and footsteps moved busily by the end of his bed. Someone was playing a mouth organ in the far ward, a conservatory, he had been told, in which those on the mend were put. Again a familiar sound to him who had heard the tune on the last day before ... before ... '

Keep the home fires burning,
Though your heart be yearning ... '

There was the sound of a dressing trolley being wheeled past, and a nurse's voice telling another to slip to the sluice for a clean bedpan for Corporal Whittaker. He had come to know all the sounds of the ward, the sighing moans of men having their wounds treated, the squeak of the trolley wheels which he wished someone would oil, the rapid footsteps when some emergency arose, the rasp of a match on a matchbox as some chap lit a cigarette. The hiss of pain frorn another bed, the crisp voice of the doctor which subtly changed when he had to

403

tell some poor sod that the gas gangrene was too far gone. The weeping and shouts of men in their sleep and the infectious chuckle of the baby which was brought in to the ward for a brief moment each day to cheer up the men whose own babies were far away. Apparently it belonged to one of the nurses, but he'd heard them say that it gave a small measure of comfort to men who had wallowed in filth and mud and blood and terror for days on end to be allowed to touch the pure, shining innocence of the child.

When it came he could not see the hand, at least no more than the vague shape of it. He could not see the owner of the hand either, for his face and head were heavily bandaged, but he knew and waited for its touch and for the gentle voice which called him James. He didn't know why. He supposed it must be his name, for the authorities would know who he was. He didn't much care at the moment. He knew her footsteps and her laugh, which was low and sweet as though it knew there were men about who could not cope with heartiness, but it was laughter all the same, like the ripple of the wind in the trees.

He knew the scent of her too, a fresh, sweet smell which, like the howling of the dogs, seemed familiar though again he didn't know why. She was a nurse, he recognised that, for she had the sharp, clean smell of carbolic about her, but underlying the hospital smell was that fragrance which tantalised him.

He could hear the rustle of her uniform as she came along the ward and something in him longed for her to hurry up with the chap in the next bed and get to him. Something urgent, compelling, something that would not wait, and without thinking he put out his hand to her and at once she was there.

'James, I'm here,' she told him and immediately the urgency was gone and the tranquillity she brought washed over him and he sighed.

'I wish you wouldn't keep going away,' he heard his own voice say fretfully, knowing he was being unfair, for all the men in the ward had as much call on her time as he did. He had been told he had been wounded, as the rest of them were, but it was only when she was with him that he had any peace.

'I'm here now,' she whispered and he felt her breath brush the skin of his hand, and something else, warm and damp which was quickly brushed away.

'What is it?' he asked.

'Nothing,' she answered him and though he was sure it was a tear he could not be certain and anyway, why should she be crying over him?

'Is Rory about?' he asked her, turning his head restlessly on his pillow as though he might see the only man he knew through the thickness of his bandages.

'No, he's been taken to the operating theatre again. His stumps are . . . need irrigating and the doctor wants to put him to sleep.'

'Poor sod. Tell me when he gets back, will you, Nurse?'

'Of course, but in the meanwhile why don't you try and get some sleep?'

He turned his head away from her and sighed deeply. 'That's all I'm ever told to do, Nurse, but . . .'

'What? What is it? Tell me and if I can I'll . . .'

405

'What will you do, Nurse, give me back my life, my thoughts, my memories?' He moved his body in the bed, twisting away from her and then back again. 'Jesus, I'm sorry, I shouldn't say that, not to you who . . . but when you know only one person in the whole bloody world.'

'I know . . . I know, James, but you will get it all back, I promise you.' Surprising him she lifted his hand to her face and held the back of it to her cheek and again he could feel a dampness there. Her lips brushed it and he felt his heart begin to race and for the life of him he didn't know why. She was a nurse, filled with a great compassion, not just for him but for them all. He had heard her in the night when he knew she was supposed to be off duty, moving along the ward, stopping to murmur to some restlessly tossing man, stopping to put her hand on his own brow though he could barely feel it through the bandages. Several times he had threshed up from the infernal depths of the blackness he was captured in, like a fish leaping from the ooze at the bottom of the ocean, to find her there, his hand in hers, her face close to his though he did not know how he was aware of this.

'James, I'm here,' she would say with a strange break in her voice and he would be comforted.

'Don't let me go to sleep again,' he would beg her, for he could not stand that blankness he tipped over into which contained, though he could not bring it to him, his past life.

'Why has Rory gone to the operating theatre again?' he asked her. Rory was the only human being in the world, in his life, his past and present, who he remembered. His life had started really when he had staggered across no-man's land with him on his back. He could remember the weight of him, the sighing rustling sounds of his moans at every jerking step, every fall and stumble. He could hear Rory's voice in his ear telling him to let him go but he couldn't do that, could he, and he had told him so, the silly sod. He didn't remember any more until he came to, lying on a stretcher among hundreds of others, the bombardment thundering over him and the bandage that had been slapped hastily on his face blinding him. He had begun to shout in panic but the voice of the wounded man on the next stretcher had reached out to him.

'Don't fret, old man,' it said weakly. 'We're in this bloody thing together. You don't think I'm going to lose sight of the stupid bugger who dragged me here, do you?'

'I must have been mad,' he said, just as weakly.

'We all are in this bloody war.'

'What's your name?'

'Rory Cameron. And yours?'

It was then that the black thing came down on him and swept him away on a tide of terror. There was something behind him that pressed against his present consciousness, pushing him and belabouring him and he wanted to turn and stare into it, sweep aside the curtain that hid himself from himself and see whatever it held, for it was his life up to the time he had carried this Rory Cameron to safety. But no matter how hard he tried it remained a vacuum.

He didn't even know his own name!

They had travelled together from that clearing station in France to this hospital, which he had been told was near Ambleside in the Lake District, and whenever they tried to separate them, he and

Rory, he had yelled and screamed and tried to do the stretcher-bearers an injury, and for the sake of peace—and what difference did it make to anyone? they asked one another—they had kept the two badly injured soldiers, one an officer, together. They had even shared a stretcher in the ambulance up to the hospital, for by then Rory was off his head, twisting and turning and throwing himself about so that the only way to keep him from falling out of the bloody ambulance had been to hold on to him.

He sensed her leaning over him. Her elbows were on the bed and he wanted to let his body fall against her but instead he gripped her strong hand with his which was ridiculously weak.

'They're trying a new treatment,' she told him. 'Rory has gas gangrene in both his legs, or rather in the stumps, as you know, and the doctor doesn't want to . . . to cut again. This new thing is called hypochlorous acid. Drainage tubes will be attached to a large syringe and the liquid will be injected into the tube every three hours to irrigate the wounds of his stumps. It will be an agonising procedure but, if we don't do it, Rory could die.'

She kept nothing from him. That was why he clung to her, he supposed. Some of the staff, and the men, too, treated him as though he were an infant or a lunatic because he could not remember . . . remember what had happened to him before this. They spoke over his supine body as though, having no memory, he also had no feelings, no adult mind and he'd had the devil's own job to force the doctor to tell him what was wrong with him. In fact had it not been for this nurse, who was his lifeline, as she was to many of the others, he would not have succeeded. The less you know the better was the attitude of the medical profession but this woman had stood beside him and fought the doctor on his behalf. He would never forget her. He might never remember his previous life but he would never forget her.

*   *   *

'Let me tell him who he is,' she wept, clinging to the doctor's hands, flinging off Sister Colyford's attempts to restrain her. She knew Sister believed she was about to do the doctor an injury in her desperate state of fear for James, but nevertheless she could see no reason why her husband should not be told that he was in his own home, that he was with his own wife, with his own family about him, and during those first days she had said so at every turn. Every time Doctor Yates or Doctor Penfold came off the ward she would be there, hovering anxiously, resolute in her determination to accost him and talk about this one patient when the doctors had over forty others to see to. The doctors were patient with her but very adamant.

'Mrs Buchanan, we know very little about the human mind and if we just ... just barge in and force on Major Buchanan the truth of who he is and where he is we might do untold harm. Here, on the ward, he is a soldier among other soldiers and that is familiar to him and for the present he can cope with that. Of course he wants to remember, to know who he is and where he comes from but we must go slowly. No, please, don't ask me why. From experience the medical profession, in these unusual times, has found that it is better to wait and see if

409

the patient recovers naturally. That whatever is blocking out his past will simply drift away. There might be some dreadful thing, dreadful to him, that is, which is putting up a barrier to help him keep it at bay. It might be a . . . a physical wound, in his head, though we don't think so,' he added hastily as Mrs Buchanan swayed and turned the colour of her own nurse's apron, clutching at his arm for support.

'May I put his child in his arms, Doctor?' she pleaded. 'He loved her so and it might . . .'

'Again you are trying to force him to remember, Mrs Buchanan. Has he shown any interest in the baby when you take her on the wards to visit the other men? They all want to pat her and talk to her, even hold her, and we know now that it does them untold good, but does your husband ask? No. Then we must not do anything which might precipitate him into something worse than his present state.'

The memory of that day when James and Rory came home together would haunt her to the end of her days. Gallant little Elsie who had wanted nothing more than to help these poor broken soldiers, had staggered back in horror, turning to Mrs Bunting and falling into her arms, the pair of them crouched together on the bottom step of the staircase, the stretcher on which Major Buchanan had been placed left to fend for itself on the floor. Sister had lifted the casual dressing which covered James's face, saying she would just have a quick look at his wound and it was the sight of that wound which had knocked Elsie for six, as she was to say later, ashamed of herself and ready to apologise to anyone who would listen.

Whatever it was that had exploded in front of

410

him, mine or shell, had taken the skin from his face as though someone had peeled it with a knife. There was shattered bone showing just below his right eye and most of his hair was gone. Had it not been for his ring they would none of them have known him. The wound had festered and it had turned Lucy faint and sick to see it but in her compassion and her love for this man whom she had come late to knowing, she sank down on her knees and took his filthy hand in hers. His eyes were open and he could see her, she knew that, thank the good God, but he said nothing, held in the deep shock that merciful nature sends to mend the injured. Would James Buchanan mend? her heart anguished. Her tears, of which she was ashamed, for what good would tears do her wounded husband, dripped on to the hand she held and his eyes moved to look enquiringly into hers but there was no recognition.

'Mrs Buchanan, please, we must take him,' Sister's urgent voice had told her. 'Let him go, my dear.'

'I must come with him, please.' She knew she was becoming distraught, hysterical and Sister moved round the quiet man and lifted her to her feet.

'No, you cannot. He needs immediate attention. That wound is ... my dear, you have seen enough wounds to know that unless ... Pull yourself together, Mrs Buchanan, and let us do our job. Go and help the others. There are uniforms that need cutting off and ... well, you know what to do.'

Please, please, Sister, let me ... .' Her tears coursed down her face and on to the hands which Sister Colyford was holding and it was not until

Sister's voice became harsh and commanding, telling her to behave herself and remember her training, that she let him go, watching the stretcher being carried along the hallway to the operating room where a queue was already forming. There were three doctors on three tables, surrounded by nurses and VADs and they would work the clock round, they were aware of that, and Lucy must do the same. She must let them do what they could for James while she put her quite considerable knowledge to work in the easing of the others. She was allowed to give injections now, to take away the agony for a while of a wounded man, to change dressings, to irrigate wounds and there were men here who needed these things. Let her do what she was capable of doing, she told herself, wiping her eyes and squaring her shoulders, for there was nothing she could do for James. Not yet.

'Lucy . . .'

The voice, so weak she could barely hear it, came from the stretcher from which James had just been lifted and for a moment, disorientated, confused, distraught as she was, she did not recognise it, or the pallid face that looked up at her from the floor. She knew who he was, of course. Silver blond curls clotted with blood and mud and what could have been manure, which she supposed was not out of the question since that was what the farmers had put on their fields before the armies of three nations tore them up in the bloodbath of war. It was that which turned so many wounds to the dreaded gas gangrene, they all knew that by now too. Pale blue eyes surrounded by long, fair lashes tried to smile at her from that filthy face and with a murmur of pity Lucy dropped to her knees again and put her hand to Rory Cameron's cheek. He turned his face into the palm and sighed in great relief and even contentment, as though he were safe now, for he was in the care of the woman he loved. He closed his eyes and for an appalling moment she thought he was dead but he opened them again and smiled that sweet smile she remembered so well.

'He . . . brought me back, Lucy. We were . . . in a shell hole together . . . I didn't know who he was, of course. Not until they read his . . . identity tags.' His voice was barely a whisper rasping from his throat and she leaned over him tenderly.

'Don't talk, Rory. It's all right. There's no need . . . later, perhaps.' She smoothed his hair, once thick and heavy and shining, from the sweated brow of his powder grey face, and she could feel the rigid strain of something in him begin to ease.

'I wanted to do . . . the same for him, my darling. I may call you that, mayn't I? I've always . . . longed to. I wanted to do it . . . for you because . . . I'

'I know, Rory, don't talk any more,' for she could see he was hanging on to life by no more than a slender thread that threatened to break at any moment. He was exhausting his already badly depleted body in his effort to explain to her how he and James had come home together.

'Sleep, Rory, and when you wake I'll be there.'

'Promise.'

'I promise.'

Then Clapcott, Licky Thripp, Jacob and someone she didn't recognise came to lift him up and take him to the doctors.

That had been six weeks ago and today, later in the afternoon, they were to remove the bandages from James Buchanan's face.

'We did the best we could, Mrs Buchanan, but he was . . . his face was . . . Well, we shall have to wait and see, won't we?' and she knew he was warning her that her husband might not look like the man who went to war nearly two years ago.

They wouldn't let her take him to a private room, her bedroom even, where she could nurse him. She had wanted to have him with her twenty-four hours a day and night, while she slept beside him in a truckle bed. He was an officer, which she didn't care about, and she knew he wouldn't either, and the rest of the wounded were ordinary Tommies, and by the military rules he should not have been with them, but again the doctors, who did not give a damn about protocol, fortunately, would not allow it.

'He feels a comradeship with these men, Mrs Buchanan. He is one of them. He has no idea who he is, whether he was an officer or not, it wouldn't matter, and to put him on his own would distress him immeasurably. Leave him with those he knows, the only ones he knows, especially Corporal Cameron. I'm sorry, Mrs Buchanan, if I seem heartless,' for she had flinched away from his words. 'They both owe their lives to the other and it seems fitting, at least to the major, that they should lie side by side in the ward.'

She had bowed her head and though she wanted to weep and even scream that she would nurse her own husband if she wanted to, for who better than the woman who loved him more than life itself, she did as she was told.

Rory was lying in the bed beside his when the doctors came. He himself had only just come round from the anaesthetic and his face clearly revealed his shock and pain, his eyes huge in his thin face. His hair had been recently washed and it shone a pure silver blond in the sunshine that streamed through the window above the two beds. His head was turned painfully on his pillow, his eyes looking directly into James's and for a moment Lucy knew these two had no need of her or indeed of anyone but each other. They had suffered together, gone through the hell of battle together, a battle from which Job Gunson, Lawrence Gunson and Roger Askew had not returned, and they were united in that mysterious bond which only another soldier would understand.

When he heard the sound of the screens being drawn round his bed James turned to glare at the nurse, or at least as much of a glare as he could manage with his face totally obscured by the bandages.

'Don't do that, Nurse,' he snarled.

'But it is customary, James.' They had all been told to call him by his given name in order to protect him from the chance of his being flung into the confusion and terror of being inadvertently told who he really was.

'I don't give a damn. Rory is . . . I don't want to. And where is . . .'

She knew at once what it was he wanted.

'I'm here, James,' taking the hand he held out to her and gripping it firmly in both of hers. She wanted to put her arms about him and hold him safe, tell him it made not the slightest bit of difference to her what he looked like but naturally she could do none of these things, He was not her husband at this moment. But he still needed her

415

hand in his.

'Right,' he said briskly, doing his best to keep his hand steady in hers. 'Let the dog see the rabbit.'

She met Rory's eyes for a moment and in them was a message of love and hope and compassion. Rory Cameron would never walk again unless his stumps healed enough to fit him with two artificial legs. He would never know the blessings that awaited James Buchanan but he let her see that though he loved her, that he, Rory Cameron, loved her and wanted her for himself, he knew she belonged to James Buchanan.

The bandages came away quite easily and the doctor grunted in satisfaction. The whole ward seemed to be holding its breath, even men at the far end knowing that this was an important day for the poor bugger who was known simply as James. Was he to be as hideous as some they had heard of, men who were burned, or shot in the face, or had the clever doctor who, before he had retired to the Lake District, been a surgeon in the field of plastic, reconstructive surgery, and who had been brought back at the beginning of the war, been able to put his shattered face together again?

His hair had grown in the six weeks since he had been brought here, falling in that way she was so familiar with in a rough tumble of darkness across his forehead, and without thought, scarcely looking at the rest of him, Lucy brushed it back from his forehead, saying, as any wife would, 'It's time you had a haircut, James.'

He turned slowly towards her, looking up in surprise to her smiling face and there were his eyes, smoky grey and as soft as velvet, the lashes thick about them, uncertain but without the fear she had

416

expected to see in them.

'You sound like my mother,' he said, the first time he had made a remark that told them he knew he was a person like the rest of them.

It was then that Lucy looked at the rest of his face. It was the bright shiny pink of newly healed flesh, clean and smooth, with a mottled creasing of scars about his mouth and eyes and a puckering beneath his right eye where the doctor had mended the broken bone of his cheek. There was a lift at the corner of his mouth that would always be there but which might have been the start of a smile and a slight dragging down of his right eyebrow. She didn't see them or if she did it did not matter. It was James, that's who it was, the James she had loved for years, she knew it now, had known it for a long time, and it shone like a candle in her eyes. A candle flame that would never blow out.

He was blinking in the bright light, despite the drawn blinds, for though he had had eyeholes cut in the bandage they had been covered thinly with gauze. It was seven weeks since James Buchanan had looked at anything, another human being, and the first face he looked up into was that of the loveliest woman he had ever seen. A face so exquisite, so young and tender he felt he wanted to hide what he was sure was his own disfigurement from her. A face in which two golden brown eyes, deep and soft as old sherry, looked into his with an expression of . . . well, what in hell's name was it that was in her face? He was damned if he knew but it wasn't revulsion and he tightened his grip on her hand.

'God, you're a handsome dog,' Rory croaked valiantly from the other bed. 'None of us will have

417

a chance now with Nurse Buchanan.'

They saw his body relax though he still clung to the nurse's hand, glancing about him as though to catch any faint shiver of distaste which might come from one of them, but they were all smiling and the doctor looked like a dog with two tails, both of which he thought he might wag.

'Perhaps Mrs Buchanan's husband might have something to say about that,' he joked, turning towards the nurse who held a mirror, not exactly eager to see what a guy he was but prepared to suffer it, he said to Rory.

He held the mirror and cautiously peeped into it but it was not what he saw there that relieved him but the expression of approval on Nurse Buchanan's face. Her great shining eyes beamed down into his, and she was nodding and he was not to know that, having seen his face, she was thinking that there was nothing on this earth that would stop her from bringing his daughter to see him.

'What d'you think?' he asked diffidently, looking not at the rest of them but into the lovely smiling face of the nurse, the one who had got him safely from there to here.

He was astonished and so were the rest of them when she bent her head and kissed him on his shiny new cheek.

CHAPTER TWENTY-FOUR

She watched him from her bedroom window, his tall, thin figure erect and easy as he strolled down the grassy slope at the front of the house towards the group of men who had already been put out there by the nurses. He had lost a lot of weight during the past weeks, and his cheeks were hollowed out below the flat planes of his cheekbones but the exercise and the sun had touched his lean, scarred face with the amber tint that had been his before he was wounded.

He was pushing Rory in what they both called the 'baby carriage', the wicker stretcher on wheels which the legless and those still recovering from serious wounds and unable to walk got about in. They were laughing at something one of them had said, James bending his dark head to Rory's silver pale one, and it was obvious even from this distance that their companionship was strong and important to them both. They wore the blue hospital uniform with its distinctive red lapels, James, the officer, indistinguishable from Rory, the corporal.

It was a glorious September day with that special crispness in the air which says that summer is almost over and autumn hot on its heels. The sun cast its benign warmth over the men and Lucy could hear their voices, accented with the brogue of Ireland, the burr of Scotland, the long-vowelled flatness of Lancashire and Yorkshire, the clipped chirpiness of the cockney and in the midst of it the well-bred drawl of James and Rory which the others seemed to find easy to accept. They might be of a different social class to the others but they were soldiers, damaged men just like them who had gone through the hell they had and their comradeship was total. They did not know who James was, nor his rank, apart from the fact that he was a soldier wounded in battle, respecting the loss of his memory, poor sod, for the doctor had impressed on those who knew him, only Sister and herself, the servants and the children, that for a while they must let him heal until, gradually, they were certain, he would find the truth of it himself.

Though the day was bright and cheerful none of them could forget that in the trenches the leaching of the nation's best blood went on relentlessly day after long day in the Battle of the Somme where so many of them had fallen and as far as those who followed it on the map could see, no realistic gains had been made by the British army. The previous month forty-nine of the new and unreliable tanks had been shipped over to France and on the fifteenth of the month they had lumbered monstrously forward with the leading infantry against the German army, three hours later moving through the third German line. It was the greatest gain since the battle had begun.

When the men heard the news they were as excited as schoolboys, telling one another that now they had the Hun on the run, but it seemed their elation was to be short-lived. From what the newspaper reports said there were too few tanks to make much difference and after the initial success the fighting had degenerated into its usual bull-headed contest for every inch of ground.

But they were out of it and for the moment that

was all that mattered, though they felt ashamed to think so when they remembered all those still out there. Some of them who were recovering quickly, the strong and sturdy country lads and those who had been built up in childhood with nourishing food their mams had cooked and so had the strength to fight the infections, knew they would have to go back when their wounds had healed but most, and these were men who had lost limbs, or their sight, would go home to their families and thanked God for it.

James placed Rory's stretcher in a patch of sunlight then flopped down in a deckchair beside him. A card game was going on round a small folding table and several men on crutches were stumbling awkwardly along the neat path Clapcott and Licky Thripp kept swept and tidy. The flowerbeds were a vivid blaze of colour, the showy splash of dahlias and stock and zinnia, sweet william, peonies and pinks, and edging the lawns an eruption of lavender, its fragrance a delight to these men who had known the stench of war, the stench of the sickroom. They did not know the names of the flowers but Clapcott, who was anxious to talk to any man who might have known his Bertie, was only too happy to tell them about mignonette and rock rose, hydrangea and delphinium and the correct growing of them.

Lucy turned away with a deep sigh, the open window still bringing in the men's voices. Her bedroom was on the corner of the house and moving slowly from the window which faced west she leaned her hands on the sill of the second and stared sightlessly in the direction of Colwith Woods. They stretched from the winding river to the fell top, hazel and birch and rowan, and so exquisitely lovely at this time of the year as autumn approached Lucy felt the pain of it enter her heart which already ached in a continuous destruction. The grandeur of the fells never ceased to bewitch her, to overwhelm her, to hurt her in some strange way and she studied the great swathe of the bracken already turning from green to brown, the heather from purple to umber, her eyes ready to moisten with tears. She cried very easily these days. The dry stone wall at the back of the house, where a couple of ambulatory wounded were perched in peaceful silence had, during the summer, burgeoned with hedge parsley, dock and nettle, meadow cranesbill, ragwort and foxglove. They were slowly dying away now but over it all the sharp smell of aniseed from the sweet cecily drifted about the gardens so that she could smell it from here.

The old cast-iron fireplace that once had graced the bedroom when Alex and Christy Buchanan had slept here was gone and in its place was an unadorned white marble surround in which a small fire burned. A pretty French clock ticked on the mantelpiece next to a small bowl of late roses. Apart from the fireplace the room was exactly the same as when James's grandparents had occupied it. The flickering flames of the fire gilded to cream and apricot the white lace curtains and the plain white walls, putting a touch of rose in the soft velvet curtains and the two small bedroom chairs, into one of which she sank. The bed, which was enormous, was new, for James was a tall man and liked a bit of space, he told her when they were first married and it had been purchased. She had kept the white theme throughout, with a touch of colour here and there in cushions and the valance above the bed, though James had told her she might change anything she wished. But she had delighted in the pale rosewood furniture, the pale biscuit carpet, rich and deep to the foot and, apart from putting a picture or two on the walls, prints of the French impressionists which she loved, and her own personal brushes, combs and the toilet things her mother had left her, it was almost exactly as it had been a hundred years ago.

There was a tap on the door and at her call it opened and Buffy entered, Alice on her hip. The child, who was thirteen months old now and the pet of every man and woman in the house, with the exception of her own father, was wriggling to get down, shouting her displeasure at Buffy, for now that she was mobile she did not like to be carried.

'I'm just going down now and I wondered if you were coming,' and perhaps this time James Buchanan might take more than a polite interest in the child, Buffy's face plainly implied, the child whose charm, laughter, innocence and total unconcern with the disfigurements the men had brought back from France was helping them to come to terms with their own particular horrors.

Looking at Lucy's bowed head, Buffy put Alice down and let her totter over to her mother's dressing-table and climb precariously up on to the stool before it. She reached for the hand mirror, jabbering at her own reflection, smiling and turning the mirror towards them so that they might see it too.

Buffy sat down in the second small chair and leaning forward took Lucy's flaccid hand in hers, her face filled with loving sympathy.

423

'Don't give up, Lucy, not now when he has come so far. He is almost himself again—'

Lucy laughed harshly. 'Don't be a blithering idiot, Buffy. He is far from being himself again.'

'Let me finish, Lucy.'

'There is nothing more to be said. A man who does not know his own child, his wife, his home where he was born, a man who prefers the company of the man whose life he saved to ... to any other, clings to him even as though ... as though he were his lifeline.'

'Perhaps he is, Lucy. Rory is the only person James remembers from his past. He *is* James's past and so James cannot bear to be parted from him. He wants to be Rory's legs. I don't know why, I suppose it gives him a purpose in life. All these men have something, a life, a family.'

'So has James.' Lucy's voice was low and despairing.

'But he doesn't know it, so he holds on for dear life to the one man who knew him before ... before ...'

'Oh, don't go on, Buffy, there's a love. I just don't know how much longer I can manage without babbling to him to ... to wake up, as though he were some bloody princess in a fairy tale. I want to put Alice on his knee and say, "This is your daughter who once you loved so much," and me ... he loved me as well, Buffy.'

'He still does, darling.'

'Then why doesn't he recognise it?' Lucy's voice rose in despair and the child turned anxiously, her eyes, so like her father's it was incredible, becoming clouded. She hesitated as though she would climb down and run for the safety of one lap or the other but Lucy quietened and Alice went back to her pleased contemplation of her own reflection.

'I've tried to explain to the children, which was the hardest thing I've ever done, especially Percy, that they must not talk to James about ... about the days before he went away but I know they don't understand. He's lost all memory of those days, I told them and he must be left to find it again by himself, but Margaret wept and said it seemed brutal, that those who loved him must not help him. Percy wasn't even sure what a memory was and I know they are trying so hard. I can see it when I'm with them and James. Just the fact that they are to call him James and not Mr Buchanan as they used to is a mystery that puzzles them. I know that it will slip out ... something, I don't know, perhaps about the motor car, or the walks we had and I'm convinced that that will be more harmful than this ... this charade we must all keep up. And then there are the others.'

'The others?'

'His family. They can't be put off much longer. He is their cousin and is dear to them. He has been home for almost three months and I am beginning to believe they think that I am holding them off for some purpose of my own. They are offended by what they see as my bloody-mindedness. They've always thought me a bit odd, Buffy, you know that. An unconventional rebel, undisciplined and not like them. I told Doctor Penfold that if James didn't recognise me how could he be expected to recognise Ben or old Mr Buchanan and so where would the harm be, but he seems to be obsessed with the idea that should one of them say anything untoward James might have some sort of relapse. It frightens me, this constant walking on a tightrope. Last week I heard Clapcott call him 'Mister James'. He was about to remind him of something that had happened years ago but he caught himself in time and fortunately James didn't notice.'

'Darling, I don't know what to say, except that you can only take the doctor's advice. There are so many men whose minds have been disturbed. That Rory is still inclined to jump at any unexpected sound and that other poor chap . . .'

'Private Matthews?'

'Yes. He'll never get over the sight of . . . you know what I mean.' Buffy's face spasmed in anguish.

'Yes, I know.' Lucy's face was dark and brooding as she looked into the dark dread which haunted poor Private Matthews who had seen his own wounded comrades, fallen in battle, go under the tracks of the British tanks that had been sent to protect them.

'They all have their own private hell inside them, Buffy, and I suppose that is what James is hiding from. At least I pray that it is,' she finished sombrely.

'What d'you mean?' Buffy leaned forward to look into her face.

'I'm hounded by the thought that . . .'

'What, darling?'

'That it might be that bloody letter Charlotte Buchanan sent him. The one that told him about . . . about me and Rory. He believed it, that is what is tearing me apart, and is that what he's hiding from? Oh, Buffy,' her voice was soft and frightened, 'it's breaking my heart.'

426

It was the dogs who got to him first and it was perhaps then that memory began to seep, like a dripping tap, drop by slow drop into James Buchanan's empty mind.

There were some children, relatives of the owners of the house, he was told, who spent a lot of time with the wounded men who were well enough to get about outside and when he became one of those, walking out into the bright sunshine pushing Rory in his baby carriage, it was then that he met them. The children and the dogs.

'This is Edward, James,' Rory said, somewhat hesitantly, James thought, 'and this is Percy, and these are their beautiful sisters, Margaret and Emily.'

James nodded pleasantly, waiting for some reaction to his scars but when none came he managed a smile and though they all stared at him with great curiosity he supposed that was only natural. He was still a bit of a freak despite the process of healing that was taking place, with a sort of half smile always about his mouth whatever his mood, but it was better than a snarl, or so Nurse Buchanan told him during one of the delightful little interludes they spent together during the night when all the others were asleep and he was wakeful. Jesus, 'one of their little interludes'! It sounded as though they got up to something they shouldn't but it was nothing like that at all. They talked. Mrs Buchanan's husband was an officer in the Border Regiment, she told him when he asked her, her face somewhat strained, reluctant to say more for some reason, and he did not press her, for he did not want to remind her of the terrors of the trenches. She already knew enough of that particular demon from the men she nursed.

The dogs, who he had never seen since it seemed, for the safety of the men who staggered about the front garden, they were kept locked up, were howling in that strangely pitiful way of animals who are distressed and he wondered why. He knew they were taken up on the fells by one of the outside chaps, the fellow they called Jacob who was, apparently, a groom. The children had ponies up in the paddock and he meant to take Rory up there to see them when he was able to get him into a wheelchair. Rory had once ridden to hounds, he told him and loved horses and these were only ponies but he thought he might like to see them. The children had names for them. Comet, Oliver, Silver and Sally, they had told him shyly, but when he had asked them the names of the dogs that howled so painfully they looked away to Nurse Buchanan, awkward and stiff, the smallest boy ready to reach for her hand. She had changed the subject brightly, sending the children off back to the schoolroom where their lunch was waiting for them, she said.

Today the boy, the eldest boy called Edward, was messing about with a bit of something mechanical, deep in conversation with Sergeant Cooper who was interested in such things. It looked like an old clock and the pair of them were doing something with a screwdriver while the elder girl, Margaret, was reading to a group of young patients, only boys themselves, every one of them taking more interest in the lovely girl than what she was reading. Their eyes were unfocused with peace, their tormented bodies relaxed in their respectful contemplation of her young beauty, while Emily, who was younger, was making daisy chains, of which she was inordinately fond, one for each of them, she told them. The boy, Percy, was darting about the grass with a wooden sword, charging and retreating in some game of his own devising and along the flowerbeds Clapcott and his workmate placidly hoed the dark earth.

It was a beautiful garden, filled with the peaceful tranquillity that the old man who had created it and tended it for so long had brought to it. The terrace, the steps of which led down to the lawns, was lined with terracotta pots of yellow-eyed forget-me-nots and violas. There were benches on the terrace on which men sat enjoying the warmth of the sun on their faces. There were more benches in the shade of the old oak trees which had seen James Buchanan's ancestors stroll under their magnificent arch and at the bottom of the garden a bed of roses: cabbage roses, old white damask and maiden's blush almost overwhelmed them with their heady fragrance.

It was as though a whirlwind had been let loose on them and for several moments there was pandemonium as men in wheelchairs did their best not to be turned head over heels and others like Rory, in stretchers, cowered beneath their blankets, some of them beginning to whimper, for they were, for a moment, flung back into a world of fear. There was the sound of a furious barking, high-pitched and ecstatic, hysterical with joy, and before he could get to his feet they were on him, two enormous black forms, leaping and jumping and placing their huge paws on his chest and his shoulders, forcing him back in the deckchair until it collapsed beneath him. They would not let him alone, licking his face and ears and neck and any bit of flesh they could reach with their rough tongues, still barking in the shrill voice that dogs, even dogs as big as these two, take on when they are overcome with joy.

Strangely, he was not afraid. 'Get off me, you devils,' he roared and all the men fell silent, recognising authority, as it seemed the dogs did. Though it was evident it would take more than a few words, a barked command to calm them, they had begun to back off a little, enough to allow him to sit up. Still they huddled up close to him, whining now, their joy almost a pain, their strong tails nearly wagging them off their feet, and when he put an arm round each neck they simply shivered against him, their eyes rolling in silent adoration.

'Well, you've made a hit there, old chap,' Rory said flippantly, doing his best to cover the total confusion that had fallen over the men. They had never seen the dogs before, and, as far as they knew, neither had James but, by God, it was evident they knew him. They were taking absolutely no notice of anyone else, even though young Edward and even Percy were doing their best to haul the pair of them off James.

'Get off, Holmes, you blighter,' Edward was yelling, pulling for all he was worth at the dog's collar, while Percy was doing the same to the one he addressed as Watson, but with little success. They would not leave James's side and, being big, strong dogs, they were having their own way.

'Sit, sit, I say,' James said quietly and at once, incredibly, they both sat, though it was very evident it would not be for long.

'You've certainly a way with animals, James,' Rory drawled. 'They must be well-trained beasts to obey ... well, someone they are not used to, wouldn't you say?'

James was still sitting on the flattened deckchair, his arms about his bent knees, his eyes looking directly into those of the two dogs who were, though still sitting, inching nearer to him. They were doing their best to obey him but for three months now they had known he was home and, having been kept from him, they were not about to do it again.

From somewhere, probably the same gate that the dogs had forced open, another streak of canine activity raced, this time in the shape of a small, brown Border terrier, prancing and leaping at every seated man, excited beyond measure, until at last it fastened its small black nose on the scent of the man on the ground and, with a yelp of pleasure, swarmed all over him.

'Dear God, not another one,' James groaned, beginning to laugh. 'Where in hell's name have you come from and why am I the recipient of all this bloody rejoicing? Go and lick some other bugger to death and let me get to my feet,' and at once they were all laughing and as Lucy ran across the lawn, Buffy hobbling behind with the protesting Alice in her arms, it was this sight that met her frantic gaze. She had seen it all from her bedroom window and after a frozen moment of horror had raced down the stairs and out of the front door, convinced that some dreadful catastrophe was to befall them all.

But it seemed James saw nothing wrong in the three dogs singling him out and though she had distinctly heard Edward and Percy call the labradors by their names, James appeared not to have caught on.

She sat down in a vacant chair after dragging Thimble on to her lap where he settled placidly enough, for by now Thimble was three years old and though still a bit inclined to disobedience, was no longer a puppy. She watched James, the expression on his face just as it used to be with his animals, though she had to admit she had never before seen him romp with his dogs as he was doing now. They had him on his back again, and when Percy, who loved a bit of male rough and tumble, threw himself into the fray, rolling over and over on the grass, shouting with laughter as the dogs and James played, not only together, but with him, which was a bit of an eye-opener since Mr Buchanan had never played with any of them before, Lucy waited, holding her breath, for surely this must be the moment when memory would return to James Buchanan. She caught Rory's eyes and she could see the same anxious thought in them. There was no one more urgently in need of James's return to his own life than she was, but James was Rory's friend by now and was this commotion to slip that friend into some sort of appalling limbo from which he would never recover? Would the disturbance—God, what a foolish word to describe chaos—create more harm to James than the gradual return the doctor wanted, or would he suddenly turn to her, recognise her, and Alice, who was ready to join in what seemed like enormous fun, and . . . and what?

Sweet Jesus, she didn't know. She couldn't think properly. She was fixed in a block of ice, in a cast of a longing so great it had set her into the pose of a statue, her face grinning in what she knew was a grotesque image of her own smile.

She turned to look at Buffy. Her heart was fluttering somewhere in her throat and her hands were wet with the sweat of terror. She wanted him back, God how she wanted him back, but she didn't want that return to harm him. What should she do, her expression asked her, but Buffy smiled comfortingly at her, then leaned to take her hand, pulling her from the chair. She led her across the lawn towards the side entrance.

'A cup of tea for everyone, I think, Lucy. Let's leave James with his new friends while you and I go and fetch it. Watch Alice, will you, Margaret,' she said over her shoulder, her arm still through Lucy's.

'I'll keep my eye on her, Miss Tyson,' Major James Buchanan called after her as his daughter, who was on the grass studying a daisy, crawled over to him, climbed on to his chest then sat on his face and chortled with laughter.

*   *   *

He was awake later that night as she made her way through the ward towards him. There was a moon and the light of it pricked in his eyes in the dark as he watched her walk to where he and Rory now lay in the conservatory. She had changed out of her uniform and for the first time he saw her in a dress, a becoming dress of some soft material, light and gauzy, the colour of which was extinguished by the pale moonlight. Her hair was brushed back and pulled into a loose knot on the nape of her neck, held there by a ribbon. He could smell that light, fresh perfume she always wore. Beside her, for the first time, was the small dog.

'I wanted to bring the labradors,' she murmured as she reached him, smiling her lovely sweet smile, 'seeing they made such a friend of you today but I knew they couldn't be trusted not to leap all over you again. Thimble is a bit of a nuisance at times but he is considerably smaller and I thought you might like to . . . stroke him.'

If Sister saw her with a dog on the ward she would be in for it, she was well aware, but this room was for men who were on the way to recovery and there was little chance of infection. She lifted the little dog on to the bed and at once James's hand went out to it, fondling the rough coat. It was a contact with normality, with the world of peace, free from fear and the horror they had all known and, like the hand she held out to them all, a healer.

'What did you call him, Nurse?' He smiled and his teeth gleamed white in the darkness of his face. 'I'm not sure that I should call you that, the way you're dressed. I haven't seen you before . . . out of uniform.'

'His name's Thimble, on account of his size. And . . . I just felt like . . . dressing up.'

She sat down in the chair beside the bed and waited. She didn't know what she expected. The conservatory, when it was turned into a hospital ward, had been cleared of all the lovely hothouse plants which a past Mrs Buchanan had put there many years ago. But since then, very gradually, Lucy had returned those that could be hung from the glassed arch of the ceiling: the pure white of magnolia mingled with hanging fern and ivy; deep pink, cerise and scarlet bougainvillaea with dark glossy green leaves flowed from their baskets, low enough for the men to see and smell but high enough to suit Sister's insistence on hygiene; camellias, the palest pink and, in a cage where it sang its head off all day, a small yellow canary. It was silent under its sheet now, sleeping with the men whose company it kept.

She knew he was studying her, as a man studies a woman, and she could feel the hot wave of blood beneath her skin, thankful for the cover of pale darkness that surrounded them. When he put his hand on hers which were clasped before her on the bed, she trembled and so did he.

'The dogs knew me, Mrs Buchanan, didn't they? All three of them.' His voice was hesitant, unsure, wary, as though he were afraid of her answer. 'Won't you tell me? Am I from round here?'

CHAPTER TWENTY-FIVE

'I didn't know what to say, Doctor. He's not a fool and even in his present state he was aware that the dogs had recognised him and that being so it made sense to him to come to the conclusion that he had been here before. In fact, if the dogs belonged to Howethwaite in some way, then so did he. He knows he's not a servant, his own speech tells him that, and so what is he to this house? I could see it going through his mind, twisting and turning but he was also backing away from it. His eyes were fastened on mine, imploring and yet at the same time afraid, as though there were something he couldn't face.'

'What did you do, Mrs Buchanan?' Doctor Penfold's voice was grave. He held one arm across his chest, resting one elbow against it, pulling at his lip with his other hand in a way she knew meant he was very concerned, They stood in her bedroom, for there was always a nurse on duty and so the only place Lucy had with some privacy was the lovely, fire-lit bedroom she had once shared with James. It was made even more cosy today as the bright fire leaped in the grate, for the rain sliced down across the hills and gardens of Howethwaite, darkening the room and putting a weight of moody depression on soldiers who had been, for several weeks now, getting about in the sunshine. There was a different feel to the wards when the sun shone through the long windows, but today it was morose and in the midst of the men James Buchanan sat beside Rory Cameron's bed in total silence, staring at the rain running down the windows, the pattern of the raindrops reflected in his blank face.

'What shall I do, Doctor?' Lucy begged Doctor Penfold. 'He was on the edge of something last night, I know he was but he drew back so . . .'

'That's what worries me, Mrs Buchanan. He drew back, which seems to say he's not ready yet to face whatever it is that he's hiding from. I know he is to be awarded a medal for his bravery in bringing back Corporal Cameron and that on that day he must have gone through . . . well, what they all went through which was, we all know, sheer hell, but I somehow cannot believe that it is that which has done this to him. Of course, the shell exploding in front of him concussed him for a while, and who knows what damage that has left, but somehow I don't think . . .'

He watched as Mrs Buchanan, so lovely and vulnerable and so very frail all of a sudden, hung her head, putting both hands to her face. She was not weeping but her expression, what he could see of it, was stricken. She turned away and went to stand by the window, her back to him and he watched her, for he was convinced that there was more to Major Buchanan's loss of memory than the extremes of war that he had gone through. He had, apparently, been a brave and resourceful officer, a striking leader of his men and had been in the trenches since the beginning and not once in that time had he shown the symptoms of shocked terror that afflicted so many. So why, suddenly, had he slipped away into the dark recesses of his own mind, to a place where memory could not reach? If he himself was any judge of the human creature, which, having been a doctor for forty years, he was, Mrs Buchanan knew more than she was telling. He admired her enormously. For two years she had moved among badly wounded men, giving them unstintingly of herself, wearing herself to a shadow of the blithe, spirited girl he had heard she used to be, in the service of these men. She had made a home, a loving home for her brothers and sisters, protecting them from the worst of what the war was doing. She gave time and patient love to her child and supervised her servants and the running of the house and the hospital, and now she was forced to pretend she didn't know her own husband who was sitting beside the man whose life he had saved with

437

a look of unutterable sadness on his face.

'Is there . . . something more, Mrs Buchanan?'

She stood for perhaps thirty seconds, staring out into the soggy landscape which yesterday had been golden with sunshine then she turned to face him.

'Yes,' she said simply.

'Would you like to tell me?'

'I'm surprised you don't know. Everyone in the area does . . . did at the time. Before last Christmas. The gossips had a high old time of it.'

'I don't listen to gossip, Mrs Buchanan.'

'No, I wouldn't suppose you did.' She sighed sadly, then moved to the fireplace and sat down in front of the cheerful fire. She picked up the brass poker which stood with a brush on a 'tidy', poking the glowing embers with a listless hand, indicating to him that he should take the other chair.

He hesitated. 'I haven't much time, Mrs Buchanan. I'm sorry, but that lad with the stomach wound . . .'

'Private Ernie Henshaw.'

'You know them all by name, don't you, lass? They're real people to you.'

'Oh, yes.'

'I cannot believe that you have done anything, *anything* in your life that would turn your husband against you, Mrs Buchanan, if that's what you're going to confess to me.'

'No, I haven't, but my husband believes I have.'

'Aah . . .'

'Or should I say James Buchanan did and the awful, ironic thing is that it concerned Rory Cameron.'

The doctor raised his bushy grey eyebrows in amazement and disbelief. 'Rory?'

438

'Yes, he's been here before, did you know that?'

'Sister did say . . .'

'Shell shock. He was in a bad way, Doctor Penfold. Out of his mind but somehow, I don't know why, he seemed to draw strength from . . . from me.'

Dear God, and could you be surprised, Richard Penfold thought. Her flawless beauty was what drew men to her initially, for they were human, male, and would find her irresistible, but what was not immediately visible was her true female compassion, her sweetness of spirit, the indomitable resolve of that spirit which she gave without stint to whoever asked it of her. They leaned on her strength, watched and waited for her, beginning to smile, even those who had suffered appalling wounds, as she came through the door. They drained her in a way, he could see that and yet she always had something in reserve for every man who needed her.

Her voice was sad as she continued, her face pensive as she gazed into the dancing coals. 'They sent him back to the trenches, of course, and it was as he left that he . . . he told me that he loved me. He knew, naturally, that there was nothing for him. I loved my husband and my child and . . . well, he asked if he might write to me and if I would answer. He needed . . . something, Doctor, and if I could give it to him by the simple act of writing a letter, was I to refuse? But his letters were . . . love letters and someone heard of them. She knew the officer who censored them, you see. She wrote to James and . . . well, that was the end for him. He . . . we had only just begun to . . . realise our love. It was very fragile and he believed her letter and I am

439

... I feel ... I am certain that that is what he is blocking out. He clings to Rory, the very man I am accused of having an affair with and if he knows the truth ... Dear sweet Christ, what will that do to him? I am torn in two. I want him to know me, and Alice, his home and family and yet I'm afraid that the knowledge, if it is because of me and Rory, will send him further out of reach.'

'So what did you tell him last night?' Doctor Richard Penfold, though he was filled with painful sympathy for this woman, kept his voice steady and calm, not wanting her to know the grave doubts he had of her husband's recovery. Not that he knew a great deal about the mental wounds these men had had inflicted on them. Shell shock, or neurasthenia, and other psychiatric disturbances were a new condition never before studied by the medical profession and loss of memory was one of them. They knew that the human mind had a talent for shutting out what it could not cope with but they had no idea how to treat it, so they walked gingerly round the men who suffered it, hoping for the best, which was all they could do. Great strides were being made in the control of infection, the advancement of surgical techniques and wound control, the management of compound fractures, wound infection and the development of plastic, constructive surgery. They had plenty of patients to practise on, he thought bitterly, and there would be more as the war raged on but at the moment he was concerned only with this woman's husband

'I was stunned when he said that ... about the dogs and he must have seen my hesitation,' she went on. 'Immediately he turned away, not waiting for an answer, saying he was tired and, in a way,

440

dismissing me. He is on the verge of knowing, I'm sure of that, Doctor. Little things: he knows his way about the grounds, for instance, and . . . oh, I can't remember, but things he wouldn't know if he had never been here before. He looks at me with those piercing grey eyes of his and I swear he knows me, but then if that is so and he believes the tale about me and Rory, why does he still stick like a burr to Rory's side?'

'I don't know, my dear. I wish I did.' A deep sigh accompanied the doctor's words. He rose to his feet, glancing at the clock. 'I'm afraid I must go, Mrs Buchanan, so all I can say is that we can only carry on in this fumbling way until we learn more and hope that it is for the best. I have several colleagues in London and I think I might write to them and see if they can shed some light on what is the safest thing to do. Just waiting like this is unbearable for you, I know.' He put a gentle hand on her shoulder. 'Bear up, my dear, and pray.'

'I do, Doctor, for all the good it does.'

*   *   *

It was a week later when the discreetly black Vauxhall drew to a graceful halt at the bottom of the sweep of steps that led up to the open front door of Howethwaite. A smartly clad but elderly chauffeur got out and opened the door at the rear. As there was no one about to welcome them in the shape of a butler or footman, the old couple who had alighted, and the young woman who accompanied them, moved up the steps and into the wide hallway. The older woman carried a bunch of chrysanthemums, glowing in a blaze of bronze and gold, tied about with white satin ribbon.

'Where's the carpet, Job?' she asked in consternation, looking about her at the chequered black and white tiles of the floor. 'What on earth have they done with the carpet? I can remember when these black and white squares were covered up by . . . oh, dear, who was it put the carpet down? Was it your grandmother, or perhaps Sara? She always hated the black and white squares, though I thought they were wonderful when we were children. I can remember playing hopscotch.'

'Yes, dear.' The stooped, white-haired old man patted her arm tenderly as they both peered round looking for someone to receive them as they were accustomed to being received, but there were only a couple of men in hospital blue, one on crutches, the other with one arm, the sleeve of his uniform neatly pinned up.

The young woman was icily beautiful, like a princess in a fairy story, the soldiers were inclined to think, staring in wonder at her magnificently clothed and curved figure and the enormous cartwheel of a hat perched dashingly on her silver pale hair. She looked quite magnificent. She had recovered from the birth of her son and though Paul had not been home since he had impregnated her, she had made a vow to herself that when he did, come home, she meant, there would be no repeat of the act that had got her that way in the first place.

Her blue eyes passed over the soldiers unseeingly as she peered distastefully along the ward on her right which had once been the splendid Howethwaite drawing-room. The rows of beds were filled with men wrapped in bandages, some with their arms held up on splints, others with a contraption of pulleys supporting a leg. Some of them were reading newspapers, others smoking a cigarette, talking to each other quietly about the Somme offensive which still dragged on and which was swallowing the thousands of young volunteers who had enlisted in Kitchener's New Army. Two nurses were bending over a dressing trolley, unaware that they had visitors and when the elegant and imperious figure of Charlotte Buchanan swept between the rows of beds, her skirts held so that they would not touch anything in this dreadful place, they were too astonished to try and stop her.

'Good morning, Nurse,' she said, just as she might address one of her own servants. 'I've come with Mr and Mrs Buchanan to see their nephew.' The men in the beds stared at her in open-mouthed wonder. 'I believe he is here and, in fact, has been here for several months. Mr and Mrs Buchanan have been very keen to visit him but . . . well, it seems Mrs Buchanan, Mrs Lucy Buchanan, that is, felt the need to keep them away. They lost their son a year ago so they are particularly concerned to visit James, so we would be glad to be shown to his room.'

'His room?' Nurse Pennington gasped.

'Yes, his room.' Her expression clearly said that she thought the nurse to be a half-wit and why she was in charge of seriously wounded men was a mystery to her.

'But . . .'

'Dear me, is there no one in charge here?' She swept haughtily past the nurses and their trolley, Job and Mary Buchanan hesitating in her wake.

They were not at all sure they should be here, but Charlotte had been so insistent and it would be lovely to see James again. Especially after the loss of Andrew, their only son. They still had Janet and Christine, of course, but the added blow, a blow which had crucified their elder daughter, of the deaths of their grandsons, young Job and Lawrence, was one they could hardly contemplate. And now Anthony, just turned eighteen, had gone, breaking his mother's heart all over again. Out of her four handsome sons, poor Janet had only young Will at home and if this war dragged on he would be the next to go. He was eighteen next year and already talking of enlisting, though not where his mother could hear him.

It was at that moment Lucy Buchanan, who was bending over the last bed in the conservatory ward where young Private Ernie Henshaw was clinging to her hand, his face grey with pain as his dressing was changed, heard the voice which, for a moment or two, she did not recognise, or if she did, at the very corners of her mind, she flinched away from in horror.

Rory Cameron was reading a newspaper to James Buchanan. There was only the one on this ward and several others were listening to Rory, trying to take their minds off the laboured breathing and harsh gasps of the boy at the end of the ward. James looked peaceful, the withdrawn expression that had hung about him for the past week gone for the moment. Rory was reading to them about the report of the poppy which was growing in the battlefields of Flanders. Legend had it that Genghis Khan, the Mongol warlord, had brought the seed of the white poppy with him in his advance on Europe during the thirteenth century. It was said that the white poppies turned red with the shape of a cross in their centre when they sprang up after a battle and certainly on the Western Front, for had they not all seen it for themselves, the scarlet poppy proliferated on devastated battlefields, particularly those of the Somme.

James's two dogs were sitting patiently on the step of the conservatory door waiting for him to emerge and take them up into the wood, a task he had taken over from Jacob since he had renewed his acquaintance with them, though it was very evident that his mind was still in a state of total confusion. It was as though he had come to some sort of crossroads in his condition and was not sure which path to take and so he stood there, waiting, no one was awfully sure for what, least of all himself. He was conscious that the dark veil which had hid something from him for almost three months was becoming lighter, not quite as opaque as it had been, and through it he had glimpsed vague shapes, sounds, smells which were familiar to him though he didn't know why. From his past life, he supposed, but still he hung back from it, immersing himself in the comradeship of the wards, the men on them, with helping Rory to recover. Rory would be measured for two false legs very soon, for there was no way he was going to sit on his arse for the rest of his life, he had laughed, and James meant to be there to get him up on them. In a way, Rory was his responsibility. He had brought Rory back from death and he meant to make sure Rory had the very best chance he could. One day, when he himself knew who he was and where he came from he would take Rory there and continue to look after him until the lad was back on his feet. He almost felt as though Rory were his son, for after all there were fourteen years between them.

Lucy had reached the chair he sat in at the same time as Charlotte and on her face was a look of such horror, Rory, who had looked up as the exotically beautiful woman approached, as they all did, for she was like a young queen, put out his hand, he didn't know why. To stop something, again he didn't know what, but there was a look of triumph on the unknown woman's face to match the horror on Lucy's.

'Lucy,' she cried extravagantly, 'how good it is to see you after all this time. And James, too. How are you, James? You certainly look well,' though it was in her eyes for all to see, including James himself, that she did not really think so, not with all that scarring which, in her opinion, made him look like some freak in a show.

James rose to his feet uncertainly, the manners taught him as a child not forgotten. He was hampered by Lucy's closeness as she did her best to protect him from this woman who had damaged their lives so dramatically. It was evident she wanted to draw him away, tell him to run up to the schoolroom where he would be safe from fresh hurt, as she would one of her brothers or sisters, to get him away from further damage and if she had to put her arms about him, even carry him on her back, she would do so to save his sanity, which she was sure would be threatened if this woman had anything to do with it.

'James, oh, sweetheart, how lovely to see you,'

quavered Mary Buchanan from behind Charlotte, doing her best to get to her nephew and put her arms about him, but she hesitated when she saw his scarred face, putting her hand to her mouth in confusion. 'It is James, isn't it?' She turned to her husband imploringly and put her hand in his and the lovely bouquet fell to the floor.

The room was in total silence, even the two VADs frozen to the polished floor in their dismay. James had been with them for nearly three months and though they knew, of course, of his condition, they had not the faintest idea who he really was. The doctors would know, and probably Sister Colyford, and until the amazing occurrence of last week when the Buchanan dogs had greeted him with such ecstatic joy had believed him to be from . . . well, somewhere, but certainly not about here. There had been talk on the wards, among the nursing staff and the men and now, from nowhere, here were three people, two of them related to him, come to visit him.

And would you look at Mrs Buchanan! if her eyes had been daggers that gorgeous creature in the cartwheel hat would be lying dead at her feet pierced to the heart. She was pulling at James's arm and begging him to come away but he seemed to be fixed to the floor, staring at the three visitors in total incomprehension.

'Go away from here, Charlotte,' Mrs Buchanan hissed venomously. 'You have done enough damage already. There are men who are ill and need peace and quiet and . . .'

'Well, I'm certainly not going to upset them, Lucy, and I'm sure Mr and Mrs Buchanan wouldn't dream of it, would you?' turning to the bewildered

447

old couple who still were not sure whether this scarred soldier was their James, though he certainly had James's build and, of course, his eyes. It was the eyes that decided them.

'Job, of course it's James. He has Grandmother Buchanan's eyes, can't you see? Oh, James, James, it's Aunt Mary and Uncle Job. We had heard you were home but were allowed no visitors so we kept away but Charlotte here . . .'

'Charlotte here had to come and stir up fresh trouble, is that it, Charlotte?' Lucy was beside herself with terror and rage, for how was this to affect James? 'Not content in writing lies to my husband about Rory . . . Dear God, let me keep calm. James, see, darling, come away with me. Let's go into the garden, shall we?' She was doing her best to be calm, normal, pretending for his sake that there was nothing untoward about these people, though her face was stiff with shock. 'Look, the dogs are waiting for you. Would you like to . . . to . . . would you like me to come with you to . . . oh, please, James, do come with me.'

Rory Cameron was looking at James who was retreating further and further from this commotion that was washing over him in great crashing waves. Rory could see it, all the progress that had been made in the tranquillity of this house and this woman whose husband he was, the other men and their acceptance of him, the children, smashed into a million pieces by the gloriously beautiful woman who had the eyes of the devil in her face. She was smiling, turning to look at him now, fully aware it seemed to him of who he was, ready to twist further in the knife she had apparently aimed at James all those months ago when she must have written to

448

him to say that his wife was . . . what? it didn't take much working out to realise that she had told him that Lucy was having an affair with a private, as he was then, by the name of Rory Cameron. No wonder James had gone mad with it, particularly when added to what he was going through at the front. It was all clear to him now. There had been no truth in it, of course, but this woman had made James believe it, totally devastating the man he had once been.

'And this is Rory Cameron, I believe?' Charlotte Buchanan's voice was a gentle murmur of politeness. 'We had heard you were James's special friend after he had saved your life which, in view of what happened here while James was away, seems very odd, but then who are we to judge what a person will do, or not do, in times of war. Now then, we mustn't keep these brave soldiers from their rest, must we?' turning solicitously to look about her at all the brave soldiers who were listening and watching in fascinated silence, knowing something was being destroyed here but having no conception of what it was. She took the arms of Mary and Job Buchanan who were like children in her grasp. 'Say goodbye to James,' she was telling them and obediently they parroted her words, but as she turned to glide away up the ward taking them with her, every man and woman in the room, including her, felt the hairs rise on the backs of their necks as James Buchanan shook off his wife's restraining hand with a roar that could be heard in the schoolroom and sent Alice Buchanan scurrying for Buffy's protective arms.

But it was not at Charlotte Buchanan that his bitter rage was directed but at the man in the bed

449

who had been, though he couldn't walk himself, his crutch for three months. Before they knew what he was about, any of them, even Lucy, who was totally unprepared for it, he had flung himself at Rory Cameron and grasped him round the neck.

'I'll kill you for this, you bastard,' he screamed, squeezing his fingers deep into the slender neck of the defenceless man. Outside, disturbed by the uproar inside, the two dogs had begun to bark furiously, leaping and crashing against the door, for all they were concerned with was the safety of their master. All along the ward men began to shout, some of them to whimper, others trying to get out of their beds to go to the aid of the soldier who was being strangled by another, while Charlotte Buchanan, who had by now reached the door into the hallway, turned round for a last jubilant look at the chaos she had caused. The old people were horrified, calling out to James to behave himself, as though he were still a boy at school having a go at another. From everywhere medical staff were racing, seeing only James apparently trying to wring the life out of Rory Cameron, his friend and support, while at his back, on his back, screaming into his ear, Nurse Buchanan was completely unsuccessful in stopping him.

'A syringe, Sister,' Doctor Penfold bellowed, medical professionalism thrown to the wind as he and several nurses flew down the conservatory ward, pushing aside anything and anybody who got in their way. It was total chaos as soldiers fell back on to their beds and even Mrs Buchanan was thrust on to her back as the doctor, Nurses Cartwright, Atkinson and Stephens, all big, strong women who were well versed in the control of obstreperous

450

patients, began to haul on James Buchanan's arms. Sister Colyford appeared, carrying a syringe containing something she knew the doctor wanted, and without bothering with anything like antiseptic, or even the barrier of his trousers, plunged it into James's buttock. It took no more than a moment or two as he struggled to fight against it, and then, for there was enough in the syringe to fell a horse, she told a distraught Lucy later, then he grew limp and fell, though he was not aware of it, into the arms of the man he had been trying to kill.

They put him to bed in the same small room where once Rory Cameron had grovelled under the bed, locking the door and barring the window. He was still deeply drugged when Lucy and the doctor looked in on him last thing that night. When they unlocked the door the next morning he had gone.

CHAPTER TWENTY-SIX

The two big, black dogs moped about the stable yard, lying down for a brief moment then getting up to sniff miserably under the gate through which James Buchanan must have gone. They had been found shut up in the tack-room, which was not where Jacob had left them the night before, so it seemed evident, the authorities said, that Major Buchanan had put them there. An ancient greatcoat, a woolly scarf knitted by Mrs Bunting and a cap belonging to Jacob were missing, along with a raised game pie, a loaf of bread, a lump of the Lancashire cheese of which Mr Dixon was especially fond, and a bottle of whisky.

Buffy sat quietly and watched Lucy stride up and down her bedroom to where, with every room in the house either packed with children or servants, wounded men or being used for some purpose in their medical care, those who wished to speak to her came. The house was in turmoil, with Mrs Bunting and Mrs Burns tearfully telling one another in the kitchen that they had known no good would come of all this secrecy in the matter of Mr James and his loss of memory. Surely, if he had been given the facts, the facts being that Mrs Buchanan was his wife, that Miss Alice was his daughter and Howethwaite was his home, he would have been far happier and none of this would have happened. It was unnatural to keep from a man his family and Mrs Bunting had told them all so, at least those in the kitchen, time and time again.

'Well, the doctors didn't seem to think so,' Elsie ventured bravely. 'I don't know the ins an' out of it, but . . .'

'Then I should keep me lip buttoned if I was you, young lady,' Cook lashed out at her, and then was sorry, for Elsie was a good girl and as concerned as them about poor Mr James. Where could he have got to? they asked one another and Cook was comforted by the thought that he had on that warm scarf she had knitted for Jacob though Jacob was not best pleased about it, nor his coat which had gone missing.

'Yer should be ashamed of yersen, Jacob,' she had cried, dreadfully upset. 'How can yer begrudge him a bloomin' old coat when the master might be wandering them there hills, and in this weather, an' all,' for it had turned cold and drizzly. 'I'm only glad he took that pie, an' bread an' cheese wi' 'im an' the whisky'll put a warm fire in his belly, poor lad.'

Lucy told herself the same thing, directing her remarks at Buffy who had not moved from her side since the discovery that James was gone. Smashed the window and forced back the shutters, he had and it was a wonder no one had heard him, they said, though Jacob did admit to hearing them dogs for a few seconds. They had settled at once and he had turned over and gone back to sleep. James must have had a key to the house since he had simply let himself back in and helped himself to the food from the kitchen. Oh, he had had his wits about him, there was no question of that, preparing himself for what lay ahead of him and really, were those the actions of a man who was out of his mind? Lucy demanded.

He had to report James's disappearance, Doctor Penfold patiently told James Buchanan's almost deranged wife, looking for confirmation to Doctor Yates who had just come on duty, holding her firmly by the upper arms as she tried to break away from him. Despite his age he was strong.

'No, oh, please, Doctor Penfold, no! Doctor Yates, tell him,' for Doctor Yates had been the Buchanan family doctor for many years before he retired. 'He's not a violent man, not usually. He was . . . not himself when he attacked Rory. He had been provoked by that bitch . . .' Her face spasmed with bitter hatred and if Doctor Penfold had not seen it for himself he would not have believed that Mrs Buchanan could summon up an expression of such malevolence.

She flung herself away from him and resumed her frantic pacing of the room, constantly returning to the window to peer out through the thin veil of drizzle that drifted across the empty garden. It was as though she might see him there, catch him before he flitted off again to some secret place only he knew of and she must be at the window or she would miss him. Her hair was wild about her, falling in a long cape of dark, glossy brown down to her buttocks, for she had been brushing it when Doctor Penfold had knocked on her door. She had on her uniform and the pristine whiteness of it was no paler than her face.

Buffy spoke for the first time, trying to catch her friend in one of her demented whirls. 'Lucy, calm down, darling. You must take a hold.'

'Don't tell me to calm down, Buffy Tyson,' she spat out. 'How can I be calm when only God knows what has happened to him? I love him so much, you see, and I cannot forgive myself.'

The two doctors were seen to bend their heads in enormous pity for the sorrowing woman, but it was Buffy who spoke again.

'Darling, it's not your fault.'

'Maybe not but that does not make me less responsible. I should have stayed with him. I was not there when he needed me and . . .'

'Mrs Buchanan, don't torture yourself like this. It is not healthy. He must be found, and soon.' Doctor Penfold put his hand on her arm but she shook him off violently and he backed away. Nevertheless he continued to speak. 'We cannot have him wandering about in his condition, whatever it might be by now. No, I'm sorry, but it must be said. We don't know how this has affected him. He may be even more disturbed.'

'He was alert enough to take some warm

454

clothing and food which surely proves he was thinking coherently?'

'True. But as I said he must be found. He might be wandering about the fells, losing himself in some—'

'He would never get lost, Doctor Penfold. He knows these mountains like . . . like he knows his own garden. And if he wants to remain hidden there is no one, whoever they may be, who will be able to find him. He has been climbing and walking this area ever since he was a boy. I think he just wants time to . . . to think; so won't you let him alone for a few days? Don't send the police out looking for him. Let him be. He loves these hills and if he could be given time, time to come to terms with who he is and . . .'

'He might still not know who he is, Mrs. Buchanan.'

'He knew Rory and what had been said about . . . us; that is why he attacked him, but he wasn't . . . wasn't . . .Oh, I know I keep repeating myself but he wasn't himself.'

Lucy slumped down in the chair by her fireside, her head in her hands and felt the comforting hands of Buffy on her shoulders. She reached up and clung to one, keeping her eyes covered with the other. It was all she could do not to leap up and put on her stout boots and go shouting up on the fells for James this very minute and as soon as this lot, meaning the two doctors and the military policemen Doctor Penfold meant to call in, were gone, that's exactly what she would do. She could not believe what the doctor had told her gravely, which was, that by leaving the hospital without permission, James was technically a deserter,

455

though it would not come to that, surely? He had been ill. The doctor would vouch for it and the authorities would acknowledge that fact and accept that as far as the doctors were concerned, he was not in his right mind.

But she did not believe it. Not for a minute. She had seen his eyes for a moment, just before he had leaped, like a man tackling another on a rugby field, on to the recumbent figure of Rory Cameron. They had looked into hers, a soft and smoky grey, the pupils narrowed to tiny black pinpoints, and in them was an expression of such love and joy, of wonder and remembrance she had been ready to lift her arms and enclose him in a miraculous embrace. It had taken no more than the fraction of a second, that glance their eyes had exchanged, then the veil had corne down and his face had twisted in a snarl of jealous rage and he had turned to throw himself at the man he thought had taken his world from him.

'There is one other thing, Mrs Buchanan,' Doctor Penfold told her hesitantly. She lifted her head eagerly and her hand clung like a vice to Buffy's.

'Yes?'

'Do you remember when your husband first came here and we took his belongings, his wallet and such like? We do that with all the men, as you know, but as soon as they are fit enough they are given back to them. We didn't give Major Buchanan his in case ... well, he would have known at once who he was, or who he had been and ... you know the rest, Mrs Buchanan. His documents were in Sister Colyford's office. Photographs of you and your daughter. They are

456

gone.'

*   *   *

The man in the long, shabby overcoat pulled his scarf more warmly about his neck and adjusted the peaked cap he wore, tugging it down more firmly over his forehead, then leaned his back against the pitted grey stone of the craggy outcrop behind him. He reached into his pocket and withdrew a packet of Woodbines, grimacing ruefully as he lit one, for it was his last.

'You'll have to do without now, old feller me lad,' he murmured softly to himself, settling himself more comfortably into a slight crevice in the rock, trying to get out of the chilly wind which whistled straight from the North Pole, or that's what it felt like. His eyes moved slowly from one horizon to the other, glad that on this, his last day, it was fine and clear, for he knew he was saying goodbye to his home and the beauty in which it stood.

He was standing on the summit of Silver How, gazing down towards Grasmere where the intermingling of crag and conifer, juniper and bracken, was breathtaking in its majestic beauty. There was a mass of timber on the lower slopes and trees persisted even in the crags which fringed the summit, guarding waterfalls, Blindtarn Gill, Wray Gill and Meg's Gill, all the names as well known to him as those of his own family. His eyes roamed over the vale and village of Grasmere far below, and the lake itself. Rydal Water lay sleeping under a silken sheet, no wind today down there in the valley and even the upper reaches of Lake Windermere to the south could be seen and a small

457

corner of Coniston Water. It was all spread out before him, this lovely land of his which he loved so well and he knew he would take it with him in his heart wherever he went. As he would take the woman he loved.

He had seen her again today with the dogs, and heard her calling his name and it had taken all his strength and resolution not to begin the mad run down the scree and slippery slopes the rain had left, to shout and wave and tell her he was here, to whip her into his arms and kiss her until her eyes were blinded with love and hold her curving woman's body which he knew so well against his and to hell with the consequences. She was so loyal and true to her promises, to those she made and those she had been forced to make, for he knew now that she and Rory had never been lovers and that Alice Christina Buchanan was his own child. He knew her and he knew Rory. Rory had been a stranger to him when he had picked him out of the funk-hole and carried him back to safety, but he had come to know him and to love him during the three months they had been together, three months which he remembered now, just as he remembered the whole of his life. He remembered her indifference to him, polite but still indifference, when they first married. She had been gracious with him, as she was gracious with everyone, even complete strangers, and only on that last leave of his had she become warm, responsive to his lovemaking. She had appeared to be sad when he left to return to France but then, perhaps that was the natural sadness anyone would feel to see a man going back into danger. Mrs Bunting had wept and so had that little maid, and to them he was just the master of Howethwaite. It was all an impenetrable mystery, a complicated web of 'maybe' and 'perhaps' but until he unravelled the complexities of it he could not stay in the same house with her.

They had been searching for him for three days now, the local police and the military police who had been brought in to find him, but he had evaded them easily enough. They had come high, the local men, looking in caves and old quarries, in worn-out mines and outcroppings, but none knew it like he did and so they had gone away, but not her!

She called his name again and again. The dogs were casting round, looking for his scent as she directed them but he had covered his tracks too well, wading in his bare feet through icy cold streams and keeping himself well hidden high above them, He had wept on the first day he saw her, for her cries were harrowing but he could not go back. Not now. He could not even explain it to himself why he should feel like this but he did. He must have time to . . . to get to know himself again. He must pick up his life somewhere and where better than in the place where he had lost it?

He watched her re-enter the belt of trees on the lower slopes, the dogs following her reluctantly, both of them stopping again and again to sniff at the air as though they knew he was here somewhere. He waited for an hour, wishing he had another cigarette as his eyes once more lifted to the hills about him. Helvellyn. Wansfell Pike. Loughrigg Fell. Pike o' Blisco and Pike o' Stickle and Gibson Knot. Loved and familiar names all of them and he printed them more firmly in his mind so that wherever he was he would only need to close his eyes and they would be there.

He looked again to the place where he had seen her disappear and his voice was infinitely soft, infinitely tender as he spoke.

'Goodbye, my love, goodbye.'

Pulling his coat and scarf more closely about him he turned away and began the long walk across fell and mountain to Penrith and the railway station there.

*   *   *

She continued searching for many weeks, weeks after she knew it was no use, for he was either dead in a gully or long gone from the area. The womanly curves her husband had longed to hold to him that last time on Silver How had disappeared, eaten up by her grief and terror for his safety, and her positive belief that it was her fault. That she was to blame. That the guilt for this could only be laid at her door and it made no difference who spoke to her, gently, or harshly, as Doctor Penfold tried to do, she would stubbornly shake her head, then, putting on her stout boots and her thick, fleece-lined coat, would call up the dogs and set off again to search for him, or at least a sign that he was still alive.

She found it four weeks after he had gone. She had taken the dogs to the summit of Silver How, going up the rough track from Grasmere, moving between waist-high bracken and a jumble of boulders. There was a cairn, several cairns at the top and a huge outcropping of rock and it was here that the dogs went wild. They began to yelp and run round in mad circles, their noses to the ground, moving outwards in circles, almost talking to one another as Holmes lost the scent for a moment and Watson picked it up again. They set off in a northerly direction, still running with their black noses to the ground, casting this way and that and it was not until she bellowed to them to come back that they stopped for a moment to look back at her as though to ask her what the hell she wanted, for couldn't she see they were on important business. Their massive heads nodded at her and their tongues hung from their mouths and she could see they longed to be off but she put that sharp crack in her voice that James used to make them obey him and reluctantly they came back to her. They sat where she put them, side by side, constantly looking over their shoulders towards the north-east but by then she had seen the cigarette stub. Only a bit of a soggy end with a shred or two of tobacco still clinging to it, and when she pointed to it with a shaking finger both dogs nosed at it curiously then sat down and began to howl. Again they wanted to be off, moving along the path towards the Langdale Edge but she had them by the collar now, and as they sat impatiently once more she knelt down beside them, an arm about each strong neck and began to weep.

'He's still alive . . . he's still alive,' she whispered into their ears. 'He had a cigarette here and then began to walk . . . you've shown me the direction. Dear God, he's still alive.'

She was jubilant for about a week, going about her work on the wards, ready to whistle and sing and the men elbowed one another saying that their cheerful Mrs Buchanan was back with them again, for they had all heard the good news. James was still in the land of the living, or at least he had been

461

... well, they couldn't really say, and, when she began to think about it, neither could Mrs Buchanan, and it was then that the euphoria of finding the cigarette end and the reaction the dogs had displayed to the spot on the summit of Silver How began to wear off.

'I'm going to go back, Buffy,' she said one night when she and her friend were sitting drinking cocoa in her room before going to bed.

'Go back where?' Buffy put her mug on the side table and leaned forward to look into Lucy's face.

'To Silver How.'

'Darling, what is the use? James isn't there now and there seems no point in—'

'No, not now, but he was there, Buffy, and the only way I'm going to find out where he went to from there is to take the dogs and let them . . . just go. They'll find his scent and—'

Buffy was aghast. 'Lucy, it's the first of November tomorrow and the winter is beginning to close in. You can't just go tramping about on those fell tracks, sheep trods, most of them, not knowing where they are going to lead you. Even Mr Buchanan . . .' meaning Mr Ben Buchanan who had been over with the rest of the family to remonstrate with her hotly over what they saw as her dereliction of duty in not consulting with them on the matter of her husband's illness. It didn't seem to concern them that she had been following Doctor Penfold's precise orders. They felt that it had been a mistake and to prove it look where it had led! Ben was the head of the family, for you could not count the old gentlemen, Job and Harry, and Lucy should have brought him over to talk to the doctors. The shouted argument had been heard on the wards and Sister had been forced to come up to her room, where they had all been perched on whatever seat they could find, to ask them to respect the men who were ill.

'Buffy, d'you think I give a damn what Ben Buchanan says, or any of them? The only one I had any respect for was Franny and as she's not here to put in her twopennyworth I shall make my own decision. I must go soon before the scent fades.'

'Perhaps it has already done so.'

Lucy put her mug on the hearth and in a great surge of pain leaned into her own arms and bent her head. Her voice was muffled. 'Don't say that, Buffy, please, it's all I have to cling to. The hope that I might find where he has gone to. He might be working somewhere quite close by and I would never forgive myself if I didn't try and find him. Oh, Jesus, why did he leave me like this? Why did he go without speaking to me? Why didn't he give me a chance, Buffy? I know he loves me and I love him but something has sent him away from me and if I can't find out what it is I shall go mad.'

'No, you won't, Lucy, not you. You're the strongest woman I've ever known and your dear mama and papa would be proud of you.'

Lucy lifted her head and her eyes were blind with tears, dewed to a deep golden honey, the lashes round them spiky and separated.

'I haven't thought of them for weeks, Buffy. Not once. Even my child has retreated from me as though she realises that I am not really giving her my full attention when I should. Well, there is only one way to settle this.' She lifted her tousled head and Buffy reached for her hairbrush and, standing up, moved behind Lucy's chair and automatically

463

began to brush the thick, gleaming weight of her hair.

'You're going then?' Buffy's voice was fearful.

'Yes. I have to, Buffy.'

But it seemed the harsh Lakeland winter had decided to thwart Lucy Buchanan's plans, for on the next day, just as Lucy was fastening the laces of her heavy boots, it began to snow, the first delicate flakes drifting down from the leaden skies Lucy had scarcely noticed.

There were not as many men on the wards now, as those who recovered and were sent either home or back to the front were not replaced, for the war had faltered into what seemed to be a winter lull. The Somme offensive was dragging on until, with the advent of winter rains which came in November, when the exhausted, hungry men could no longer drag themselves through the deepening mud, it died away in disappointment and despair. The BEF was astride the ridge originally occupied by the Germans but for this ridge the British and the French between them had lost in the region of 600,000 men. Time to call it a day until the next battle, those high up said and the poor tattered armies, on both sides, breathed a collective sigh of relief.

'Damn and blast it to hell,' Lucy swore when she saw the snow. The time was ideal for her to take some days off, for with the wards quieter she could easily be spared, but with this snow, which even after half an hour was beginning to drift, she could not chance it.

'I'll wait until tomorrow,' she promised Buffy, then went along to the schoolroom to spend some time with her sisters and her daughter. Edward and

Percy had set off for school early that morning, riding their bicycles at breakneck speed down the drive, turning to wave at the men who watched them go, some of them scarcely older than Edward.

'They'll not get far on them things,' Sergeant Higginbottom remarked sagely, lighting his pipe and turning round to nod at the younger men. Sergeant Higginbottom was a country man, a farm labourer from Lancashire and knew the look of the weather like no other man on the farm he had worked. This wasn't no bit of a snowstorm, he promised them, and them lads'd not be seen again today, which turned out to be true, for just before the telephone lines came down, dragged by the weight of snow, Mr Joliffe, headmaster at Fellthwaite Grammar School, telephoned to say that he was keeping Dean Major and Dean Minor overnight and Mrs Buchanan was not to worry about them. He and Mrs Joliffe would look after them and send them home as soon as it was fit.

Those at Howethwaite did not see them for three whole weeks, though Edward was furious about it, saying that old Jollops was nothing but a Mary Ellen since he and Percy could have walked home after three days if they had been allowed.

'And wouldn't be able to get back,' Lucy told him, raising her eyebrows with some irony.

'Well, probably not,' Edward grinned, 'but have you any idea what sort of food Mrs Jollops serves up? Dear Lord, I've seen Mrs Bunting put better stuff in Mr Clapcott's pig bucket.'

The children had been quite devastated by James's disappearance. The two girls and Percy had wept bitterly, begging anyone who would listen to them, including the police who combed the area, to allow them to go too. They knew the hills, Percy said seriously from his manly position of just eight years old. James, as they had got used to calling him, had taught them all sorts of things like which side of a tree trunk moss grew on and things like that and if only he could be allowed to give them a hand he was sure, with Thimble and Holmes and Watson to help him, he would soon track James down. He had been incensed when Lucy had forbidden any of them to go out with her, saying it was better for the dogs to be undistracted.

'I wouldn't distract them, Luce, honest,' he told her earnestly. 'Please let me go with you,' for Percy had found he had liked the new Mr Buchanan enormously. He was quiet and patient and of course they had all heard of his bravery in bringing Corporal Cameron back from the funk-hole. And his face hadn't been bad at all. At least Percy didn't think so. It was a bit puckered and a funny colour at first but nobody had minded, not even baby Alice.

The snow grew deeper and deeper, the next morning when daylight came, what there was of it, revealing the still solidly eddying curtain of it stretched from tree line to tree line. It reached up to the windowsills and covered the drystone wall that surrounded the house and it had taken Jacob almost an hour to flounder from his room above the stable to get something to eat in the kitchen and then to wallow back again to see to the ponies in their warm stalls. The men were quiet, absorbed with the sheer magnitude of it, for they were from cities like Manchester and Liverpool and Bolton and were only used to the poor stuff which fell there and which turned to grey slush the minute it

466

hit the ground. When it stopped and the sun beamed from a hard blue sky, they looked out to the frozen, crystallised whiteness of trees and shrubs which were hung with a sparkling, breathtaking loveliness. Every branch and leaf was illuminated a thousand times over with a dazzling reflection from the sun's rays and they told one another in awed voices they had never seen anything like it before. They simply sat or lay in their beds and gazed at it in silent, stunned wonderment.

As they watched there was a great shout and the children erupted from the side gate, wrapped about in scarves and mittens and bobble caps, for by now Mrs Bunting's efforts with her knitting needles had become very creative. Margaret, at almost sixteen, was quite exquisite with that fresh and innocent look of a girl on the threshold of womanhood and the men were almost ashamed to find themselves watching her as she threw snowballs at the windows, making them flinch back for a moment as though the snow could reach them. The boy, Edward, was just seventeen and thought himself to be no end of a fellow but he was a nice lad and full of fun. He was busy in the construction of a snowman, for he liked to build things, did Edward, whether it be mechanical or something simple such as this. The two younger ones were pelting one another with snow, their faces a laughing poppy red and when Mrs Buchanan came to join them, waving to them all and laughing as she had done before James left, they all told one another wistfully that, given his legs, or his arm or even his sight, for the men who were blinded were having the scene described to them, they would be out there too.

Winter moved on with its inevitable mixture of snowstorms, aching days of bitter frost, of blinding sunshine and deep blue skies and it was not until April when the United States of America entered the war that the next blow came to break the already fragile heart of poor Mrs Buchanan.

CHAPTER TWENTY-SEVEN

The Battle of Arras, as it was later to be called, began on 9 April, the very day young Will Gunson left to join the Border Regiment into which all his relatives had gone and in which, on his eighteenth birthday, he had enlisted.

It was a bank holiday and the two boys were not at school, so they did not discover Edward was missing until nightfall. His bed had been slept in, for Elsie had made it, and that of young Percy, and in her fluster to turn out Mrs Bunting's and Mrs Burns's bedrooms, which she had been ordered to do by Mrs Burns, she completely overlooked the envelope with Miss Lucy's name on it which stood on the dressing-table propped against a pile of books. The room always looked as though one of them there shells had hit it, she had been known to say to Mrs Burns, even when they had lived at the rectory, littered with whatever them lads had been busy with when called away. A jigsaw puzzle half done, school books opened and scattered on the beds, an 'airieplane' Mr Edward was trying to build, only a little one, of course; clothes strewn about though she had heard Miss Lucy tell them many times that they were to tidy up after themselves, for Elsie had enough to do without clearing their mess up, which was true.

They all ate in the schoolroom now. Lucy and Buffy and sometimes Miss Bradley before she rode home on her bicycle to Fellthwaite, the four older children and Alice. It was more convenient to bring up trays from the kitchen; besides, where else would they eat with the dining-room turned into a ward and the breakfast-room into a second operating theatre? Even James's study had gone, though Lucy had promised not to touch it, but with so many men needing peace and quiet, no room could be spared. All his books, the furniture, the horse prints which lined the walls, his guns and fishing rods, lamps, desk, chairs of glowing leather, his decanter cabinet, all had been carefully wrapped away and put in the attic with so much of Howethwaite's lovely things to await the day when they would be brought out and lovingly restored to their rightful place.

Edward was often at the last minute for his meals. He had so much to do in his busy day, not only his schoolwork, which would come to an end in August when Lucy prayed he would go on to university, but his hobbies, matters he was deeply interested in, first and foremost, of course, his love of things mechanical. The motor car, the aeroplane which was performing such useful and daring activities in the skies above the battlefields of France, and the contraption he was building in the tack-room which he swore would make Mr Clapcott's work with the lawnmower considerably easier.

Lucy sighed and indicated to the others that they

were to start. Cook had made a splendid steak and kidney pie, the pastry crumbling, the steam rising and the smell which came from beneath the crust making all their mouths water as it was cut into. There was mashed potato, sadly without the knob of butter Cook usually mixed in with it, for butter was very short, and cauliflower done to perfection, for she did not like to see vegetables turned to mush with overcooking.

'Has anyone seen Edward in the last hour?' Lucy asked irritably, looking round the table at the intent faces of her brother and sisters as they tucked into their evening meal. Even Alice, who insisted on trying to feed herself with the spoon and pusher which had once been used by all the Dean family, was making short work of the plain but delicious meal. On the table where he usually sat Edward's meal was going cold,

'Well?' Lucy asked, exchanging a glance with Buffy, for Edward loved his food and though he might be late when time got away from him he always turned up eventually. Now, as they were about to lay into the apple pie and custard which had been keeping warm on the hearth, he had still not come and Lucy began to feel the creeping dread of something stir in the middle of her chest. She didn't know what the dickens it was but so many dire misfortunes had befallen this family she was frightened, which was silly, she knew, by the smallest thing that happened out of the ordinary.

They all shook their heads and picked up their spoons in preparation for the pie, even Alice waving hers to indicate to her mother that she was ready as well. She babbled something in her new-found vocabulary, for she was getting on for two years old now, something which might have been, 'Pie, Mama,' and, leaning forward in her high chair, banged in a peremptory fashion on the tray.

'Yes, yes, darling, it's coming.' Lucy smiled, for a moment distracted from her small worry by the charm and loveliness of her daughter. If only James ... if only, if only ... How many times a day did she say that? she wondered, particularly when she was with Alice who had James's colouring and even in a strange way, the shape of his chin. She looked at Lucy, with James's eyes, a sparkling merriment in them, sometimes a turbulent rebelliousness which Lucy recognised as her own nature but her charm and sweet ways were being missed by the man who was her father, wherever he was, for he had vanished off the face of the earth as though he were dead and buried in it. He wasn't, Lucy was convinced of that, for she felt that her heart would know if his was no longer beating, but it was very hard not to throw a few things in a bag and set out to look for him. The thought was ridiculous, she knew that, for he could be anywhere, north, south, anywhere, so where was she to start? Sometimes when she lay sleepless in the night she became angry with him. Enraged that he should have done this to her and Alice, deserted them both and gone off on some private pilgrimage which had left her bereft and grieving. It was cruel of him, a cruelty which was not like him, but then he had suffered a great trauma and could he be blamed if he no longer thought in that precise and logical way which had once been his?

'I'd better go and look for Edward,' Buffy said with an edge of anxiety in her voice and at once Lucy was aware that she was not the only one with

471

a sense of something wrong. 'You stay and finish your meal,' Buffy went on. 'I'll just go and ask the servants, or perhaps the nurses . . . he might have been on the wards; you know how he loves to talk to that private who was wounded on an airfield. He was going on about a Sopwith Camel whatever that is, the other day.'

'It's an aeroplane, Buffy,' Percy said, round a mouthful of apple pie.

'Don't speak with your mouth full, Percy,' Lucy told him automatically and he subsided with a resigned sigh, which said he was only trying to help.

Buffy put the envelope in Lucy's hand, her face drained to the hue of suet, her ginger freckles standing out on her skin in tiny spots the colour of Cook's marmalade. Lucy's hand wavered, for it very badly wanted to refuse what Buffy was offering her and every child at the table stopped eating, even Alice, as though she sensed the bleakness that had swept over them all.

'It was in his bedroom,' Buffy said simply.

'Well, I never saw it,' Percy retorted defensively, ready to cry, it seemed, for these were days when the simplest thing could turn into a tragedy.

'It's all right, darling. It's not your fault.' Again Lucy's response was automatic. She pushed her chair back from the table and stood up and they all watched her. Thimble, who had been stretched out before the fire, got to his feet and moved across to her, nosing her hand.

'Well . . .' Her voice was barely more than a whisper. 'I suppose . . .' With a sharp movement as though she hated the thing and couldn't wait to get it out of her hand and on to the back of the fire, she ripped it open.

It was very simple.

Dear Luce,

'I couldn't stand back any longer, not with all of them gone now. Will was the last. Then there's James, wherever he is and even Franny Buchanan and can I sit at home messing about with schoolboy stuff when I'll be eighteen this year and would have to go anyway. I'm hoping to get something with the . . . no, I'd better not tell you, for I know you'd try to bring me back. Give my love to the brats and say you forgive me.

    Your loving brother,
      Edward Dean

Not Edward, not her baby brother who had been her boyish support for as long as she could remember, even when Papa was alive. Not cheerful, good-natured Edward who had kept up the spirits of the men on the wards with his passion for making things, things he had shared with them, often bringing one of them back from the brink of hell with his innocent belief that they were as interested as he was in motor cars and aeroplanes and even the motorbike he was hoping to build himself when the war was over. He was no more than a child and someone, herself probably, for she could trust no one else, must go down to the railway station and find out where he had gone. What in hell's name were the military authorities thinking of taking schoolboys into their dreadful war, she demanded. She couldn't bear it, her voice becoming shrill, fighting Buffy off, until they brought Doctor Penfold to take her away, for she was terrifying the children. She'd had enough, she'd hissed at him, breaking away from his arms. She couldn't bear it, she repeated over and over again, and it was not until the wail of the baby and the gasping sobs of Margaret, Emily and Percy finally followed her down the deep well of terror into which she had fallen, that she managed to get a weak hold on to her flailing senses.

'I'm sorry, really I am. It was the shock. I didn't mean to frighten you all, darling,' she told Percy who cowered on her lap alongside Alice, both of them fighting for space. Margaret and Emily were held in Buffy's strong embrace on the other side of the fire and at their feet Thimble licked any hand that came within his reach, his eyes dark and sympathetic. 'But you see, Edward should not have gone . . . yet. He is not eighteen and besides he had not finished his schooling,' as if that mattered, her bruised heart whispered, only his safety. If only she had him here, where he belonged, where he had been last night, lying his full length, which was quite considerable, on the floor, fiddling as usual with something or other, his face absorbed. Where . . . and how had he persuaded the recruitment centre that he was old enough to go for a soldier? But then he was a big lad, strong and well fed and with the war machine gobbling up men, and boys, like some malevolent and greedy giant, would they refuse him, for they needed more and more fodder to feed the monster.

'What will you do, Lucy?' Margaret quavered. 'Will you bring him back? I don't want him to . . . to be like those men in the wards. I don't want him to fight.'

'I wish I could go with him,' Percy said defiantly, though he still clung like the small, frightened boy

474

he was in the only really safe arms he had ever known. 'I'd kill all those—'

'Don't, Percy,' Emily shrieked, setting off Alice again and there was bedlam for several minutes as Lucy and Buffy and Elsie, who had been sent for to help, since she was part of their family from the old days, calmed them down. Doctor Penfold gave each of them, except Alice who had fallen asleep on her mother's knee, a small sleeping draught and it was not until they were all in their beds, Percy tucked in with Emily, that Buffy and Lucy were able to discuss what should be done.

Buffy spoke first. 'I think you should call Mr Buchanan. He knows a lot of people, probably in the War Office, or wherever it is records are kept and they'd be more likely to help him. After all, it's his bloody gunpowder that keeps this war going.' Buffy's voice was bitter and Lucy reached out to take her hand. She turned it over, looking at the small palm which still retained the rough calluses gained in her service to the Dean family.

'I honestly don't know what I would do without you, Buffy,' she said in a low voice, 'and I bless the day my mother brought you home to us. You're like a sister to me.'

'Lucy . . .'

'And it follows that Edward is your brother as well as mine. I want to dash off to Windermere and see if he left from there and yet he could have gone up to Penrith, or even Carlisle. His bicycle has gone, Jacob told Elsie, but I know it makes more sense to let Ben Buchanan do the searching. Perhaps a few telephone calls is all that it needs. I know if James was here he would move heaven and earth . . . Oh, God, oh, dear sweet God, don't take

475

my brother as you took my husband. Buffy ... Buffy, hold my hand, for I feel I'm going to fall into that deep black hole again. I love them both so much, and I have lost them.'

'They're not lost, Lucy, only mislaid for the moment.' Buffy shook her hand, trying to lighten the moment but Lucy wept again.

The Battle of Arras continued and in many places the British troops advanced triumphantly. The Canadians captured Vimy Ridge and the Australians broke through the dreaded Hindenburg Line which the Germans had built over the winter months, and the doughboys, the name given to the American soldiers, were coming.

April drifted into May and May into June and the war which had swallowed up Edward Dean guarded him jealously, for he was a brave soldier and a grand lad, those who shared his scrape-hole with him, a small burrow dug out of the side of the trench, told one another. He had had, like all the other young lads who came out with him, no more than a rudimentary bit of training, which, for all the good it did, was a total waste of time, and had it not been for them, old hands, some of the youngsters would not have survived a week. Though he was a big chap he was no more than a boy and his innocent cheerfulness in the face of terror provoked admiration in them and they adopted him as a kind of mascot. Aye, Private Eddy Fellthwaite was a good lad, a toff, they could tell that by the way he spoke, but he never held himself above them. All he wanted was to get posted to some airfield, for his passion was flying. He'd spend hours, when he could, of course, watching the tiny birds swoop about the skies, tracer bullets zipping among them like demented wasps, his face white, his eyes glittering as our lads gave what for to theirs, though sometimes it was the other way around. The trouble was, he told them earnestly, that with the movement of troops and the constant change of the position of trenches as advance or retreat took place, airfields were constantly being changed from one place to another, but he meant to see one, and if he could manage it, work among the aeroplanes he loved. One day, he told them, he would learn to fly and be up there with the other men of the Royal Flying Corps. His hero was Captain Albert Ball, VC, DSO, MC who, at twenty years of age, had shot down forty-three aircraft. He had been devastated, sobbing like a child when they had heard that Captain Ball had been shot down in his turn and, rough chaps that they were, they had held him in their arms and comforted him. They loved him and his tales, the old sweats, of whom there were not many left, and the boys, and when it was rumoured that they were to be on the march again, this time to the Messines Ridge that ran south from the Ypres salient, they jostled to march next to him, for he was their good-luck mascot.

They sang as they marched, even young Eddy Fellthwaite joining in the gruesome words that he had soon learned.

If you want to find the old battalion,
I know where they are, I know where they are.
If you want to find a battalion,
I know where they are,
They're hanging on the old barbed wire . . .

Lucy wouldn't leave Ben alone, even after weeks of telephone calls and urgent messages left on the desks of all the men he knew who were influential in the War Office and Foreign Office.

'I can't keep on and on at them, Lucy,' Ben told her impatiently. 'I've tried everybody. They've gone through the enlistment records with a fine-toothed comb and could find no Edward Dean among them. There is only one conclusion to be drawn, lass,' softening, for this wife of his cousin's was wearing herself to skin and bone, not only trying to find that bloody young brother of hers, but James as well.

'Yes?'

'That he enlisted under another name.'

Her face whitened and seemed to sink in on itself and he remembered thinking that if she lost any more weight she'd be a bloody skeleton.

'Oh, Lord,' she whispered. 'How are we to find him?'

'You're not, Lucy. There are many men in the army who enlisted under names that are not their own. God knows why. Perhaps men doing their best to escape from something.'

'But not Edward,' she cried. 'He had nothing to hide from.'

'Only you, lass.'

She looked horrified and he went on hastily, 'Oh, I don't mean that how it sounds, but he knew you would do your best to fetch him home and if he had gone in under his own name you might have found him.'

'Oh, Ben,' she whispered brokenly. 'Why must men feel the need to fight?'

'They fight for what they believe in, Lucy.'

478

'But it is so futile.'

'Is it? You were willing to knock the block off anybody years ago who stood in the way of women getting the vote, as I recall.'

They were in his office at the Emmerson Gunpowder Works beside Elterwater. It was the seventh day of June and across the Channel the Battle of Messines had proved an outright victory for the Allies though the couple in the office were not yet aware of it.

'But that was not the same at all, Ben. We were not willing to spill blood to attain our aims.'

'Some of you were pretty violent, as I remember.'

Lucy got up and moved to the window, still holding the cup of tea Ben's lady clerk had put in her hand. It was a fine day and the start of a long spell of good weather which again she and Ben were not aware would affect their troops in France. There was a turbulent area of activity going on in the yard as carts were loaded with the barrels of death the Buchanan family manufactured and Lucy shuddered. There were many women among the men, for the war had taken much of Ben's workforce.

'When will it end, Ben? When will they come home to us? Haven't enough of them died yet? Your Henry is sixteen now, so is he to be dragged into it soon? What about poor Janet and Angus? Three of their sons gone and yet young Will still breaks his mother's heart by—'

'He had no choice, lass. They would have conscripted him and let's pray to God that the bloody thing will be over before . . .'

'Before Henry goes?'

'Aye.' Ben's shoulders slumped, for the image of his tall, handsome elder boy marching off as Janet's lads had, put a cold ring of despair about his heart. They all grieved for Janet and Angus, who would never be the same again, even if Will was spared. They were like two old people whose lives were nearly done with, creeping about their empty home in bewilderment, the sharp-tongued, witty woman who had disapproved of this lass standing dejectedly before him, gone for ever.

The victory at Messines prompted those in the know to begin a new offensive at a place called Passchendaele at the end of July, for the weather was good. For two weeks the heaviest bombardment of the war churned up the land into a sodden mass of mud, for by now the rain had begun. A vast morass of craters appeared filled with water and it was across this that the British troops began their attack. Not deterred by the shattering losses on the Somme last year, the soldiers were thrown into battle as though they were invincible, and like the Somme, it was found that they were not and again the hospital at Howethwaite was crammed to the doors with men who had come straight from the trenches. Lucy looked for Edward among them, her heart almost exploding in fear, and at the end of each convoy, gasping with relief when he was not among them. Foolish, she knew, for even as the last one drew away she was aware that he could be lying dead or dying on some battlefield, or having his blood-soaked, mud-encrusted uniform cut off him as she was doing to the lad on the stretcher.

The telephone shrilled in the night and it woke her but she turned in her bed, ready to drift off

480

again into the exhausted sleep her body craved. It would not be for her, she had decided, and when the quiet knock at her door brought her to a rigid sitting position in the bed she could feel her heart begin to leap like a fish on a hook.

Drawing on her robe, she opened the door and was surprised to find Sister Colyford there, immaculately starched as usual but with an expression of some anxiety on her face.

'What ... what is it?' Edward ... or James? Dear God ... Dear God, would she ever know peace again, the thought flashed through her mind while she waited for Sister to strike her down with some appalling news.

'A telephone call, my dear, from a Mr Alex Buchanan.'

'Alex ...' For a moment she was astonished and vastly relieved, for what possible bad news could Alex have to tell her? He worked in London, certainly, but he had nothing to do with ...with ... what did he do? She couldn't even remember anyone telling her exactly what Alex Buchanan did for the war effort but she was sure it ... Oh, God, please ...'

'Mr Buchanan wants to speak to you, my dear. I asked him what he wanted, for if it was ... bad news I felt it should be told you by ... by one of us,' who are your friends after all this time. It was in the compassion on her face and in her hands which reached out to Lucy in case she needed something to hold on to.

The voice at the other end of the line was tinny and faint, fading and roaring suddenly into her ear in the most odd way. There were crackles and buzzes and for a while she had not the faintest idea

481

what Alex was trying to say to her. She could feel
Sister at her back, ready to catch her, she supposed,
if the news proved to be too much for her to bear
but when she at last heard the name she was so
stunned she could not at first take it in. It was
soldiers who were wounded, or killed, and those
who were out there to help them just did not fall in
battle, or so she had liked to believe, though she
knew that was absolute claptrap.

Slowly she replaced the receiver, beginning to
shake, allowing Sister to lead her to the chair that
stood by the telephone.

'Who . . . ?' Sister paused delicately.

'It's . . . that was James's cousin in London.' Her
voice sounded hollow even in her ears and she
could feel shock beginning to take her over but she
must not give in to it, for she was needed and she
must make arrangements . . . trains . . .

'Is it a relative?'

'Yes, his wife.'

'His wife?'

'Yes, she's an ambulance driver . . . *was* an
ambulance driver in Flanders. She was changing a
tyre . . . Oh, Franny, how you laughed when you
said you were to learn the . . .' She could feel an
almost hysterical need to laugh herself, for she
could clearly remember that day when Franny had
told them in that droll way she had that she was to
learn how to service her own vehicle, but she thrust
it away, clinging to Sister Colyford's kind hand and
being dragged back to reality by her wise eyes. She
had waited for this telephone call for weeks,
months, dreading it but expecting it daily, waited to
hear a voice at the other end of the wire telling her
that her beloved husband was dead, that her

482

beloved brother was no more and not once had it occurred to her to give a thought to Franny who was the most courageous woman she had ever known. Franny who had gone to Flanders for a bit of adventure.

'She was hit by shrapnel, Sister, and they are bringing her home. Alex has asked for me and I must go.'

'Of course you must. I'll send for Miss Tyson to help you to pack and I myself will telephone the railway station to find out the times of the London trains. You did say London, didn't you?'

*   *   *

The journey from Windermere was long and wearying. At every station the platforms were crowded with soldiers but she had little luggage and she had been lucky at Windermere to find a seat. She felt quite strange in her elegant dress and flowery hat and she could see the men eyeing her as though wondering who in hell she was, travelling down to London in a crowded train looking as though she were off to Ascot. She had no conception of her own beauty but they had and she found one or the other of them looking at her as though she were some miracle that had come among them. They smiled when she did, shy with her but there was little conversation. These men knew they were going back into battle and that the likelihood was that they wouldn't ever come this way again. They were weary of war after three long years but when the train steamed into Euston station in the light of a chilly grey dawn they jostled with one another to lift her small bag down from the luggage rack.

She had never seen so many soldiers in her life and so many trains taking them away, while others brought back those who were no longer any use at the front. The sound of marching feet drifted in to the station hall and she watched until they came into view, uniformed men moving steadily in columns of four, their heads held high, their shoulders erect, betraying no sign of their reluctance to go back to the trenches.

She managed to get a taxi-cab to Kensington where Franny and Alex's smart little house lay, though she had never been there, or even to London. A milkman clattered his way along the road and he eyed her with the same degree of astonishment the soldiers on the train had done. She moved slowly up the steps and rang the bell and when Alex, his face white and strained, opened the door, she fell weeping into his arms, the first tears she had shed for Franny Buchanan who had teased her and provoked her but who had always been her friend.

CHAPTER TWENTY-EIGHT

'She's being brought back today. I've arranged for her to go straight to a private hospital. After all'— Alex gave a shaky laugh, reaching for Lucy's hand—'she can't be expected to be put among all the other wounded soldiers, can she, though if I know my Franny, that's exactly what she would have relished. And she is a soldier, Lucy. She was wounded in battle just like all the other brave and broken men who are pouring back across the Channel. The hospital is quite near here and the sister in charge has promised to ring as soon as Franny arrives. I wanted to go the station and meet ... meet her, but they advised against it. An ambulance will pick her up and take her to ... to the hospital and then, when ... when she is ... when they can tell me ... I am to go ... Dear God, Lucy, what am I to do if she ... They said, others said, that I shouldn't have let her go but you know Franny. When did she ever listen to anything anyone advised her? I couldn't stop her, wouldn't stop her, for like you I believe women, as well as men, must decide their own course of action but if ... if she should ... if she doesn't recover I'll never forgive myself.'

'Don't think like that, Alex.' Lucy was appalled to see the anguish which had Alex in its frightening grip. They were sitting in a pleasant room furnished in the style of the new look the Edwardians had given to their drawing-rooms. It was lighter, brighter and less formal than the Victorian, elegant with a few simple pieces of furniture and pleasant chintzy fabrics, with unpretentious pictures on the plain walls which toned in with their surroundings. A white marble fireplace, in which stood an enormous vase of mixed flowers, occupied the wall opposite the long windows which overlooked the street, and above the fireplace was a vast mirror in a plainly carved frame. There were crystal light fittings on either side of the mirror and pretty lamps to match on the small polished tables of light English wood. There was a deep sofa in a shade of biscuit velvet and two chairs to match and the sun streamed across the pale patterned carpet, reaching up to touch Alex Buchanan's haggard face.

Lucy's heart, which was enormous in its compassion, went out to him and she leaped up, drawing him to his feet. She folded his enormous frame in her arms, drawing his head down to her shoulder where he rested his forehead. She knew he was close to breaking point, this big man who once she had described to herself as a shambling bear. Good-natured, even-tempered, wanting to please, that was the way she had always known Alex Buchanan, and to see him now, ready to weep over the woman who, though she loved him, had never been faithful, was almost more than Lucy could bear. If she could comfort him, reassure him, give him some of her own strength, though sometimes she admitted she had little left for herself, then she was ready to do it.

Alex relaxed and leaned his not inconsiderable weight against James's wife and felt the tension ease out of him. She once had been almost Junoesque in her young beauty, broad-shouldered, tall, full-breasted. All men's fantasy of the perfect woman. Though she was still tall, her eyes almost on a level with his own, now she was slender, frail bones at her shoulder blades, and yet he sensed something powerful in her transfer itself to him. He didn't know what it was. Perhaps it was to do with her upbringing in the house of a man of God where goodness must surely have rubbed off on her since that was what she was. Good! A simple word which had connotations of virtue and purity and Lucy Buchanan had these characteristics too, but she was far from being a prude, and very far from being the self-righteous paragon so many raised as she

486

had been might be. No wonder James had loved her, he remembered thinking in a kind of disjointed way. Different she had been, when first Franny had invited her to Grange House, undisciplined and naïve, rebellious to their code but, by God, she was a rare bird, then and now, and when James came home from wherever the fool had hidden himself, she would make him a wife and a soulmate that any man could treasure. He had been right to send for her and not one of his other cousins' wives, for this woman's durability, which had been proved a hundred times in the four years since he had known her, would support and strengthen Franny's recovery as no one else's could. It did not occur to him to question Lucy Buchanan's own frailty and need of support.

'Alex,' she was murmuring, her hand stroking his dishevelled hair and he felt the tears come to his eyes. All night he had walked the floor of this room, waiting for morning and the moment when he would be told if Franny was to live or die. He had eaten nothing and drunk nothing but now Lucy was leading him to the sofa, sitting him down with that smiling grace she had, looking round for the bell and when she spotted it, pulling it vigorously. An elderly housemaid popped her head round the door, then, on seeing the poised and lovely creature who raised an imperious head as though to say, 'What took you so long?' bobbed a creaky curtsey.

'Some tea, please, er . . .'

'Whittaker, madam.' Whittaker came with the house which Alex and Franny had rented. Whittaker had been born and bred in London and when the family who owned the house and who had young children had moved to their country place in Derbyshire for the duration of the war Whittaker had been kept on here, with a scullery maid, an ancient cook and an equally ancient gardener, to look after the place and see to Mr and Mrs Buchanan. It had turned out very well, for Mrs Buchanan had taken herself off to Flanders, of all places, the minute she got here and Mr Buchanan had been out such a lot and, like all men, when he was at home scarcely noticed what went on, especially in the servants quarters. They virtually pleased themselves what they did and when they did it. Whittaker was not awfully sure who this haughty young woman was who was sitting on the sofa holding Mr Buchanan's hand, but it looked as though she might be a bit of a tartar by that glint in her eye. Used to having her own way, the elderly housemaid thought. Whittaker, who liked to know what went on in her own place, had overheard several telephone calls Mr Buchanan had made, and received, and they had all been astounded, and sorry, of course, though she shouldn't have been over there in the first place, to hear that his wife had been injured at the front and was to be brought home. So how was this young woman to be involved?

'And perhaps some sandwiches for Mr Buchanan.' The young woman turned solicitously to the man beside her. 'Have you eaten, Alex?'

'I don't remember,' Mr Buchanan mumbled, and really, you couldn't help but feel sorry for the poor bloke, Whittaker said a few minutes later to Cook who had her feet on the fender in the kitchen, her stockinged feet to the fire.

'Well, 'oo is she then?' Cook asked, ready to

enjoy any bit of a change so long as it didn't involve extra work for her. Mind you, if she had been a bit younger she would have gone with the family to Derbyshire, especially after that air-raid on London last month and then, blow me, another a week or two back. Twenty German aeroplanes, it was said, in the skies above London, bombs dropped and folk killed and injured and what was the world coming to when a body wasn't safe beneath her own roof.'

'Eeh, I dunno, though she acts as though she were Queen Mary 'erself.' Whittaker spread margarine on a thin slice of bread and reached for the potted meat, which was all there was in the house to make a sandwich with.

The telephone shrilled and Whittaker sighed, laying the knife on the table beside the bread board, turning towards the kitchen door and the hallway to answer it, but as she opened the door Mr Buchanan had beaten her to it.

'We'll be there at once, Sister,' he was saying, while at his back the lovely young woman was straining her neck to hear what was being said at the other end of the line. 'Is . . . how does she seem, Sister?' Whittaker heard Mr Buchanan say from behind the door where she hid, pulling a face at Cook to be quiet.

There was a small silence as Mr Buchanan listened to whatever was being said by the sister then, 'Thank you, Sister. We'll be there at once.'

Clinging to the hand of the young woman in the most peculiar way, Mr Buchanan flung open the front door, almost dragging her off her feet.

'We shall need a taxi-cab,' Whittaker heard him mumble, then the front door slammed behind them.

*   *   *

The hospital showed none of the chaos the mass of suffering humanity brought from the trenches to Howethwaite and the other military hospitals up and down the land. It was a place of calm and order. The corridor was filled with sunshine, highlighting the exquisite polish on the floor put there by several hardworking VADs. Though the walls were painted a somewhat sombre green it was bright and smelled of disinfectant and on several polished tables along its length were bowls of flowers. A porter directed them to the ward they asked for and when they got there they were told to wait, since, the pursed-lipped nurse said, this was not visiting time, looking ominously at the ticking clock on the wall.

This was a general hospital, a civilian hospital and in a tiny ward lit by a tiny lamp, for by now it was evening, Franny Buchanan lay, the sheets smoothed across her and tucked in in that strangling grip so beloved of sisters and nurses the world over. It was as though they imagined patients might escape if they were not firmly anchored to their beds. Lucy nearly smiled. Even if Franny had been feeling up to it she could not have moved.

She and Alex moved slowly across the threshold, their hands still clasped for comfort, their total attention on the white bed and the white face on the white pillow. Franny looked peaceful, too bloody peaceful, Alex was to tell Lucy later, for a less peaceful woman had never been born, her hair brushed tidily across her forehead and if they

490

hadn't known they might have thought her to be asleep, uninjured. There wasn't a bandage to be seen but the bandages and the hurt were underneath the immaculate sheets, the hurt which, the doctor had just told her husband, would never allow her to walk again.

Alex had wept, again in Lucy's arms, but now he was dry-eyed, composed, ready, should his wife be conscious, to tell her to keep her chin up, old girl, and what the hell did she think she was doing, putting the wind up him like this.

She opened her eyes as Alex gently placed a kiss on her cheek, then, when she saw who it was, she smiled, doing her best to struggle out of the cocoon that held her rigid, wanting to put a hand up to him, to tell him that he was not to be upset.

'Don't try to move, Mrs Buchanan,' the nurse on the other side of the bed warned but Franny Buchanan was not one to be told what to do, even now.

'Oh, go to . . . blazes, Nurse,' she said. 'I want to give my . . . my husband a hug.'

'Now then, old girl, behave yourself and do what the nurse tells you. There'll be time enough for hugs later.'

A flirtatious smile wisped about Franny's pain-drawn face and Lucy felt a small cry of painful admiration catch in her own throat. 'Is that . . . a promise, Alex?' Franny whispered, then winked in that wicked way she had, a slow wink, merely a small drooping of one eyelid, but a wink just the same.

'It is, and it won't be long, either,' ignoring the small moue of disapproval on the nurse's face. Not that she objected to Mr and Mrs Buchanan's words, or what seemed a promise to one another that they would soon resume their ... marital relationship, but her concern was that Mr Buchanan must not promise something that would, in all probability, never come about. Mrs Buchanan had been hit in the back by shrapnel from a shell which had exploded quite close by, killing a dozen of the wounded she was about to lift into her ambulance. She had been changing a tyre on her vehicle, it was reported, and though she had not caught the full blast, the shrapnel had lodged in her spinal column. In fact it was still there and it was imperative that she lie quite still until the doctor, who was a specialist in that field, could operate on her.

'Who ... who's that with you, darling?' Franny's voice was barely audible. Her eyes wandered past Alex's bulky shoulder, doing their best to focus on Lucy's shadowy figure at the end of the bed.

Alex turned and the nurse frowned her disapproval again. Her patient must not be tired any more than could be helped and this was not doing her much good, but she supposed the husband was entitled to see his wife. She didn't know who the woman was but her face was calm and her eyes, as they met hers, told her that she would not be long.

'It's only me, dearest,' and it was a measure of Lucy's love that she called Franny by the endearment her mama and papa had exchanged and which, up to now, had been used only for those of her own family. 'I've come to keep Alex company. No, you must not speak. Not again. I'm a bit of a nurse myself now,' managing a quirky smile, 'and I know what's best for you and there's no need to raise your eyebrows like that. I'm staying with Alex and then, when you can be moved, you shall come to Howethwaite and I will look after you myself. Is that clear?'

'What a tyrant she . . . has become, Alex, but may I . . . say one thing?'

'No, you may not.'

'I did not . . . come home alone, Lucy. Someone brought . . . me,' and again her eyes moved but over Lucy's shoulder this time. 'Look,' she whispered.

Lucy wanted to turn but dared not. There was something warm and loving in Franny's eyes, something almost impish, as though she was pleased with herself and knew Lucy would be too. She knew there was something . . . someone of importance there, something that was to mean life itself to Lucy Buchanan and she was afraid to turn in case she had been mistaken in Franny's expression and it was not . . . not . . .'

She sensed the movement behind her in the corner of the room as someone she had not even noticed sitting in a chair in the deep shadows stood up. A tall figure. A man. A quiet man, and when Alex gasped sharply, a gasp cut off in mid-breath, she found the courage to turn her head, looking for the first time in two years into the eyes, the true, knowing eyes of James Buchanan.

'We brought . . . one another . . . home, Lucy . . .' The whisper from the bed trailed away as Franny Buchanan lapsed into unconsciousness and the plain truth of their deep, enduring love stood between Lucy and James Buchanan.

'You must all leave now,' the nurse told them firmly, quite put out by this show of emotion, feeling under the curve of Franny's jaw for her pulse. She had wanted the man in the filthy

493

uniform with his arm in an equally filthy sling to wait outside while Mrs Buchanan's husband visited her, but he had flatly refused, saying he would deliver her to her husband and then he would go. Apparently he had been the same all the way through from the Ypres salient where he and Mrs Buchanan had been wounded. He had fought like a tiger any move on the part of the authorities to separate them, and so, after he had had his own wound seen to, they had let him be. He had been no trouble as long as he had his eye on Mrs Buchanan who was a relative.

They waited until they were outside the door before James and Alex fell on one another and pummelled each other's arms and back in that strange way that men have when they are deeply moved. They hugged and pounded and it was not until they were done that James looked at Lucy.

She looked back at him with a sort of drifting, dream-like expression in her eyes, telling him that she was in no way put out that he should greet his cousin before her. She knew why, naturally.

'James.' What else was she to say to this man who had broken her heart and yet had loved her as she had loved him? Oh, yes, there was no doubt about it now, since the day they met, though in her innocent girlhood she had not known it. She had loved him then, she loved him now and would never stop until they both died, which she hoped earnestly would not be for a long time but would be on the same day, for she could not bear to be parted from him again. Tonight, in the bed she and he were to share at Alex's house, make no mistake about that, she would tell him so, show him how it was, but it seemed she did not need to speak, for

494

her eyes were soft and unfocused with the love she bore him. They were warm and deep and incredibly lovely, her smile welcoming him home where he belonged, for it was not her nature to bear a grudge. They had hurt one another badly but she loved him, it was all there for him to see in that one look and he fell into it as it cherished him, enfolded him in the knowledge that nothing would ever change in her heart.

She could see the strain run out of him, empty from him in a weary torrent. His mouth had been held tight and drawn in a grim line as though he could not remember a day when he had not been weary and in pain but now that day had come again, brought to him by her.

The wariness in his eyes was replaced by a drowned sweetness, a sweetness put there by her, by the shining knowledge that at last they were meeting as equals in their love. He smiled gently and his uninjured hand rose to cup her cheek.

'My love,' he said softly and neither of them noticed as Alex Buchanan tiptoed quietly back along the corridor.

They scarcely noticed him when they got back to the house either, for he diplomatically slipped away upstairs to his room, leaving them to whatever it was they were to do. It was no business of his, though the servants, who were still up, were open-mouthed in wonder, gawping at her as the young woman, whose name turned out to be Buchanan, walked into the kitchen and demanded a fire in the rather small bedroom where Whittaker had decided she was to sleep. In fact, she said, since her husband . . . husband mind you, was to share it with her she rather wondered if there was a bigger room, with a double bed, please, where they might spend the night? Was there hot water, good, and the bathroom ... yes, that would be splendid ... clean towels, good, and she'd be obliged if the fire was lit at once since her husband, who had just come from the trenches, was cold.

The trenches! Well, that was a turn-up for the books and no mistake, though they could well believe it when they saw the state of him and would you look at her now. A bit different to the pale and peaky thing she had been earlier in the day. Now she was all shining eyes and flushed cheeks and looking as pretty as a picture and no wonder! She also wanted hot water in a bowl, she went on, scissors, any sort of antiseptic ointment they might have, carbolic and clean bandages. They could tear up a sheet if such things were not available, she told them, and they did not mind her high-handed manner at all now, for nothing was too good for a man who had been in the trenches.

She undressed him while his dreaming eyes studied her face, not looking away from her as her fingers unbuttoned and gently removed his tunic and then the rough khaki shirt he wore. She smoothed his chest and shoulders with wondering hands, making him tremble and his nipples peak, then she pulled off his trousers, and he obeyed her when she told him to stand or lift his foot. He was totally absorbed by her, by her hands on him as she removed his muddy, bloody—thankfully not his own—clothing, easing the filthy bandage away from the gaping hole where the shrapnel had hurriedly been dug out of him and which it had stuck to with dried blood. Thankfully there was no sign of the infection she had dreaded. The shrapnel wound was in his right shoulder which, naturally, meant as a right-handed man he could not perform any of the duties a private soldier was asked to do in the trenches. He could not dig a hole in which to shelter. He could not hold his rifle or draw a bayonet. He could not salute his officer or go over the top with the other lads so they had sent him home. He was no longer of any use to them, was he? Nevertheless he had no trouble getting his arms round his wife!

She cleaned the wound and expertly re-bandaged it, her professionalism not allowing her to begin what they both wanted, which was to make love to her husband and have him make love to her, not before she had tended to his wound.

She had put him in the bath, aware with her breath catching that though her husband's naked body was thin and undernourished, it still had the virile power to become erect with his need.

'Is this the kind of treatment I may expect when we get home, wench?' he asked her drowsily as she soaped his aching body with hands which were gentle but at the same time searching. He groaned a little as her hands found his penis.

'My love, I shall be no good to you at all if you continue with that, delightful as it is,' he told her, so would she stop it at once and let him get out of the bath, for he had better things to do than succumb to her nurse's need to boss him about. Was she always to be as masterful as this? he murmured into her hair as she bent to dry his body and would she be careful with that bit ... yes, there, for he had great plans for it later. He would have had her in the bath with him, he told her, bemused and bewitched by her, but as she had seen for herself, he had been covered in what could only be called . . . well, it was worse than filth, for he had not had a bath, or even a proper wash, since he couldn't remember when and why in the name of all that was wonderful, hadn't they done this before, he begged her to tell him, his breath catching in his throat as she began to remove her own clothes.

She found that though he murmured soft words and endearments throughout the whole joyful encounter, she couldn't speak. Her heart was too full. It was as though it were so filled with emotion it had cut off her ability to utter a word, to tell him how she felt, but it seemed her hands on his body and the adoration in her eyes as they met his was enough for him.

The firelight was a gentle glow on their naked bodies, turning them both to burnished gold as he began to tell her what had happened to him since he last saw her, but before that they had loved one another in the deep enchantment their need and their long separation had created. He did not hurry. His concentration was complete as he studied her body, the beauty of her breasts which he told her were smaller but he liked them just the same. He cupped them awkwardly, for his arm, which he had refused to allow her to put in a sling, stabbed him painfully as he moved it to lift his hand to her nipple. He turned her this way and that, telling her smilingly, wonderingly, that he must inspect her for change, satisfied when there was none, speaking with that loving humour he had kept well hidden for so long. He caressed her slowly, carefully, surely, smoothing his hands down the length of her slender body, not wishing to neglect any of the sweet sensations his hands and loving heart created, for himself or for her. He put his face against her flesh to smell the musky fragrance of her willing, female body, pressing his lips to every inch of her, groaning when his shoulder tore at him but refusing to stop. His hands slipped down her back and across her buttocks, moving to her flat belly and into the dark, mysterious bush between her thighs, making her sigh and stretch until his fingers found the sweet, moist centre of her when she began to cry out in need. They were overwhelmed by the sensual renewal of what they had known only twice before, glorying in this love that they had thought to be lost but which was found.

'I will never leave you again,' he told her harshly as he thrust into the waiting centre of her.

'I wouldn't let you and if you try I will follow.' She gasped in exquisite pleasure and her body arched to meet his.

'I will never . . .'

'What, my love?'

'Love anyone as I love you.'

'I know. I love you the same. Not grammatical but true.' There was laughter in her voice but he silenced it with his mouth.

'Always?' he managed a moment later.

'Always.'

'I'll kill any man who tries to take you from me.'

'No one will.'

'I know that now, my dearest love. And when morning comes . . .'

'Yes . . .' Her voice was no more than a sigh.

But he had put his head on her breast and was asleep.

CHAPTER TWENTY-NINE

They did not return to Howethwaite until the middle of September and when they did Lucy was already pregnant with her second child. Was it any wonder, she giggled to her besotted husband, when he wouldn't leave her alone for a moment, day or night.

'Do I hear a note of complaint in your voice, my darling,' reaching out to put his hand on her leg, then beginning to slide it up beneath the hem of her skirt.

'James! Whittaker might come in at any moment. I know she takes an age to carry out an order, poor old soul, but if she brings the tea in and finds you with your hand ... where it is, she'll possibly faint, or run screaming to Cook.' She gasped and arched her back and her husband smiled complacently, ignoring her words as his fingers found that sweet place they could not resist.

'Put this shawl thing over your knee,' he suggested, smiling with pure devilment, but Lucy pushed him away and just in time, for there was a knock at the door. It opened and Whittaker came doddering round it pushing a trolley on which were the teacups and saucers, the teapot, sugar basin and milk jug and the cakes, scones and biscuits Cook made in an endless orgy of activity in her attempt to 'put a bit of flesh on that lad's bones', for it seemed that the whole household now revolved round the wounded warrior who had come back from the war.

Whittaker would report fondly back to the

kitchen that 'they were at it again' but they all thought it was lovely for a man and his wife to be so much in love. She gave her whole attention to the pouring of the tea, handing a cup to Major Buchanan with what could only be called a dimpling smile, though she hadn't a dimple in her. James took it from her and winked, and Lucy smothered a smile, for she knew the elderly housemaid was as under the major's spell as she was herself. It was not fair to the poor dear to tease her the way James did, but James insisted she loved it and perhaps he was right. She knew *she* did. She couldn't get enough of his attentions, his kisses, his whispered remarks in her ear on what he was to do with her later in their bed. Sometimes it was his hand reaching out blindly for hers as something from the war came to plague him in a way that told her she was loved and needed, and that he must touch her at once to reassure himself that she was really there. He needed protection, his hand told her, comfort, like a small boy whose mother has momentarily strayed from his sight.

He had nightmares. She would be woken from her own sleep by a voice chanting in her ear, a chant of fear which was very familiar to her, for had she not heard it a hundred times on the wards at Howethwaite?

'Don't go, Joe ... Pass me my rifle ... a dozen killed ... poor old Dick ... there's Alf with all his ribs broken ... 5,000 bombs gone up ... Oh, God ... Oh, God ... Joe said he wouldn't last three weeks and he bloody didn't ... his glasses blown into his face ... poor sod, they've blown his balls off as well ... Oh, God ...' and in the way she had learned she would wake him carefully, shielding him from his terror, holding him until he quietened, then fell asleep again in the safety of her arms.

They had given him the Military Cross for his courage in rescuing a corporal on the Somme though when Major Buchanan deserted and Private Jimmy Johnson took his place it caused a great deal of confusion in high places when it was discovered he was one and the same man. Could he be described as a deserter when, strictly speaking, he was still serving bravely in the king's army and if not then he must surely be entitled to keep the medal he had won. There must be some sort of enquiry, they all agreed, some discipline taken against Major Buchanan, some punishment, but as he had now been medically discharged from the army with a shoulder which a shrapnel wound had permanently stiffened, what were they to do? He was thirty-eight years old, a married man with a child and really, they had enough to trouble them, for by now the army, which they had expected to break out of the Ypres salient and be halfway to the ports of Ostend and Zeebrugge, was bogged down in the tides and storms of autumn which was now upon them. The troops were still painfully inching upwards and onwards through the slough of shell holes and mud towards the village of Passchendaele, which was finally taken, but with winter upon them again it was going to be a hard push.

Sometimes, in the aftermath of their loving, when he lay with his cheek against her breast, relaxed and at peace, he would talk about it, about the waste, the sheer bloody brutality, the slaughter of a whole generation of the country's young men, the irony, the humour, the simple bravery of them all, whether they be peers or peasants.

'I was having a quiet smoke among the men, I can't remember after which battle since they all became the same one, when I overheard one chap say to another, 'D'you remember halting here on the retreat, George?' His mate answered simply, 'Can't call it to mind somehow. Was it that little village in the wood down there by the river,' pointing to the desolate and empty landscape, 'or was it that place there with the cathedral and all them factories?' Do you see, Lucy, they were looking at nothing but an ocean of mud, shell holes, devastation for as far as the eye could see, but in their mind's eye they still saw what had been there once. They were wonderful men, all of them, and brave, for they go back again and again, even though they know what it is they are going to. They are always cold and wet and tired and yet they remain cheerful. They are mown down like wheat before a scythe, often getting no further than the parapet of the trench and the bloody officers, myself included once, keep urging them to get up and go on. Dear God, Lucy . . .'

'Don't . . . don't . . . you're home.

'But they're not, Lucy, they're not.'

She knew she kept him with his head above water at times like these, above the stinking mud he dreamed he floundered in, holding him in her compassionate arms and gradually, as the weeks passed slowly by, she knew she was winning. She was one of the lucky ones and so was he.

They talked about Edward and again she cried in his arms for her little brother who had gone to 'do his bit'. Edward was not as ignorant of war as were many young men, schoolboys really, who marched away with colour blazing in their cheeks and their eyes shining with pride. He had seen in the wards of Howethwaite what war could do to a man and yet he had still gone.

One night, after a long silence in which James seemed to be making his mind up about something, he suddenly said, 'I saw him, my darling.'

She sat up in his arms, flinging her hair back from her face and stared at him, not knowing whether to be horrified or glad. Edward had written to her. She knew the name he had enlisted under. It had caused her a wry smile, but he wanted her to write to him and so he had been forced to tell her. He spoke of the men he was with, Bert and 'Rosie' and George, all men from the original British Expeditionary Force which must prove, or so she told herself, that if they could survive for so long there was hope that he would come back home again. He did not speak of the march to Ypres where the men lived in shell holes and were afraid to leave them, for the whole earth was ploughed up and the holes were filled with water and if the shells didn't get you the deep waters in the craters might.

'Where?' she whispered.

'On the road to Ypres. He was marching with his platoon. They seemed to be very attached to him, watching out for him, if you know what I mean, but he was in good spirits, Lucy.'

'I want to bring him home, James. He's only a boy.'

'No, he's a man now, and would not thank you for it.'

'But he's not eighteen yet,' she wailed.

'Oh, yes he is, in experience if not in years and you must leave him where he is, my darling.'

'It's so hard . . . so hard.'

'I know, my love, but we can only hope and pray that someone . . . perhaps your mama and papa are watching over him.'

Comforted by the thought she fell asleep at last in the shelter of his arms.

He did not tell her that when he met Edward the boy was in a rapture of enchantment, for he was to report to an airfield behind the lines where his hopes of becoming a pilot might be at last fulfilled. Edward was a clever lad, well educated and with a gift for machinery, and when it became known to his officers they had done all they could to have him moved. It meant that he would transfer from the army into the Royal Flying Corps and would probably be sent home for his training, but it also meant, which was why James didn't tell his wife, that her brother's expectation of life once he became a pilot was seventeen and a half flying hours.

*   *   *

He was longing to return to Howethwaite to see his child but Lucy refused to leave Franny and he refused to leave her. And not only Franny kept her in London. She was sadly aware that Alex would simply fall apart if there was no one to share his devastation, to tell him constantly that Franny was a fighter and would come through this. To hold his hand each time he came back from a visit to the hospital, to see that he ate something and changed his underwear, for of everybody, including Franny

505

herself, he seemed the worst hit by the tragedy.

Franny had had her operation and was out of danger now but there was no way she could be moved just yet, the doctor said. She and James and Alex went to see her every day but Alex was still in the war, though what good he was in his present state, Lucy often wondered, and could not spend as much time with her as he would have wanted, so it was up to Lucy to be with her as much as she was allowed.

It was on one of Lucy's visits when she had gone alone, that Franny talked of what the future held for her. James had gone to call on the mother of one of the men killed in his platoon. She lived somewhere in the warren of working-class streets near the docks where Fred's family had always worked and though Lucy had offered to go with him he said that he would rather go alone.

'His mother will want to talk about him, how he died, was he brave, did he speak of her when he was wounded, where his grave is, was it a nice funeral, that sort of thing, and she probably won't be able to do it if you're there.'

'Why not? I have every sympathy for her.'

'I know that, my darling, but you are so obviously not like her. It will inhibit her. You're a lady and she's just the mother of a simple working-class lad and besides . . .' He hesitated and bit his lip, staring sombrely out of the long window to the busy street beyond.

'What? What is it?' At once she was kneeling beside him, her lovely face passionate in her dedication to his welfare.

'I may not be able to lie as easily with you there.'

She looked astonished. 'Lie?'

'Yes, you see her Fred died by a bullet from the rifle of one of his own men.' His face was livid with pain.

She put her hand to her mouth and leaned back on her heels. 'Dear God . . .'

'He . . . hung on the barbed wire, you've heard the song, calling for his mother . . . for seventeen hours. We couldn't get to him, you see. We kept hoping the German machine-gun fire would finish him off but . . . It didn't and so . . . one of us . . . stood up and took aim and shot him.'

'You?' she whispered.

'Yes.'

'Oh, my darling, have you any idea how much I love you.' She began to weep, laying her face against his knee. He lifted her up and cradled her against him, shushing her tenderly but his face was bleak with memories.

It seemed Franny Buchanan wasn't going merely to loll—her word—about all day when she got out of this bloody place, she told Lucy on that day. She didn't believe it when they told her she might not walk again and anyway, she meant to have a damn good try at it and if it turned out that they were right, then she was going to have a chair made, a motorised chair.

'Perhaps that lad of yours might be able to come up with something,' she mused, gazing out of the window towards a stand of trees which were already beginning to lose their leaves. The lawn beneath them had a thin carpet of gold and amber and bronze and there was a chill in the air, a feeling that winter, the winter so dreaded by soldiers in trenches, was creeping inexorably closer.

'That lad of mine? Which lad?' Lucy was

bewildered.

'Edward, of course. As I remember he was for ever fiddling about with bits of wire and a spanner. He was obsessed by anything mechanical. I can see him now sitting in that little Austin of mine, his face absorbed, his eyes sort of unfocused with wonder. Do you remember—?'

Oh, yes, Lucy remembered. She remembered all those lovely days with her brothers and sisters, the long innocent days of their childhood, for she had been no more than a child herself then. Their 'expeditions'. The bicycles which Edward had cobbled together from bits and pieces of scrap and dear Papa, so wrapped up in his butterflies and his memories of his beloved Evelyn that they might all have cycled to John o' Groats and back and he would have smiled that sweet smile of his and asked them if they'd enjoyed themselves!

'Lucy.' Franny took her hand and squeezed it gently, looking into Lucy's bent face. 'He'll come home, darling, really he will, and when he does, he'll design me a chair with a motor on it so that I can get about the gardens and the house and then he can start on the Austin. I want to be able to drive and the vehicle will need to be adapted to my needs. Edward will do it for me so take that look of woe from your face and tell me how you and James are getting on. Aha, that brought a flush to your cheeks, lady, so I gather that everything is pretty good in that department.' Her voice was low and sad. 'Treasure it, darling, and him, for it's very special, what you and he have.'

The great day came when the doctor told Alex that as long as he promised that Mrs Buchanan was to go straight to the hospital where the other Mrs

Buchanan nursed, then she could go home. She must have a well-padded mattress to lie on in the railway compartment and he himself would accompany her if Mr Buchanan could give him a bed for the night. He had already had lengthy telephone discussions about Mrs Buchanan's condition with the doctors in the Lakeland hospital but he wanted to speak to them face to face. Mrs Buchanan must be brought back to him—yes, he knew it was a long way—at regular intervals but she was healing nicely, at least physically, though he did not add this last to Mrs Buchanan's husband.

*   *   *

If the doctor was amazed at the reception committee Mrs Buchanan had waiting for her on the steps and spread out in the lovely autumn gardens of the hospital, he managed to keep it to himself as he supervised the tender lifting of her from the ambulance which had brought them from the station at Windermere. There were people everywhere. Men in wheelchairs, children doing cartwheels, women weeping and wiping their eyes on their aprons, dogs barking and racing round like mad things, so that he began to wonder if this was going to be the right environment for his patient to recuperate in.

Lucy was overcome, blaming her tendency to weep at the slightest thing on her pregnancy, as she climbed down from the ambulance. Margaret and Emily and Percy had her in a stranglehold the minute her feet touched the gravelled drive, laughing and crying and begging her not to go away

509

again. Percy must show her the cartwheels he could now do, flying at once to the lawn where he proceeded to throw himself about in a mad arc of joy, his face beaming.

'Look, Lucy, look, Mr Buchanan,' he cried, including his brother-in-law in his delight.

'I think I liked it better when you called me James.'

'Look, James, watch me, watch me.'

'I am, old chap, and when you've a minute to spare you shall teach me. I've always wanted to do cartwheels.'

Percy was enchanted and when James opened his arms to him flew into them without hesitation, for it seemed this new Mr Buchanan was going to be enormous fun.

There were shouts of 'Welcome home, sir,' from Clapcott and Licky Thripp and even old Bibby who had brought Mrs Hutton across from the cottage they now shared. Mrs Hutton was Mrs Bibby now, and a prouder man never walked the earth, he was fond of saying to all and sundry. She'd done right well for them all, had Miss Lucy, but then hadn't he always said to anyone who would listen what a grand lass she was.

The two big black dogs frightened the life out of the doctor as they hurtled towards him but it was not him they were after but Mr James Buchanan who was swept off his feet, lucky to be standing on the grass at the time as they got him down and sat on him as though determined he would never escape them again.

'Get off, you daft beggars,' he was yelling at them, just as he had a year ago but now he knew they were his dogs, that he belonged to them. And as for that mad imp, Thimble, he was no better behaved than when James clapped eyes on him four years ago and would need taking in hand, he told his wife, helping her solicitously up the steps which made Mrs Burns and Mrs Bunting, who were the ones shedding the tears, nudge one another and exchange a significant look.

Buffy was there and in her arms was Alice. A shy Alice who hung back for a moment, hiding her face in Buffy's neck, her finger in her mouth, but when Lucy held out her arms, Alice held out hers and in a moment Lucy was being besieged by a torrent of words which seemed to imply that Alice had missed her and she was not to go away again. There were open-mouthed baby kisses and strangling hugs and then the moment they had all waited for when father and daughter met one another for what was really the first time. She did not remember him, for a year or more is a long time in a young child's life, but she had been accustomed to sitting on soldiers' laps, to being petted and gently hugged by men who could not get enough of her infant sweetness and when James held out his arms she went to him willingly enough.

The moment was fraught with emotion. They all cried then, even Sister Colyford who had taken Lucy's hand in greeting but was swept into her affectionate embrace instead. Then they all turned to watch James and Alice.

'Darling . . .darling . . .' James seemed unable to say more than those words as the memory of his love for this child rushed back again and became real.

Alice turned away in his arms, directing her gaze at Buffy.

'Daddy?' she asked questioningly, pointing a plump finger directly into James's face.

'Yes, it's your daddy,' Buffy told her. 'Give Daddy a kiss.'

Turning back to James, who was himself weeping unashamedly by now, Alice pursed her rosy lips and placed them gently on his cheek where the tears were. 'Daddy cry,' she said softly, then put her arms about his neck.

It was all too much for Franny Buchanan, who lay on the stretcher holding her husband's hand. She looked up and in that whimsical way of hers sighed heavily, theatrically.

'Well, I can't stand much more of this, really I can't. You'll have me in tears next and that would be a catastrophe. Now, will someone get me inside and, Lucy, will you ask that butler of yours if there's any champagne in the cellar, for I do believe this calls for a celebration. And there's no need to look at me like that, Doctor. It's my back that's injured, not my innards and a glass of champers would go down very nicely.'

They moved slowly up the steps, the stretcher carried carefully by the ambulance driver and his aide, and there, at the top of the steps and just inside the wide front door, was Rory. He was in a wheelchair, the stumps of his legs sticking out over the edge of the seat. To Lucy's consternation Margaret flew up the steps beside her, standing at Rory's back, her hands on the wheelchair as though she were ready to take him wherever he wished. She was smiling, a lovely luminous smile that transferred itself from Lucy to Rory, who put up a hand which she instantly took.

'Lucy,' he said quietly, clinging to Margaret's

hand. 'Welcome home. We've missed you. And . . . and James. How are you?' And in all their minds was the memory of that last day when James and Rory had been together and James had tried to kill Rory and what were they to make of one another now?

But James Buchanan had his daughter in his arms and his wife by his side, both of whom he loved more than life itself. Lucy was his now, totally and irrevocably, as was the child growing in her womb. He was whole and slowly healing the wounds of his mind and could he turn away from the man who had none of these things, though by the look of him and Lucy's sister things might be different one day.

'Rory. Good to see you, lad. And out of that bloody bed as well. We'll talk soon.' He placed the hand of friendship on Rory's shoulder.

There was a great letting out of breaths on a sigh of relief, and though Lucy wasn't sure she cared for the way Margaret was fussing about Rory Cameron, she merely smiled, bending to kiss Rory's cheek.

'You look well, Rory. As James says, we'll talk later but now we must get Mrs. Buchanan to bed.'

'Never mind bed, Lucy Buchanan. I haven't had my champagne yet and here is Dixon with the bottle. Now then, Doctor, remove that sour look from your face and take a glass with me. Let's drink to . . . to absent friends.' Her face saddened, thinking of Andrew and the three sons of Janet and Angus and all the other young men who had gone so gladly off to war and would never come back, and for a moment they were all silent then Franny laughed, 'and to happy homecomings,' and with that special no-nonsense magic that was hers she had them smiling again.

*   *   *

There was just one more thing that Lucy had to do and the cause of it was her sister Margaret, or rather what had been done to Margaret.

They had been home a week when she had been startled by the sound of desolate weeping. She had gone up to check on Alice who was having her nap and intended, if Alice was still sleeping, to persuade James to walk with her up through the woods at the back of Howethwaite. It was a glorious winter's day with a light frost and a smoky, opalescent haze above the treetops. The grass was stiff with the cold and the path up through the gardens was like a ribbon of tawny brown, the bricks in it brushed with white. Just the day for a walk.

She could not at first identify where the weeping came from, or even who it was who was so grief-stricken. It seemed to come from the attic, the stairs to which were beyond the nursery door. Buffy would be in the nursery with Alice so, without going inside to check on her daughter, she moved slowly past it and climbed the stairs to the attic. Putting her head through the trap-door which had been left up she peered round, trying to pierce the gloom which was thick and heavy among the unidentifiable shapes, small, large, square, piled on top of one another or stacked against the wall.

The weeping continued, not loud but heart-wrenching in its poignancy. Lucy moved further up the narrow staircase and stepped quietly into the attic. Brushing past all the odds and ends of unwanted furniture which the years of Howethwaite occupancy had accumulated, she saw, to her horror, that it was Margaret. She sat on the floor between two boxes, her knees up to her chest, her arms about her knees and her head resting on her arms. Her hair fell about her in a dark curtain, covering her shoulders which shook with her distress.

'Darling ... oh, darling, what is the matter?' Lucy blundered into a packing case, knocking it to the floor as she rushed to get to her sister, flinging herself down beside her and clutching her in frantic arms. 'Whatever has happened? Why are you crying? Tell me ... dearest, I cannot bear to see you in such a state. You're not hurt, are you? Has someone hurt you?' though she was not certain what or who she meant, for who would hurt Margaret in this place where they all loved her?

'Has ... is it to do with ... Rory? Please tell me, dearest. Perhaps I can put it right. Dear God, I'll have no one upsetting you like this. What is it?'

Blindly, without lifting her head or responding in any way to Lucy's determination to have her arms about her, Margaret thrust a piece of paper into Lucy's hands, then with what seemed to be a movement of distaste, drew herself away from her, her head still hanging in despair.

'What?' Lucy reluctantly took the piece of paper, a sheet of good quality notepaper and glancing quickly at it saw that it had no address nor a signature.

'Who?' she said, foolishly she knew, but something was ringing alarm bells in her head, remembered alarm bells, though they eluded her

515

for the moment.

She began to read it while Margaret continued to sob, though the storm was lessening somewhat.

It has come to my notice that you have become involved with a man called Rory Cameron and I am concerned that you might not know of his history, or that part of his history which involves your sister, Lucy Buchanan. Perhaps you are not aware that some years ago he had an affair with her and the child she passes off as James Buchanan's is, in fact, that of Rory Cameron. I could not have it on my conscience if you were to marry a man who will toy with the affections of two women, indeed two *sisters*, so disgracefully and felt it was my duty to warn you.
A well-wisher.

Lucy felt the nausea rise to her throat and for a moment she thought she would be sick, but it didn't last long, for hot on its heels came a rage so dreadful she wanted to scream and shout and fling herself about in a way a child will who is frustrated beyond measure. But she was not a child. She was a woman and this was her little sister who was weeping so broken-heartedly and all over what was a tissue of lies.

'Dear God,' she hissed. 'Dear sweet Jesus, is there no end to her madness. It was not enough for her to do her best to destroy James and me, now she is bent on doing the same to you and Rory. I can't believe it and really, Margaret,' her voice stern and forbidding, 'I'm surprised to find that you do.'

Margaret had lifted her head and turned her

swollen face to Lucy, her expression uncertain, frightened even, for she could see that Lucy was as mad as a wet hen, which was one of Lucy's favourite expressions. She brushed her long tangled hair back with a trembling hand then wiped her nose on her sleeve.

'Lucy . . . I didn't . . .'

'You didn't think, did you. That's what the trouble is, you didn't think this out or you would have come to the proper conclusion, which is that this letter is a load of . . .' Here she used an expression she had heard from James which was very rude and Margaret gasped.

'Do you honestly believe that that child downstairs, who is as dark as the night and with James Buchanan's eyes smiling out of her face, can possibly have been fathered by Rory Cameron? Margaret, I thought you had more sense. Rory is fair, fair-haired and fair-skinned and has blue eyes, and apart from that Alice is so like James in her ways it is quite uncanny. We've all said that, haven't we? Go on, admit it. Even the way she laughs. And apart from that, you who have known me all your life, can you believe that I could be so dishonest, so dishonourable, so deceitful that I could have an affair with a man while my husband was fighting for his life in the trenches? Have I ever told you a lie?'

'No . . .' no more than a whisper.

'Well then . . .' She took hold of her sister by the forearms and turned her fiercely to her. 'Do you believe me or this . . . this sick person, whoever it is,' though of course she knew, 'and who is bent on making trouble?'

'Lucy . . . oh, Lucy, it's just that I love him so much and I do remember when you were . . .

517

special to him.'

'He was desperately ill, dearest. He needed something I could give him. Now you are giving it to him because you love him and believe me, he loves you. Can you not tell that?'

Margaret's eyes, though still wet with tears, had begun to shine and with a little cry she flung herself into her sister's arms.

'I'm sorry, Luce. Oh, Lord, I'm sorry. I should have known. Forgive me.'

'There . . . It's all over now,' Lucy said, knowing it wasn't. 'Go and kiss Rory and then dare to tell me it isn't you he loves. Go on. Get out of here. Wash your face and brush your hair and don't let me hear another word.'

*   *   *

James was doing what he had done ever since they had got home which was thoroughly spoiling his daughter when Lucy told him she had to go out for an hour. He could scarcely bear to have the child out of his sight and Lucy had told him she would become decidedly jealous if this went on much longer. What about her? she asked him plaintively, but he merely smiled and said her turn for spoiling would come later unless she would like to go up to their room now when he would spoil her until she screamed for mercy.

'D'you remember me telling you about that chap who wrote to his wife that she was to have a good look at the floor, for when he got home she would see nothing but the ceiling? That's how I feel, as I think I've demonstrated ever since I came home.'

'Darling.' Her smile melted his heart which he

518

had thought would not be big enough to encompass both her, his daughter and the new little one to come, but it seemed hearts were designed to expand as and when necessary. This house was filled with love and affection as it had not been since before his own mother's death.

Margaret, who was sixteen now and quite old enough to know her own mind, she had told him and Lucy firmly, spent most of her time with Rory Cameron who, in his early twenties and come from a decent family, not that that mattered, she had added scathingly, was very suitable for the daughter of Edward and Evelyn Dean. It made no difference to her that he had no legs. Rory meant to have false legs fitted as soon as he could and she would have him up in no time at all. Yes, she loved him and he loved her and that was that, she had said, lifting her head defiantly, looking the image of Lucy, James thought, and Rory was a lucky chap. He knew Lucy had pulled strings to keep him at Howethwaite when really he should have gone to a convalescent home. He had become almost one of the family and everyone, including the children, had become so fond of him.

She drove the Rolls herself, telling no one, not even James, where she was going. She had put on her most elegant oufit which she only just managed to get into. It was what was known as a coat frock, double-breasted and buttoning down to the waist where a broad sash was tied. The skirt was slightly flared, ending six inches above her ankle bone. It had a definite military look about it and was made in a soft woollen material the colour of burned almond. Her hat was the same shade, close to her head, the small brim framing her lovely, serene face and had a ribbon the same coffee colour as her sash. She looked well and very, very fashionable.

He would see if madam was in, the high-nosed butler she remembered from the last time told her, gliding away to the door of the drawing-room, but she did not wait as he had asked her to, but followed on his heels as he tapped discreetly then opened the door.

Charlotte Buchanan might have been frozen to the same chaise-longue she had occupied over eighteen months ago. She was in exactly the same position, leaning back and flipping moodily through the pages of a magazine. There was a box of chocolates on the table beside her and as Lucy strode in she was just about to stuff one in her mouth. She had put on weight.

'Those won't do you much good, Charlotte, not if you're to regain your figure. I know it's hard after having a child but after all it is over a year since your son was born.'

Charlotte Buchanan, for the space of five seconds, was struck dumb. The chocolate hovered at her lips as though she were not quite sure whether to pop it in or not, then, with what sounded suspiciously like an oath to the astonished butler, she sat up and threw it back in the box.

'What the devil are you doing here, you bitch?' The words were spat out with all the venom that had lain like a cancer inside Charlotte Buchanan ever since James Buchanan had married Lucy Dean. She turned on the butler. 'And what the hell d'you mean by letting her in? You know my father does not like riff-raff in his house.'

'But, madam . . .' the butler stammered, then, seeing that retreat was his best course, almost ran from the room.

'Don't worry, Charlotte, I can't stay long so don't bother with tea. My husband is expecting me home. As you will have gathered you did not succeed in parting us, and I'm happy to say he can't bear me out of his sight for more than half an hour. Yes, isn't it a marvel after all you tried to do to us? He loves me and I return his love and we are to have another child because of that love. I don't suppose you know anything about that since it seems to me that it is unlikely ever to happen to you. I can't say I lose any sleep over it except that it saddens me to know that Paul will never know what James and I have.

'But that is not why I'm here. James and I have resolved our differences, no thanks to you but it seems you are not satisfied with doing your best to destroy us, you are determined to destroy my sister as well with your hatred and envy. Yes, I believe it is envy that eats away at you and turns you into a malevolent shrew. You cannot bear to see anyone have what you wanted and couldn't get, and even after all these years your twisted little mind is still scheming on how to avenge yourself on me. Oh, yes, I am aware that it is me you want to hurt but you have not succeeded and never will. I will just say this. If we have another of your vituperative letters I shall take it to the authorities which will cause such a scandal your poor mother will not be able to hold up her head again. Do I make myself clear?'

Charlotte's face was a bright crimson and her eyes were slitted with rage. She stood up, then seemed undecided on what course to take, twisting her hands together in the lovely silk folds of her tea gown.

'Get . . . out . . . of . . . my . . . house.'

'Your house. I thought this was your father's house. Oh, I see, you are still his little girl, is that it? Dear God, I pity you, Charlotte, I really do.'

She turned and before Charlotte could say another word, she left the room, swept through the door which the smiling butler opened for her, having heard 'madam' get what for, she supposed, and ran lightly down the steps.

'Good day to you, Mrs Buchanan,' he called after her as she started the motor and, as she turned into the road she began to sing.

'Rule Britannia, Britannia rules the waves . . .'